THE
FOUR

A Novel

ELLIE KEEL

WILLIAM MORROW
An Imprint of HarperCollins*Publishers*

THE FOUR. Copyright © 2024 by Ellie Keel. All rights reserved. Printed in the United States of America. No part of this book may be used or reproduced in any manner whatsoever without written permission except in the case of brief quotations embodied in critical articles and reviews. For information, address HarperCollins Publishers, 195 Broadway, New York, NY 10007.

HarperCollins books may be purchased for educational, business, or sales promotional use. For information, please email the Special Markets Department at SPsales@harpercollins.com.

Originally published in Great Britain in 2024 by HQ, an imprint of HarperCollinsPublishers Ltd.

FIRST U.S. EDITION

Library of Congress Cataloging-in-Publication Data has been applied for.

ISBN 978-0-06-339438-4

24 25 26 27 28 LBC 5 4 3 2 1

For my Four: M, M, P, and H

HIGH REALMS
Map of Property

PART I

Chapter 1

It would have made our lives a lot easier if Marta had simply pushed Genevieve out of our bedroom window on our third day at High Realms. Certainly, it would have been tragic. The Main House was six stories high, and our room was at the very top. Genevieve would have fallen hundreds of feet through the clear Devon air, landing on the smooth lawn, which ended just short of the sandstone wall of the East Wing. She would have died instantly.

But Marta didn't push her that day, or—if you choose to believe me—at any other time. Things ultimately got pretty bad for Lloyd, Sami, Marta, and me, but already on day three I had an uneasy sense that we weren't going to be able to make things work at this school. My skepticism was largely based on Marta's inability to follow rules, even simple ones, which was getting all four of us into trouble: Marta and I had had two unofficial sanctions and a withdrawal of privilege already, and lessons hadn't even begun. That first Tuesday—a golden, early September day in 1999—we'd been warned about the Senior Patrol Inspection, which would take place between Games and Formal Supper, and I'd asked Marta to make sure she tidied up, but when I returned to our room after my first hockey practice with the Hillary First XI, I pushed open the door to find Room 1A in a worse state than ever.

Marta was standing on her bed, arranging books on the shelves above it. "Hiya!" she said, beaming at me.

"What the—" I stared at the scene. When I'd left for hockey, my bed and my half of the long desk had been fairly neat, but now Marta's possessions were strewn everywhere. Items of uniform—not all of them clean—smothered every surface, including the floor. I picked my way over to my bed and plucked Marta's running shoes off the pillow. "We need to tidy up," I told her.

"I *am* tidying." Balanced precariously on her bed, her dark hair disheveled, Marta pointed to the shelves. "I'm putting these books in alphabetical order. I'm doing yours, too."

"OK, but . . ." I swallowed, staring at the mess. "We've got twenty minutes before Genevieve comes. Let's clear the floor, at least." Before I could continue, there was a sharp rap at the door. "*Shit.*"

Marta bounded off the bed and across the room, yanking the door open with misplaced enthusiasm. "Hello!"

"Senior Patrol Inspection." As I'd feared, it was Genevieve Lock's voice. She had the room next door, 1B, and was a member of the Senior Patrol—High Realms's word for prefects—for Hillary House. She was also on the hockey First XI. In our first few interactions she'd treated Marta and me with lofty derision, but I'd put two goals past her that afternoon, and now, as she stepped over the threshold of Room 1A, I saw anger simmering in her high-cheekboned face. "Oh dear," she intoned. "Am I early?"

Marta and I watched as Genevieve picked her way between

the twin bedsteads, across the cluttered floor toward the two sash windows. She'd already changed out of her hockey kit and was wearing her gown over a tartan dress and high heels. The gowns were made of black crepe, with billowing sleeves and hems that brushed the floor, making the Senior Patrol homogeneously intimidating. The first time I'd seen all twelve of them together I'd found their appearance absurd, but my impression had quickly changed when I realized how much power they had. Only that morning, I'd witnessed Genevieve and the Captain General of School, Jolyon Astor, terrorizing a group of First Formers who had mistakenly attended the early breakfast sitting. *There are one thousand fucking students here, and you think you're getting in first?*

With one motion, Genevieve swept all of the objects on my side of the desk onto the floor, swung herself onto its surface, and tugged the lower half of the window up to above her head. She crossed one slim leg over the other, leaned nonchalantly against the wall, and lit a cigarette with an ornate silver lighter.

"So," she said, exhaling sharply out of the corner of her mouth, "our suspicions are confirmed."

"What do you mean?" Marta's brow was furrowed.

"We all rather presumed you'd be slovenly little toads," Genevieve replied. "But I told Sylvia and Bella we'd need to wait until the first SPI to know for certain. And here we are. Vindicated." Her eyes hardened as she absorbed the squalor of Room 1A. "You can both miss Formal Supper tonight and tidy the fuck up. Fucking freeloaders," she added calmly.

There followed a long silence in which I sat down on the edge of my bed while Genevieve smoked thoughtfully out of the window, and Marta stared at Genevieve. Amid my humiliation at receiving yet another punishment, I felt a prickling anxiety about Genevieve's cigarette. Its acrid smell was permeating our room, despite the open window. This would no doubt lead to more trouble with our Housemaster, Major Gregory, who'd summoned Marta and me to his study that morning and told us that *nobody*, in his twelve years at High Realms to date, had ever made a worse start at the school, and that we could consider ourselves on probation. That all of "our" misdemeanors had been Marta's: as her roommate, I was destined to be tarred by the same brush. I was, therefore, relieved when Genevieve reached under the window to stub out her cigarette on the outside of the frame. I hoped she would leave, but instead she settled herself more comfortably on the desk and surveyed Marta contemplatively. "It's for your own good," she remarked.

"What do you mean?" Now Marta was glowering at her, her fists balled in her lap.

"You'd do well to remember that boarding schools are *communal* environments. A degree of consideration for your fellow students is an essential courtesy." Genevieve's eyes darted from Marta to me, but I knew that her anger had nothing to do with concern for my personal space, and everything to do with the goals I'd put past her an hour ago. "But perhaps you already know that. Perhaps you've been to boarding school before. Have you?" Her eyes bored into Marta's.

"I've never been to *school* before," Marta retorted, and Genevieve's eyes widened. She glanced at me, apparently to see whether I'd registered the same surprise, but her homeschooling had been one of the first things Marta had told Sami, Lloyd, and me about herself. *I don't know how to behave in public*, she'd said cheerfully, and it had rapidly become clear to us that this was true, to an even greater extent than Marta herself seemed to realize.

Now Genevieve's eyes were narrowed. "Explains a lot," she told Marta. "You're a fucking savage, aren't you? An unsocialized little—what the hell are you doing?" For Marta had moved swiftly toward Genevieve, her body suddenly taut with anger. "Sit the fuck down."

"Marta," I began, feeling helpless, but she'd already retreated. She sat down slowly on the edge of her unmade bed, her face pinched with tension. My roommate was small: shorter than Genevieve and me, and very thin; almost emaciated. Marta's pleated school skirt swamped her knees, which were tightly pressed together, and her shirt sleeves were so baggy that they enveloped her fists, which I knew were still clenched.

"What about you, Rose Lawson?" Genevieve demanded, pronouncing my name as though it tasted sour. She withdrew a fresh cigarette from inside her gown. "You don't say much. Were you homeschooled, too?"

"No," I said, relieved that her attention had turned to me, and like a fool I haltingly began to tell Genevieve about my ambitious, no-nonsense comprehensive school in Hackney, spinning out the story in an effort to distract her from Marta, who slowly began to pick up clothes from the floor around her bed. But Genevieve's cold eyes repeatedly flickered toward her, and I realized then—as I would sense so many times during our time at High Realms—that we hadn't got away with it; that more trouble was fast approaching. Genevieve couldn't have cared less about my old school. She was focused on her target. Her silver lighter clicked.

"Your name," she interrupted suddenly, her voice louder than previously. She was speaking to Marta, who was kneeling on the floor, scooping socks into the drawer under her bed. "It's foreign." Genevieve pointed to an exercise book on the desk, near her foot, on the front cover of which Marta had written her full name: *Marta De Luca*.

Slowly, Marta turned to face her. "Yes."

"Where's it from?"

"Italy."

"Is that where your parents are from, then?"

"My mother's family," Marta replied. She got to her feet, gazing over Genevieve's head out of the window at the high, heather-blazing hills.

Genevieve wrinkled her nose. "Your mother? But then—"

"My father took my mother's name when they got married," Marta said. Almost imperceptibly, she took a step closer to Genevieve.

Genevieve nodded, and I detected a gleam of approval in her cold eyes. "So your mother's a feminist," she stated.

"She was. She's dead."

Now it was my turn to stare. Marta hadn't told me that her mother had died, even when I had mentioned my own mother's death—of leukemia three years previously—during dinner on our second day. But before I could say anything, Genevieve spoke again. "So that's why you're so strange," she stated languidly. "God, your dad must be weird. Look what he's done to you. You're a fucked-up, feral, motherless little gremlin."

And there it was: the first turning point in our difficult, dangerous story. It's so easy for me to identify it as such, for if Marta had acted on her clear impulse in that moment—to

8

push Genevieve so that she toppled, lit cigarette in hand, from the seat we had not offered her, out of the open window, hurtling to her death on the lawn below—all of what we went through would not have happened, *could* not have happened, and perhaps we would have been able to find happiness, even as scholarship pupils, at one of the most exclusive schools in the country. If not happiness, then at the very least a quiet, bearable existence. We would have been without Marta, of course. At that juncture, I don't think I would have lied to the school or the police and tried to say that Genevieve had fallen. I had no skin in the game; no greater affinity with Marta than a couple of nights sharing a room, and I doubted that we would ever really be friends.

Marta took two rapid steps toward Genevieve, and Genevieve recoiled, her eyes now widening in panic rather than scorn, reaching for the window frame as though she hoped to cling on to it. I saw Marta's arms swing upward, and jumped to my feet, hardly knowing what I would do. But at that moment there was a knock at our door, and three people burst into Room 1A, laughing uncontrollably. Genevieve's boyfriend, Max, and our fellow Millennium Scholars Lloyd and Sami were dressed in dinner jackets that were too large for them. Lloyd's camera hung from a strap around his neck, and their cheeks were flushed with—I assumed—the wine they'd drunk from the three-quarters empty bottle Max was carrying.

The spell was broken. Max marched across the room, flung his arms around Genevieve, and kissed her on the lips—*missed you!*—and then began to tell Marta and me about the tour of the Estate (they never said *campus* or *grounds*), that he'd taken Lloyd and Sami on. They'd followed Donny Stream for miles, he said, until they were finally out of sight of the Main House. Lloyd had managed to get a photograph of the deer they'd come across; they'd sat on the bank and drunk the communion wine that Max had pilfered from the antechapel—drunk more than they'd intended, actually, and here they were, ready for Formal Supper, and why hadn't Marta and I gotten changed yet? It was plump, fair-haired Sami who noticed that something was wrong—Sami who picked up on the odd atmosphere; that sense of something having *nearly* happened—and gave me the searching, anxious look that I would come to know so well. He said nothing, but put his hand on Marta's shoulder as she stood silently amid the clamor, still gazing out of the window.

We never talked about that encounter, Marta and I; never told the boys about it, or openly acknowledged its significance in any way. But it's so clear to me now that it was what awoke Genevieve's hatred. Before Marta stepped toward her, arms outstretched, Genevieve had disliked us on principle because we were on full scholarships. But that afternoon, her resentment transmogrified into something else. At the time, I couldn't have said what it was, but now I know: it was fear.

"Sylvia's doing the First Form uniform check in the Atrium," Max was saying. "Let's go down early and see how many of them cry." Genevieve suddenly laughed, slipping her hand into Max's, and the vestiges of tension in Room 1A were dispelled. Lloyd, Sami, Genevieve, and Max went down to Formal Supper. That was High Realms: they hated you to be idle, and so there was always another activity to get to, another match to play or meeting to attend or piece of prep to finish. Whatever happened, you just carried on, and if you didn't, you were weak. Marta and I stayed behind to tidy up, silently folding the endless items of the High Realms uniform into drawers, stacking textbooks on the desk, stowing our trunks under our beds. Marta did not resume her task with the books. For half an hour or so longer, Room 1A was filled with radiant evening light. Then the sun dipped behind the hills, and dusk began to gather around the Main House. For everyone else at High Realms it was just another day, but for us, the Millennium Scholars, it was the start of a journey that would define the rest of our lives.

Chapter 2

The next day was a Wednesday and our last off-timetable day before lessons were due to begin, and Marta and I felt like the only members of the Lower Sixth who weren't hungover. On the way down to breakfast, a bleary-eyed Sami told us that a huge amount of alcohol had been consumed during and after Formal Supper—bottles and cans concealed in dinner jacket pockets and under tables—and that, far from prohibiting this, the Senior Patrol had been the ringleaders.

There was a lot of sex at High Realms. The shouted cross-corridor conversations on the day we arrived were all about the parties that had happened over the summer and who had slept with whom, which relationships had survived vacation, who had cheated (and with whom), and whether or not they would be taken back. The stakes seemed to be much higher than at my old school, where people gossiped briefly and then moved on. I was getting the impression that, at High Realms, who you were going out with was an even more significant factor in determining your social status than how much money you had or who your parents were. Max Masters and Genevieve Lock were the celebrity couple of our year, having been together since Fourth Form, and they were glamorous and unassailable:

she a Senior Patrol member, the daughter of the Leader of the Opposition; and he the handsome, gifted recipient of the Burne Organ Fellowship, which was a scholarship, but apparently carrying none of the ignominy that ours did. Then there was Genevieve's roommate Shana Hussain, a sheikh's daughter who, according to Max, rarely did any work but was never punished for it. Shana's boyfriend was Jolyon Astor, the Head of the Senior Patrol and Captain General of School. Genevieve wasn't as close to Shana as she was to Sylvia Maudsley, who was Vice-Captain General and a Senior Patrol member for Raleigh House. We hadn't come across Sylvia yet.

I sensed a febrility in the air as we scrambled downstairs at ten o'clock for the Lower Sixth briefing. Hillary's Sixth Form Common Room was an airy, wood-paneled space; high-ceilinged enough to have a gallery that wrapped around its four sides, accessed by a spiral staircase. It wasn't really large enough to accommodate all four Houses, and that morning there was a lot of dehydrated bickering as we all tried to find somewhere to sit. Lloyd, Marta, Sami, and I ended up on a small sofa right at the back of the crowded room. Wedged between Sami and Marta, I stared around at my braying classmates with their immaculate uniforms and perfect teeth. *This is your home now,* I thought. *You wanted this. You've got to make it work.* Next to me, Marta had extracted a book of poetry from the pocket of her blazer and was reading it intently.

"Silence." Our Housemaster addressed us from a dais in front of the fireplace. Major Gregory was a short, balding man in his late fifties who'd attended High Realms as a pupil and had returned to the school as Master of Laws and Founding

Head of Hillary House after what the prospectus described as a *distinguished army career, truncated by injury*. Pedantic and irascible, Major Gregory was no less intimidating to me this morning than when he'd collected Lloyd, Sami, Marta, and me from the Atrium three days ago. He'd taken an instant dislike to Marta, chastising her for ordering her uniform in the wrong size and for arriving at High Realms unaccompanied. He'd ignored my father, who'd been standing to one side, holding the keys to his cab, but he'd shaken Sami's parents' hands, addressing them both as Dr. Lynch.

The noise died down. "Before we commence notices," Major Gregory began in his clipped voice, "I'm deeply displeased to hear about some of the events that took place after Formal Supper. Those who were involved—you know who you are—should report to my study directly after this briefing."

Intrigue and amusement rustled through the Common Room. Major Gregory called for silence, but I'd already caught Genevieve and Max's names amid the hissing. I could see them sitting next to each other on a sofa near the fireplace, Genevieve's legs draped over Max's knees. She was examining her fingernails, smirking.

"They were caught having sex in the organ loft at two o'clock this morning," Sami murmured to me. "Max told Lloyd at breakfast." With difficulty, as we were so tightly wedged together, I turned to look at Sami, but another voice now rose above the muttering.

"Good morning, everyone." The speaker was a woman in her early forties: tall and slim, with an astute, scholarly face and wavy dark hair. I took her to be a Mag—High Realms's word for *teacher*, which Marta had guessed was short for the Latin *magister*—although she was wearing jeans and a sweater, and no gown. "For those of you who don't know me, my name is Isobel Reza, and I'm the school doctor. For those of you who *do* know me: a warm welcome back to school. I'm delighted to see you all."

There were a few languid cheers. As far as I could tell, this reaction was atypical of High Realms, where the default attitude toward staff seemed to range from indifference to outright scorn.

Dr. Reza went on, with a quiet, assertive warmth to her voice. "I know most of you well, and it's been my privilege to look after you during your time at High Realms so far. You're all now at least sixteen years of age. You're still welcome to come to the infirmary at any time, and I or one of the nurses will see you as soon as we can. There may be new things you want to discuss with us, and I'd like to remind you that you can talk to us in confidence."

There was an outburst of sniggering. Next to me, Marta's body was rigid with tension. The book of poetry lay open in her lap, but she was no longer reading it. I followed her gaze to Dr. Reza, who was ignoring Major Gregory's red-faced glare. He opened his mouth to speak, but a cold voice rang out from the gallery. "I think we can all be sure that Gerald Foster will have absolutely *nothing* to talk to you about, Dr. Reza."

All heads swiveled upward. The speaker was a dark-haired girl I'd seen exchanging smirks with Genevieve earlier, who was wearing a Senior Patrol gown with silver braiding on the collar and sleeves. She was as tall and slim as Genevieve and even more striking, with pale, glossy skin and sharp features.

The way she was surveying us from the gallery made her look like the captain of a ship, I thought.

"Good morning, Sylvia." Dr. Reza said, raising her voice above the whispering. "Shall we try to start the year on a pleasant note?"

"Oh, spare me. My only *note* is that Gerald Foster is a pathetic sneak who's bitter because he isn't getting any, and never has." Sylvia Maudsley wasn't looking at Dr. Reza, but toward the corner of the Common Room, where a broad-shouldered, red-haired boy with pockmarked cheeks was sitting on the floor. Alone of our number, he was wearing jodhpurs and a filthy waxed jacket rather than his uniform. His face was aflame as the room rocked with derisive laughter.

"That's enough, Sylvia." The new voice was the Head of Raleigh House, a stern woman whose name I didn't know. Sylvia shrugged and turned away, vanishing into the shadows at the back of the gallery. I felt lightheaded and anxious because of how Sylvia had described Gerald Foster, but also because of the glee with which her viciousness had been received. What was more, I'd heard that Sylvia was on the U18 School Hockey team, which I was scheduled to try out for in two days' time. With a stick in her hand, I was certain she would be lethal.

Finally we were dismissed for Elevenses. Lloyd, Marta, Sami, and I extracted ourselves from our sofa, and had just joined the tide of students heading for the door when we heard Major Gregory summoning us. We fought our way back to the fireplace. A few feet away, Dr. Reza was deep in conversation with the woman who had silenced Sylvia.

"A word with you all," Major Gregory said. "Classes

begin tomorrow morning. As Millennium Scholars, I expect you to be top of every class." We nodded: this had been made clear in the letters that offered us the full scholarships. "Normally I would be reluctant to admit four scholarship pupils to Hillary at the same time, but in light of your scores in the examination . . . Miss De Luca, yours were particularly impressive." He looked Marta up and down. "Which is more than can be said for your uniform."

"I'll grow into it." Marta's jaw was clenched. The scholarship fund hadn't covered our uniform and equipment, and I assumed she—like me—had decided to buy one set that would last the two years. At that moment Dr. Reza turned around.

"Hello," she said, smiling. "It's very nice to meet you all."

We shook hands with her as Major Gregory looked on coldly. Dr. Reza glanced at him. "Did you say there's a problem with Marta's uniform?"

"Clearly."

"That's easily solved—there's plenty in the lost and found at the infirmary. We'll find you some replacements when you come for your start-of-term checkup, Marta."

Marta looked panicked. "I don't want—" she began, but she could not continue: Major Gregory pulled Dr. Reza away from the group and began to remonstrate with her.

"Come on," Lloyd said, glancing at Marta, whose expression was mutinous. "Let's get to Elevenses."

As we passed Major Gregory's study, I saw Genevieve and Max waiting outside, talking to Sylvia and Bella Ford, the Captain of Games, whom I knew slightly from hockey. Bella's muscular arm was clamped around Sylvia's shoulders, her thumb jerking from side to side across Sylvia's collarbone. The four of them broke off their conversation as we approached.

"Millennium Scholars?" Sylvia demanded, looking us up and down. We nodded.

Her lip curled. "Fuck me." She considered each of us individually, her gaze falling on me last. "Where the fuck did they find you?" Max, Genevieve, and Bella laughed, but Sylvia's eyes lingered on me, her expression still hostile. "You won't last five minutes," she said coldly, and then she turned away to continue her conversation.

I remember that day, that Wednesday, was the day I fully appreciated how many stairs there were at High Realms. We descended six stories to the Atrium for Elevenses, taking the steep main staircase they called the Eiger, whose two hundred steps were almost twice as deep as normal ones, and so highly polished that I saw several First Formers slip. Then we returned to Hillary for a short ceremony known as the Distribution of Duties, in which Marta and I were told to report to the stables at half past two that afternoon, and thereafter at quarter to seven every morning. We surged back down to the vast Dining Hall on the ground floor for lunch, and then it was back to our rooms to put on the overalls and work boots prescribed on the uniform list for outdoor duties. It took me several attempts to persuade Marta to change out of her uniform and accompany me to the stables, but I cajoled her for my own benefit as much as hers: I didn't want to go to the induction on my own.

Did Lloyd, Sami, or I wonder then why Marta's behavior was so strange, or guess that she was troubled rather than rebellious? The simple answer is no. Those first few days at boarding school were so busy, so overwhelming. We were wrapped up in our own problems, which were to do with fitting in, and the fact that Marta was one of the factors preventing us from doing so. For different reasons with a common denominator, we'd all desperately wanted to come to High Realms. We'd been enticed by its renown (*everybody* had heard of it), by the glossy prospectuses it had suddenly sent to high-achieving state schools like mine, and—particularly in my case—by the list of *destinations of leavers* and alumni profiles at the back of the brochure. These pages made it clear that Old High Realmsians ran the world. They went to Oxford, Cambridge, and other top universities, and subsequently ascended to high office in governments, armies, and corporations with mind-boggling rapidity. But now it was rumored that High Realms's exam results were slipping, and that the school's charitable status was looking shaky: they needed an injection of impoverished talent. So Lloyd, Sami, Marta, and I took the fiendishly difficult scholarship exams. Over a thousand other applicants did the same, but we won the places. We were in.

I'd hoped that High Realms would be fun. Boarding schools had a fairy-tale quality in my mind, an allure generated by the books I'd read about them as a child. After my acceptance letter arrived, I'd revisited those fabled institutions—Malory Towers, Trebizon, the Chalet School—and my nerves had been soothed by the familiar stories in which misfits became leaders, the ostracized were gradually accepted, and nothing too terrible ever happened. I'd been so focused on my academic work that I hadn't had many friends at my school in Hackney, and so I'd found the idea of inbuilt—even enforced—camaraderie at boarding school appealing. A few months later, as my father and I had first approached High Realms in his cab, along that broad drive lined with stately plane trees, I'd felt as though my imagination was being colored in, to a vividness and a grandeur that exceeded all my expectations. I'd felt thrilled. But as soon as we had entered the bustling Atrium with its dozens of portraits and towering staircase, my excitement had fallen away. I'd looked up and around; I'd seen the hundreds of students who exuded their confidence and beauty even more than their affluence, and I'd felt tiny. I'd felt as though I didn't know anything, that nothing had ever happened to me, that nothing *would* ever happen to me because I was insignificant, unworthy. I'd hoped to metamorphize as I stepped through the door—but compared to this tribe of elegant, technicolor creatures, I'd felt monochrome, inexperienced, and dowdy.

Now it was day four, and Lloyd, Sami, Marta, and I had clubbed together in a fragile, crucial camaraderie. There had been limited time to talk, so we'd gleaned only the scantest of details about each other. Even this meager information was woolly and, in places, confusing. In the Atrium on the first day, Lloyd had introduced his foster parents, who'd affectionately hugged him goodbye, but Lloyd had since told us that he didn't expect to see them again. *That can't be right,* Sami had said to me afterward; but in reality we had no idea how such things worked. Sami had been dropped off by his parents, whose Yorkshire accents were even thicker than his own. They'd helped Marta unload her luggage from the taxi she'd arrived in, and then chatted warmly to my father while Sami said goodbye to his three sisters. The smallest girl had clung to Sami until he'd picked her up, her arms winding around his neck as she'd cried. I remember eyeing Lloyd and

Marta for their reactions, sensing that they, like me, had no siblings. Lloyd had looked on, his expression calmly cynical, but Marta's head had tipped back and she'd gazed at the vaulted ceiling of the Atrium, a slight smile on her pale face.

As little as we knew about each other, we'd found out even less about our fellow pupils, because the majority of them hadn't spoken a word to us. Lloyd had palled up with Max, but only because Max gave organ lessons as part of the Burne Fellowship, and Lloyd—who turned out to be a talented pianist—had decided to have a shot at it. Otherwise, it was already a lonely experience amid the cultish atmosphere of High Realms—where, we were coming to understand, the students danced a complex polka of loyalty, honor, and revenge, the steps of which we had not yet learned.

Perhaps it would have been better to have stayed on the sidelines. There was no need for us to get involved in what happened that afternoon—unlike those that followed, it wasn't our battle to fight. I remember hurrying down the Eiger with Marta, stumbling slightly in our thick-soled boots, through patches of dusty sunlight in the empty Atrium. We dashed out of the front door on to the drive, which was also deserted, and stopped right there at the foot of the stone steps, blinking in the bright sun. We looked to the right, across rippling lawns to the Klein-Portman Building and the Straker Library. To our left the Chapel's vast facade glowed in the sun, its bell placidly chiming three o'clock.

"The clocktower," Marta said suddenly.

"What?"

"You can see it from our window. It's in the stable block—I remember it from the prospectus." Marta pointed to a passage between the Main House and the Chapel. "It's that way."

I followed her through a maze of redbrick buildings containing classrooms and boardinghouses, clumped around grassy quadrangles. Then, suddenly, there was a high archway leading to a hexagonal courtyard with a fountain in the center. Marta consulted a sign next to the arch we had passed through. As we scanned the list of arrows, we heard raised voices in the distance: a kind of chanting.

"What's that?" The intensity of the voices was making me uneasy.

Marta shrugged, her finger landing at last on the word *stables*. "This way," she said, and we hurried around the grass to a second archway. The chanting grew louder as we rushed through it, becoming more aggressive by the second.

We saw the stables: a set of two-story buildings arranged in a square, more run-down than the rest of High Realms, on the far side of which was the clocktower Marta had glimpsed from our room. Through another archway we saw the stable courtyard, this one full of students dressed in overalls. They had been chanting, but now they were completely silent, their backs to us, staring at something we couldn't see.

Lingering out of sight in the archway, several feet away from the back of the crowd, Marta and I glanced at each other. It was obvious that something bad was happening; almost certainly another bizarre High Realms ritual. *You don't need to see this,* a voice murmured at the back of my mind. *Go back to the Hexagon and wait for it to end.* I reached for Marta's arm to pull her away, but then we heard hooves crunching on gravel, and an enormous black horse came into view around the edge of the crowd. The rider steered it into the group of students, parting them, and we saw what they were looking at.

The red-haired boy who'd been sitting under the window in Hillary Common Room was tied to a statue in the middle of the courtyard. Naked from the waist up, his body was contorted by the shape of the statue, his neck twisting helplessly to one side. The statue was a rearing horse, its head tossed back and its front legs pawing at the air. Gerald Foster was strapped to the stone head and flank, held in place with leather cords around his torso, arms, and thighs. His feet dangled into a circular trough, from which the horse's lower legs emerged. As we looked on, he kicked violently. Water flew everywhere, and the crowd backed away.

"Stop struggling." The speaker was Genevieve, who was riding the black horse. Across the courtyard, I saw Sylvia patrolling the perimeter of the crowd on a second horse. "It won't do any good, and anyway, we thought you were so fond of horses."

"Let me go, bitch!" Gerald strained against the cords, his arms pinned to his sides. He was extremely tall, and despite his helplessness there was enormous power in his body. "You're going to pay for this!"

"No." Genevieve's voice was high and cold. "It's *you* who's going to pay, Gerald. You're going to pay for being a traitor and a sad, jealous virgin." Gerald snarled at her, but she spoke more loudly, her horse now stationary in front of him. "It's not as if you're unfamiliar with how things work at High Realms. You've been here as long as any of us." Her expression hardened even more as she surveyed him. "You know the rules."

"You broke them!" Gerald yelled, struggling against the

ligatures, which I suddenly realized were not ropes, but reins. "We're not allowed out at night! You think you can do whatever you fucking want, but now I'm Senior Patrol—" He broke off as one of the reins suddenly slipped, and his body slid down a few inches into the basin.

"I'm not talking about the *school* rules, as you well know," Genevieve said. She was holding a riding crop in her right hand. "Your ill-advised appointment to the Senior Patrol doesn't change anything, Gerald. You will never sneak on me again." She lifted her riding crop, and I felt a surging dread, but she pointed it at the assembled students, who began to chant. Now we could make out the words. *Sneaking virgin. Sneaking virgin. Sneaking virgin.*

As the crowd chanted, I looked over at Sylvia. She was sitting astride her horse, dressed in a blue Raleigh riding jacket. Her face was creased in a frown, her gaze flickering between Gerald and Genevieve before settling on her friend. Her horse tossed its head restlessly. Sylvia reached down to stroke between its ears, her eyes never once leaving Genevieve. Although Genevieve appeared to be in charge, I had the impression that Sylvia was the referee, making sure that things went the right way for her friend.

With expert ease, Genevieve steered her horse around the crowd so that she was next to Sylvia, and together they watched Gerald fight desperately against the reins, water still flying everywhere as he attempted to use the power of his kicks to work the knots loose. To my horror, I saw that his body was slipping farther and farther down as the lower reins began to yield to his force. The top one had been looped around the stone neck of the horse and bound across his chest and arms.

Without the support of the lower reins I knew it would slide upward to his neck. Sylvia's eyes were narrowed.

"We don't sneak on people because they're getting something we'd like for ourselves," Genevieve now told Gerald, her voice close to a hiss. Gerald's face was puce as he wrestled even more frantically to free himself. He appeared to be in the grip of a panic attack as well as severe physical pain. As I stared in horror, he suddenly gagged, vomiting copiously down his bare chest. A roar of laughter rose from the crowd.

I heard hooves very close to us, and Sylvia's gray horse blocked the archway, obscuring our view of the scene. Marta and I drew back into the shadows, watching Sylvia bend down from the saddle. She used the tip of her whip to prod a younger student in the back row of the crowd. He jumped, looking up at her fearfully as she mouthed something at him. He blinked in surprise, then nodded, and Sylvia's heels brushed the flanks of her horse, steering back toward Genevieve, whose back was turned.

Several things followed almost simultaneously. A high, trembling cry rose up from the back of the crowd—*Mag! Mag!*—and the crowd of students scattered, dashing into the surrounding stables, seizing rakes and buckets and wheelbarrows as they went. Genevieve and Sylvia maneuvered their horses into the corner of the courtyard, where they paused as if they'd just mounted them. Gerald kicked even more desperately, freeing his legs, and at once his body jerked downward, the upper rein sliding up his chest and around his neck. He choked.

"*No!*" Marta rushed toward the statue. She leaped onto the rim of the trough, scrabbling at the reins that bound Gerald.

His face was contorted in pain, and water flew everywhere as he continued to kick. His panic was hindering Marta's attempts to help him: she couldn't get close enough to unpick the knots around the horse's head. Suddenly Marta dropped to her knees on the rim of the basin and flung her arms around Gerald's legs, holding them tightly to prevent him from moving. "*Rose!*" she yelled.

I unfroze. I rushed to the statue, clambering onto the rim as Marta had. Ignoring the knots, I worked at a buckle, trying to ease the leather out of its metal casing. Just as I managed to release the strap, Gerald gave one final, almighty kick, and both he and Marta were flung onto the ground, Gerald landing on top of Marta. They rolled over in the dust.

"*Fuck.*" I jumped down, crouching next to Marta, who lay with her cheek pressed to the gravel. I put my hand on her shoulder as she struggled to sit up. "Are you all right?"

"I think so." Blood was beading in the corner of her mouth, and her overalls were covered in dirt and Gerald's vomit. She looked over at him. "Are *you* OK?" she asked.

He was kneeling on all fours, coughing, his cheeks scarlet with shame. "Fuck off," he managed to say. He heaved himself to his feet and limped across the courtyard toward the other archway, his pale back streaked with blood.

Marta and I were left standing in the middle of the court-yard, staring at each other in mute shock. Around us, the stables were a hive of plausible activity. The sun glinted on the hands of the clock. There was no sign of any teachers.

"Losers helping losers. How charming." We turned to see Genevieve and Sylvia approaching us on foot. They were both taller than us, with a willowy kind of toughness. "Which one of you broke up the party?" Genevieve demanded.

"We didn't—" Marta began, but Sylvia's eyes narrowed, and I realized what she'd asked the younger student to do. I interrupted Marta without knowing exactly why.

"It was me." I swallowed hard as Genevieve and Sylvia's eyes swiveled to me. "You can't treat people like that."

Genevieve's expression was one of implacable contempt. "I don't believe you," she told me. She glared at Marta. "It was *you* who called out, you ghastly little gremlin. You've got a lot to learn if you don't want to end up like him." She jerked her head to where Gerald was just visible inside one of the stables, standing with his forehead pressed against the neck of a horse. His broad shoulders heaved. "Get out of here," Genevieve said suddenly. She pointed at Marta, and then to the Main House. "Go on—fuck off. Your copybook's marked, gremlin."

For a moment Marta hesitated, and I feared she would not obey Genevieve. Then she sighed, and shuffled off in the direction that Genevieve had pointed, without looking back. Genevieve made a noise of contempt and marched off into a nearby stable, leaving Sylvia and me standing together in the courtyard.

Sylvia scrutinized me, her cold features overlaid with something close to curiosity. "I didn't see you in the crowd," she said.

I shrugged. My lie now felt pointless, even stupid, but somehow I knew that attempting to backtrack would make things even worse. Sylvia opened her mouth to say something else, but at that moment Genevieve shrieked her name. Her eyes bored briefly into mine, and then she turned on her heel.

I knew I should go after Marta, but nausea was rising within me. I sat down on the edge of the basin from which the enormous stone horse reared. I was horrified by the cruelty I'd witnessed, but it was more than that. Despite Sylvia's quiet act of mercy—now blamed on Marta—I was shaken by the conviction with which she and Genevieve had behaved. They had appointed themselves moral arbiters in a world without morals, with a system that worked only for the strongest. We already knew that we were not the strongest, and I felt a deep sense of dread about the fact that I had chosen this place as my home for two whole years: a world whose understanding of good and evil was entirely and terrifyingly its own.

Chapter 3

She didn't turn up *at all*?"

I shook my head, and Lloyd and Sami looked incredulous. We were eating breakfast in the Dining Hall, the morning after Marta and I had witnessed the attack on Gerald. Classes were due to begin in half an hour, but none of us had seen Marta that morning. Her bed had been empty when I got up at quarter past six for morning duty, and she hadn't appeared at the stables, either. A surly Gerald had assigned me to Block C, but I hadn't managed to finish the sweeping, hosing down, and other tasks before the breakfast bell rang.

"Does she normally get up early?" Sami now asked me.

"Yes," I replied, but as I spoke I realized that I had never actually seen Marta get up or go to bed, despite the fact that we shared a room. In defiance of the rules, every night she'd remained at her desk after the bell rang for lights out, bent low over her books, and until today she'd always been working there when I woke up, too.

"Morning, campers." To my surprise, Max plonked his tray down next to mine, splashing milk from his cereal bowl over the table. "First day! How're you feeling?"

"Pretty good," said Lloyd at once. Max grinned.

"Even the First Stream will be a breeze for you guys," he said, digging his spoon into his cornflakes. "I tried to make Keps put me in Seconds for English because I'm all for an easy life, but she insisted on me and Sylvia joining you." He beamed at us, and I thought how charming he was, with his wavy dark hair and olive skin. "Hey—where's Marta?"

"We don't know," Sami said, looking troubled. "Rose hasn't seen her this morning."

"Maybe she's run away," said Max cheerfully.

"*What?*" Sami looked horrified. Max laughed.

"I'm joking!" he said, through a mouthful of cornflakes. "But seriously—she doesn't seem to like it here much, does she?"

"What do you mean?"

"Well, she doesn't even seem to want to *look* the part. That enormous uniform . . ." Max took a swig of coffee. "And all the WPs and sanctions. I *know* Gin gave her most of them," he added, seeing the look on my face, "but she's only trying to make sure Marta gets the hang of how things work around here, for her *own good*. Gin told me what happened with Gerald. Marta's not going to do herself any favors by sticking up for people like him."

Lloyd, Sami, and I looked at each other uneasily. "Max," Sami said suddenly, "that's not fair. It sounds like Genevieve and Sylvia could've really hurt Gerald. I think Marta did the right thing."

Max gave him a look of amused pity. "You don't understand. Gerald can look after himself. Shopping me and Gin to Major G is the *least* he's capable of. He's had it in for us for years."

"Why?" Lloyd was watching Max closely.

"He kept asking Sylvia out when we were younger. She said no."

We waited, but Max said nothing more. He was buttering his toast, glancing imperturbably around the Dining Hall. "Wish Gin would come to breakfast sometimes," he began, but Sami interrupted him.

"Is that *it*? Sylvia turned him down—years ago?"

For a moment I thought I glimpsed irritation in Max's expression. Then, "People here bear grudges," he said evenly. "We spend too much time together to forget things. There's a . . . shared history, I suppose." He stirred his coffee, apparently lost in thought, before smiling at us engagingly. "That reminds me: you're getting to know all about *us*, but we don't know anything about you two." He was eyeing Sami and me. "I know Lloyd's situation, but where d'you both come from? What do your parents do?"

I looked down at my half-empty cereal bowl. Max sounded too casual, I thought; his manner too studiedly offhand, like a detective gathering evidence from an unwitting suspect. Feeling it would be rude not to answer, I said, "I live in Hackney. My dad drives a taxi."

"And your mum?"

"She's dead," I replied, trying not to sound curt. Max's eyes widened, and he put his hand over mine and gave it a gentle squeeze. It was the first physical contact I'd had with anyone at High Realms, and for a moment I felt I wanted to cling on to his hand all day.

"I'm so sorry," Max told me. "That must be *awful* for

31

you." He gave my hand another squeeze and turned to Sami. "What about you, lad?" he asked, in a poor imitation of a Yorkshire accent.

"I'm from Leeds, and my parents are doctors," Sami replied cheerfully. "My father's a psychiatrist, and my mum's a gynecologist."

"And you're hoping to follow in their footsteps?"

"How did you know—" Sami began, but Max was already speaking again.

"That box you arrived with," he said. "The wooden chest. Got anything fun in there?"

"Fun?"

"Any booze, cigs? Anything we might be interested in?"

"Oh," Sami said, half laughing. "No, afraid not. It's my care package." Seeing Max's raised eyebrows, he went on, "My parents told me people brought care packages to boarding school. It's just got chocolate in it, really. Some biscuits, sweets—"

"OK!" Max chuckled. "That's a shame, but never mind. I wouldn't mention it to the others, though, if I were you. We gave up our care packages after Third Form." He winked again. At that moment a bell rang shrilly, and Max drained his coffee cup. "We'd better go—Keps'll kick off if we're late."

"Rose!" Halfway up the Eiger, we turned to see Marta several steps below, pushing past people to catch up with us. She had no schoolbag, but her arms were full of books.

"Where've you been?" I demanded, trying not to show how relieved I was that she'd turned up.

"The Library!" She showed us one of the books she was carrying: our AS-Level poetry anthology. "I hadn't finished reading the poems, so I got up early." She was breathless and holding her skirt up by the waistband to stop it falling down. A large scab had formed in the corner of her mouth.

"But—" I stared at her, torn between which objection to raise first. *You were supposed to help me at the stables? I had to cover for you at roll call? Our room is a mess again?*

"We don't have to have read them all before class," Lloyd told her. "That's not how lessons work, Marta."

"I *like* reading—"

"OK, but you let Rose down." Lloyd sounded like he was trying to stay calm. "She had to do morning duty by herself."

"I'm sorry." Marta gave me a smile of such sincerity and contrition that I felt my resentment thaw. "I just got overexcited. It's my first proper day at school." She looked so happy that I couldn't bring myself to chastise her.

The English Department was on the fourth floor of the Main House. Max led us down a corridor to a door that stood ajar. "This is Keps's room," he said over his shoulder, pushing it open. Inside, the wood-paneled room was full of sunlight. Looking out of the high windows, I realized that we were almost directly below Room 1A. We were facing east, over the greenish roof of the Chapel toward the Hexagon and the stables, identifiable by the clocktower.

"Good morning, First Stream." The stern woman who had rebuked Sylvia during yesterday's briefing entered, her arms, like Marta's, full of books. She wore a black suit under her gown, and her dark hair was swept back. "Take your seats." She watched with narrowed eyes as we sat down, and a sudden jolt of determination pierced my dread. I'd excelled at academic work since primary school, supplementing my natural ability with hours of hard work that had earned me the admiration of my teachers, if not my peers. As tricky as High Realms was proving to be in other ways, the lessons themselves would surely be my chance to shine.

"Introductions," said the teacher briskly. "My name is Miss Kepple. I am Head of Raleigh House and Higher Mag for English."

We went around the small circle, introducing ourselves. Marta had just given her name when the classroom door swung open and Sylvia strode in, her Senior Patrol gown whipping around the door like a cape. She flung herself into an empty chair near Miss Kepple, who gave her a tight smile. "Good morning, Sylvia."

"Hello." Sylvia propped her chin on her hand, her gaze traveling haughtily around the horseshoe of desks. *Oh, to have your power,* I thought.

"Now," said Miss Kepple, after a moment, "our first term will be spent on the poetry component of the course. Do you all have the anthology?"

There was a rustling as we made to pull the book out of our bags, but Miss Kepple held up her hand. "To begin with, I'd like you all to have a look at this." Sheets of paper were handed around, and I looked down at what I'd been given.

since feeling is first
who pays any attention
to the syntax of things
will never wholly kiss you;

wholly to be a fool
while Spring is in the world

my blood approves,
and kisses are a better fate
than wisdom
lady i swear by all flowers. Don't cry
– the best gesture of my brain is less than
your eyelids' flutter which says

we are for each other; then
laugh, leaning back in my arms
for life's not a paragraph

And death i think is no parenthesis

I looked up and met Marta's gaze across the room as she, too, raised her eyes from the page. She smiled at me. Two seats down, Lloyd was underlining something, and next to him Sami was also studying the poem, frowning slightly. On Sami's other side, Max was gazing out of the window, his eyes unfocused.

"Let's see what you're made of, shall we?" Miss Kepple's eyes swiveled to me. "Miss Lawson. Perhaps you could tell us what you think of the poem."

I'd expected her to ask a more specific question, and could not, for a few moments, think of a single thing to say. I looked down at the poem and swallowed. "I think it's about spontaneity," I said finally. "And truth."

There was a silence, during which the teacher regarded me coldly. Opposite me, Sylvia smirked. "I see," said Miss Kepple. "Would you care to expand?"

I felt a warm blush rise to my cheeks, and gripped my pen hard, staring down at the words on the page. Out of the corner of my eye I saw Marta open her mouth, but it was Lloyd who spoke first. "I thought the poet might be trying to tell us that love can be illogical," he said. "That it's an instinct, rather than something you decide on rationally."

Miss Kepple looked at him dispassionately and said nothing. Marta tapped her pen on the desk excitedly. Then Max said to the room at large, "I agree with that. Love *isn't* logical."

"We're studying poetry, Mr. Masters, not your unsolicited opinions."

Max smiled amiably. "Well, it does say that kisses are better than wisdom, so I thought—"

"A better *fate* than wisdom," Miss Kepple corrected him. "Be precise. Mr. Lynch, what do you have to say?"

Sami ran his fingers through his hair. "I don't know that it's saying that love is *irrational*," he said. At the sound of his accent, Miss Kepple winced. "Or at least—not entirely." Sami hesitated, scanning the page.

To his right, Sylvia laughed: a low, scornful sound. " 'Not entirely,' " she echoed. "Do enlighten us."

Sami returned her gaze, his head tilted to one side. "I was looking at the word 'syntax,' " he said cautiously. The nib of his pen fell on the word. "I think the poem might be saying that common sense, or rules, or whatever it really means by 'syntax,' might mean that you feel things *differently*, and express them differently. Less intensely, maybe."

"Yeah," said Lloyd immediately, "and he says 'wholly to be a fool'—he's undermining the role of reason in emotion, he's saying that emotion is purest when it's free from conventional structures or whatever—that's why the line breaks are so weird—"

"He's saying that emotion can't be *governed* by reason—"

"You assume the poet is a man," interrupted Miss Kepple.

"But it is a man," said Marta, speaking for the first time. "It's Cummings, isn't it?"

Miss Kepple glanced at her repressively. "Mr. Masters. What do you have to say?"

Max looked idly at his sheet of paper. Before Miss Kepple could question him further, Sylvia spoke again, her voice clear. "The poet is downgrading intellectual prowess in favor of simple, physical, natural truths," she said. "That's why he doesn't use proper grammar."

There was a short silence in which the whole class looked down at the poem again. I felt coldly trepidatious. It was us, Millennium Scholars, who were supposed to be leading the class, but we'd been outpaced by a High Realms native in the first ten minutes.

"Thank you, Sylvia," said Miss Kepple after a moment. "I think we might be getting somewhere. The poet is suggesting that syntax, which here becomes a metaphor for structure, or rules, or restrictions, can obfuscate and even diminish true depth of feeling."

Sylvia looked triumphant. I ran over what Miss Kepple had said in my mind. There was something that I felt didn't add up in her summation of the poem, but I couldn't put my finger on what it was.

Then Marta's voice rang out, loud and clear. "I don't entirely agree."

We all stared at her, including Miss Kepple. "I'm sorry?" said the teacher after a few moments.

"I don't think Cummings really *is* undermining the value of the intellect," said Marta. "I think the poem expresses a contradiction."

Miss Kepple glanced down at the poem, and I saw her eyes narrow a fraction. I couldn't tell whether she was impressed or annoyed that she was being challenged. She looked up at Marta. "Explain."

Marta tapped her pen on her sheet of paper. "There's a tension at the heart of this poem," she said slowly. "Ostensibly, the poet is cynical about syntax—I think that's right." She nodded at Sylvia, who glared at her. "He seems to say that a preoccupation with detail, or overintellectualizing stuff, somehow distracts from true feeling . . . I think that's right, too."

"What is your point?" snapped Sylvia.

"You said it's important to be precise," Marta went on, now addressing Miss Kepple. "Well, this poem is *really* precise. Like Lloyd said . . . every line break is deliberate; none of it's random. And that's only possible because of syntax. That semicolon at the end of the first stanza—it's such a clear sign. The thing is, he's *had* to use syntax—the kind of detail he seems to say irrelevant to true feeling—to convey his own feelings in the form of a poem. So I think he might be saying—in real life, in 'live,' situations, we can sidestep detail, because true beauty is in the real and the spontaneous . . . but when it comes to art, to capturing and immortalizing emotion—well, structure of *some* kind, even if it's unconventional, is fundamental to beauty."

There was an awkward silence. I glanced at Sylvia, whose expression was one of hard resentment. Then Miss Kepple said, very quietly, "And how, then, would you account for the final line?"

Marta shrugged. "Death is permanent," she said. "It's not an aside, or an interlude. What will be left of us is our words—which for him are his 'best gesture.'" She hesitated. "I'm not sure about that part, though."

We all stared at Marta. The sun was behind her, casting her face into shadow, but I could see that her expression contained no hint of complacency. There was only a kind of restrained, hopeful energy; a palpable excitement, as though she couldn't wait to be asked another question. For the first time since I had met her four days ago, she appeared content, at home—as confident as any of the High Realms students I'd seen.

Then Max broke the silence by beating a short, merry drumroll on the desk. "Wow," he said. "*What* a performance, what a triu—"

"That's quite enough, Max." Miss Kepple's voice was harsh. She glanced at Marta, looking rattled, just as Sylvia did the same thing. "Miss De Luca, I will review your analysis of the poem. You may have a point." Marta shrugged, reaching for her pen. "Now, First Stream, let's begin the syllabus proper. Take out your anthologies."

That first lesson was followed by Elevenses. Marta, Lloyd, Sami, and I traipsed downstairs to the Atrium, tailing Max, who strolled beside Sylvia, the two of them deep in conversation. Marta chattered, but the boys and I were virtually silent.

In the crowded Atrium, the four of us collected mugs of

tea and handfuls of biscuits from one of the trestle tables set up under the Eiger. We retreated into a corner, trying to listen to Marta gabbling about how much she was looking forward to her other subjects. She and Lloyd had chosen identical A Levels—English Literature, Latin, History, and Philosophy—but Marta had persuaded High Realms to allow her to pick up a fifth subject, Physics.

"So you're an all-rounder," Sami said admiringly. "Wish I was. I'm rubbish at English—I'm only taking it because my parents say good communication skills are important if you want to be a doctor." He paused, looking worried. "They helped me a lot with preparing for the scholarship exam. I'm OK at Biology and Chemistry, but Math is going to be *hard*—"

"I'm good at Math," Marta butted in, cramming a biscuit into her mouth. "I'll help you. And Rose is actually *taking* Math, so between us we've got you covered." She grinned at me through a mouthful of crumbs. "It feels so weird being in a *class*—"

"Millennium Scholars?" The interruption came from Bella Ford, who was even more tough-looking than I remembered. Her blond hair was scraped into a French braid, and she was flanked by Sylvia and Genevieve. "I want a word with you all about your athletic commitments," she said without preamble. "You"—she pointed at me—"are accounted for with hockey. You two"—she gestured to Lloyd and Sami—"can go and speak to Rory F-S now about rugby." She pointed to a muscular boy in a Senior Patrol gown standing halfway up the Eiger, tossing a rugby ball to and fro over the banister with Max and Jolyon Astor. She looked Marta up and down.

"I've got no idea what to do with you. You're too small to be of any real use."

"That's fine by me," Marta returned at once. "I hate sports. I'll sit it out."

"You bloody won't." Bella glowered at her. Sami started to say something conciliatory, but Bella snapped, "Off you both fuck and talk to Rory before the bell rings."

Reluctantly, Sami and Lloyd obeyed her. Bella took Marta by the arm and pulled her several feet away from me, hectoring her about Games. Sylvia followed them, her arms folded. I was left with Genevieve, who appraised me spitefully. "Which one are you sleeping with?"

"What?"

"Fatty, or the orphan?" Genevieve jerked her head at Lloyd and Sami. They were standing at the foot of the Eiger, talking to Rory Fitz-Straker, who was gripping the rugby ball between meaty hands. Lloyd was almost as tall as Rory, but Sami was a head shorter than both of them, and was fidgeting apprehensively. As we looked on, Rory chucked the ball at Sami's stomach, winding him. "Which one?" Genevieve repeated.

"Neither of them," I replied, bewildered. I wondered whether Genevieve thought that all four of us had come from the same school, rather than the truth, which was that we had only met five days ago.

"Right. So you're shagging the gremlin?" Genevieve pointed at Marta, who was now arguing heatedly with Bella. I shook my head. "So you've got someone at home," Genevieve sneered, pulling her cigarettes from the inside pocket of her gown.

"No." Suddenly I'd had enough. "I've never been out with anyone. OK?"

She raised her eyebrows. "How sweet," she commented, and I immediately regretted telling her. My instinct had been that divulging the information would protect me, because then there would be nothing she could sniff out, or task Max with doing so, but I sensed that I'd been mistaken. "What do you think's wrong with her?" Genevieve asked, indicating Marta again.

"What do you mean?"

Genevieve's expression was difficult to read. "There's something weird about her," was all she said before Sylvia and Bella wandered back over to us. There was no sign of Marta.

"I've told her she's playing lacrosse," Bella told Genevieve, ignoring me. "She might be OK on the wing. You're right, she's a cheeky little toad."

"Max says she's causing trouble in class, too," Genevieve said, glancing at Sylvia. "Being a smartass. Showing off."

Sylvia shrugged. "There's an argument that Keps shouldn't set work she doesn't understand herself," she said. I looked at her in surprise, and Genevieve scowled.

"She's going to have to buck up her ideas, or we'll do it for her," she snapped. "I'm not having—"

"Where's Marta gone?" I demanded.

Sylvia glared at me. "Don't interrupt," she said coldly. She took Bella's arm, and the three of them prowled out of the open front door, Genevieve lighting up as they went.

Feeling rattled, I looked around the Atrium, which was emptying of students ahead of second study. I spotted Marta, half-hidden in the shadow of the Eiger. The back wall of the Atrium comprised almost a thousand pigeon holes, one for every student at the school, the top rows of which had to be reached by wooden ladders. Marta was standing at the foot of one of these, holding a piece of paper in her hand. She was reading it with fierce concentration, one hand gripping the paper and the other the edge of the ladder. The part of her face that wasn't hidden by her tangled hair was deathly pale.

My first thought was that Bella and Sylvia had upset her. She'd seemed so cheerful until only a few moments ago. I began to move toward her, but then I heard someone call my name. It was Dr. Reza.

"How was your first lesson?" She smiled at me, and I felt disoriented.

"Fine, thanks—" I glanced past her, trying to keep an eye on Marta, but a large group of students was crossing the Atrium to the Eiger, blocking her from view.

"I've found Marta a smaller uniform," Dr. Reza said. She held up a suit carrier. "Do you know where she is?"

"She's over there," I said, pointing, but Marta had vanished again. Dr. Reza looked puzzled.

"Is everything all right?" My expression must have betrayed me. "Why don't you take this to her?" She held out the bag and pointed up to the Lower Gallery, where Marta's small figure was just visible, pushing through the crowds of students on their way to second study.

"Thanks," I said, and I pulled the bag out of her grasp and ran up the Eiger after Marta, who had disappeared yet again.

Marta moved quickly, but I guessed where she was going. There was precious little privacy at High Realms, and although there was no lock on the door, our shared room was the only space we could call our own.

Hesitating outside Room 1A, I contemplated knocking. Then I compromised by tapping on the door and pushing it open. I saw Marta sitting on the desk in front of the window, irradiated by the sunlight slicing either side of her, her skirt pulled up on one side to her thigh. She was holding a burning match.

As I entered, she whipped around, pulling her skirt down. We looked at each other silently for a long moment, absorbing our new truths. Then, incredibly, Marta smiled. "I suppose it was inevitable," she said. "I'd rather you knew sooner rather than later. It makes it easier."

I crossed the room and sat down slowly on my bed. "Why?" I asked her.

"Why is it easier, or why do it?" Marta replied calmly.

"Both."

Marta looked at me thoughtfully. "It's a solution. Of sorts. Or at least it sometimes is. Sometimes it's just a . . . mitigation."

I stared at her, stunned by her eloquence, which jarred with the raw brutality of what I'd seen her doing. "Marta," I began, but I didn't know what else to say.

"As for you knowing," said Marta loudly, ignoring me, "that's a solution to the awkwardness of you *not* knowing, which frankly would've been a logistical nightmare." She folded the spent match into a piece of paper and dropped it into the bin beside her. "But please don't mention this to anyone," she added. Seeing my expression, her tone changed. "*Promise* me."

"OK. I won't." *At the end of the day, it was her business,*

I thought. Marta sighed and gazed out of the window. Then she indicated the suit carrier. "Is that from Dr. Reza?"

"Yes."

She sighed again, and muttered something about an interrogation. Taking the bag over to her bed, she began to take off her uniform and replace it with the smaller size. I looked on silently as she pulled her cardigan and shirt over her head, with no need even to unbutton the clothes, so small was her body relative to them: and there were her wasted, skeletal arms, and the shoulder blades and vertebrae that jutted out beneath her skin like a relief map; and below them her painfully narrow hips, and the scarred and freshly wounded thighs which she did not, now, try to hide from me.

I knew I should leave her be, but I couldn't stop myself. There was something about witnessing someone cause themselves such excruciating pain that offended my sense of logic. To me, pain was something to be avoided or minimized at all costs. I had known pain, both emotional and physical. I'd felt the former most acutely after my mother had died, and the latter when I took up hockey as a way of exorcising my grief. It was the *absence* of pain that brought me relief, but in the split second between me pushing open the door and her removing the match, Marta had looked almost as content as she had in Miss Kepple's lesson.

"What happened at Elevenses?" I asked her.

"It doesn't matter."

"Was it Bella?"

Marta nodded, but as she did so I spotted a piece of paper lying near where she'd been sitting on the desk. It was covered in dense, sloping handwriting. "What's that?"

She sighed. "It's a letter."

"Who from?" I could tell she didn't want to talk about it, but there was something in Marta's expression that made me keep asking questions: a kind of terrified, suppressed shame.

"Rose—"

"Who's it from?" I took a step closer, trying to read the signature, but Marta picked up the letter and crushed it in her palm.

"It's nothing, Rose. Leave me alone." Sometimes, in my more cowardly and self-interested moments, I wish that I had. But something inside me had shifted when I'd seen Marta help Gerald, and again when she'd run up the Eiger behind us this morning, her face shining with anticipation. I'd realized that she was more than just a troublemaker. I felt closer to her, and I wanted to help her.

"If it were nothing, you wouldn't be hurting yourself." I spoke more bluntly than I'd intended, but it worked. Marta looked defiant.

"The letter is from my father," she said curtly. "He wants me to leave High Realms."

"Why?"

Marta flinched. "It's complicated. He's on his own."

"My dad's alone now, too. But—"

"It's not the same. My father can be very difficult. And he's not well." She sighed again, her face pinched with strain. "If my mother were still around, things would be different."

"When did she—"

"In February," Marta said repressively, and I was shocked at how recent it was. A lump formed in my throat. My mother was dead, too, and since I'd arrived at High Realms it had been easy to forget that fact—to imagine, even subconsciously, that she was at home; that when I went back to London for Christmas, she would be there. The reminder of the finality of her absence was more than I could bear. I looked up at Marta and saw that her green eyes were full of tears. "I've got until Christmas," she said.

There was a knock at the door. I assumed it was Major Gregory, and wanted to scream at him to go away. I felt close to reaching an understanding with Marta; an empathy sparked by the fact that we'd both gone through the same thing. I remembered how limp and devastated I'd still been six months after my mother died. I would have been in no condition to come away to school, but here Marta was, trying to make the best of things. I felt determined to help her, but I also knew that attempting to avoid Major Gregory would have been fatal. I called for him to enter, but it was Dr. Reza who stepped into the room.

"I'm sorry to turn up unannounced," she said. Marta and I stared at her, stunned by her courtesy. "I've just been speaking to Bella Ford."

"I'm sorry I was rude to her," Marta said at once. "I'll do lacrosse."

"I told Bella that I've signed you off Games for the foreseeable future," Dr. Reza went on, as if Marta hadn't spoken.

"Why?" Marta asked eventually. She looked wary.

"We can talk about it when you come and see me for your next appointment," Dr. Reza replied, and I guessed where Marta had really been first thing that morning. She smiled at Marta. "Did we say Monday afternoon?"

Very slowly, her expression somewhere between mutiny and resignation, Marta nodded.

"Good." Dr. Reza nodded. "Would you give me a moment with Rose, please?" Marta and I stared at her in surprise. "It won't take long."

Marta left the room. As she did so, she glanced warningly at me, her meaning plain. Then Dr. Reza and I stood together on opposite sides of Room 1A.

At last she spoke, her tone gentle. "I wanted to ask you how you're getting on, Rose."

My instinct was to bristle. Had I shown signs of being intimidated, overwhelmed? I'd taken such pains to appear breezy and unconcerned; focused on the next activity, like everybody else at High Realms. "I'm fine," I said bluntly. I looked down at my feet, encased in the stiff leather of my new shoes.

"Have you lived away from home before?"

"No."

"High Realms can take some getting used to," she said, and on the final word I realized that her tone had changed. I looked up and saw that her gaze had landed on our desk. There, in the pool of light beneath the window, were half a dozen spent matches, and the screwed-up letter from Marta's father.

I will never understand exactly why Dr. Reza came to Room 1A that afternoon. With the benefit of hindsight, I suppose she'd guessed that morning that something was seriously wrong with Marta, and her enquiry about my welfare was really only a prelude to asking about my roommate. What I know for certain is that I failed Marta—and Lloyd, Sami, and myself—in my answer to the question Dr. Reza went on to ask me. There were other turning points, other grave mistakes, but when Dr. Reza asked me, very quietly, whether I had noticed anything unusual or worrying about Marta, I should not have lied; should not have said brusquely—or in any other way—that yes, she was fine; that she'd only come back to 1A to pick up a book she'd forgotten. I should not have obeyed Marta's look of warning as she left the room. Most of all, I should not have promised Marta that I wouldn't tell anyone about what she was doing to herself or her father's demand. I regret my own naivety for thinking that it was the right thing to do. Looking back, I suppose I had already started to enter into the High Realms covenant that asking for help was simply not the done thing.

Chapter 4

A strange mixture of dread and exhilaration pervaded the rest of September. My memory of that time has been largely eclipsed by what followed, but I do remember that Marta, Lloyd, Sami, and I tried to find ways to overcome the hostility we faced at High Realms, with varying degrees of success. Genevieve, Sylvia, and the ten other members of the Senior Patrol seemed to make it their mission to make our lives at their school untenable, but they hadn't factored the very thing that had brought us there in the first place: our determination to succeed. We still felt lucky to be at High Realms, and we were reluctant to give up, even under such intense pressure.

Lloyd's growing friendship with Max contributed significantly to the modicum of acceptance we gained among our peers. Max was very popular—an alpha figure despite his status as a scholar—and Genevieve's obvious disapproval didn't deter him from sometimes hanging out with Lloyd and the rest of us. He gave Lloyd several organ lessons a week, from which Lloyd often returned worse for wear. Alcohol flowed into High Realms via two groundsmen who'd been bribed with the pooled resources of the Senior Patrol, and Max was in charge of hiding it in the organ loft until it was required for parties. Drugs were in shorter supply, and seemed to be the preserve of a small core of the richest students, who tended to keep their stash for themselves and their partners.

Sami and I found our niches, too. I got into the hockey First XI, which earned me the grudging respect of my teammates—with the exception of Sylvia and Genevieve. Sports turned out to be a good niche because the loyalty the players held to the team was greater than their antipathy to me. For an hour every morning, and three hours on a Saturday afternoon, I had a license to communicate with people who completely ignored me the rest of the time. Sami joined Medical Society, which was run by Dr. Reza, and soon became the star of the group. This was a relief, because he and Lloyd were put in the Ds for rugby, neither of them having ever played before. As the weeks wore on, I became accustomed to seeing both of them—but particularly Sami—with numerous minor injuries from training and matches.

Marta refused to take part in any activities, and was bullied even more badly when Bella and the others found out that she'd been signed off Games. Often they targeted her in the bathroom at the end of the girls' corridor, because Major Gregory never went near it. One of the horrors to which they subjected Marta was dubbed *the sauna*. One Saturday afternoon they closed the windows, turned six showers up to the highest temperature and tied Marta to a radiator, her mouth gagged with a pair of tights. They left her there for two hours, keeping guard outside. As soon as I heard about what was happening, I ran for Lloyd and Sami, and together we pleaded with Bella and Genevieve to let her out, hearing Marta's muffled moans from inside the bathroom.

They refused, ultimately releasing her just in time for late roll call. I will never forget seeing Marta emerge from the dense clouds of steam, coughing, her hair plastered to her head and her uniform drenched in sweat, shaking from head to toe. We half carried her back to 1A and sat with her for several hours, talking about prep and doing crosswords to distract her from what she'd been through.

We tried to encourage Marta to keep a low profile, but she seemed unable to help herself. The fact that she'd never been to school meant that she lacked social awareness at the best of times. All too often this manifested itself as a flagrant disregard for the hierarchy that governed High Realms, and all four of us suffered as a result. It happened with depressing frequency, but certain incidents stick in my mind. One or two evenings a week, Max would sneak into Hillary House, and I remember a night in mid-September when I was kept awake by him and Genevieve giggling next door in 1B. On the other side of our room Marta was curled under her blankets, reading. Then Genevieve started to moan softly. I lay there for a few minutes, ashamed of the prickles of titillation that spiked my embarrassment. Genevieve's moans grew louder. I turned over, ready to roll my eyes at Marta, but she was staring at the ceiling, her body rigid. Suddenly Genevieve emitted a muffled shriek of pleasure, and without warning Marta jumped out of bed, rushed to the party wall and hammered on it with balled fists for over a minute. In retaliation, Genevieve ordered the Senior Patrol to deny us access to the Dining Hall for three days. We knew better than to complain to Major Gregory or anyone else, and managed to survive on the contents of Sami's care package and a few surreptitious handouts from Max.

On so many nights, I saw Marta burn herself. She never attempted to hide it from me. As she'd realized on the first day of lessons, to do so would have been virtually impossible. She and I spent almost every hour together, every day of the week. On top of sharing a room, we were in nearly all the same classes—except that I studied Math while Marta took Philosophy and her extra subject, Physics—and we did the same morning and evening duty in the stables. The enforced closeness meant that we came to know a lot about each other. The shyness that characterized our behavior in the first few days and nights of sharing Room 1A swiftly fell away, and Marta's body became almost as familiar to me as my own. I grew used to seeing her scars, and to her physical frailty, which contrasted so starkly with her mental agility, and with my own increasing fitness. Every so often I mentioned my mother's death, hoping she would talk to me about her own feelings, but she never did, instead withdrawing into herself in a way that made me think it was better to stick to talking about homework.

I didn't fight Marta's impulse to harm herself, viewing it as a coping mechanism for her grief that I had no business interfering with. On the mornings after I'd heard the rasp of a match being struck in the early hours, followed by the hiss as it met soft flesh, I stole ice packs from the Pavilion freezer after hockey, and watched Marta press them against her inner thighs, her expression carefully blank as she avoided my eyes. I began to wonder whether she resented me for knowing how much pain she was causing herself. Then, one night, my period arrived early and without warning, badly staining my sheets with almost a week to go before wash day.

In the morning Marta marched downstairs to Major Gregory's study and demanded clean linens, refusing to leave until he'd provided them. She helped me make up my bed, only shrugging when I thanked her. "You help me all the time," she said, and the small smile she gave me seemed to acknowledge multitudes.

The letters arrived a couple of times a week, and again Marta made no attempt to hide them from me. She read each one very carefully, bolt upright on the window seat, the paper crumpling where she clutched it. Sometimes, tentatively, I asked her what the letter said. I felt certain that Marta's father would soon change his mind about withdrawing her from school; that he was simply adjusting to life without her. But Marta shook her head every time, her face pinched with disappointment. She would sit down at our desk and write back to her father: three or four pages in her trademark red ink, never uttering a word to me.

Apart from what he'd told us in the first few days, Lloyd guarded his privacy closely. Eventually he revealed that he'd been in a children's home until he was eleven, before being fostered by several different families. "The most recent couple were OK," he told us, sprawled on Marta's bed in his rugby kit. "They're musicians. They taught me singing and the piano, and that was cool. But I'm not under any illusions—fostering was their job. *I* was their job." He glanced at Sami, who'd shown us a long letter and several photographs from home just that morning. "This place is hard work, but it's a means to an end," he told us.

It *was* hard work, but the lessons and the vast amounts of prep didn't bother me: it was the fact that only Lloyd, Sami, Marta, and Max talked to me, which meant that

I sometimes felt lonely. Back in London, my father had only driven his cab during the hours I was at school. His presence was dependable: whether in the next room while I did my homework, or across the table as we ate dinner (always at half past five—I never got used to "supper' at High Realms, which was at eight o'clock), or on the touchline, bundled in his fleece as I played hockey. His main reason for supporting me in applying to High Realms was his belief that my mother's death had come at a crucial moment in my adolescence, and that I'd been robbed of one of the most important periods in which to make friends. In his view, a fresh start in new surroundings, and what the prospectus called a *ready-made social life,* was exactly what I needed. I'd been more interested in the *destinations of leavers,* but even so, during those first few weeks at High Realms, I often felt guilty for not having made more friends. The company of other people was a powerful currency within that harsh regime; a protection that no amount of personal strength could match. On the occasions I ate alone in the Dining Hall, which I had to do if the others were busy, I felt an odd, appetite-diminishing shame.

The weekends could be particularly difficult, and I clearly recall one Saturday in early October—the Saturday on which everything changed again, in fact—I had lunch on my own after lessons finished. Marta had beetled off to the Library to verify something Major Gregory had said in History, and Sami and Lloyd had a rugby match. I ate at a table in the corner, surrounded by the happy uproar of High Realms celebrating the beginning of the weekend, trying to console myself with the fact that I had a hockey match to play that afternoon.

I was stowing my tray when I felt a tap on my shoulder. I wheeled around to see Max, his springy hair held back with a headband. "Congratulations!"

"What for?"

"Come with me." He tucked his arm in mine and marched me into the Atrium. "You're third in the Rankings," he said, swatting some younger students away so I could read the notice. The Lower Sixth had been ranked in order of attainment, with scores awarded for each subject and averaged to determine our positions.

Summa Cum Laude
M. *De Luca: 99*
Magna Cum Laude
L. *Williams: 95*
R. *Lawson: 93*
S. *Maudsley: 93*
Cum Laude
S. *Lynch: 87*

There followed a few more names, and then Max's. I felt a quick surge of relief, mingled with concern for Sami. I was sure he would be worried about his score and the fact that Sylvia had beaten him. Major Gregory reminded us on an almost daily basis that he expected us to be top of the year in return for our scholarships, insisting that they could be retracted at any time. As worrying as this was, coming out on top seemed achieveable for now: most of our classmates were mediocre at best in intellectual terms and didn't bother to work hard, either.

"So that's the *first* bit of good news," Max said, his arm still in mine as he led me out of the front door on to the drive. It was a misty sort of day with an autumnal chill in the air, and I was grateful for the confident warmth of Max's body next to mine as we began to cross the lawn.

"Where're we going?"

"To find Marta, of course," he said, looking at me in surprise. "I thought you'd want to tell her she's got the SCL spot. Normally Sylvia takes it."

"OK." Privately, I doubted that Marta would care. She was devoted to her studies, but apparently out of genuine enjoyment rather than a desire to be on top. Unlike Lloyd, Sami, and me, she seemed indifferent to her grades, although she'd grasped High Realms's unnecessarily complicated marking system long before I'd managed to do so. I said none of this to Max, but allowed him to escort me in the direction of the Straker Library. "Are the Rankings a big deal?" I asked.

"Yup. If you're near the bottom, you get shat on by the Mags," he replied succinctly. "Worst-case scenario—you get house arrest. You're not allowed to leave your room until your Ranking improves."

"*What*?"

Max nodded. "It's pretty rare. I got it once. It was *terrible*. You feel like you're going mad. They double all your prep, too."

"But you can't go to lessons, so how're you supposed to—"

"Well, that's Dr. Reza's view, too. She opposes house arrest." Max laughed unconvincingly. "She tries to get people out early, but it never works—it just antagonizes whoever put you there. Another tip for you," he said, squeezing my arm, "don't tell Reza any more than she needs to know. About *anything*. In my experience, when she starts interfering, things take a turn for the worse."

I absorbed this, thinking of how wary Marta seemed of Dr. Reza. "She seems OK," I said at last.

"Hey—who's been here longer? She's *fine*, but honestly, she's caused trouble for us in the past. Keep her at arm's length, would be my advice." Max grinned at me, but I felt a strange stiffness in the arm that was looped under mine. "Look," he said, shaking his arm free, "there's Marta."

I followed Max's gaze to the Library steps, down which Marta was scurrying, her arms loaded with books. As we looked on, Jolyon Astor ran up the steps, jostling her. She stumbled, and the books scattered.

"Hey!" I couldn't stop myself from shouting after him. He turned in the doorway.

"Can I help you?"

"You did that on purpose," I said, his haughty expression making me feel foolish. Marta was collecting up the books, wiping their covers carefully. Max spoke, his tone light.

"They're so easy to trip over, aren't they?" he said, gesturing to Jolyon's gilt-braided Captain General gown and his own, less ornate one. "You didn't mean any harm, mate."

Jolyon's eyes glimmered unpleasantly. "I suppose not," he said. "Watch *you* don't come to any harm, though, won't you, mate?" He disappeared into the Library.

I went to Marta and began to help her pick up the books. There were at least a dozen of them, mostly on subjects unrelated to our A-Level courses. "Thanks," she said. "Hello, Max."

"Hiya." He bent down and handed her the last book. He

smiled at her in his usual engaging way, but I saw a flicker of tension in his eyes. "You're on top of the Rankings!" he told her.

For a moment, Marta looked confused. "Oh," she said. Max watched her expectantly, but she turned to me and said, "I *knew* it. Major Gregory isn't unbiased about what happened in Northern Ireland. This book says—"

"Marta," I interrupted, seeing Max's expression, "aren't you pleased?" I stared at her, hoping she would realize that she'd been tactless, but she only looked bewildered. Finally, after several awkward moments, she turned to him.

"Thank you for coming to tell me," she said stiffly.

He shrugged. "I just thought you'd be pleased to—you know—*have* something." Marta looked more confused than ever. "Scoring ninety-nine in the Rankings is pretty special. The whole school will know your name. You'll get a Privilege— maybe even a Bonus. *Free time*," he clarified exasperatedly.

"Oh," Marta said again. She looked down at the books in her arms, and I knew she wanted nothing more than to cart them up to our room and start reading them. "Sorry," she said. "This is all quite new to me."

"Sure," said Max easily. Then, "I'd better go. I'm teaching Lloyd in a few minutes."

He patted me on the shoulder and started to hurry away, but I suddenly realized something. "Max!"

He turned, still smiling.

"Lloyd's playing rugby. Didn't he tell you?"

"Oh." Max ran his fingers through his hair. "I'd forgotten."

"And you said there was more good news."

"Right, yeah . . ." Max ran his fingers through his hair again. "I don't know whether—"

"Go on, tell us," I said, and even Marta looked intrigued. Max pressed his lips together for a moment, appearing to deliberate with himself. Then he smiled winningly again, and came over to us. He slung an arm around each of our shoulders and began to walk us away from the Library.

"There's a party tonight," he said in a low voice. "Down by Donny Stream, out of sight of the Main House. We've been going there since Fourth Form. We drag some wood down from the barns and build a bridge over the water, so we can get into the woods. For—you know—*privacy*." He winked, then gazed at us impressively, waiting for our response. "Bridge Night is a pretty big deal. Attendance is by invitation only. I'm inviting you—and Lloyd and Sami, of course."

"*Really?*" The word had slipped out of my mouth before I could stop it.

"Yup." Max grinned, but Marta suddenly swore. "What is it?" he demanded.

"I've got another WP this afternoon. From Genevieve," she said, her color rising in frustration. "I completely forgot. I'll be late." She looked down at the books in her arms.

"Don't worry," said Max, but I could tell he was irritated. "I'll tell Gin you were with me."

"Maybe you could also tell her to stop being so fucking unkind to us." Marta's voice was suddenly hard. There was a short silence in which Max looked at her in surprise.

"Easy there," he said after a few moments. "Gin's Senior Patrol."

"She's given me more WPs than the rest of the year put together," Marta shot back. She glanced at me, apparently looking for support, but I said nothing. "She's got a serious anger problem. I don't know how you can stomach her, Max."

She'd gone too far. Max's handsome face twisted momentarily, and I tried to think of something placatory to intervene with, but he spoke before I could. "There's more to Gin than meets the eye," he told Marta, his tone both defensive and warning. "She's been through a lot."

"Yeah, OK." Marta turned to walk away, but Max grabbed her arm, pulling her none-too-gently back around to face him.

"Seriously, Gin's had a really tough time," he told her, looking at us both intently. "Her younger sister died two years ago, right here at school. If she's angry, she has a right to be."

Marta and I stared. Our reaction appeared to mollify him, because he sounded calmer as he went on, "She doesn't talk about it, and she doesn't like anyone else to, either. Persie was Gin's best friend. She was also fucking great." He bit his lip. "Just because it isn't mentioned doesn't mean Gin isn't hurting. I reckon it's a good thing I've told you. Nobody speaks to you except me, so you'd never have found out otherwise."

Marta and I looked at him silently. My scalp prickled with embarrassment. Judging by Marta's flushed cheeks, even she felt abashed. Max's expression softened further. "You weren't to know. You're still invited tonight, yeah? And don't worry about being late for your WP. I happen to know that Gin's at an appointment with Dr. Reza." He winked and strode away across the lawns, his gown billowing behind him.

The task Genevieve had assigned Marta was clearing manure off the stable courtyard. Marta reluctantly went to get started while I hurried off to my hockey match. Genevieve and Sylvia weren't there, which was almost unheard of.

We lost to Roedean that afternoon, and, although I dreaded Genevieve and Sylvia finding out, I was still excited about the party. Bridge Night seemed like an opportunity to meet some new people in a more relaxed setting than High Realms generally permitted. Lloyd and Sami sometimes came to lounge around in Room 1A after supper, but if Genevieve heard us from next door she would barge in and send them away, citing a rule about no-boys-in-girls'-rooms, which nobody else obeyed—least of all Genevieve herself. After the boys had gone I tended to read silently or go to bed early while Marta worked. Being alone and unoccupied was making it easier to sink back into the grief that I'd worked hard to erode over the past few years, and to submit to the low-level homesickness that was setting in as time went on and life at High Realms got no easier. I decided to go and help Marta with her WP, to make sure she finished in time to come to the party.

As I strode across the Hexagon toward the stables, I thought of what Max had told us about Genevieve. I was horrified by the idea that Genevieve's sister had died right here, at High Realms, but the longer I reflected on it, the less surprised I was. Genevieve's anger frequently seemed disproportionate, even irrational. In the years after my mother's death, I too had sometimes experienced burning, irrepressible rage: rage that threatened to become all-consuming unless it had a target. What I didn't fully understand was why Marta was so often the focus of Genevieve's anger. Marta could be tactless and willful, and her academic success would be easy to envy at a different school, but none of these things seemed commensurate with Genevieve's loathing of her.

Marta was shuffling across the gravel, pushing a wheelbarrow full of manure toward the clocktower arch. I called her name, and she smiled grimly, pushing her hair out of her eyes. The smaller uniform Dr. Reza had given her hadn't included new overalls, and her frame was drowned by the ones she was wearing. "I'll give you a hand."

"Don't bother. I'm nearly done." Marta was tenaciously independent, even masochistic, about her punishments.

"I don't want to miss out," I said, picking up the shovel. "What was this WP for, anyway?"

"Bad table manners. She said if I'm going to eat like an animal, I can clear up after them, too. What a bitch." Marta grinned, but then she caught the look on my face. "Yeah, yeah—poor bereaved Genevieve. I'm not sure I believe it, you know."

"Max wouldn't lie."

"Come off it—he's no saint." Marta gave me a sly look. "Are you into him, Rose?"

"Into him?" I stared at her, baffled as to how she had picked up on my feelings for Max, the nature of which even I didn't fully understand. "I don't—I mean, I like him, but as a friend. I don't think he's a liar," I said, trying to distract her. Marta was looking over my shoulder.

"We can check that," she said. "Hey—Sylvia!"

I turned. Sylvia was leading her horse, an enormous thoroughbred called Cleopatra, out of the Senior Patrol stable. She looked over at us, her expression coldly quizzical.

"Hello!" Marta marched toward her, while I trailed behind, feeling awkward. Most people found Sylvia deeply intimidating and would never approach her without an invitation. "Can we ask you something?"

Cleopatra snorted, and Sylvia ran her hand over her nose. Ignoring Marta, she looked me in the eye. "What was the score?"

I swallowed. "Four–three."

"To us?"

"To them."

Her lips thinned. "I leave school for *one* afternoon—"

"Have you been out?" Marta's surprise was justified. It was very unusual to be allowed to leave the Estate for day leave, and even rarer to be permitted a night away from school, which they called extraneous leave.

"Clearly." I thought Sylvia looked more rattled than the Roedean defeat warranted. She glanced at Marta. "What did you want to ask me?"

"It's about Genevieve's sister," Marta began, and Sylvia's face paled, her eyebrows raising in shock rather than disdain, but at that moment Gerald cantered into the courtyard on his horse, Whistler. He rounded the statue, his body rising and falling effortlessly with the horse's gait, and came to an abrupt halt next to us.

"You're not taking her out," he told Sylvia without preamble, indicating her horse. "It's too late in the day."

She looked up at him, her expression growing even colder. "What on earth makes you think you can tell me what to do?"

Gerald jumped down from the saddle. "I've been promoted,"

he said, his pockmarked face very close to Sylvia's. "Briggs has given me a special role. Wardlaw signed it off this morning—I'm Head of Horses."

She took a step backward, sneering at him. "You'll need more than a new job title to start bossing me around. It's a shame Briggs can't promote you to having friends. We'll be thinking of you tonight, Gerald—"

"*Bitch*." Gerald suddenly squared up to her. "You frigid bitch."

"No." Sylvia spoke over him, her eyes hard. "I know what I want. And it's not a filthy, flame-haired stable hand, as I think I've made very clear." She thrust her foot into the stirrup and swung herself onto her horse. Then she looked down at Marta and me. "You two," she said curtly, "keep your noses out of what doesn't concern you." Her heels tapped the flank of her horse. "Stay away from the stream later on, Gerald," she called over her shoulder as she rode away.

For a fleeting moment, confusion rippled over Gerald's face. Then he emitted a mortified snarl, jumped back onto his own horse, and galloped after Sylvia out of the courtyard. Marta and I looked at each other. "So it's true," Marta muttered. "The look on her face . . . you'd think she saw it happen."

"Maybe she did." I recalled the mask slipping from Sylvia's face. "She must've known her."

"Yep." I could tell Marta had lost interest. "I'd better get on. Don't worry about me, Ro. Go back to Hillary."

I shook my head. I could hear Sylvia and Gerald's raised voices from beyond the clocktower arch, and didn't want to leave Marta alone in the vicinity of their aggression. Nor did

I want to return to our empty room by myself. "I'll stay and help you," I said.

It took us half an hour to finish clearing the manure. We were just returning the wheelbarrow to Block A when we heard footsteps on the gravel behind us. It was Gerald, on foot this time, his swagger diminished. "This party tonight," he said, addressing Marta.

She looked at him in surprise. "What about it?"

"You been invited?"

She shrugged. "Yes."

Gerald cleared his throat, his bearing suddenly awkward. "Want to come with me?"

His question couldn't have come as more of a surprise, and I immediately doubted his motivation. Gerald had never treated Marta with anything other than total scorn. Furthermore, Sylvia's parting shot had been clear: he was not welcome at Bridge Night. Marta was twisting the sleeve of her overalls in her hand. "Thank you," she said after a few moments, "but I can't."

"Why not?"

"Because I—" She looked down at her Wellington-clad feet and was silent. "Because I'm not going," she said at last.

"Oh." For a moment, Gerald looked relieved, but then he scowled. "You're just saying that to get rid of me."

"No," Marta interrupted, "I'm definitely not going." She looked Gerald in the eye. "I'm sorry," she said quietly.

He glowered at her. "Fuck you, gremlin," he spat, and stormed away across the courtyard.

Marta was worrying at the gravel with the tip of her boot, her face creased. Suddenly I felt frustrated by her behavior.

I was sure that her refusal to attend would offend Max and whoever had sanctioned our invitation to Bridge Night. I took a step closer to her. "Why?" I asked.

She looked up. "Rose," she said, her expression suddenly full of despair, "look at me. Do you really think I'm fit to be anyone's date?"

I'd been referring to her decision not to come to the party, but to this day, I'm glad that Marta misunderstood my question. If she hadn't, I'm convinced that I was sufficiently annoyed with her that I would not have been kind to her that evening. As it is, I know I didn't do enough to help her. I should have responded more considerately; asked her what she meant, or simply reassured her, but I am sorry to say that I did not. I was self-absorbed enough to be irritated that even Marta—strange, bullied, bedraggled Marta—had been invited on a date, whereas I, who felt acutely lonely, and cared much more about fitting in, had not been asked out by anyone.

Chapter 5

Lloyd and Sami dropped by 1A while I was getting ready for Bridge Night, toweling my hair dry after a shower. Marta was lying on her front on her bed, muttering to herself as she did her Physics prep. When the boys learned that she was planning not to come, their disappointment was even greater than mine.

"Come *on*, Marta," said Lloyd. "You can't study all the time." She ignored him, carefully writing down an answer. He spoke more loudly. "*Marta.*"

She looked up, startled. "What?"

"You should come with us tonight." Lloyd stood over her. "We need to integrate. Have some fun."

Marta put down her pen and rolled onto her back, looking up at him through candid green eyes. "I am having fun."

He sighed and sat down next to her on the bed. "Mar," he said, "I worked hard for this invitation."

From the window seat, Sami raised his eyebrows at me. "Are you worried about the others?" he asked Marta. I assumed he was referring to Genevieve, Sylvia, and the rest of Marta's coterie of tormentors.

"No more than usual."

"I don't think Genevieve will bother you this evening," Lloyd told her. "She's got her own problems."

"Like what?" I asked, thinking of what Max had told us.

Sami looked warningly at Lloyd, but Lloyd went on, "She got pregnant."

Marta and I stared at him.

"Max said she dealt with it this afternoon," Lloyd added nonchalantly. I couldn't help but think that it was indiscreet of Max to tell Lloyd that his girlfriend was having an abortion, but before I could say anything we heard loud, jeering voices in the corridor. There was a knock at the door—the bassy thud of a balled fist—and Sami jumped up to open it, putting himself between us and the visitors.

"Where's the happy couple, then?" It was Sylvia's voice. She was craning her neck, looking over Sami's shoulder into Room 1A.

"What do you mean?"

"Gerald and the gremlin." Sylvia pushed past him into our room, followed by Genevieve, who looked subdued. Sylvia stopped next to Marta's bed and stared down at her. "What are you doing there? You should be meeting your boyfriend."

Marta pushed her books away. She seemed to have had enough of being harangued, and I didn't blame her. "What the hell are you talking about?"

"I'm talking about your date with the new *Head of Horses*."

"*What?*" Sami demanded, looking scandalized, at the same time as Marta told Sylvia sharply, "I told him no. Not that it's any of your business."

Briefly, Sylvia looked stunned. She looked around at

Genevieve, who was smoking silently out of our window, a bottle of sherry by her foot, paying no attention to what was going on. Slowly, Sylvia turned back to Marta. "I mean, it *is* our business," she told her slyly. "We're the matchmakers here. Or we would have been."

"Matchmakers?"

Sylvia jumped up from the seat she'd taken, uninvited, at the foot of Marta's bed. "I told Gerald he could come to Bridge Night if he managed to get you to be his date," she said. "When we spoke to him just now, he seemed to think you'd said yes. Fucking liar. Come on, Gin," she commanded. "We'll have to deal with him." Genevieve did not seem to hear her. "*Gin.*" She nodded briskly and got up, stubbing out her cigarette.

"Wait a minute," Lloyd called as they reached the door. His expression was puzzled. "Why did you do this?"

It was Genevieve who turned around, her eyes glittering malevolently. "You and Gerald could have helped each other out," she said, addressing Marta. "Two lonely virgins together. It's not like anybody else will ever touch you." She and Sylvia left, banging the door behind them.

"Ignore her," Sami said to Marta at once. She was sitting cross-legged on her bed, staring at the wall. Sami watched her for a moment, then turned to us, clearly angry. "What's with their obsession with people being virgins?" he demanded.

Lloyd returned Sami's gaze, his head on one side. "Some would say that sex is power."

My face grew warm, and I looked away. I rummaged loudly in my washbag as Sami snapped, "I can guess who's planted that stupid idea in your head."

"It's not stupid. It's true."

"Just because *he* climbed the greasy pole via Genevieve, and now you're—"

"Shut up." Lloyd's voice was suddenly hard. "You don't know what you're talking about, Sami. Genevieve *needed* Max. He looked after Gin after her sister died—without him Gin would've fallen apart." *So Lloyd already knew about Persie*, I thought, but had not shared the information with me and Marta.

"If that's what he's told you, feel free to believe him. But I'm still calling bullshit on your twisted idea that *sex is power*."

I glanced around to see Sami pulling at his shirt collar, his cheeks flushed with anger.

"You know," Lloyd said goadingly, still sprawled at the foot of Marta's bed, "anyone would think I'd touched a nerve."

Sami's flush deepened, but he didn't give up. "Sex is *love*," he said, his voice trembling unhelpfully, "and *love* is power."

"Is that what your mummy told you?" Lloyd snapped, at the same time as Marta said, "Only the second one is true." Her voice was quiet compared to Lloyd's, almost inaudible, but we all heard it.

Slowly, I turned to face the room. Marta was staring down at her Physics textbook, her finger on the page as though she were reading it, but her eyes were glazed and her bearing totally rigid.

"Mar," said Sami, his tone drained of pugnacity, "what's the matter?"

"Nothing." She looked up sharply. "Can I borrow something to wear, Rose?"

"To wear?"

"For the party. I haven't got any smart clothes. Can I borrow something?"

"Yes," I said, dazed, "but I thought—"

"I've changed my mind." Marta scrambled off her bed, tossing her textbook on to the floor. "The four of us need to stick together. But first"—she pointed at Lloyd, then Sami—"you two've got to leave Rose and me to get ready. You're always in here, loafing around."

"Come on! You love it," Lloyd replied, grinning. He was leaning back in my desk chair, his arms tucked behind his head, while Sami looked anxiously from him to Marta. "You can get changed with us here, Marta—we won't look—"

"No," Marta said obstinately, "go away. We'll see you at roll call." Sami got to his feet, and Lloyd reluctantly followed suit. Marta hustled them out of 1A, ignoring Lloyd's grumbling. "Bye!" she said, shutting the door. She turned to me and smiled, although she looked a little weary. "Are you pleased I'm coming, Rose?"

"Yes," I said, realizing how true the words were as I spoke them. "I really am." Without thinking, I reached for Marta and pulled her into a clumsy hug. I felt her forehead rest on my shoulder for a moment, her tangled hair brushing my jawline, but her body remained stiff. "It'll be fun," I told her.

"I hope so." Marta stepped backward, her tone brisk. "So. What shall I wear?"

I remember being bemused by the way Bridge Night began. After roll call everyone went down to the Dining Hall for supper as usual. Most of the Lower Sixth were dressed up to the nines, and I was worried about how this would look to the Mags, but Max reassured us. "It's the first Saturday of the month, which means Dr. Reza will be driving most of them to the pub in Lynmouth," he said, loading his plate with lasagna. "They won't be back till gone midnight."

So we ate our supper—as the only source of food, meals were important fixtures at High Realms and rarely missed—and afterward Lloyd, Sami, Marta, and I wandered into the chilly Atrium, unsure what our next move should be. Marta was tense, tugging at the dress I'd lent her, which didn't fit her very well. The absence of a clear plan was making me uneasy, too. I began to prepare myself for the possibility of our invitation being a trick, just like Sylvia and Genevieve's taunting of Gerald.

Next to me, Lloyd was tapping his foot, glancing around the emptying Atrium. "What's up?" I asked him.

"Max said he'd show us the way."

"Rose," said Marta suddenly, "do you think I should've washed my hair?"

Lloyd, Sami, and I looked at her. Her hair stuck out in matted clumps around her pale face, and there was a long smudge of ink on her cheek. "Brushing it would've been a good start," said Lloyd heartlessly.

Marta looked at him in surprise. "Maybe I'll go upstairs and do that," she said.

Sami glared at Lloyd as she moved toward the Eiger, but Marta was halted in her tracks by Major Gregory, who was descending the stairs, wearing a khaki greatcoat and a Hillary scarf. He looked Marta up and down with less contempt than usual. "I hear congratulations are in order."

Marta blinked warily, and he pointed to the Rankings noticeboard. "*Summa cum laude*, Miss De Luca. You're clearly in the business of compensating for the many areas in which you are deficient. Your scores were rather good, too," he added, nodding at Lloyd and me, while Sami shuffled his feet uncomfortably. "Hillary House may be proud of you yet."

"Are *you* proud of us, sir?" Marta demanded. Lloyd winked at her, and she grinned back at him.

Major Gregory looked disarmed. "I am satisfied," he said at last. He cleared his throat, looking at Lloyd and Sami's suits. "I wasn't aware there was an event this evening."

"Sir!" Max was galloping down the Eiger, taking the stairs three at a time. "Sir, I forgot to tell you. We're doing a memorial recital in the antechapel—for Persie."

Major Gregory looked as though he had been slapped. "Ah," he said after a moment. "I see. I see." He looked past us to the front door.

"*Nimrod*, sir. She loved it."

"I am aware of that," Major Gregory snapped. "Late roll call will be at ten o'clock as usual."

"Of *course,* sir." Max gave him an unctuous smile. "You'll be wanting to get to the minibus," he offered, and Major Gregory nodded, walking stiffly away across the Atrium.

"*Phew.*" Max grinned at us. "I knew you wouldn't know what to tell the old bastard. Mentioning Persie always shuts him up." He led us up the Eiger, beckoning to a few other people to follow us.

"Why?" I asked, hurrying to keep up with his long strides.

"He liked her. Said she was a credit to Hillary. Then she died on his watch," he added carelessly. "You know what he's like—Hillary first, and all that." He goosestepped along the Lower Gallery, stopping at the look on Sami's face. "Oh, lighten up! He fought to get you four. Even if only to bump Hillary up the House Rankings." He looked around at us, his expression sly.

"What happened—" I began, but Sami broke in, his tone anxious.

"I hope he doesn't suspect what we're up to. I can't afford to get in any—"

"Don't worry. He's not very clever. And he'll be so wasted when he gets back after an evening jerking off about Roman legions with Briggs that he won't check Upper House." Max laughed, glancing over his shoulder at Lloyd.

"What about late roll call?"

"Oh, get with the program, Sami. The *Senior Patrol* take late roll call on Saturdays."

We followed Max deeper into the school, through departments I'd never visited before, where all the lights were off and the classroom doors were closed for the weekend. At the entrance to Raleigh House we were joined by Sylvia and Bella, who were both dressed in black. Then Max opened a door to what looked like a store cupboard, and led the way down a narrow staircase. He and Bella were talking loudly and excitedly about the last Bridge Night, which had apparently gone on until dawn. I felt full of a blazing energy at being involved, a delight that only increased when we burst through a door at the bottom and found ourselves beneath the night sky. We were in a small paved courtyard surrounded by a high brick wall. Glancing behind me, I saw that the door we'd come out of was almost entirely camouflaged in its position in the wall by a thick coat of ivy.

The space was full of bins, onto one of which Max and Bella now swung themselves. With an agility that suggested they'd done it many times before, they helped the rest of us climb up and then onto the brick wall. Crouching there in the dark, I felt sweat spring onto my palms as I looked down and saw how far away the ground was. I paused, hearing the gleeful chatter of the others around me, and wished that I could hold on to the moment for longer. Then I heard a voice beside me. "It's not as far as it looks," Sylvia said, and she jumped, her silk scarf flying behind her as she landed on the gravel path.

We ran across the rugby pitches, looping the Hexagon in favor of the cover of Lime Grove, and then traversed the croquet lawn behind Drake Cottage, which backed onto the stables. We reached the high, steep bank of Donny Stream and slithered down it, the long grass damp around our ankles, and then we were beside the rushing water, and there were the lights of many torches. Dozens of students were gathering there, each group arriving by a different route. I looked back up the bank and saw more of them running down in suits and evening dresses, the clocktower framed darkly against the night sky behind them. All around me was the glow of cigarettes, the clink of bottles, and the rasp of cans being opened. The Sixth Form of High Realms raised their drinks in the moonlight and toasted each other.

Max, Bella, and Rory and Alice Fitz-Straker ran up to the barn, returning several minutes later carrying several long planks of wood between them. They laid these over Donny Stream, supervised by Sylvia, who pulled her dress up to her waist and waded fearlessly through the deep water to secure the bridge on the muddy bank opposite. For a moment she was lost in the shadows. Then she jumped onto the planks and danced back across them, her legs gleaming wetly in the torchlight. "It's Bridge Night!" she shouted, and for once her face wasn't hard with condescension or hostility: it was full of happiness.

Marta, Lloyd, Sami, and I stood apart from the others, watching Bridge Night unfold with a mixture of thrill and apprehension. It had felt exciting to make our way to Donny Stream, but now that we were here, the coldness of the night air and the wild abandon of our classmates made the venture seem riskier than ever. None of them seemed to have the faintest concern about being caught. A bonfire was being built on the bank, and soon flames were leaping high into the air. Max left Genevieve's side and came over to us, his bow tie loose around his neck. "Guys," he said, slinging his arms around Lloyd and Marta's shoulders, "you gotta have a drink. C'mon."

He led us to where boxes and crates nestled in the long grass. "Champagne!" he said, tugging a gold-labeled bottle out of its case. "Rory nicks it from his parents' wine cellar," he said, wrenching the cork out. "They never notice. And his older brother posts us something even more useful." He winked, tapping his nose. "Go on," he urged. "You'll have more *fun*."

Lloyd, Sami, and I each drank in turn. Its acidity made me want to gag, but I swallowed, and after a burning sensation in my chest I almost immediately felt a swell of excitement, of confidence. I held the bottle out to Marta, but she shook her head.

"Oh, no," said Max, grabbing the bottle. "You *gotta* have

some Taittinger. It's the good stuff. This lot"—he pointed to our classmates—"were practically breastfed with the stuff. Open wide!" he commanded, and Marta was so surprised that she allowed him to pour some of the champagne into her mouth. She coughed, but then she grinned.

"You're right," she said to Max. "It's good."

He gave her a smacking kiss on the cheek. "It'll help you relax," he said. "High Realms doesn't have to be a battle, you know, Marta. Take it from me." He winked again, and tipped the bottle quickly, forcing her to take another large gulp. Some of the yellow liquid trickled down her chin. "These are pretty awesome, too," Max said, opening his palm to reveal some small white pills. "Want one?"

Sami, Marta, and I shook our heads, but Lloyd shrugged, swallowing one of the pills as though it was a painkiller. "You're a pal," he told Max.

Max nodded. "Where would you be without me? Now," he said firmly, "we're gonna dance the night away. Come on!"

We drank the rest of the champagne and danced under the crescent moon, in the capering light of the bonfire. Someone brought a stereo down from the barn. My inhibitions left me as Max led us in a strange, almost tribal dance in the moonlight, half ballroom, half freestyle, moving lithely between partners. He seized Lloyd and waltzed a full orbit of the bonfire with him, their movements synchronized and powerful. As he reached my side of the group he held out both of his hands to me. I took them and danced with him, our bodies helplessly colliding, his arm around my waist. The feeling of being so close to Max was as intoxicating as the champagne. He spun me around and pulled me against him, and as my arms fell around his neck I felt a new warmth: a strong and exciting desire for him that was different to anything I'd ever felt before. I leaned in closer, feeling the alcoholic sourness of his breath against my cheek. I looked up at him just as he glanced down at me. His dark eyes flickered contemplatively, and he tipped his head toward mine. I felt his lips brush my cheek, seeking my mouth.

Then somebody seized my hand, and Marta pulled me away, all the way to the other side of the bonfire. She slung her arms around my neck, acting drunker than she was, and spoke into my ear over the music. "He's not worth it, Ro. Imagine if Genevieve saw." She turned her head and kissed me quickly on the cheek, where Max's lips had just been. "Don't be embarrassed," she said. "I won't tell anyone. It'll be our secret."

At that point Lloyd and Sami came to join us, bringing another bottle of champagne, and the dancing grew wilder. Marta danced a jig on her own, her small body empowered. Passing me, she seized my wrists and pulled me toward her again, and we danced together, clumsy and free and full of sudden joy. Marta bumped into Genevieve, but Genevieve didn't snarl, because she was caught up by Max, who swept her into his arms and kissed her, her arms around his neck and his hand at the small of her back. I looked away and saw Sylvia and Bella sitting on the grassy bank, Bella's lips on Sylvia's neck. Suddenly Sylvia looked up. Her eyes caught mine.

Some moments later, I pulled my gaze away. Marta and Lloyd were standing together near the stream, their arms around each other. Marta's head was on Lloyd's chest, and

Sami stood next to them, his hand on Marta's shoulder. I went over to them. Marta was crying, the tears sliding helplessly down her cheeks. Seeing my dismay, she smiled. "I'm not sad," she said, her speech thicker than usual. "It's the opposite. I'm so happy here, with you three. I never want it to end." I pulled my sleeve over my hand to wipe away her tears. "You're my best friend," Marta told me, and I felt a rush of affection for her that was more than just the champagne. *You're mine,* I wanted to tell her, but the words wouldn't come soon enough. Marta stepped away from Lloyd, seeming to pull herself together. "Let's dance some more," she suggested.

The four of us stuck together for a while, close to the bonfire to keep the coldness of the night at bay. Max came over and gave Lloyd another bottle of champagne. We all drank from it, and my head began to spin. It was the first time I'd drunk alcohol in any significant quantity. I needed someone to hold me up, as Lloyd had done for Marta, but when I looked around for him, I saw that he and Marta had their arms around each other again. This time, they were kissing. I stared at them, feeling like I was watching a pair of strangers, unable to understand how things had evolved so quickly. Marta's hands slipped beneath Lloyd's jacket. I looked away, hoping to find Sami, but there was no sign of him.

The number of dancers on our side of the stream was dwindling as more people began to coalesce into couples. They started to spill onto the bridge, a temporary stage, and across it into the dark woods. As they stepped onto the bridge they passed Sylvia and Bella, who were stationed on the bank. I saw Max and Genevieve kiss Sylvia on the cheek before vanishing into the darkness. As they did so I knew a twinge of grief for the fact that Max had gone. I wanted to follow him to the other side, but I had no one to go with. I squinted into the darkness for Sami, and my eyes found him in a clinch with a red-haired girl, not far from where Lloyd and Marta had been kissing. Now they, too, had crossed the bridge together.

I took another swig of champagne, relishing its numbing effect. I was very cold, and with my friends gone, I had no reason to stay at Bridge Night any longer. *It had been a mistake to come at all*, I thought; a grave error to believe that partying with the High Realmsians could help someone like me make friends. I set off, making my unsteady way up the bank toward the barn. Halfway up I slipped, landing heavily on my hands and knees. My forehead brushed the wet grass.

"Rose!" Sami was hurrying up the bank behind me, his collar loose. He hauled me to my feet. "Where're you going?"

"To bed."

"Where are Marta and Lloyd?" I pointed silently to the other side of the stream, and Sami's face fell. "*Together?*"

I shrugged. "They were kissing."

Sami's expression was part horror, part sadness. "Christ," he muttered. "Shit."

"What's the problem? *You* were getting off with—"

"Ingrid and I were just messing around. Lloyd and Marta—that's different."

"*Why?*"

Sami bit his lip, gazing over the stream. The far side of Donny Stream was another steep bank, this one densely wooded, and all the sound from that direction was strangely deadened. My frustration with his silence was reaching its peak when he muttered, "Max gave Lloyd those drugs."

"What does it matter?"

Again Sami said nothing, and his reticence made me very angry. Coming to Bridge Night had not resulted in me making friends, let alone anything more. I felt excluded, and fearful that my immaturity and isolation were obvious to everyone. I thought of the warm arms around each other in the woods, the closeness I was craving, and turned away from Sami, intent on returning to the Main House. "Rose, wait. I'm sorry. I just—I don't quite know how to put it, but—"

"But *what?*"

His eyes were round and luminescent in the darkness. "Sharing a room with Lloyd," he said at last, "means I notice things . . . I know things about him. Things that not everyone sees. It must be the same for you and Marta, right?"

"What do you mean?"

"You must've picked up on it. There's something . . . something not right with her. We need to look after her, Rose. I don't think Lloyd understands that. I don't think he gets that she's—vulnerable."

I hesitated. I was cold, exhausted, and drunk, but I was still not prepared to divulge to Sami what I knew about Marta. "She's grieving," I said.

He shook his head, speaking more firmly this time. "I don't think so. *You're* grieving, Rose. I can see that. But Marta—"

"Shut up." Suddenly I was furious with him. "You've got no idea. None at all. You have *no idea* about me, Sami."

"It's nothing to be ashamed of—"

"It is. It is." I'd spoken the words before I knew what I was doing; before I even knew that I believed them. "I thought coming to High Realms would help. I thought it would make me better, but I feel so much worse." A wave of unhappiness crashed over me, and I turned away from Sami, pressing the back of my clammy hand against my mouth.

A moment passed, and then I felt Sami's hand on my shoulder. "Rose," he said gently, "Rose, I'm sorry. I shouldn't have said anything." He paused. "You're not on your own. We've all got different stuff going on, but that means we can help each other, right? It'd be different if one of us was thriving here, but"—he laughed shakily—"we're not. Not yet. Least of all me. Sometimes I don't even feel clever enough to be a Millennium Scholar." I felt a rush of sympathy for him, sullied by a guilty sense of relief that there was one problem I didn't have. "That's not the worst thing. I asked Lloyd not to tell anyone, but they've got it in for me."

"Who?"

"The rugby boys. Rory and Jolyon and the rest of them." He took a deep breath. "They say I'm rubbish at rugby because I'm too fat. They're probably right, to be honest. I promised to lose weight but they said I needed some encouragement. They smashed up my care package with a hammer. Then they made me climb into my empty trunk and tried to shut it, but it wouldn't . . . it wouldn't close. So they got a rope and tied the lid down, and left me in it for hours. Lloyd tried to let me out, but they stopped him." His voice cracked. "They're going to do it every week until it'll close without the rope."

"Fucking hell. *Sami,*" I said, reaching for him, but he shook his head.

"It's OK. *I'm* OK. Lloyd and I, we're dealing with it. We're going running—four miles every morning before breakfast. And I've stopped eating dessert—"

"Sami, this isn't right. Tell someone—tell your parents—"

"Rose, I *have*." Sami gave me a small smile. "They said they'd come and get me. Said I didn't have to stay here a day longer than I want to. But they really wanted me to come to High Realms. They kept telling me what a brilliant time I'd have. To give up after a month seems . . . unfair to them, somehow. I want them to be proud of me, of the things I do." He paused. "You, me, Lloyd, Marta—we're a team, right? I'd do anything for you guys."

I didn't know what to say. I was torn between admiration for Sami's stoicism, guilt that I hadn't known what he was going through, and surprise at how fierce his loyalty to us already was. I wondered whether I could, after all, tell him what I knew about Marta, but suddenly a muffled yell came from the woods. Sami and I looked at each other.

"What was that?" Sami ran his hands through his hair, looking apprehensive. We were the only ones left on our side of the stream. The bonfire was smoldering gently. Empty bottles shimmered in the long grass.

"I don't know." The yell had sounded to me more like one of anger than of peril, but I could not be certain.

"I'm going to have a look." Sami stared over the stream to the woods. "Someone might be hurt—"

"I'll come with you."

"No, wait here. If I'm not back in fifteen minutes, go and get help." He shrugged off his jacket and handed it to me before stomping down the slope and across the bridge: a stocky, determined figure soon swallowed by the darkness.

He was gone for about ten minutes, during which I felt

steadily more anxious, and extremely cold. Finally I heard footsteps on the bank. I leaned forward, trying to make out who it was.

"It's me," said Marta, stumbling up the bank toward me.

"What's going on? Did you see Sami?"

"Yes," she said. Her teeth were chattering. "He's fine. Everyone's fine," she added.

"Really? Lloyd, too?"

"Yeah." She looked down at me. "I want to go to bed," she said. There was a tremor in her voice that I didn't think had anything to do with the cold.

"OK," I said after a moment, and got stiffly to my feet. "But Mar, are you sure Sami and Lloyd are—"

"I'm certain," she said. "I think we should go."

We tramped up the bank, both of us shivering. I felt profoundly uneasy. I wanted to ask Marta about what had happened between her and Lloyd, as well as what Lloyd and Sami were now doing, but I was worried that if I did it would make Marta feel she could ask me about Max, which I was desperate not to go into. Marta marched ahead of me, making for Lime Grove. Then she stopped, looking over at the stables. "What's the time?"

"Half past one."

"Christ," she said. "There's no way I can be up again in five hours to muck out those fucking horses." Apart from the reprieve from lessons, which were replaced by Chapel and prep, the Sunday schedule at High Realms was no different to any other day.

Marta's eyes gleamed obstinately in the darkness. I was

annoyed, but too tired to argue with her. "I'll do it, then," I said. "Let's go to bed."

"Let's do it now," said Marta suddenly. "It'll only take us half an hour, and then we can sleep in. Gerald'll never know—"

"OK," I said after a pause. I didn't fancy the dank stables at this time of night, much less the hard physical work of mucking out, but at least this way I might hear Lloyd and Sami returning from the woods and would know that they were all right.

We looped around to the entrance of the stables and crossed the courtyard to Block C, the clocktower looming above us. We unbolted the door and stepped inside, hearing the three horses shifting in their stalls. The metal buckles of the tack hanging on the back wall shone in the moonlight. Marta snapped on the light, and we blinked in its halogen brightness.

We began to rake out the soiled straw from the stalls and piled it into the wheelbarrow, refilled the water barrel, and poured feed into the buckets. Within minutes our hands and clothes were filthy. I was unsteady on my feet with alcohol and exhaustion, and my mouth was dry. I felt as though I couldn't go on for much longer, but there was still the concrete floor to wash. Marta got out the pressure hose and had just attached it to the tap when we heard shouts coming from behind the stables. We stopped. "What's that?" said Marta.

"I don't know." The shouts were growing louder: a combination of male and female voices. I strained to try to make out who it was. The horses began to snort restlessly, as though this fresh nocturnal disturbance was a step too far, and George began to toss his head in frustration. He whinnied. The shouts reached a crescendo just behind Block C, and then died down as the voices moved farther away in the direction of the Hexagon. I looked over at Marta. She was biting her lip, clearly troubled.

George was still roaming his stall, bumping against the walls, and stamping at the ground. His behavior was starting to perturb the other two horses, who began to toss their heads and flick their tails. From the adjoining blocks we heard a chorus of answering whinnies. Marta and I looked at each other anxiously. The stables weren't far from the Hexagon, where several Senior Patrol members slept, including Gerald.

Marta went over to George's stall and spoke to him from a safe distance. "You've got to be quiet now," she said sternly. "Rose and I aren't going to hurt you." George snorted again, and Margot and Polly answered with their own noises. George butted the door of his stall, and Marta jumped backward in alarm. "For God's sake," she said, her voice rising in anger. "You beasts are just like the people here, aren't you? You're overbred, practically anything sets you off, and you're *so fucking arrogant*—"

"The feeling is mutual," said a smooth, clear voice.

Marta and I wheeled around. Genevieve and Sylvia were standing just outside Block C, their faces illuminated by the harsh halogen light, and the rest of their bodies obscured by the half door.

"Fuck," muttered Marta. Genevieve pulled back the bolt, and she and Sylvia stepped into the light. They were both disheveled, with smears of mud on their dresses and leaves in their hair. Genevieve, I saw, was deathly pale. Her eyes were full of the usual spite, but there was something else there:

a new, aggressive vulnerability. Sylvia, meanwhile, was calm. Her arms swung gently at her sides.

"You know," said Genevieve quietly, looking at Marta and me, "we've given you so many chances."

"*Bullshit*!" Marta burst out. "You've hated us from the start, it's obvious you don't want us here, and what the hell have we ever actually *done* to—"

"Oh, I wouldn't ask that now, if I were you," said Genevieve, and now her face was all blazing fury. "I really wouldn't." She looked sideways at Sylvia, her chest heaving, and I saw the precipitate of tears in her eyes. Then her head whipped around again. "I let Max invite you tonight," she said, a sob catching in her throat.

"Sylvia," I said, speaking directly to her, "it's really late. Marta and I have finished now. We know we're not supposed to be here." I was so desperate for her to use her influence over Genevieve that I was almost pleading.

Sylvia shrugged. "You go, if you like," she said. She jerked her head at Marta. "Leave the gremlin."

"No, I—" I was shocked at the reprieve, but couldn't entertain the idea of abandoning Marta. "Come on. Let's all go to bed." I looked from Sylvia to Genevieve. There was a moment in which Genevieve's shoulders sagged slightly, and I thought the fight had gone out of her, but then her body grew rigid again.

"No," she said slowly. "No, I don't think so. You see, I don't think you have finished here."

"What?"

"You're mucking out, aren't you?" she stated. "You're cleaning up filth."

"Yes, but—"

"Well, you've missed a bit." Now Genevieve was looking directly at Marta, and I felt a surging dread. "In fact, you've missed the filthiest thing in here."

Marta stood by the back wall, a shrunken figure in the dress I'd lent her. Her bare arms and knees were covered in mud.

"You need a wash, Marta," said Genevieve. She paused, appearing to deliberate. Her gaze flickered from the hose, to Marta and finally to Sylvia, whose eyes widened a fraction. Genevieve darted to the spigot and twisted it, hard.

Water shot out from the end of the hose as it lay on the floor and hit the opposite wall, sending a fine mist of spray over the stable. Genevieve seized the nozzle and twisted it, increasing the pressure so that she could barely grip the hose. She wrestled to control the jet of water, and then pointed it directly at Marta.

What followed was like a scene from a horror film, except that there was no blood. Marta flung her arms over her head, uttering a scream of pure terror that cut me to the core. The jet hit her first in the stomach, then swung down to her thighs. She caved inward against the pain, dropping to her knees. The water now blasted over her entire prostrate body, boring into the skin of her arms with terrible intensity. Her face was buried in her knees, and the jet hit the crown of her skull and her hands and any part of her body, in fact, that was exposed. Frozen to the spot, I saw red welts appear on the skin of her arms and knees, and still the water kept coming. Marta rolled over onto her side, drawing her knees up to her chest, and Genevieve moved closer, her expression entirely without mercy. As Marta screamed a second time, I saw Sylvia run to the tap. Genevieve took another step closer to Marta, now holding the hose above her prone figure and directing it at her neck. I knew it would soon reach her face, and could not let that happen. I launched myself at Genevieve, forcing her off balance, just as Sylvia's hand folded around the spigot. Genevieve stumbled, dropping the hose, and the jet of water was pushed away from Marta and against the back wall, scattering the tack and drenching the rugs that hung there, spraying them with mud whipped up from the floor. Sylvia wrenched the tap closed, and the jet stopped.

I picked myself up from the floor, where I'd slipped after forcing Genevieve to drop the hose. I went to Marta and crouched down next to her. She was curled in a pool of water, coughing, her face buried in her knees, which were still pressed against her chest. Her skin was red raw. As I reached out to touch her wrist, she suddenly screamed again. The sound was so terrible to me that I backed away.

There was a silence of indeterminate length, and then I heard footsteps on the gravel. I turned to see Dr. Reza and Gerald hurry into the pool of light spilling from Block C. Sami was a short way behind them. Dr. Reza wore a long coat over a pair of pajamas, but Gerald was fully dressed in his overalls and steel-toed boots, as if ready for the day's work. Genevieve and Sylvia had vanished.

"What on earth is going on?" Dr. Reza's voice was quiet, but deep shock was written over her face. She knelt down next to Marta, putting her hand on her shoulder. Marta yelped, shifting away as though stung by her touch.

Gerald didn't even glance at Marta, but went to the stalls and made soothing sounds to the three horses. Dr. Reza glanced at him.

"Go and get some dry blankets, please." Gerald didn't move away from the horses. "*Now*," Dr. Reza said, and there was an urgency in her voice that he couldn't disregard. He marched out into the dark courtyard.

Marta was still coughing, and her whole body was now shaking violently. Dr. Reza took off her coat and spread it over her. Marta whimpered. "Rose," I heard her say.

I went back to her, kneeling down in the pool of freezing water in which she lay. I reached out and moved some of her sodden hair off her face. Her green eyes were full of shame. "You stopped them," she said, in a voice that was more like a sob.

"Yes." *But I hadn't acted quickly enough*, I thought, looking at Marta's inflamed skin. I glanced over at Sami, who was standing just inside the stable, his face half in shadow. He seemed frozen to the spot. *Genevieve,* I mouthed to him. *Genevieve and Sylvia.*

Dr. Reza was examining the welts on Marta's arms as Gerald returned with an armful of horse blankets. He dumped them on the floor next to Dr. Reza and went back to caressing the horses. As he passed Marta he looked down at her prone figure, his expression full of disgust.

Dr. Reza and I helped Marta sit up, and wrapped her in the towels and two of the rugs. Her shaking had subsided a little, but her shoulders still curved inward, as if to shield herself from further harm. We draped Dr. Reza's coat over the rugs around her shoulders. Marta looked around the stable as if realizing where she was.

"I'm taking you to the infirmary," Dr. Reza told her. Marta shook her head, trying to move away, but Dr. Reza said,

"I won't examine you if you don't want me to. It's just because it's much closer, so we'll be able to get you warm sooner."

Marta blinked. She looked at me. "Are you coming?"

"Rose and Sami need to go to bed," said Dr. Reza gently. "They can come and see you in the morning."

She helped Marta to her feet and led her out of the stable, leaving Sami and me alone with Gerald. Sami and I looked at each other for a long moment. Then Gerald broke the silence, his voice harsh.

"You can fuck off now," he said. "But get back here in the morning to clear this mess up, or I'll make sure you're in even bigger trouble than you already are." He gestured to the water all over the floor, the tack that had been sprayed off the wall by the hose, and the sodden rugs.

Sami and I left Block C. The night had grown even colder, and a light rain was falling. Ahead of us, I could see Dr. Reza supporting Marta as they passed through the South Arch toward the Hexagon. When we reached the statue, Sami stopped walking and reached for my arm. "Do you understand now? What I said about Marta—about how vulnerable she is? She's not safe here. Next time Genevieve and Sylvia could do her serious harm."

I returned his gaze, which was deeply troubled. "Sylvia helped me stop Genevieve," I said at last. "I don't think she'd let it go too far."

"*Too far?* Rose—did you *see* Marta's injuries? She's not safe at High Realms," he repeated. "It's too rough. It's relentless. Maybe she'd be better off going home—"

"She burns herself," I interrupted. Sami stared at me, and after a few seconds I continued, trying to keep my voice steady. "Marta burns herself with matches every night. Her father writes to her three times a week telling her she's got to leave High Realms at Christmas." I hesitated. "I don't think . . . I don't think she should go home, Sami."

Sami closed his eyes for a moment. When he opened them it was as though all the fear and confusion that I felt about Marta had transferred itself to him, wrapping itself around his disgust at what Genevieve and Sylvia had done. I will remember that moment forever: the moment I betrayed Marta's secrets, the moment I stoked Sami's fears about her suffering, the moment I made the selfish decision to unburden myself rather than ask Sami what had happened in the woods to provoke the attack on Marta. I remember that moment because it was the start of Sami's anger. I remember it because it catalyzed our silent, unshakable complicity. But most of all, I remember it because it was the quiet expiration of denial: the true end of our innocence, which High Realms, with its relentless and alluring power, had already begun to erode.

Chapter 6

I woke early the following morning, and for a moment couldn't think where I was. I lay still, the events of the night compiling in my mind like a fast-forwarded film, rushing into place with the same crushing inexorableness with which they had happened. My head was pounding.

The covers on Marta's bed were rumpled where she and Lloyd had sprawled on it before Bridge Night. I looked over at our worktable, hoping to see Marta bent over some extra task she had set herself, every now and again firing a newly discovered fact at me, but of course she wasn't there. I only had myself to blame for that, I thought glumly. I got out of bed and pulled on my uniform, my tired fingers struggling with the buttons.

I found Sami and Lloyd in the stable, carefully drying and hanging up the tack that had been forced off the shelves by the hose. They'd removed the wet, mud-spattered rugs from their rails and piled them in the corner, revealing a back wall boarded up with plywood.

"Hi," I said.

"Hi." Lloyd's face was puffy with tiredness. He was wearing his suit from the previous night, which was creased and smeared with mud. He bit his lip. "You OK?"

"Yes," I said, and then realized that I didn't know why I was lying. "Actually, no, I'm not." I glared at him, and how good it felt to be the one glaring: the satisfaction of exuding opprobrium for once, rather than absorbing it.

"Ro," said Lloyd apprehensively, "Sami told me what happened to Marta. I'm sorry I wasn't there, but—"

"It happened *because* you weren't there," I cut in harshly. "It happened because you slunk off into the fucking woods—*you* took Marta in there and did God knows what—*you* didn't come back—"

"OK. OK." Lloyd held up his hands. "I'm sorry, I really am, Rose. I can explain."

"Save it." I felt an oppressive tiredness. "I want to go and see how Marta is, and then I want to face the music from last night sooner rather than later. Dr. Reza found us in the stables, drunk, at two o'clock in the morning. I wouldn't be surprised if we were kicked out."

There was a short silence in which Lloyd and Sami stared at me. "What do you mean?" said Lloyd. "They're not going to expel us for going to a party that forty other people also went to."

"Oh, wouldn't they?" I said, my temper rising. "I suppose you think that wouldn't be *fair*?"

"Rose, don't worry," said Sami, looking bewildered. "I really don't think we're going to be expelled."

"Then you're fucking deluded!" Lloyd's complacency and Sami's determination to think the best of people infuriated me, and all of a sudden I was shouting, shouting in a way I'd never shouted before. "You think anyone here gives a shit about fairness? You think we'll be given the same chances as the others? If you think that, you're wrong, Sami, you're *so, so wrong*—"

"Rose," Lloyd said, looking amazed, "calm down—it's going to be fine—"

"*Don't tell me to calm down!*" His attempt to dampen my fury had enraged me all the more. My only release was yelling. I felt as though I'd been holding in the emotion for years rather than weeks.

"What's going on?" A voice came from behind us. "Rose, why're you shouting?"

Breathing heavily, I turned around to see Marta standing in the doorway of Block C. She was still wearing the dress I had lent her, now creased and patchy with damp spots. Her skin was red, raw, and pockmarked. "I could hear you from the Hexagon," she said.

"Sorry," I said, after a moment. "I just—got angry."

Marta nodded. "Oh." A pause. "Hi, Lloyd. Hi, Sami."

"Mar." Lloyd went straight to her and hugged her. Seeing his hand fall on the back of Marta's head, and her body hanging limply in his arms, I deduced that Sami had already passed on to Lloyd what I had told him about Marta the previous night. "I'm sorry about last night," Lloyd said. "All of it." *Sorry for what?* I thought, but he did not elaborate.

Marta shrugged and wandered into the stable. Her green eyes flitted around the space, taking it all in: the mopped concrete floor, the newly polished tack, the rugs ready to be washed. "Thanks for doing this," she said. "It was a bit of a mess, wasn't it?"

"Yeah," said Sami. There was a short pause. "How're you feeling?" he asked her.

"Oh, I'm fine," said Marta. She was standing next to the back wall, avoiding our eyes by examining the plywood boards. It was a long time before she turned to us. "Time for Chapel soon," she said simply.

We all stared at her. The thought of the Sunday routine continuing as normal after the events of the previous night hadn't crossed my mind: nor, by the looks on their faces, Sami or Lloyd's.

"Marta," I said. "You've got to go and find Major Gregory and tell him what Genevieve did. We'll come with you—"

Marta shook her head. "No," she said. "I don't want to do that."

"What?"

"I don't want to tell anyone about what happened last night." Almost absentmindedly, she ran her hand along the plywood.

"Why?" I couldn't keep the incredulity out of my tone. I was frustrated by her lack of fighting spirit, at this of all moments. "Marta—she attacked you. If Sylvia and I hadn't stopped her she could've *killed* you. And she just ran away." Marta shrugged maddeningly, and I was compelled to invoke her own words against her. "They've hated us from the start. Why are you protecting them?"

"I'm not." Marta looked up at me. There was a finality in her tone that told me she'd thought all of this through; had perhaps not slept the previous night in pursuit of this conclusion. "I assure you, I have no interest in shielding Genevieve from what she deserves. But it's not as simple as that."

"What do you mean?" This time it was Lloyd who spoke. He wore a disconcerting expression of dawning comprehension.

Marta looked around at us all. "I suppose I'd really like to be sure that if I told Major Gregory what happened last night, he'd believe me," she said slowly. "I'd like to believe that Genevieve would be punished. But we all know it wouldn't work like that. There's a good chance he *wouldn't* believe me, or that Genevieve and Sylvia would somehow twist it so that I was in the wrong. Then I'd get into trouble, and they'd come after me again for telling on them. You know how it is," she went on, her voice oddly flat. "Sylvia's Vice-Captain General, Genevieve's Senior Patrol. We're the nonpaying guests. I've decided it's far too much of a risk." She hesitated for a moment before looking directly at Lloyd and Sami. "My father wants me to leave High Realms at Christmas," she stated quietly, and paused for expressions of surprise that didn't come. "I don't know whether I'll be able to persuade him to change his mind. So I want to make the most of the time I've got here. That's more important to me than getting revenge."

"It's not revenge," I said immediately. "It's justice."

Incredibly, Marta smiled. "I'm sorry, Rose," she said. "I've made up my mind." There was a hint of her usual defiance. I tried to think of another approach, but it was difficult when she had just encapsulated the unfairness that I had accused Sami and Lloyd of being blind to.

"What about Dr. Reza?" asked Sami. "Didn't she ask you what happened? She likes you—she'll want to help—"

Marta shook her head impatiently. "I didn't tell her anything. I don't trust her—she's been badgering me since day one. Prodding and poking, asking me stuff . . . I can't stand it." She scowled before continuing. "Oh, and she doesn't *like* me. She just feels sorry for me."

We were all silent. Marta looked down at the backs of her hands, which were scarlet with soreness from Genevieve's attack. Then she looked up. "I need you to promise that you won't tell anyone," she said simply. She looked at me in silent acknowledgment of my betrayal. "Partly because you know I'm right, and it'd never work out in our favor—but mostly because it happened to me, and I get to decide."

There were no arguments left to make. We all mutely nodded our agreement.

"So," she said, "let's go to Chapel. And then this afternoon, I thought maybe we could go for a walk."

We hung up the rest of the tack and took the rugs over to the workshop to be washed. Then we made our way through the archway to the Hexagon. I allowed Lloyd and Sami to get a few paces ahead before taking Marta's arm and drawing her to a standstill. "Why did Lloyd apologize to you?" I asked her directly.

Marta bit her lip, looking down at her crumpled dress. "I—" She stopped. "Something happened between us," she said at last.

"I saw you kissing."

"Yes." She looked upset. "It was after that. I'd rather not talk about it, Rose. It's . . . private."

"But—"

"No." Now her voice was firm, even harsh. "It's no good, Rose. I'm not going to tell you. Can you—can you just leave it, please? Sometimes there are things we don't want other people to know." Her eyes met mine, knowing and fierce. "Surely you understand that," she said.

I nodded. I felt humiliated, but I saw Marta's point. There *were* things I didn't want people to know, and even after being friends with her for such a short time, I felt sure that Marta would never divulge them or pester me for more information. It was not her style. The fact that we shared a room and a dead parent did not entitle me to know everything about her or vice versa, I acknowledged; I would not demean myself or risk causing Marta more pain by asking her again. I heard the cloister bell start to chime insistently. "Let's get going," Marta said, absolving me from replying, and we set off again together toward the Chapel.

Lloyd, Sami, and I kept our promise to Marta, and never told anyone what really happened in the stables on Bridge Night. That decision marked a shift in my relationship with the truth. Before High Realms, before knowing Marta, I thought of myself as a truthful person; or at least as someone who believed in the importance of the truth, even if I didn't always manage to communicate it. After October 1999, there were crucial, untruthful narratives that came to live in my mind *as* the truth, and my moral compass spun so that truth-telling was no longer an imperative or even a priority.

Apparently in return for our silence, the Senior Patrol called a ceasefire in their campaigns of aggression against us. They showed us no warmth, but the landmark acts of violence stopped. We weren't sure whether Dr. Reza told anyone about finding us in the stables, but if she did, we suffered no consequences. If anything, I recall Major Gregory's hostility toward us abating slightly as our grades stayed high and Marta's behavior stabilized, and the four of us were able to immerse ourselves in the happier parts of life at High Realms. I remember playing my fourth hockey match of the season, just as the leaves on the plane trees surrounding the Astroturf were turning golden. As I sliced the ball into the back of the net to score my third goal, Marta, Lloyd, and Sami erupted in cheers on the steps of the Pavilion. A week or so later I turned seventeen. "Let's have a party," Marta suggested, and so we met up in Room 1A after supper, knowing Genevieve would now let us get away with it. We shared a cake that my father had sent with one of his frequent letters (*I hope this is big enough for the four of you,* he wrote, in response to my pointedly enthusiastic anecdotes about my new friends), and two bottles of wine that Lloyd filched from Max's organ loft stash. "He sends his love," Lloyd told me. I nodded, avoiding Marta's eye, and held out my glass. With my friends around me, I found I didn't care that Max hadn't come to wish me happy birthday himself.

On that evening and others around that time, I was aware that my growing sense of security was rooted in incomplete information. Something bad had happened on Bridge Night; something I hoped would gradually lose its significance, and become part of a story about how we had settled down and made a success of our time at High Realms. I was so keen for this to be the case that I ignored signs to the contrary: looks that occasionally passed between Lloyd and Marta, or between Sami and Lloyd, or—perhaps most troublingly—the way Sami would sometimes watch Marta sadly, as though he feared that something was unresolved and festering. But it was also the case that Marta appeared, on the whole, to be improving. The number of matches in the wastepaper bin in 1A were dwindling. She seemed to be receiving fewer letters from her father; or perhaps she was dwelling on them less, trusting that he would ultimately change his mind about her leaving High Realms. She could still withdraw into herself from time to time, and she never mentioned her mother, but despite this she and I were growing closer. "She relies on you," Sami told me quietly one day, as we watched Marta rampage around 1A in search of a lost textbook, pausing every so often to ask me a question about our English prep or tell me about something that had happened in her Physics class. Sami was right, in a way, but I knew that the opposite was also true, and that I needed Marta. It was this, her discretion about what had nearly happened with Max, and the fact that she seemed to be settling down that stopped me demanding the truth about Bridge Night from Lloyd or Sami. I didn't want to risk Marta finding out that I'd asked them, and losing the friendship with her that was bringing me such happiness.

By mid-October there had still been no repercussions from Bridge Night, and I dared to believe that we would be OK. In the boarding school stories I'd read, outsiders flourished after the stickiest of beginnings, and I hoped that would be our fate, too. When I shared my theory with Marta she laughed, saying she'd read the same books with her mother. We compared characters from the stories to people at High Realms, finding equivalents in almost every case. The only person we were unable to categorize was Sylvia. We were coming to understand that Sylvia was different to her colleagues in the Senior Patrol. Everyone was afraid of her quick temper, but the reality was that she was less inclined to the mindless cruelty that everyone else at High Realms embraced without question. She used her power as Vice-Captain General to bolster Genevieve and Bella and to keep Gerald in his place, but the rest of the time she seemed somehow to be above it all. She was high-minded and clever, darkly glamorous and elusive: glimpsed as she descended the Eiger, her hand encased in Bella's; or riding Cleopatra in the distance; or on the other side of the hockey pitch, passing to me in a fleeting, enforced moment of allyship. Gradually, I came to realize that I envied Sylvia. Not so much for her place at the top of the food chain, but for her close friends and her steadfast loyalty to them; her dignity; and her sense of self, which nothing and nobody seemed able to shake.

I remember our first and only Bonus, gruffly bestowed on us by Major Gregory after our grades carried Hillary to victory in the first House Rankings of the year. The four of us took cartons of juice and pastries from the pantry, packed them into our schoolbags, and set off straight after Chapel. Max's jubilant chords receded as we strode toward Donny Stream: not to the Bridge Night spot, which we tended to avoid, but past Drake Cottage to beyond the barns, where the stream began to widen and deepen. We walked and walked, until the Main House was out of sight. I remember Lloyd striding ahead, his blazer slung over his shoulder, Marta scampering to keep up with him. Sami and I walked behind them, just out of earshot. Marta gesticulated. We caught Lloyd's deep, cynical tones on the breeze.

The Estate boundary was a decrepit wooden fence that straddled both sides of the stream. "Come on," called Lloyd as he vaulted it, "I've missed the real world." Our world that afternoon was the lushest of green grass, speckled with the first fallen leaves, and the smooth boulders by the stream. We lounged on the bank. Lloyd, Marta, and I dozed and read fiction, but Sami had brought his prep, and sat with his books open around him. Nobody ever mentioned it, but we were all aware that he was the least gifted of the four of us; the one who had to labor hardest and longest for the smallest rewards—even if, in the wider context of High Realms, he was still one of the brightest. That afternoon, I recall Marta's eyes drifting from *Anthony and Cleopatra* toward Sami's prep, which lay beside him while he looked something up in his Math textbook. I remember her green eyes narrowing thoughtfully, and the fleeting pause in which tact would usually intervene. "You're using the wrong formula," she told Sami. "All your answers are wrong."

Again, something hung in the air. This time it was the moment in which anybody else would have snapped at Marta: not because she was right, but because of the *way* she was right; the way she was so often, so unapologetically correct, even when it came to subjects she didn't study. But Sami never snapped at Marta. As calmly as she'd spoken, he took the cap off his pen and drew long diagonal lines across three pages of equations. "Can you help me?" he asked Marta, who nodded, and I watched as they bent over his exercise book together: one fair head; one dark. Sami's hair grazed his collar—it was several inches longer than most boys wore it at High Realms—and Marta's tangled curls were lustrous with grease in the autumn sun.

Later, Marta would stand up. She would wander the short

distance to the water's edge, and step down into the shallows without removing her shoes and socks, wading deeper until her calves were submerged. Lloyd, Sami, and I would look at each other, realizing once again how unusual she was; how she sometimes seemed to withdraw from reality, as though it no longer interested her. We would watch her bend down and scoop water in her cupped hands; watch her daub it purposefully over her exposed knees, then her thighs. The stream flowed tranquilly around her. Marta took another two steps forward. The water reached the hem of her skirt, and she turned to us, her face breaking into a grin, just as she slipped. She made a noise of surprise, pitching to one side. Momentarily her hands and the shiny toes of her shoes protruded from the water, and then she was thrashing around, trying to stand up. Sami and Lloyd strode into the stream without a second's hesitation, grabbing Marta's upper arms and pulling her upright, supporting her between them.

That was the third time—and the last, it would transpire—I saw Marta soaking wet, fully dressed. For months it was just another panel of the tapestry of my memory: memorable for having happened on that happy afternoon, and for its fleeting, picturesque drama—*You looked like Ophelia without the flowers*, Lloyd told Marta—but unpossessed of wider significance. Later, I would remember how quickly Marta let go of Sami's arm. I would remember how willingly she leaned on Lloyd as they walked toward me. I would remember Sami kneeling beside Marta, encouraging her to take off her wet blazer and put on his dry one, and how Marta still only had eyes for Lloyd. I was close enough to Marta that I should have realized how she felt about him, but I didn't—not then, not yet.

The sun was low in the sky. We had to get back for supper, and we were all quietly glad to do so. The four of us walked back to school along Donny Stream, relieved that our Bonus, those precious hours of liberty, were at an end, and we were free to submit to the timetable once more.

Chapter 7

The first frost settled over the Estate on a Friday in late October, at the end of our eighth week at High Realms. Fallen leaves crunched under our feet as Marta and I rushed up to the Main House for breakfast after mucking out. Friday mornings were special, because I didn't have hockey practice, and because we were given a full English breakfast, as a sort of bribe to keep us going for one and a half more days of lessons.

Marta was talking to me at great speed about *Jane Eyre,* one of our set texts. "I mean, Rose," she panted as we ran up the steps toward the Atrium, "did they actually *know* people who kept their wives in the attic? Was that something people really *did* then, or—"

"It's fiction, Mar," I said, as we stood on the threshold of the school, wiping the worst of the stable muck from the soles of our Wellingtons. For all Marta's intelligence, she had a propensity to take things very literally. "But now you mention it—" I broke off, seeing Dr. Reza coming down the Eiger. Marta was kneeling on the huge, bristly doormat, banging one of her boots on it to remove some entrenched dirt, and didn't notice her approaching.

"Hello," said Dr. Reza. Marta looked up at her in surprise, her cheeks flushed with exertion. "How are you?"

"I'm great." Marta bounded to her feet. "Look, my hands are so much better! That cream did the trick." She held out her hands, her palms downturned and fingers splayed.

Dr. Reza extended her own hand. "May I?" Marta nodded, and Dr. Reza took one of Marta's hands in hers, examining it carefully. "Very good," she said after a moment.

"Cheers," Marta said, turning to me. "Is it time for bacon?"

"Actually, I wondered whether I might have a quick word," Dr. Reza said, and Marta looked dismayed. "It won't take long."

Marta stared at her. "OK," she said, after a moment. She thrust her feet back into her boots and followed Dr. Reza toward the Eiger.

I collected two plates of food from the kitchen, one each for me and Marta, and carried them over to an empty table. I sat there, devouring my breakfast. Unlike the early days, when my isolation had taken away my appetite, I seemed now to be constantly hungry, and hankered after mealtimes like all the other High Realmsians. After a few minutes, Sami and Lloyd appeared, red-faced and sweaty after their morning run. "Where's Marta?" Sami asked, pouring himself coffee.

"She had to see Dr. Reza," I replied. "I don't think she'll be long."

"Good," he said. "We bumped into Major G—he wants to see her, too."

"What about?"

"She probably forgot wash day again," Lloyd speculated. "Oh—wait. He said there was a phone call for her. Whoever it was is going to ring back after breakfast, apparently."

I stared at him. "Who would be phoning her so early in the morning?" I asked, but I felt a rising unease.

"Dunno," Lloyd said with a shrug, turning back to his breakfast.

Marta stomped over a few minutes later. "I've got to bloody well do Games now," she said without preamble. She dropped into her chair, glowering. "This is a fucking nightmare. I *knew* I was right not to trust her—"

"Come on, Marta," Lloyd said impatiently. "Surely you didn't think you'd be exempt forever?"

"I was misled," Marta replied through gritted teeth. She was staring at her plate, her face red with anger. "Dr. Reza promised me she'd signed me off till Christmas at the *earliest*."

"So why—" Sami began, but he broke off, looking over my shoulder. I turned to see Jolyon Astor approaching our table, wearing his Captain General gown and an expression of distaste.

"Tucking into another free meal, I see," Jolyon said. His hard eyes fell on Sami. "Not that Mr. Blobby from Bradford here needs it."

"That is *so unkind*—" Marta burst out, but Sami met Jolyon's gaze, his hands steady as he held his knife and fork. I smiled at him, trying to be supportive, but Jolyon was already speaking again.

"Dr. Wardlaw wants to see you in her study at Elevenses," he told Marta.

Marta's face paled. "What have I done?"

"Well, you exist"—Jolyon looked disgusted—"but it seems you're earning your keep. You've been recommended for the Persephone Lock Memorial Prize."

"What's that?"

"It's a prize for academic excellence," Jolyon said disparagingly, "awarded annually by Sir Jacob Lock, Genevieve's father, on what would've been Persephone's birthday. I need hardly say that the decision that you of all people should be its recipient is—*controversial*."

"Someone recommended her for it, though," Lloyd said loudly. "She's won it fair and square."

"She's won it because the Master of Laws, who is hardly unbiased, insisted she should," Jolyon snapped. His hard eyes swiveled from one to the other of us. "I suppose he's trying to make sure his gamble pays off."

We all looked at each other as Jolyon walked away. "Well *done*, Mar," Sami said warmly, but Marta wasn't listening. Her head was between her hands as she stared down at the cold bacon on her plate.

"Why," she muttered, "do they all still hate us so much?"

"What d'you mean—*still*?" Lloyd asked, reaching for the coffee pot.

"I thought they'd have got over it by now! Can't they see that we're not really any different from them? Why are they all so fucking *entrenched* in the way they think?"

"Oh, come on, Marta." Lloyd's voice was calm as he poured us all more coffee. "I think it's fair to say that between us we cover everything your typical High Realmsian dislikes." He smiled. "First off, we're clever."

"Sylvia's clever, and they don't—"

"Yeah, but she's got *power*, right? So she's exempt." Lloyd's smile widened. "Let's take Sami. He's got an accent, he was a bit porky at the start of term"—he winked at Sami—"and he's not very good at sports, although he's improving. Ro: well, they know her dad drives a cab for a living, and *that's* not acceptable. She's better than them at hockey. And she's quiet, which they misread as aloof—"

"What?" I demanded, but nobody was listening. Marta was staring at Lloyd.

"What about me, then?" she said. "Why do they hate me?"

"For all the reasons we like you," Lloyd replied simply. "You're the cleverest in the year, but you're not interested in the Rankings. You don't care what you look like. You hate horses. You hate Games even more—you'd rather be in the Library—but you come to support us in our matches. You argue back, but you forgive them when they bully you . . . they'd have more respect for you if you hated them. You laugh out loud in Chapel, you won't sing the National Anthem. You're—*unembarrassable.* You genuinely don't notice hierarchy, and when it's shoved under your nose you just take the piss." Lloyd looked Marta in the eye. "They know you don't need their money, their status. They know you could do anything, be anything . . . they know you'll go to the best university in the country and that'll only be the start of all the things you'll achieve, all the ways you could change the world."

Marta gazed at Lloyd, her arms folded. For once she seemed entirely lost for words. Finally she said, "And you?"

"Me?"

"I don't know why they hate you." Marta was still looking straight at Lloyd, her cheeks slightly pink. "There's nothing hateable about you. Except"—she hesitated—"you don't know who your parents are. And they don't like that, do they? They want to know where everyone's from, who everyone is."

The warmth drained from the atmosphere as Lloyd and Marta stared at each other as though they were seeing each other properly for the first time. Sami shifted uncomfortably in his chair. After a moment Lloyd told Marta abruptly, "Someone phoned you this morning."

Marta's eyes widened. "What?"

"You were at the stables, so they're going to phone back after breakfast. Major Gregory said to go up to the Call Center." The Call Center was the colloquial name for a room full of small telephone booths on the third floor, where calls were put through from a switchboard in the school office.

All the color had left Marta's face. "Fuck," she said quietly. She looked down at her tray, biting her lip. "Have I got to go now?" she asked, looking up at me.

"After breakfast," said Sami. He glanced at me, and I could tell he now shared my fear about who the call was from.

"Do you want me to come with you, Mar?" I asked.

She shook her head, looking dazed. "No," she said quickly. "No, thanks. I'll be fine." She got to her feet, her food still untouched. "I'm going now," she said.

"But—"

"I don't want to miss any of English," she said, and with that she was gone, plodding across the Dining Hall in her overalls, her thin shoulders slumped.

"What can we do?" Sami demanded. Lloyd stared sullenly into his coffee cup, and Sami spoke again, his tone urgent. "We need to help Marta—that phone call could be bad news—"

"She'll be fine."

"*Lloyd*. You *know* there's something not right with—"

"So you say." Lloyd drained his coffee cup, his expression

hard. "You two are so sheltered," he snapped, as Sami and I exchanged glances. "You've had such cozy little lives. I've seen people in a far worse state than Marta, I can tell you. I've known people with *real* problems." He got to his feet and strode away, out of the Dining Hall. Sami looked at me pleadingly.

"I don't think there's much we can do," I said. How badly I wish that I'd thought harder at that juncture—that my mind had been clear and focused enough to suggest something, rather than being distracted by so many inconsequential things to do with the day ahead, and prep, and a hockey match the following day against another famous school. More than anything, I wish that I'd jumped up and followed Marta to the Call Center. Instead, Sami and I finished our breakfasts, cleared our trays, and left the Dining Hall to climb the Eiger to Hillary House.

Sami and I arrived at our English classroom half an hour later. We'd looked for Marta in Hillary, but had been unable to find her. There had also been no sign of Major Gregory, which was unusual, because he usually spent the hour before lessons stomping around Upper House, expressing dissatisfaction with his holy trinity of dislikes: slovenliness, tardiness, and noise.

Lloyd was already there. Sami took our seats and pulled out our poetry anthologies, but didn't open them. Miss Kepple had continued to start every lesson with an unseen piece of poetry or prose, calling it our "starter for ten." By now it was not always Marta who had the last word on the interpretation of the text in question. Often she, Sami, Lloyd, Sylvia and I hashed it out together, while Miss Kepple grew steadily more frustrated. I'd come to understand that Miss Kepple, like many of the Mags, had been hired on the basis of a prestigious educational background (in her case, High Realms itself) rather than actual teaching ability—or indeed, as Marta had remarked to me in a rare caustic moment, any appreciation of literature whatsoever.

That morning, Sylvia was in her usual seat opposite me. She looked sleekly alert, her sleeves rolled up under her gown. Marta was nowhere to be seen, and there was also no sign of Max. The boys and I took our seats, Sami flashing me an anxious glance, but before I could respond Miss Kepple swept into the room. "Settle down," she said curtly, and handed around some sheets of paper. I looked down at the poem.

> After great pain, a formal feeling comes—
> The Nerves sit ceremonious, like Tombs—
> The stiff Heart questions "was it He, that bore,"
> And "Yesterday, or Centuries before'?
>
> The Feet, mechanical, go round—
> A Wooden way
> Of Ground, or Air, or Ought—
> Regardless grown,
> A Quartz contentment, like a stone—
>
> This is the Hour of Lead—
> Remembered, if outlived,
> As Freezing persons, recollect the Snow—
> First—Chill—then Stupor—then the letting go—

A chill came over me. I resented the poem: hated it, in fact. Reflexively, I glanced over to where Marta usually sat, hoping for her quick smile of camaraderie, but she had still not arrived. By now I was very worried. I pushed the poem to the edge of my desk, and looked up to see Sylvia watching me.

"Your thoughts, please," said Miss Kepple. She looked around, but nobody spoke. "Come on," she snapped.

"It's about grief," said Sylvia in a bored tone. "The numbness of grief." She was sitting back in her chair, her slim arms resting lightly on the desk, her silver fountain pen propped between her fingers. In that moment, I hated her even more than the poem.

"Explain," said Miss Kepple, her tone evincing the same if not greater boredom than Sylvia's.

Sylvia raised her eyebrows. "Emotional freezing," she said laconically. "Refusing to accept what's happened to you. Not feeling anything, like a lump of stone. Resilience."

"Not quite," said Miss Kepple, and Sylvia, predictably, looked annoyed. "However, I'm interested that for 'great pain,' you read 'grief.'"

Suddenly Sylvia looked flustered. She hesitated, and I felt a grim satisfaction in watching her trying to find her words. "Well," she replied, "I suppose it's that the greatest pain I've known is grief."

Miss Kepple looked wary. "I see," she said. "And what do you understand by—"

"Not me," Sylvia said sharply. "By 'known' I meant— I should've said—*seen*. The greatest pain that I've known *about*, that I've seen, was grief. When Persephone died," she added, in a clearer voice. "Gin didn't speak for weeks. You remember. You were our form tutor."

"Of course I remember," snapped Miss Kepple. "However, I'd like us to entertain the idea that 'great pain' could mean something other than grief—could in fact refer to *any* type of emotional pain," the teacher said. "Can anyone tell me—ah, there you are." She looked over our heads to the door at the back of the classroom. "Good of you to join us, Miss De Luca. Have you seen Mr. Masters?"

Marta shook her head and slid into her chair. She looked more or less normal, except that her uniform was perhaps slightly neater than usual, and her face a little paler. She didn't look at any of us, despite my attempts to catch her eye. She pulled her copy of the poem toward her.

"I was just posing the question," Miss Kepple went on, her voice now edging toward the dangerously quiet tone she used whenever she felt her lesson was not progressing in the way she'd planned, "of whether this poem is about hardness, or non-feeling, as Miss Maudsley would have it."

Marta sighed. It was not a sound of frustration, or anger, but full of weariness, as if she knew that she had to explain something virtually incommunicable to someone who could never understand it, even if they wanted to. "No," she said, and Sylvia's head whipped up. "You see, the contentment is described as 'quartz.'"

"Yes, and quartz is *hard*—"

"It is," said Marta. "But it's also brittle. It's more fragile than it appears. And if you look at the second half of the line—it says '*like* a stone.' Not 'a stone.'"

We all looked down at our sheets of paper. Marta spoke

again. "That isn't to say that the contentment doesn't exist," she said. "It does. But when I read 'quartz contentment,' I think of a contentment that's easily shattered. I think of words like 'quarter' and 'quasi' . . . she's saying that the contentment is *similar* to—but still different from—insensate stone."

Sylvia stared at Marta. "You're reading this too negatively," she said, and I heard the faintest undertone of coaxing in her voice. "There's hope—there's the 'letting go' at the end—"

Again Marta shook her head. I realized that she'd barely glanced at the poem. "That's not what that means."

"Oh, tell us what it *does* mean, then. Help us poor mortals out." Now Sylvia's voice began to rise with anger and humiliation, and I felt a fleeting, vicious delight in the spectacle of her being rinsed by Marta's superior brain. But then I noticed Marta's strange lack of pleasure in the debate. She was sitting in a patch of watery sunlight, her body limp in her chair. Her face exuded a fierce sadness.

"It might be a sort of letting go of pain, if that's what you mean," she said tiredly. "But not in any truly hopeful sense. There's a fallacy in '*as Freezing persons, recollect the Snow.*' If you're frozen, you're dead—you can't recollect anything. The 'letting go' is capitulation to death, which I suppose does mean a release from pain, but . . ." She gazed sightlessly into the middle distance before continuing, her tone one of dreadful finality. "After great pain, there is no recovery. Only a kind of non-progression, from wooden to quartz to stone to lead. None of those things are any better than the last . . . they're just the next step on the journey of this 'formal feeling.' I'd never really understood that bit before," she said suddenly, looking up at me, and I saw that her eyes were full of tears. "I used to agree with you, Sylvia . . . I thought the bits about the feet continuing to move, *outlived*—I thought they meant a sort of convalescence. That you could emerge from the other side, perhaps even stronger than before. But that's impossible," she said, her voice catching. "There's only frozen insensibility. Obliteration. Death."

There was a long silence in the classroom. The noiselessness swelled in the space until it seemed to blare within my own mind, as I entered a kind of furious reckoning with the futility Marta had identified, and with the terrible fact of her own total lack of hope. I wanted to reach across the horseshoe of desks, grab her hand and tell her that I would fix it: that this time I wouldn't sweep what was happening to her under the carpet; would not rush off to play hockey or go to lessons or blithely be happy in the face of her misery. I wanted to tell her that her survival was paramount. Lloyd and Sami's faces were grim with tension.

I dared to look at Sylvia. All the belligerence had drained from her expression, and her dark eyes were traveling between Marta and me, full of a curiosity that was rapidly metamorphosing into solicitude. I had never seen Sylvia look like that before. All the times we'd interacted, there had been no possibility of real communication, because her status within High Realms rendered her unreachable to me. Our eyes met for the first time since Bridge Night, and I felt as though she saw every secret I possessed, every iota of shame that prickled beneath my skin, every private sorrow and joy I had ever known. In that moment, her power did not frighten me. I believed that her power was good, and could help me, help Marta, in a way that nothing else could. *Come with me,* I wanted to say. *Come with me and I will tell you everything.*

"An interesting reading," said Miss Kepple, and we all jumped. "Not the most optimistic interpretation, but valid nonetheless." She glanced at Marta, whose head was bowed over her desk, her thin fingers curled doggedly around her pen. There was unfamiliar concern in her voice as she said, "Let's turn back to the syllabus now. We'll look at *Jane Eyre.*" Her eyes darted again in Marta's direction, hoping, I believed, for an iota of her usual excitement, but she didn't even look up.

The double period seemed to go on forever. I wanted nothing more than for it to end, so that we could talk to Marta about the phone call. At last the bell rang. Before most of us had left our seats, Marta had pushed her books into her bag, swung it onto her shoulder, and left the classroom. Lloyd threw Sami and me a look of extreme apprehension, jerking his head in the direction of the door. We nodded, and he departed at great speed, leaving his books scattered over the desk.

Sami and I crammed Lloyd's things into our own bags before following him into the corridor, which was full of pupils surging down to the Atrium. We tried to weave through the crowds, craning our necks over their heads in an attempt to glimpse Lloyd or Marta, but there was no sign of them.

We emerged onto the Upper Gallery. This was the oldest part of the Main House, and the paneled landing was narrow, with barely enough space for three to walk abreast. The bottleneck caused a deceleration as the crowds of chattering, blazered students made their way downstairs. The noise was tremendous. I glanced over the wooden balustrade to see the first students spilling from the foot of the Eiger into the Atrium, swiftly dispersing to the Elevenses tables set up in the four corners. I couldn't see Marta or Lloyd among them. I turned back to Sami, only to see him dive through a gap between two First Formers ahead of us.

I made to follow him, but at that moment a scream rent the air. It came from below, and was a sound of such appalling panic that I thought I would hear an explosion, or smell smoke, or see a balaclava-clad figure wielding a gun. The reality was worse. A girl's body was splayed on the flagstones at the foot of the Eiger, her blond hair fanned around her head. Her arms and legs were bent at crooked, almost comical angles, her neck bent grotesquely to one side. A pool of blood was spreading around her scalp. Even in their misshapen, damaged state, there was no mistaking those elegant limbs. It was Genevieve.

Time seemed to suspend itself, or perhaps stop entirely. My head swam. My first instinct was to swing over the balustrade and drop down to the Atrium like a cat, landing lightly on all fours, but of course I could not. There was only the convoluted, undignified reality of pushing relentlessly through the crowds, their shouts of panic now mingled with indignation as I battled my way around two sides of the Upper Gallery. I knew that I had to get downstairs; that I had to be one of the first to reach the scene. I elbowed my way down the top section of the Eiger, the crowds thinning now. By the time I was halfway down I could see more of the Atrium. Two people were now kneeling next to Genevieve. I pushed on toward the Lower Gallery, but then the shouts changed, and were no longer directed at me. "Where'd she *go*?" a voice was yelling.

I broke through the final frontier of the crowd to stand at the top of the stairs. Somebody grabbed my wrist. It was

Sami, his eyes glassy with fear. I followed his gaze down to the flagstones, and saw that the two figures kneeling next to Genevieve were Sylvia and Lloyd. Of Marta there was no sign.

From his crouching position on the flagstones, Lloyd glanced up the stairs. His hands were covered in blood, which was spreading thickly from Genevieve's head. "Sami!" he shouted. "Get down here—we need you—"

Sami seemed frozen to the spot. I shook the arm whose wrist he held and he seemed to awaken, the vivid horror of the situation blossoming over his face. He stumbled down the staircase and I followed, putting my hand under his elbow to steady him.

We reached the bottom of the Eiger. There was no sign of any Mags. Sami dropped to his knees beside Genevieve, whose body, I now saw, had been flung onto its side by the force of her fall. Her face was in profile, one side of it pressed to the flagstones, and her eyes were closed. Her expression was strangely peaceful.

"Has someone called an ambulance?" asked Sami.

Lloyd nodded. He and Sylvia were kneeling on either side of Genevieve's head, the cloth of her skirt and his trousers stanching the blood that flowed from beneath her hair. Their hands hovered helplessly over her body.

"Don't touch her." Sami's voice shook, but his hand was steady as he reached out and gently picked up Genevieve's limp arm. He pressed his thumb to her wrist and held it there for a moment. "There's a pulse," he said.

There was a choking sound, and Sylvia rocked back on her heels, her bloody hands pressed to her face. I saw tears pouring from her eyes, mingling with the blood as they streaked down the backs of her hands. She reached out to touch her best friend's cheek, but I grabbed her hand and pulled it away from Genevieve's crumpled form.

"Sylvia," I said, as another racking sob forced its way out of her mouth. She wrenched her arm out of my grasp and twisted around to face me.

"*You!*" she said, her voice somewhere between a whimper and a snarl. "You and your fucking weirdo *freak* of a friend! She did this—she pushed her—she's a fucking psycho, we all knew it. Someone call the police!"

"She didn't push her!" cried Lloyd. He stood up, Genevieve's blood dripping from his knees. "She didn't—you're a liar!" He stopped, seeing Dr. Wardlaw and Major Gregory hurrying down the Eiger toward us, their faces pale with shock. Dr. Wardlaw raised a hand to her mouth in a bizarre parody of Sylvia, uttering a low moan.

All around us the Atrium was now filling up with figures of authority. Dozens of gowned Mags flooded down from the first floor and fanned out around Genevieve. Others began to assist in shepherding the hordes of students away from the Atrium and the galleries, directed by Major Gregory, whose terse commands were for once obeyed without question. Then he approached us, his jaw set, and I thought he would tell us to stop ministering to Genevieve: that we were not needed, that we should leave the Atrium with the others. I felt almost relieved at the prospect. But as he got closer to Genevieve, the remaining color drained from his face, and I saw that he was terrified. He backed away, gripping the banister of the Eiger.

"We have to do something," I muttered to Sami, who nodded. His lips were white. He took off his sweater and rolled it up, holding it to the side of Genevieve's head, where the blood was thickest.

"Where the hell is the ambulance?" he muttered to me, looking around at the doors of the Atrium, which were open to the impossible sunshine of the morning and the vast, empty drive.

"I don't know." I thought of the endless country lanes my father and I had driven along to reach High Realms. We were a long way from the nearest village, let alone a large town with a hospital. I glanced at Genevieve's pallid face, and at Sami's sweater, which was soaked in blood. I ripped off my cardigan and handed it to him, and he switched the garments as quickly as he could.

"We need Dr. Reza," said Sami suddenly, without moving his arm. Genevieve's blood was now seeping up the sleeve of his white school shirt. "Has somebody gone to get her—she'll be in the infirmary, she won't have heard—"

"We've rung her," a clipped voice answered, and I looked up to see Jolyon Astor and Rory Fitz-Straker standing behind Dr. Wardlaw. "There was no answer—the answerphone said she's doing Third Form checkups this morning—"

"Then fucking run over there and get her!" yelled Sami, his face red with frustration, but at that moment Dr. Reza appeared in the doorway of the Atrium, silhouetted against the perverse brightness outside. I saw horror flood her face for a single moment, and then she was beside us, kneeling next to Genevieve's head.

"Pulse?" she said. Sami nodded, but she put two fingers on Genevieve's neck and held them there. Her lips were white as she asked, "How long has she been like this?"

"Fifteen minutes," said Sami wildly, but I shook my head,

knowing it was far less. I met Dr. Reza's dark eyes over Genevieve's body, and could no longer contain the panic that had been rising in me since I had heard her scream. I looked down at Genevieve, at the life ebbing inexorably out of her, and knew with terrible certainty that this was the end of our time at High Realms as we had known it; that there would be no return to even the modicum of happiness that we had grasped.

Someone dumped a first aid kit on the flagstones beside Sami, from which he now extracted several large gauze pads. Very carefully, Dr. Reza moved aside a chunk of Genevieve's hair, revealing a gaping wound in the side of her head. Sami handed her the pads and she placed these against the cut. I watched as their whiteness was instantly flooded with red. Dr. Reza bent lower over Genevieve, her face taut. Then she glanced over her shoulder. "Can someone find out how far away the ambulance is, please," she said, her voice full of urgency.

Lloyd jumped up again and ran to the reception desk in the corner of the Atrium. There was a long silence as he lifted the phone to his ear, and we all froze in an absurd tableau: Dr. Reza pressing the gauze against Genevieve's bleeding scalp; Sami holding out more bandages; Sylvia gripping Genevieve's limp hand, her face streaked with blood and tears. Dr. Wardlaw and the Senior Patrol were standing around us like sentries. Then, just as Lloyd began to speak into the receiver, two things happened simultaneously: we heard the distant wail of a siren; and Max stepped through the door of the Atrium.

For a moment he was still, taking in the scene almost as a conductor might survey the orchestra before lifting their baton. There was profound grace in his handsome face: that passion and strength of spirit that I found so compelling. Then his bearing was complete terror, and he rushed to us. He stared down at Genevieve.

"What on—" he said, his voice strangled. He looked over at Lloyd, who was speaking quickly into the receiver. He raised his eyes to Max's, and their gazes met in equal and extreme fear.

Max dropped to his knees next to Genevieve. The siren was growing louder.

"Gin," said Max, and reached out his hand to touch her hair. "Gin, Gin, Gin. Wake up, please wake up—"

"Max," said Dr. Reza in a low voice. He looked up at her at once, his dark eyes full of tears. For the first time, I saw Dr. Reza's arm tremble slightly as she held the gauze. She locked eyes with Max until he broke away, keening over Genevieve's body.

"I'm sorry," he gasped, almost inaudibly. "I'm so sorry." His face was inches from hers, and his tears dripped onto her pallid cheek.

The siren now swelled through the Atrium. I heard a vehicle rushing up the drive. I thought inexplicably of Marta arriving on that first day in her oversized uniform, and my mind then surged to a parallel reality in which we were now milling around the Atrium as usual. But that life was lost to us, and Marta was nowhere to be seen.

Three paramedics now hurried across the flagstones in their green uniforms, clutching reflective holdalls. I saw the scene through their eyes: the baronial hall with its portraits and honors boards, the dozens of students dressed in tweed blazers, the helpless Mags and Senior Patrollers in their gowns, the cluster of bloodstained attendants around Genevieve. Somewhere, far away in another world, the bell rang for second study.

Dr. Reza was talking to the lead paramedic, giving him the little information she had, her face pinched with deep anxiety. He nodded as his colleagues unloaded oxygen and other equipment.

"We're going to need clear access," I heard him tell her, motioning to Max and Sylvia, who were still crouched next to Genevieve. He glanced incredulously at Major Gregory. "If you could ask the students to move away . . . it may not be wise for them to—"

"Help her. Please help her." Sylvia's voice was shaking so much that the words were almost unintelligible. She let go of Genevieve's hand and stumbled backward, but Max stayed where he was, bent over Genevieve's body as though to protect her. His shoulders heaved as he stroked the hair from her forehead. One of the paramedics touched his wrist, trying to pull him back, but he wouldn't move. Dr. Reza went to him and took his upper arms in her hands, drawing him away from Genevieve. She motioned to me, Lloyd, Sami, and Sylvia to follow her to the back of the Atrium.

The paramedics set to work. Sylvia was now trembling so severely that she could not stand. She gripped the edge of the desk and lowered herself into a chair. I looked down at her and saw that her face was ashen between the smears of Genevieve's blood. Before I could stop myself, I crouched down in front of her, putting my hands on her quaking knees. Her head was bowed, and half a dozen tears splashed onto my knuckles before her shaking abated a little. She raised her eyes to mine for the second time that day. It was a few seconds before they hardened, and she twisted away from me, pushing my hands away.

We waited for ten more minutes as the paramedics worked on Genevieve, expertly pumping oxygen and fluids into her prone body, stemming the flow of blood from her head wound, talking among themselves in low, urgent voices. We were silent. We were helpless sentinels, spaced out in the vastness of the Atrium, as if our watchful presence could somehow breathe life into Genevieve like the drip the paramedics had set up. I felt full of a strange, dual agony. I desperately wanted Genevieve to live. My dislike of her, and my bitterness at the way she treated us, was vanishingly, hilariously small in relation to my desire for her not to die. But as I stood there, my view of Genevieve obscured by the cluster of paramedics and their equipment, my fear that she would not survive was almost eclipsed by my terror at what Sylvia had screamed at us. *She did this—she pushed her.* My longing for this allegation to be explained or extenuated by some fact Sylvia had failed to incorporate, or for it to simply not be true—for Marta not to have done it, to have been elsewhere, to be incapable of such a thing—ran alongside and within my fear of Genevieve's death. It was a terror whose very enormity frightened me.

Finally the paramedics slid Genevieve's limp form onto a stretcher, and carried it across the Atrium and out to the ambulance. We followed them out of the front doors, now able to see Genevieve again as they carefully maneuvered the stretcher down the stone steps. One of the back doors of the ambulance had swung shut in the breeze, and Sami and I ran over to open it for the paramedics. They nodded briskly at us as they prepared to lift Genevieve in. I glimpsed the pale serenity of her face beneath the oxygen mask, her high forehead and fine nose, her slim neck emerging from her bloodstained collar. Even incapacitated, she was statuesque and hard. The stretcher rose into the air to be passed into the ambulance.

We stepped back to allow the paramedics to close the doors, but at that moment a blazered figure hurtled past us and tried to climb into the ambulance. It was Max, and he was sobbing. His face was screwed up with misery and panic, his body flailing powerfully as the lead paramedic tried to pull him away. I saw Dr. Reza rush to help, but Lloyd and Sylvia got there first. Together they seized Max's arms and held him back as the paramedics leaped into the ambulance and the doors were slammed closed. Still Max fought, straining against Lloyd and Sylvia's combined strength, kicking his heels fiercely in the gravel and twisting his wiry body in the loop of Lloyd's arm around his chest.

Then the ambulance was roaring down the drive, and when it reached the gates we heard its siren wail as it disappeared onto the lane. Only then did Max stop struggling and hang lifelessly in Lloyd and Sylvia's arms. We all stood still beneath the clear blue sky, and the plane trees were aflame with color, and I seemed to rise above it all: to float in the autumn air and look down at the somber figures on the drive. I looked down at Lloyd, Sami, Sylvia, Dr. Reza, Max; and then, having seen them all for the last time, I seemed to fly away from them, over the hills of Devon and the villages, along the coast road to the motorway, and all the way to London, back to the life I had left for this one.

Chapter 8

Inside. Now." Major Gregory stood at the top of the steps. His face was in shadow, but I glimpsed an unfamiliar distress in his bearing, and his hand shook as he pointed.

We obeyed him, climbing the steps into the Atrium. There was a pool of blood at the foot of the Eiger, and the first aid kit was scattered impotently across the flagstones. Dr. Wardlaw and a few other Mags stood in a huddle, talking in low voices. The Senior Patrol roamed the space, their movements jerky and restless. There was the clatter of dishes from the Dining Hall to the left, and the low murmur of lessons from the corridors above us. The world had not ended. The school day at High Realms was continuing.

Dr. Reza crossed the Atrium to join the Mags. She cut across Major Gregory, addressing her colleagues in a quiet, urgent tone. As she spoke, Dr. Wardlaw's expression modulated from tension to displeasure. She stared accusingly at Major Gregory, who glowered back at her.

Lloyd, Sami, Max, Sylvia, and I waited by the door, having no idea where we should go or what to do. I looked down at my hands, which were sticky with Genevieve's blood, and at Sami and Lloyd, both of whom were ashen and disheveled.

They looked back at me, and I knew that we were all thinking the same thing. *Where is she?*

Sylvia was crying. She had her back to us, facing the honors board that bore her name in gilded letters, her shoulders shaking. Max was sitting on the floor, his elbows propped on his knees and his head in his hands. His body was entirely still as he stared at the flagstones. I saw Lloyd glance down at him, biting his lip. Then Major Gregory and Dr. Reza broke away from the huddle of Mags and came over to us. Major Gregory looked angrier than ever, but Dr. Reza was calm, although her face was full of strain.

"A word with you all," said Major Gregory tersely. He waited for a moment, and Sylvia turned around, her face an appalling mess of tears and blood. Major Gregory looked pointedly down at Max, and cleared his throat. Slowly, Max got to his feet.

"I have many questions about what has just happened." Major Gregory looked around at us all, his gray eyes glinting dangerously. "Dr. Reza will follow the ambulance to the hospital. I would like you all to clean yourselves up, and locate Miss De Luca. You are then to come directly to my office. Your Head of House"—he nodded curtly at Sylvia—"will meet us there."

"I want to go to the hospital," said Max. He was looking at Dr. Reza, his eyes full of tears. "Please. I have to—"

Major Gregory cut him off. "That won't be possible."

Suddenly Max let out a small, strangled howl. "She might die," he said. "She's going to die, I know it, *she's going to die.*" He put out his hand to the wall of the Atrium to hold himself up.

Dr. Reza took Max's other hand in hers. "Max," she said, "try to calm down. Wait for me in the infirmary. I'll phone as soon as I know anything—"

"Please," said Max. He looked at her imploringly, like a small child begging for a treat. "*Please*—I have to see her—I have to tell her that I—"

"That's enough." Major Gregory's voice was harsher than ever, and I saw a frightening absence of compassion in the thin line of his mouth. "Go and get cleaned up, immediately. Find Miss De Luca and come to my office, no more than fifteen minutes from now." None of us moved. "*Go!*" he thundered.

I had no choice but to obey him. I turned away with the others, Max tugging his hand out of Dr. Reza's grasp. Sylvia, Lloyd, Sami, and I climbed the Eiger to the Lower Gallery, where Sylvia wordlessly turned right to go to Raleigh House. We continued our path up to Hillary, hearing the muffled, perversely ordinary sound of lessons issuing from classrooms. Numbly we scaled staircase after staircase, and finally we were back in our boardinghouse, which was empty. Dust motes swirled in the patches of sunlight in the girls' corridor. I pushed open the door of Room 1A, and we stared at its deserted interior.

"Fuck," muttered Sami.

Lloyd shook his head. "She was never going to be here."

Suddenly Sami was angry. "What happened to Genevieve? Did Marta push her?"

It was the question I hadn't had the courage to pose. Lloyd stared at us both, his brow furrowed. "No," he said at last. "She didn't."

"So Genevieve fell," stated Sami, his voice full of relief.

Again Lloyd shook his head. "Not exactly." His tone was tight, as though the words were being dragged from the back of his throat. "At least—yes, she did fall, but—"

"But *what?*"

"Marta slapped her," said Lloyd heavily. He wasn't looking at us, but at the floor, and I realized how unlike him it was not to meet our eyes. "Mar was running downstairs to the Atrium—Genevieve ran up toward her. I was coming down from the Upper Gallery, but I couldn't get there in time. Genevieve said something to Marta—Marta said something back—then Genevieve had Mar backed up against the wall . . . that's when I got to them. I pulled Genevieve away from her," said Lloyd, finally looking up at us, his dark eyes full of unfamiliar, fearful hesitation. "She was so angry. She said something to me, and that's when Marta slapped her. It wasn't that hard . . . you know Mar, she isn't vicious, she was just upset . . . but Genevieve was already off balance, and she fell sideways down the stairs. She barely seemed to touch them." Lloyd's voice cracked. "I'm sorry."

"It wasn't your fault," I said at once. "You were trying to protect Marta—Genevieve's always had it in for her—"

"No," said Lloyd, his voice heavier than ever. "No, it's not as simple as that."

"Tell us, then!"

For a moment, I saw despair fill Lloyd's countenance. "You see—" he began, but we heard Major Gregory's door slam downstairs, and with one horrified glance at me, Sami and Lloyd hurried away toward the boys' corridor. I stepped over the threshold of Room 1A.

Our beds were unmade from where we'd left them at dawn

to rush down to the stables. Marta's bed was a jumbled nest of scrunched-up pajamas, dog-eared textbooks, pieces of paper covered in scrawled equations, and a ballpoint pen that was leaking over the sheet. On my pillow there was a scrap of paper folded over, with my name written on the outside.

Ro, the note read, in a hurried version of Marta's precise handwriting. *I'm writing this in case I don't get the chance to explain in person. He says he's coming to get me today—he's already on his way. He wants me back at home, and he won't wait till Christmas. Probably he thinks I'll run away before then—but I'd never run away from High Realms. I tried to tell Major G about him, about what he did to me. He wouldn't listen to me, he sent me away, so I'm going to find Dr. Wardlaw at Elevenses and tell her everything. I'm not going to go with my father, and if she believes what I'm going to tell her, she won't let him take me. But she might not believe me, in which case I lose. Have loved knowing you and the boys.*

I stared at the note, my body slowly filling with abject horror. This was worse than I'd expected. I knew that for Marta to have sought out a figure of authority—let alone Major Gregory—she must have been beyond desperate. Panic swelled in my chest, and I knew that I could not keep the contents of the note private.

I went to the sink in the corner and scrubbed Genevieve's blood off my shaking hands. Despite the lack of time, I didn't dare present myself at Major Gregory's office looking anything less than immaculate. I found clean versions of all my clothes, dragging on shirt, cardigan, skirt, long socks, and tie as quickly as I could. The cuffs of my blazer were stiff with dried blood. I shoved Marta's note into my pocket and left the room.

Major Gregory's office door was closed. There was no sign of the boys or Sylvia. I heard a low murmur from within the office, and Lloyd's deep voice. Panic gripped me, but I forced myself to knock on the door.

"Come in."

The small office was full of people. Lloyd, Sami, and Sylvia were seated on a row of hard chairs in front of Major Gregory's desk, behind which he sat bolt upright, his back to the window. Miss Kepple sat next to him in her dark suit. Major Gregory frowned. "Where is Miss De Luca?"

You've failed her, I thought. *We've all failed her.* "She wasn't in our room."

"Have you looked for her?"

"There wasn't time."

His mouth twitched irritably. "We will have to hope that she appears in short order," he said. "This is a very grave situation. I only hope that it can be dealt with internally in the first instance."

There was a short silence in which we heard the wind blowing outside, and faint shrieks rising from the Astroturf through the open window. Major Gregory was fanatical about fresh air.

"Now," he said softly. "I would like somebody to explain to me the events that led to Miss De Luca pushing Genevieve Lock down the stairs."

Immediately Lloyd, Sami, and I burst out in a volley of protest. To hear Major Gregory factualize the uncertain cause of Genevieve's fall in his opening gambit was unacceptable to us, but our Housemaster held up his hand. "Miss Maudsley has already told me that she saw Genevieve Lock fall as a result of being slapped by Miss De Luca, and there were a number of other witnesses at the scene who have attested to that. I want to know what took place *before* Miss De Luca slapped Genevieve. I want to know why she did it."

"Sir," said Sylvia sleekly. I looked to one side and saw that she'd regained some of her poise: her skin was clear and there was color in her fine, high cheeks. Only the redness of her eyes and the tremor in her voice gestured to the trauma she was enduring. "Sir, I'm not sure you understand. I didn't see what happened before Marta hit Genevieve. Lloyd Williams was there, but the three of us"—she indicated herself, Sami, and me—"were on our way down from the Upper Gallery, a long way behind. I don't know what happened." *That's right, Sylvia.* I thought glumly. *Distance yourself from what's happened. Let us take the blame.*

To my surprise, Major Gregory glared at Sylvia. "Miss Maudsley, I'm not asking you to explain what happened just before the attack took place. I am asking you all, as the people who spend the most time with Miss De Luca and Miss Lock, to give me the *context* of the altercation that took place on the stairs." We were silent, and Major Gregory spoke again. "Genevieve Lock is, at best, grievously injured. There's every chance the police will be involved. Incidents like this do not simply *happen*. There is information here which I am missing, and until I have received it, you are all in equal danger of very severe repercussions. Miss Maudsley, you are Genevieve Lock's closest friend, and also Vice-Captain General of School. If you wish to continue in that role, I advise you to suspend any discretion you may currently be exercising with regards to today's events. *Immediately.*" His mouth snapped shut.

Sylvia examined her hands, which were resting on her knees. One of her slim fingers had a long, rust-colored smudge of blood on it. Major Gregory's threat had given her the same expression that I recognized from English lessons, when she would consider her position after a difficult question. Her transparent habit was to ponder whether to venture an answer in which she was not entirely confident, thereby risking the humiliation of it being wrong, but also the glory of it being correct. "I'm afraid I don't know the *full* picture, sir," she said at last. "But one person here does." She looked up at Lloyd, her eyes full of a quizzical beadiness. "You can fill Major Gregory in, can't you?" she said lightly.

Lloyd raised his head. I saw the muscles in his neck contract as he swallowed. "I—I'm not sure what you mean," he said.

I darted a look at Sami, wondering whether he, too, had noticed the unusual tremor in Lloyd's voice, but he was looking at his knees, his expression full of a strange bitterness. I realized that this was about Bridge Night, and wished desperately that I had found out the truth rather than going along with Marta's wishes.

"Well?" demanded Major Gregory. "Speak up, Mr. Williams."

There was a deathly silence. Lloyd swallowed again, his eyes flickering with an emotion I thought I recognized. It was shame: the same shame that I'd seen in Marta's eyes on the night Genevieve had blasted her with the hose. Then Sylvia spoke. "I'll tell him, Lloyd, if you won't," she said flatly.

Lloyd looked up at her, his expression almost weary. "All

right," he said. "All right." I saw the moist sheen of sweat on his cheek. "The fact is, Genevieve was very upset this morning," he said. "She'd just found out—I mean, I think she *must've* found out"—he glanced at Sylvia, who nodded coldly—"that Max . . . her boyfriend, you know . . . that Max had feelings for someone else. Perhaps even that he was—that he was leaving her . . ."

"I see," said Major Gregory, after a moment. The reference to emotion seemed to have flummoxed him. I was equally confused: the idea of Max leaving Genevieve was anathema to me. Perhaps Lloyd was making it up, I thought. Perhaps he was trying to distract Major Gregory from what Marta had done.

Miss Kepple cleared her throat. "And the person he had feelings for was Marta, I assume?" she asked.

At this Sylvia laughed: a strange, mirthless sound. That laugh and its derision awoke fury in me, and a new contempt for Sylvia, whose only concern appeared to be preserving her own reputation and place in the hierarchy. Nobody was on our side; nobody would help us. We could only fight for ourselves.

"Genevieve wasn't the only one who was upset this morning," I said, as clearly as I could. "Marta was very unhappy, too. You know why." I addressed this last comment to Major Gregory, who stared at me.

"What do you mean?" he asked, his voice tight, and I realized at once that he was very afraid; that he had not wanted this to come out: that it was, for him, wonderfully convenient if the problem had existed between Genevieve and Marta, rather than with Marta herself.

"I'm talking about the phone call from her father," I said. "You knew about it, sir. You sent for her."

"So?" he spat. I hated his cowardice; hated that he did not apply his obsession with fortitude and accountability to himself.

"So you knew she was upset," I said. "You knew because she tried to tell you. You sent her away."

"I did nothing of the sort."

I hadn't expected him to lie so flagrantly. Anger bubbled inside me. "I know she did," I said firmly, and saw Major Gregory's eyes widen. I opened my mouth to continue, but before I could speak there was a brisk knock on the door, and Bella Ford stepped into the room.

"Professor De Luca has arrived, sir," she said. "Dr. Wardlaw would like you to come downstairs."

Sami, Lloyd, and I stared at each other in horror. Before anyone could say anything, Sylvia spoke. "Has there been any news about Genevieve?"

Bella's gaze softened as she looked down at Sylvia. "No," she said. "No, Sylv, I'm sorry—"

"Thank you, Miss Ford," Major Gregory cut in. "I take it there has been no sign of Miss De Luca?"

"No, sir."

"Then gather some of your colleagues and start looking for her," said Major Gregory to Bella, his voice hard. "Find the groundsmen and ask them to assist you. I want the whole Estate searched."

"I want to help," said Sylvia. "I'm Senior Patrol, too—let me help track her down—"

"You may be Senior Patrol, Miss Maudsley, but given your proximity to today's events you will remain where you are. You of all people should be aware of the severity of this situation,"

Major Gregory snapped, and Sylvia's body jerked as though he had hit her. "You will all wait here with Miss Kepple while I go downstairs. Nobody is to leave this room until I get back." He got to his feet. "Come with me, Miss Ford." The door closed with a firm click behind them.

The hours that followed were some of the longest I have ever known. Lloyd, Sami, Sylvia, and I remained on our hard chairs in Major Gregory's office, supervised by Miss Kepple, who decreed absolute silence. The boys and I were unable to communicate: unable to discuss what each of us knew, suspected, or feared; unable to offer each other comfort, or make any kind of plan. We knew nothing of what was going on outside the office. We were only aware of the sky, which grew steadily darker as the afternoon wore on, of the squalls of rain that began to whip against the mullioned window, and of intermittent flurries of voices from the Common Room. I caught Genevieve's name several times, in tones which were alternately somber and scandalized. I held Marta's note scrunched up in my palm. There was no opportunity to pass it covertly to Lloyd or Sami, because Miss Kepple watched us closely throughout, her eyes narrowed as if she thought we might try to run away. Sylvia lolled against the bookshelf, gazing out of the window. Once or twice I saw her glance at Lloyd, her expression inscrutable.

As the hands on the small clock on Major Gregory's desk nudged interminably toward two, half past two, and then three o'clock, I couldn't stop thinking about the same time the previous day, when Lloyd, Marta, and I had been in Latin with Mr. Briggs. Marta had been in one of her restless, mischievous moods—bored because the work was too easy for her, although she hadn't said so. She and I had shared a desk in the middle of the room, in front of Lloyd, whom Briggs had told to sit next to Rory Fitz-Straker. Briggs had been delivering a monologue about Cicero's use of rhetorical devices. Marta had swung on her chair, her hand on my shoulder to steady herself, and chewed her pen, which was gradually leaking more and more ink. She'd alternated between gazing out of the window and leaning toward me to whisper anything that occurred to her: what she hoped was for dinner that night; how many minutes of the lesson there were remaining; her opinion that Briggs could have used some lessons in public speaking from Cicero. Every so often she'd twisted around mid-swing to grin wickedly at Lloyd. The fourth or fifth time, she'd suddenly lost her balance, toppling backward onto Lloyd and Rory's desk. In the commotion that had followed—Rory's snarl, Lloyd's repressive words to him, and Briggs's droning admonitions—Marta had only laughed and laughed, picking herself up from the floor, ink all over her chin and dust in her hair. Now, sitting in Major Gregory's cold, silent office twenty-four hours later, Marta's laughter echoed in my mind as distantly as if I'd heard it many years ago, and I longed to feel the pressure of her hand on my shoulder, even for the briefest of moments.

Finally, at about six o'clock, there was a soft knock on the door. Lloyd, Sami, Sylvia, and I whipped around, our bodies stiff with lack of movement. Dr. Reza entered. Her clothes were streaked with Genevieve's blood.

"How is she?" Sylvia asked immediately, her voice hoarse.

Dr. Reza's dark eyes flickered over the scene, taking in Miss

Kepple behind the desk, and the four of us on our wooden chairs. "Are you all right?" she asked.

"We're fine," replied Sylvia brusquely. "How's Gin?"

Dr. Reza pulled up a chair and sat down next to the desk, closest to Sylvia. She opened her mouth to speak, and I felt a rush of terror that Genevieve was dead, but Miss Kepple cleared her throat. "I think it would be best to wait for Major Gregory to return before any news is shared," she said.

Dr. Reza glanced at her, her expression impassive. "I've just seen him," she replied. "He was on his way to Higher Mags' Tea, and asked whether you might join him, Anna."

It was obvious to me that this wasn't true, but Miss Kepple accepted the dismissal without question. She moved awkwardly around the desk, before sweeping from the room with as much dignity as she could muster. The door closed behind her, and for a moment there was silence apart from the rushing of the wind outside.

"Tell me, *please*," said Sylvia. Her eyes were fixed on Dr. Reza, who looked steadily back at her.

"Genevieve is alive," she said quietly. "She had surgery on her head wound, which was very serious. She lost a huge amount of blood. It was very fortunate that Sami and Rose acted as quickly as they did." Dr. Reza paused, still looking Sylvia in the eye. "Genevieve suffered cardiac arrest in the ambulance, and had to be resuscitated twice. She has a broken ankle, a broken wrist, and several fractured ribs. She's in intensive care. The next twenty-four hours will be critical."

Sylvia's hand was pressed to her mouth. A choking sound came from behind it, and she leaned forward, reaching for the desk in front of her to support herself. "Oh my God," she said, in a voice that was close to a moan. She rocked back and forth, appearing to panic at the strength of her own emotion. Very gently, Dr. Reza took her hand, and to my great surprise Sylvia did not pull away.

"All right," Dr. Reza said, after a minute or so. "Go down to supper, Sylvia—or if you don't feel up to it, you can go back to Raleigh, and I'll ask for a meal to be sent up. I'm going to sign you off evening duty—"

"No," said Sylvia at once, her tone strangled. "I want to hear—I want to know what's going on. Have they found Marta?"

"They have not," said Dr. Reza, and a flare of fear ignited in my chest. "Go back to Raleigh, please, Sylvia. I'll come and find you when I've phoned for an update on Genevieve. I promise I'll do that." Her eyes met Sylvia's, and Sylvia nodded reluctantly, accepting the trade-off. She left the room.

Dusk was falling outside, and the only light came from a small lamp on Major Gregory's desk. Dr. Reza looked at us all, her brown eyes full of deep solicitude. Eventually Lloyd cleared his throat. "So there's no sign of Marta downstairs?" he asked.

"No," said Dr. Reza quietly. We waited, but she said nothing else.

"And—Marta's dad?"

"He's with Dr. Wardlaw," said Dr. Reza. "He intends to stay at High Realms tonight."

There was another pause. I fumbled for the words to seek more clarity from Dr. Reza, but before I could find them, she spoke again. "How long have you been up here?"

"Since before lunch," replied Sami. Dr. Reza frowned,

opening her mouth to reply, but Sami continued, his tone strained. "Dr. Reza, do you know what's going to happen to Marta?"

"That's a very good question," she said heavily. She regarded us all with a tense, careful expression. "I think the answer will depend partly on whether Marta has to be found, or whether she returns to school of her own accord. She's been missing for several hours now, and I'm afraid it doesn't . . . it doesn't look good for her to have disappeared like this, whether what happened was her fault or not." She paused. "The hospital rang the police," she said, and the boys and I looked at each other in alarm. "They're coming to High Realms in the morning. Of course, I hope that Marta will have come back by then. I understand that she has needed time to . . . calm down, but we—some of us more than others—need to hear her side of the story." She looked around at us all. "Do you know where Marta might be?"

We shook our heads. I realized that if the Senior Patrol hadn't managed to locate Marta, then I had absolutely no idea where she could be. All the places she went—the Straker Library, the Private Study Rooms, the stables, classrooms, the Dining Hall, Hillary House—were obvious, and would already have been searched.

Dr. Reza was watching me. Suddenly I shivered: Major Gregory's office was full of the cool dusk air. Frowning, Dr. Reza got up and went to close the window. "What is it, Rose?" she asked.

I hesitated. I ran over in my mind all that had been said: about Genevieve's critical condition, about Marta's father staying at High Realms overnight, about the police, and the likelihood of Marta being expelled or suspended. Both outcomes would entail her leaving High Realms with her father. It was now or never. There was no time to wait to speak to Dr. Wardlaw, or to consult Lloyd and Sami. Most of all, there was no time to wait to find out the full truth from Marta, or obtain her blessing to confide this most private of matters. It had to be now, to somebody I was sure would, at the very least, listen to us. She might even go so far as to understand, and help us to keep Marta at High Realms with us, in an environment of relative safety and manageable risk.

"Dr. Reza," I said, "I need to tell you something about Marta."

"All right," she replied swiftly.

I uncurled my fist from around Marta's note, weighing up whether it would be better to explain in my own words, or to read to Dr. Reza what she had written. Dr. Reza glanced at the piece of paper, seeming to take my hesitation for reticence. "Do you want to go somewhere private, Rose?"

"It's OK," I said. "Sami and Lloyd know most of it. I think—"

"Rose," interrupted Lloyd suddenly. "Wait. Let me tell her."

I stared at him. Forthright though Lloyd generally was, this was unlike him, and I was sure that he didn't know all the details I was about to impart. He gave me a look of warning.

"OK," I said, bewildered. Lloyd leaned forward in his chair, opening his mouth to speak, but at that moment the door opened and Major Gregory entered, his face dark with anger.

Dr. Reza glanced at him. "Might you give us a couple of minutes?"

"I will not." Major Gregory stomped across the room, glaring at Dr. Reza. "Where is Miss Kepple?"

"I believe she's at Higher Mags' Tea," said Dr. Reza evenly. Despite everything, I saw Sami suppress a smile.

"And Sylvia Maudsley?"

"I sent her to go and have dinner."

"Without my permission."

"Yes," said Dr. Reza, whose eyes now flashed. "I understand that these students have been detained in your office all afternoon, Nicholas. Was that necessary?"

"It was absolutely necessary," spat Major Gregory. "*These students* are the closest friends of somebody who has committed a very serious crime. That person has now absconded from school and cannot be found." He rounded on us. "Do any of you know where Marta De Luca is?" he demanded.

We all shook our heads, and his chest swelled with rage. "If Miss De Luca doesn't give herself up tonight, the consequences of her actions will be even more severe than the expulsion she already faces. She will—"

"Hold on a minute," said Lloyd loudly. "You still don't know what actually happened. You're jumping to conc—"

"*Enough!*" thundered Major Gregory, and we all jumped. He slammed his hand down on the desk. "Miss De Luca is required by the police for questioning, first thing tomorrow. She was last seen by a Second Former just after the incident, running along the southern wall of the Hexagon in the direction of Donny Stream. The Senior Patrol and the groundsmen have now combed the woods beyond the stream as far as the school boundary. There is every reason to believe that Miss De Luca has run away." He paused, chewing his bottom lip ferociously. "I want you to tell me anything you know, or suspect, about where she might have gone."

"We have no idea," said Sami flatly. Major Gregory glared at him.

"In that case," he said, his eye twitching with rage, "you will all now go and do your evening duty. You will do it *impeccably*. You will then come straight back here and tell me anything that has occurred to you with regards to Marta De Luca's whereabouts. We will sit here *all night* if we have to—"

"Nicholas," said Dr. Reza, her voice low, "they've already told you they don't know. I'm going to take them down for dinner, and then—"

"You will do nothing of the kind." Major Gregory fixed her with a mulish stare. "This is a House affair, Dr. Reza, and above that, a School one, which I am dealing with as Master of Laws. It is not your remit."

"It's my remit if I believe there is a danger to their health or welfare," Dr. Reza responded calmly. She didn't seem remotely cowed by Major Gregory's bullishness. "If you insist on them doing their evening duty, I will allow it, but after that they must have supper and go to bed, without being questioned further by you. That's my final word."

Major Gregory seemed to grope for an objection. I couldn't tell whether his look of loathing came from an abstract hatred of his authority being challenged, or a personal antipathy to Dr. Reza, or a combination of the two. Finally he jerked his head toward the door. "You may go," he told us. "In your place, I would be thinking very carefully about your position at this school. You are here by invitation only, on an extremely generous scholarship. A scholarship that could be withdrawn at any time." He glowered at us. "Get on with your duties."

As we reached the door, I glanced back. Major Gregory was opening the window behind him, scowling into the dusk. Dr. Reza was looking at us. Her eyes flickered to the note I held in my hand, and she moved her head slightly to the left, in the direction of the Hexagon, which could just about be seen from the window.

We took the back stairs to the ground floor. It was now almost seven o'clock, and the sky was a deep gray. Rain whipped against the windows. The corridors were very quiet, even though it was prime time for people to be coming back from matches or going to supper. The few students we did see avoided our eyes, looking somber and almost scared. We didn't dare converse until the door had swung closed behind us and we were hurrying across the damp grass. To our left the floodlights were on over the Astroturf. I could hear the sharp, intermittent yells of a hockey match.

"Rose," said Lloyd, before I could speak, "I'm sorry I didn't tell you any of that stuff before, but—"

I stopped walking and wheeled around to face him. "Why didn't you let me tell Dr. Reza about Marta's dad?"

Lloyd's face was in shadow, but his dark eyes found mine. "I didn't think it would help Marta," he said.

"What the hell do you mean?"

"Think about it." Lloyd's tone was aggravatingly calm. "If word gets around that Marta's—mentally unstable, or whatever—it'll change the way the school and the police look at what's happened. They're already determined to think it was Marta's fault. If you ask me, Dr. Reza knows there's something wrong with her. She probably means well, but in my experience meaning well isn't enough . . . if people find out Marta's not right in the head, they could use it as more ammunition. They'll say she slapped Genevieve for no good reason; that she's just some crazy—"

"Yeah," I cut in. My temper rose, exacerbated by my reluctant concern that Lloyd was right. "And we know that's not true, don't we? I'd never have told Dr. Reza that Marta's *not right in the head*. Marta's as sane as any of us. It's like you said earlier, Lloyd—she slapped Genevieve because of something Genevieve said to *you,* about something *you'd* done. Something none of you will bloody tell me."

We stood there in the cold dusk, rain falling around us, glaring at each other in the semidarkness. Nobody spoke. I heard Sami's stomach rumble, and my body responded with its own acidic jab of hunger. "For fuck's sake," I said, to no one in particular.

Lloyd shook his head. "I didn't mean for any of this to happen. I didn't mean for Genevieve to blame Marta for what I . . . for me and Max." He swallowed, looking at me almost beseechingly.

"You and *Max*?" I stared at him through the darkness. "But—but you—"

"Rose, I can explain. It's not what you think."

"Tell me the truth, then!" I snarled, my body flooding with anger. "I can't believe this—Marta's run away, and all because *you*—"

"I don't think she's run away," Sami interrupted. Lloyd and I looked at him in surprise. His fair hair was covered with a fine mist of rain, and his face gleamed with dampness. He looked steadily back at us. "I don't think she's run away," he repeated. "She likes it here too much."

There was a short silence in which Lloyd and I stared at him. Then: "They saw her running toward Donny Stream," Lloyd said, but I was thinking about Marta's note.

I pulled it out of my pocket and looked at it. *I'd never run away from High Realms.* Lloyd and Sami leaned in, their eyes darting back and forth as they read what Marta had written, the crumpled sheet of paper growing speckled with rain. Then both boys raised their gaze to mine.

"She's still here," said Lloyd slowly.

Sami nodded, his forehead creased with concern. "But where?"

I thought hard, trying to piece together what we knew. Marta had last been seen running this way, toward Donny Stream. The woods on the other side had been thoroughly searched. If we were correct in our realization, she had not gone beyond them. That placed her somewhere between here and the stream.

"She's in the stables," I said.

"How can she be? They'll have searched them."

"She's in the clocktower," I said, and as soon as I spoke the words I knew that they were true.

"How on earth—"

"We've got to find her," I said, and I began to run across the pitch, my body feeling strangely light.

The boys ran after me. We didn't cross the Hexagon, but instead ran around the southern perimeter of the buildings and down Lime Grove, as I was sure Marta herself had done eight hours earlier. We looped around the back of the stables, past the barn, and approached the courtyard through the clocktower arch, breathing heavily. The courtyard itself was dark, but there were lights on in a few of the stables, where a handful of younger students were mucking out. There was no sign of Gerald, and I assumed that he was out searching the Estate with the rest of the Senior Patrol.

"Slow down," Lloyd muttered to me, as we slipped through the archway. "Don't make it look like we're on a mission."

I glanced at him, annoyed that he was giving instructions, and pulled open the door of Block C. The three horses snorted hopefully as we stepped inside. I strode to the back wall, and Lloyd followed me.

"Keep a lookout," I said to Sami over my shoulder, and he nodded, pulling the upper half of the stable door almost closed.

Lloyd and I examined the back wall. Part of it was covered with tack, which hung on metal hooks, and part of it with shelves, which were laden with paraphernalia: buckets, tools, bags of feed, crates of apples, and the dreaded pressure hose. Behind both tack and shelves, the wall of the stable was plywood. Looking around, I noticed for the first time that the other walls were covered with plaster.

Wordlessly, Lloyd and I began to remove the rugs and the tack from the back wall, piling it at our feet to reveal a smooth expanse of plywood, with no sign of a door. I stared at it with a sinking feeling of anticlimax, but Lloyd bit his lip, looking sideways at the stalls.

"It's got to be behind there," he said.

"What?"

"The way up." Lloyd reached out and knocked softly on the

plywood. The resulting sound was deeper than I had expected, and distinctly hollow. I looked to one side and saw that the plywood ended just after it crossed into the back of the first stall.

We pulled open the door of George's stall and squeezed past his huge body to the back. He shuffled restlessly, but otherwise didn't protest. There was a net of hay tied to a hook on the cement-coated wall, and beside that was the edge of the huge plywood board. It wasn't flush to the wall.

"Help me," said Lloyd, and he curled his fingers around the edge of the plywood and pulled. It inched toward him. I wrapped my own fingers around the rough edge of the wood, and we both gave it a tug. It moved another few inches.

We peered around it. There was now enough space for a small body to slip through. I saw the cavity beyond, and the narrow flight of concrete steps that twisted up above our heads. There was even a light: only a bare bulb, but a light all the same, and it glowed in the darkness, illuminating our path up the stairs. I heard the thud of the stable door being pulled totally closed, a scrambling sound, and an indignant harrumph from George, and then Sami was behind us, taking the long flight of steps two at a time to catch up. We hurried up them, feeling sick and fearful and excited, and the stairs curved around, and within moments we were at the top, outside a closed wooden door. Lloyd knocked. No sound came from within. He pushed the door open, and there was the clocktower room. It was larger than expected and dark, apart from a perfect halo of milky light on the floor, tumbling down from the translucent face of the clock. The space was empty except for a bare mattress, and curled on that mattress was Marta, soaking wet, her arms over her head as though she were about to be shot.

When we said nothing, shocked in spite of ourselves, our friend raised her head from her knees and stared at us. Her tearstained face was full of the utmost fear. On seeing who had entered, her eyes widened. Almost at once, she spoke, in a voice that trembled with trepidation and hope. "Please," she said. "Please, don't tell them I'm here."

PART II

Chapter 9

One of my clearest memories from the period just before the incident on the Eiger is of an English lesson with Miss Kepple. We were studying *Jane Eyre,* and Miss Kepple was drilling us on what she called the "turning points' in the novel. Her index finger tapped lightly on her desk as she gave several examples: Jane meeting Rochester for the first time in the woods, Jane finding out about Bertha, Jane's decision not to marry St. John Rivers. Miss Kepple told us that these were "points of no return." They were the events that formed Jane's character, making her who she becomes at the end of the novel: the woman who could marry Rochester without compromising herself.

Not unusually, Marta disagreed with Miss Kepple. Again not unusually, she was quick to say why, but the reason I remember this particular dispute is that Sylvia agreed with Marta. Both of them maintained that the evolution of Jane's character wasn't entirely contingent on these events. According to Marta, Jane was primarily shaped by her background and circumstances, and that—though traumatic—these events gave her the tools she would need to grow strong and independent. Anything that happened to her later—her feelings for Rochester, his deception, her relationship with St. John Rivers—was less important than what had happened to her before she ever met Rochester. I distinctly remember Marta and Sylvia's rare nod of concurrence as they explained their theory to the class. According to them, the real growth in Jane's character took place in the gray matter *between* the so-called turning points; the emotional work that Jane did in coming to terms with the abuse she'd faced as a child, Rochester's duplicity, and so on; and the self-knowledge she gained during her temporary departure from Thornfield, when she worked, met other people, and had time to reflect.

At the time, I remember being unconvinced by Marta and Sylvia's argument. To a certain extent I still am. Looking back at what happened to us at High Realms, I can identify several moments that clearly were—in Miss Kepple's phrase—points of no return. They were obviously significant events, and they were often vividly—sometimes painfully—dramatic. But it's also clear to me that there were events that at the time seemed impactful, and were not; decisions that seemed irrevocable, but were not; and plans that seemed destined to be fulfilled at any cost that were, perhaps, not as necessary as they might have been. There were times when it seemed like the world was ending, and mornings after nights when it felt as though everything had changed forever. But in reality, the true change in us didn't take place in those moments. To use Marta's words this time, it happened in the gray matter: in the time between the huge things, and in all the mending and sewing and striving that we did in those periods.

That night—the night we found Marta in the clock-tower, white-faced and drenched and with a badly sprained ankle—was one such event. It felt pivotal at the time, but ultimately it was the decisions we made afterward that were important. We couldn't spend long with Marta that evening. We knew that someone could come into the stable below at any time; that late roll call was imminent and that the Senior Patrol would still be prowling the Estate. We tried to persuade Marta to come back to school with us, promising that we would not leave her to face the music on her own, but our efforts were futile. As soon as she learned that her father was at High Realms, there was no question of her coming back to Hillary with us that night.

The three of us tramped back to the Main House, damp from the rain and colder than ever, because we'd given our sweaters to Marta to try to keep her warm overnight in the unheated clocktower. In a voice that was more like a moan, she'd told us she'd waded through Donny Stream and hidden in the woods for several hours until the Senior Patrol had started to search them. Her panic and her pain, both physical and otherwise, was extreme. We had not hidden from her the reality that Genevieve was fighting for her life, which had sent Marta into further paroxysms of fear. It was obvious to all of us that she'd never meant to cause harm, let alone on this scale; but then we'd always known that Marta meant no harm.

As we crossed the Hexagon, I felt nothing but dread. It seemed to me that by running away, Marta had sealed her fate. She'd lost any shred of credibility she might have had; any opportunity to give a reasonable explanation for slapping Genevieve, and thereby mitigate the possibility of being expelled. I felt many things, but among them was an oppressive sadness that my best friend would be leaving High Realms.

I could not see any way around that fact. More powerful than that sadness was my certainty that Marta would not be heading to a safer environment—that she was, in fact, destined to be in great danger.

We saw the Main House towering above us, its many windows still ablaze with light. I looked back through the archway to the infirmary, where several lights also burned. I knew that Dr. Reza had meant for me to come and find her after evening duty, to finish telling her what I'd started to explain about Marta. There was a part of me that still longed to do that; to run straight to the warm and peaceful San, the safest place at High Realms, and tell Dr. Reza everything. In my imagination she listened while I poured it all out, her expression devoid of judgment or criticism, and she and I worked out what to do together. But another part of me had stirred defiantly when we'd found Marta in the clocktower and looked into her trapped, terrified eyes. The same part of me remembered what Marta had said about Dr. Reza at breakfast that very morning: *I knew I was right not to trust her.* I remembered Marta's references to interrogations; her reluctance to attend appointments with Dr. Reza, which I'd never understood but hadn't bothered to investigate. *Meaning well is not enough,* Lloyd had told us; and that was assuming Dr. Reza did mean well, of which there was no evidence other than my own, fallible instinct.

So I did not go to Dr. Reza that evening. We entered the school via the front door and the Atrium, where the floor had been scrubbed clean of Genevieve's blood, and went to the almost empty Dining Hall. We began by devouring our food, but I quickly lost my appetite, thinking of Marta alone and starving in the clocktower room. A hard lump formed in my throat, and I put down my knife and fork. Sami looked over at me, and I knew he understood. Silently he passed me a napkin; then he unfolded his own, and surreptitiously piled the leftover food from his plate into it. Lloyd, meanwhile, steadfastly continued eating, his head bent over his plate.

When we got back to Hillary House, we encountered far worse than the usual pre-retiring bell hyperactivity. As I slipped down the girls' corridor to Room 1A, door after door opened, and the Lower Sixth Hillaryians emerged into the passageway and shouted. *Your friend's a psycho. She's a coward. She's a criminal.* There was no sign of Major Gregory.

I shut the door of our room behind me and tugged the bookcase part of the way across the door, as Marta and I had learned to do in order to stop Genevieve from barging in to smoke out of our window. I went straight to my bed and sat down, burying my head in my hands. I felt a cold dampness beneath me. Feeling over my bed, I found that the whole thing was soaking wet.

They'd opened the window, and the wind was blowing in. I didn't close it immediately, but instead flopped onto the desk in front of it, as Genevieve had done many times, cigarette in hand. I stared into the darkness, craning my neck to one side, and for the first time from this position, I could just about make out the silhouette of the clocktower: tall and elegant, the clock face gleaming faintly in the moonlight. My only thought was of how Lloyd, Sami, and I could extract Marta from it before the police found her.

Chapter 10

I can't come with you. I won't."

It was dawn. Lloyd, Sami, and I had scrambled down to the stables in the half-light, sneaking out of the Main House via the Ivy Door, and now stood in the clocktower room. Marta was standing next to the clock, slightly to one side, in the shadow of its circumference. Her dark hair stuck out in clumps, and her face gleamed as palely as the clock face. She hadn't touched the food that we'd unwrapped and laid out on the mattress.

"I can't do it," she repeated. "I can't leave here, with him."

"It might not come to that," Lloyd replied.

She shook her head vigorously, wincing as the movement traveled down her body to her sprained ankle. "It will," she said. "You said the police are coming."

We were silent. On our walk down to the stables we had hurriedly agreed that we would tell Marta about the impending school and police investigation. We'd hoped to convince her that her position would be improved, and her case strengthened, if she came out of hiding and cooperated. In response she'd curled into a ball on the mattress, her eyes glassy, and hadn't spoken for a full ten minutes.

Now she was up, and was leaning against the bare bricks of the clocktower wall. The room was freezing cold, and she wore Lloyd's pullover and my cardigan over her own clothes, with her blazer over the top. She shivered, drawing it around her.

"Was there any more news about Genevieve?" she asked. We shook our heads. "And—did you see my father?"

"No," said Sami. He waited for a moment. Then, "Marta," he said, his voice gentle. She looked up, her face pinched with anxiety. "We think you should tell the school about him."

"How will that help?" she snapped. "It doesn't change the fact that I slapped Genevieve. It doesn't change the fact that she fell."

"No," said Sami. "But it would change the way they'll treat you. They won't be able to send you away with him."

She shook her head stubbornly, staring at the wall. "No way. I'm not telling them anything. I tried to talk to Major Gregory yesterday—he didn't take any notice. It won't make any difference."

"But Mar," said Lloyd, an unwelcome trace of impatience in his voice, "we've seen the note you left Rose. You went to Major Gregory . . . you were even going to tell Dr. Wardlaw yesterday. What's changed since then? This is your chance to—"

"Lloyd," Marta cut in heavily. Her eyes flickered with grief. "*Everything* has changed since yesterday."

We were silent, faced with the strength of her despair. She swallowed. "Everything has changed," she repeated. "My father is here. He'll have spent hours with Dr. Wardlaw by now—and with Major Gregory, and all the rest of them."

"Yes, but how does that—"

"You don't know my father." Her voice was harsh. "You have no idea what he's like—how he can be. I can't explain it."

"Fine," said Lloyd, glancing at me. "But I still think you should *try* to tell them. What's the alternative, Mar? You can't stay up here. You've got to fight this. You've got to tell them what's happened to you."

"Oh yes?" said Marta, her voice rising. It was the first time I'd seen her truly angry with him. "And what's that, Lloyd? What's *happened* to me?"

"I don't fucking know," said Lloyd, who looked bewildered, and increasingly angry himself. "I've got no way of knowing that, do I? I've never asked you, and you've certainly never bloody told us, but we can see that you're—"

"I'm what, Lloyd?"

"Well, you're—you're—*sad,* aren't you?" Lloyd spat out the words, his own voice trembling with emotion. "You're upset—you're unstable—your behavior isn't nor—"

"*Lloyd,*" I said, but it was too late: the damage was done. Marta's eyes were brimming with tears. She put her hand out to the wall to steady herself, her entire body shaking. For a moment I thought she would drop to her knees, that the fight was over, that she would wrap her arm around my neck and allow me to support her up to the school. But then she rounded on Lloyd.

"You dare to say those things to me," she said in a choked voice. "You dare talk to me about my behavior—my decisions—*my life*—after the things you've done, Lloyd, caused the trouble you have, hurt people the way you have. I never asked you anything," she went on, her voice now trembling uncontrollably, "after Bridge Night. I never asked you about what I saw, and I've never told anyone. Even when Genevieve came after me, I let everyone think it was just because she hated *me*. I've never asked you why you did it, Lloyd. And I never will." She gazed at him, tears now rolling down her pallid cheeks. "We have to respect each other. Respect that there are things that aren't—that can't be said. That are made worse by the saying of them."

She and Lloyd stared at each other for a long time. Then Marta's narrow shoulders slumped in exhaustion, and she sat down against the wall, under the clock face. Lloyd watched her for a moment, and then turned on his heel and marched out of the room. We heard his light footsteps on the concrete steps, and a few moments later the stable door banged.

Marta looked up at Sami and me. "He's gone to tell them I'm here, hasn't he," she said dully.

"I—don't know," I said. I no longer knew what was right or best to do. I glanced at Sami, and read the same dilemma in his expression.

"Go after Lloyd," I told him suddenly. He nodded quickly and departed.

That left Marta and me in the clocktower, alone together for the first time since we'd woken up twenty-four hours previously. Staring at my friend hunched up against the wall, I felt a burning empathy. We had both lost our mothers, but I'd been left with a father I trusted implicitly, a father who loved me above all else. Marta had nobody, or worse than nobody. Compassion raged in my chest, but I was too tired and scared to know how to communicate it.

In the end I reverted to practicalities, gesturing to the food on the bed. "Want something to eat, Mar?"

To my surprise, she nodded bleakly and hobbled over. We sat together on the mattress and had a breakfast of cold baked potato and sausages and broccoli. As soon as I started to eat I found that I was ravenous, and Marta seemed to have an appetite, too. Sami had even slipped in a couple of sachets of ketchup, which we slathered over the food. We didn't speak until we'd finished every bit of it.

I checked my watch and saw that it was twenty to seven. There were a thousand questions I wanted to ask Marta, but there was no time now. The stables would soon start filling up with students doing morning duty. "I've got to go," I said.

"OK." Marta wiped her mouth on her sleeve. "Can you do something for me, Rose?" I nodded. "Can you bring me my matches?"

The food churned painfully in my stomach. "Why?" I asked stupidly.

"I need them." Her ashen face was taut with misery.

"You can't ask me to do that." Suddenly I was angry with her; angrier than I'd felt in a long time, and my anger made me unguarded. "It's not fair. How can you expect me to help you hurt yourself?"

Marta turned away from me, drawing her knees up to her chest. She let her forehead drop onto her knees and closed her eyes. It was only then, as something severed between us, that I realized how close we'd become lately. But I suddenly doubted the premise of our friendship. I'd kept Marta's secrets; had proven that I was trustworthy, but Marta had still chosen not to confide in me about Bridge Night, or about anything else. I felt manipulated.

"I'm going now," I told her, but she didn't respond. "See

you," I said lamely, but I had no idea when, or where, or in what context I would see Marta again.

The few hours of normality that followed were more disarming than reassuring. I went to breakfast, not because I was hungry, but to look for Lloyd and Sami. With every minute that passed I expected to hear an officious voice call my name, or feel a cold hand on my shoulder, but none came.

I lingered for as long as possible, but there was no sign of the boys. I began to worry that Lloyd really had gone straight to Dr. Wardlaw and told her where Marta was. Another part of me thought this unlikely. Annoyed though I was with him, I knew that Lloyd was not an impulsive person. He tended to think things through carefully, weighing up evidence, options, and opinions with his forensically analytical mind. He would know how crucial it was to her fate that Marta's whereabouts were divulged—or discovered—at the right time, in the right way.

The bell rang for first study. As I stepped out into the Atrium, I came face-to-face with Max and Sylvia. Max looked as though he hadn't slept. His hair was matted, his clothes were rumpled, and there were dark grooves under his eyes. Sylvia was as well-groomed as ever, but beneath her glossy composure she looked tired.

"Hi, Rose," said Max.

"Hi," I replied. For a moment I couldn't think what to say. "How're you?"

"I've—been better," he said. "We just got an update on Gin. She's still alive, they think she'll pull through, but she—they think—" His voice cracked.

Sylvia spoke. "Her brain might be damaged," she said expressionlessly.

I stared at her. "What?"

"You heard me." Sylvia's eyes suddenly gleamed with malice. "So, has there been any sign of your bloodthirsty coward of a friend?"

Rage flooded my body like hot oil. "No, there hasn't," I said. "And it's a bit rich of you to talk about cowardice, Sylvia, after you tried to wriggle out of trouble by dishing the dirt on Lloyd and Max. I think you're disgusting." I walked away, but not before I saw Max's face cloud with horror and Sylvia's with furious humiliation.

I went to Latin, from which Lloyd was absent. I felt ashamed of causing Max more pain, but exposing Sylvia's hypocrisy, and insulting her, had somehow eased some of my own aching dread. Mr. Briggs set us a translation into English, and I immediately relished the immersion in the pleasing rigidity of the language, and the respite from my own racing thoughts. I'd been working for about fifteen minutes when there was a knock on the door.

"Come in," said Mr. Briggs. Jolyon Astor entered. His hard eyes found me almost instantly.

"I've come for Rose Lawson," he said. Mr. Briggs nodded somberly.

"Off you go, then, Rose," he said, and I had no choice but to slide my books into my bag and leave the room.

Jolyon walked me downstairs, his face impassive. He didn't speak to me, nor I to him, knowing that it would be futile to ask where we were going, or what I was about to face. The tension within me rose as we reached the Lower Gallery, where Jolyon stopped abruptly and knocked on the door of the Old Library. A voice answered with a summons.

It was the first time I'd been in the Old Library. As I looked around I felt a familiar, bittersweet pang: an assault of beauty and fear. It happened to me so often at High Realms, among the old buildings and those endless, rolling grounds. I'd be walking along a corridor, or playing hockey, or sitting in Chapel, and a particular impression would present itself—a shaft of light on honey-colored stone, a chord from the organ—and I'd be shot through with the beauty of the place: its austere elegance, its unapologetic oldness, its proud belonging in its surroundings. I'd be struck with a powerful incredulity that the beauty was mine to behold, not just for a minute or a day, but for two whole years. The other side of this wonder was overpowering fear. Such majesty made me scared that it was somehow unreal, some kind of trick, and not for the likes of us—that we were being mocked by sheer aesthetics. I was fearful that, in blessing us with this beauty, the world would also have to take something away.

I felt that very thing as I stepped into the Old Library that morning and saw Lloyd and Sami sitting on one side of a large table, and Dr. Wardlaw, Major Gregory, and a third Mag on the other. The view from the mullioned windows was of sports pitches and green fields and a glittering strip of Donny Stream, and so many trees, each of them a different autumnal hue: reds and ochers and rich browns. The sky was high and bright and clear. For a moment I felt a flare of hope that this could be sorted out. We would be reasonable and strategic; we would find a middle ground between breaching Marta's privacy and advocating for her. At the same time I was full of dread. The beauty of this room was a threat. It told me, *Be careful. Look what you stand to lose if you get this wrong.*

"Sit down," said Dr. Wardlaw, and I took the vacant seat between Lloyd and Sami. She surveyed us for a moment. "Thank you for joining us," she said stiffly. They were the first words she'd ever spoken to me.

I nodded, realizing that I didn't know how long Lloyd and Sami had been in the room, and what they might already have said. I instantly felt on the back foot, a sensation that only increased when Dr. Wardlaw gestured to the man on her right. "This is Professor De Luca," she said.

I stared: I couldn't help myself. I'd pictured Marta's father very differently to the man in front of me. He was in his early sixties, with wispy gray hair and a gaunt, heavily lined face. One side of his mouth drooped helplessly below the other. He wore a brown corduroy jacket, and below it a baggy knitted sweater and a collarless shirt. "You're Rose?" he asked.

"Yes," I said. I could feel tension seething from Lloyd and Sami.

"You share a room with Marta?"

"I'm her best friend." The words surprised me, but I knew they were true.

Professor De Luca nodded, his gray eyes flitting between me, Lloyd, and Sami. "Marta has never had many friends before now," he said quietly. He looked down at his hands, and I noticed that he wore a gleaming wedding band. "I'm very worried about my daughter."

I stared at him. Then Lloyd cleared his throat. "We were

told the police were coming," he said. He was looking at Major Gregory, who wouldn't meet his eyes.

"The police are speaking to Sylvia Maudsley and the rest of the Senior Patrol," said Dr. Wardlaw tightly. "They are gathering the facts of yesterday's incident and establishing where to begin the search for Marta."

There was a short silence. I looked over the heads of Dr. Wardlaw, Major Gregory, and Professor De Luca, and saw birds freewheeling in the air over the hills. I was suddenly so afraid that I felt sick.

"However," Dr. Wardlaw added unexpectedly, her voice bracing, "we hope that they may not need to look for her."

There was another pause. Then, "What makes you hope that?" asked Lloyd.

Dr. Wardlaw's face was stiff. She held a fountain pen, and I saw that the knuckles on the hand that gripped it were white. "We hope that you will be able to help us work out where Marta is," she said. "If we can find her, and bring her to the police before they have to search for her, she may be treated more leniently. The same goes for the three of you," she added.

Again we were silent. I looked down at the coarse, sharply pleated material of my skirt, realizing that we had no choice but to cooperate. I was about to reply when Professor De Luca suddenly spoke. "Please," he said, looking at us all, his voice cracking with emotion. "Tell me what you know. Tell me where my daughter is."

I looked back at him in shock, at the pale eyes behind thick-framed glasses, and felt inexplicably that he knew: knew that Marta was hiding from him, that we knew exactly where, perhaps even that we knew why. I saw his face crumple, and felt a bewildering pang of sympathy.

Then Lloyd spoke, his words dropping like stones into the middle of a glassy pond. "I'm afraid we don't know where she is," he said.

I continued to stare at my knees, determined not to show my surprise. "You must have some idea," I heard Professor De Luca say. His voice sounded distant, as though he were many miles away.

"No," said Lloyd firmly. "We don't. How could we? She ran away before any of us had a chance to speak to her."

Professor De Luca's face was twisted with pain and misery. "You're her closest friends," he said. "She must have talked to you. Told you things."

"She didn't," said Lloyd flatly. "We have no idea where she's gone."

Professor De Luca's shoulders began to shake, and tears rolled down his cheeks. He raised his hands to his face and pressed them to his cheeks. He gasped as if the very breath inside him was painful. "Please," he said. "Please, *think*. I need to find her—I need her back—"

Dr. Wardlaw's expression was nauseated. She made no move to comfort him: the man who, to her, was surely just a father desperate to know the whereabouts of his missing daughter, his only child. She knew—*wanted* to know—nothing of what I understood about his oppressive, intimidating behavior toward Marta. I saw this, and decided that we were doing the right thing in not telling these people where Marta was. They knew no mercy. They were concerned only with their own reputations. Yesterday Marta had been Dr. Wardlaw's star pupil, but today she had no interest in Marta being treated leniently by the police. She wanted Marta found so that she didn't have a missing pupil on her hands as well as a near-fatal accident. She wanted her found because, as soon as she was, Marta would be the focus of the police's investigations, rather than High Realms.

"You may leave," she told us, glancing at Marta's father.

We got up and crossed the polished floorboards to the door, but as Lloyd pulled it open I heard a voice behind us that was almost a moan. "Rose."

I turned. Professor De Luca was standing up, leaning on the table with one hand and reaching toward me with the other. For the first time I saw that he was injured or incapacitated in some way. He couldn't stand unaided, and his left shoulder had a strange, involuntary slump to it. "You will think about it, won't you, Rose?" he asked, his voice rasping. "You'll think about where she could be?"

"Yes," I said, because I could think of no other answer, and because, absurdly, I didn't want to distress him any further. "Yes, I will, I promise—"

"She's all I've got," Professor De Luca said, "all I have left . . . I knew she should never have come here, I knew it." His voice cracked again, and he seemed unable to go on.

I expected to return to class, but Lloyd motioned to us to follow him upstairs to Hillary. We went to his and Sami's room, where he shut the door and pulled his desk across it. Sami went straight to the window. "They've started looking for her," he said quietly.

I went to stand next to him, my heart beating very quickly. Sami pointed, and I saw three policemen striding over the Astroturf toward the Pavilion. They were accompanied by Alice Fitz-Straker and her boyfriend—both Senior Patrollers. *She'd never hide in the Pavilion, you idiots,* I thought, but my complacency shriveled as I followed Sami's gaze to Drake Cottage, the closest boardinghouse to the stables. Half a dozen policemen were gathered in front of it. Horrified, I turned around to see Lloyd dragging a large hiking rucksack from under his bed.

"I've got some of the stuff we'll need," he said, extracting a sleeping bag, a first aid kit, a small camping stove, and a bottle of propane gas from the rucksack.

"Where'd you get all this?" asked Sami, staring.

"From the Duke of Edinburgh Award storeroom," said Lloyd. "It's crammed—they won't miss it. We'll need to get her some clothes, though—"

"Lloyd," I interrupted, "I thought you wanted Marta to turn herself in."

Lloyd hesitated, fiddling with the buttons on the stove. "I did," he said, not looking at me. "But I've changed my mind."

"Why?" I demanded.

"For two reasons," he replied heavily, finally glancing up from where he sat on the edge of the bed. "I thought you had a point, Rose."

"What about?"

"About all of this being my fault." Lloyd's voice was as calm as ever, but I heard the strain in it. "If I hadn't—you know, if Max and I—" He took a deep breath. "If Max and I hadn't gotten together on Bridge Night, if I hadn't pissed Genevieve off so badly—hurt her—then we wouldn't be where we are now. Genevieve wouldn't have gone after Marta. Marta wouldn't have tried to stick up for me on the stairs. She wouldn't have slapped Genevieve."

I followed his logic, and couldn't deny the truth of his deduction. I also knew enough not to patronize him by offering any kind of reassurance. "What's the second reason?" Sami asked, his tone cold.

Lloyd shrugged. "It's hard to explain without going into a load of stuff you wouldn't be interested in, but . . ." he exhaled briefly, looking around the room. "Decisions were made about my life," he said haltingly, "that I had no control over. I was moved around so much . . . I changed schools three times before I was nine. They held me back a year because I'd missed so much school that they thought I was stupid. I hardly ever had the chance to make friends or get close to anyone—and when I did, I was made to leave them. It wasn't fair." He swallowed, tugging the sleeves of his sweater over his hands. "I can't do that to Marta. It's like you said, Sami—she loves it here, and she doesn't want to leave. I want to help her stay."

The three of us sat in silence. I thought of the things Marta had said to Lloyd that morning; of the way Lloyd had left the clocktower room so angrily. I thought of the police fanning out across the Estate, and of Marta's terror. "What're you saying we should do?" I asked finally, looking at the stuff strewn over Lloyd's bed. "She can't hide in the clocktower for long. The police are bound to find her."

Lloyd shrugged again. "I don't know about that," he said.

"The Senior Patrol and the groundsmen haven't managed to track her down, have they? I don't think many people know about the room in the clocktower. With a bit of luck I think we could protect Marta for a few days—maybe even distract the police with some kind of false trail . . . you know, buy ourselves a bit more time with her, to work out the best thing to do about that father of hers."

There was a short silence. Then Sami said, "He was different to how I thought he'd be."

Lloyd nodded. "Yeah." He paused. "Look, I don't have a plan, as such. But I want to give Marta the chance to make a choice. I think she deserves to be able to make a choice."

I looked at the shelf above Lloyd's bed. Unlike Sami's, which was crowded with photographs of his parents and sisters, Lloyd's shelf carried only music books and one framed document, headed with the High Realms crest. I recognized it as the letter High Realms had sent offering us the Millennium Scholarships. The frame had been polished until it shone. I looked from the frame to the pile of things Lloyd had procured. He wanted to fit in at High Realms even more than I did, and yet he was prepared to risk everything for Marta.

"What do you think, Rose?" Lloyd glanced at the window, and I knew that time was very short.

I swallowed. "OK. Let's do it."

"Yes?"

"Yes," I said.

Together Lloyd and I divided the things he had brought up from the storeroom into three piles, cramming one each into our schoolbags. Then Lloyd looked around at Sami. "Can I put this in your bag?"

Sami looked up. "Yeah, OK," he said. His voice was quieter than usual.

Lloyd frowned. "Are you on board with the plan?"

"Yes," said Sami. "I guess so." He bit his lip. "So, Lloyd. Are you and Max—"

"Are we what?"

"Well, you know—"

"No, I don't know. Stop being so bloody coy."

"Well—are you an *item*? Or are you just . . . seeing each other?"

"Oh." Lloyd stared at Sami as though he'd expected a different question altogether. "I'm not sure," he replied. "It's become a bit complicated." I thought this was a glaring understatement, but Sami nodded. Lloyd glanced at me. "I care about him so much," he said quietly. "It took me by surprise."

Sami nodded again. "Yeah."

"So," said Lloyd, hefting his bulging schoolbag onto his shoulders, "is that cool?" He looked steadily at Sami with his deep brown eyes. "Because if it isn't, mate, now's the time to say so."

"It's cool," said Sami after a moment. He shoved the pile of things into his schoolbag. "Let's go," he said, and we all left the room.

Chapter 11

The twenty-four hours that followed our conversation in Lloyd and Sami's room were eerily uneventful. We were not summoned to speak to the police, or to anyone else. There was no sign of Marta's father, Major Gregory, or Dr. Wardlaw. The police combed the Estate for Marta until darkness fell, and they paused the search. A thunderstorm broke over High Realms just as prep finished, and under the cover of the wind and hail Sami and I ran down to the clocktower to take the things to Marta. We decided it was too risky for all three of us to go, and after the row that he and Marta had had that morning, Lloyd accepted that he should be the one to stay behind. We didn't know what kind of state we would find her in.

She was in a bad way. Sami and I couldn't stay long, because we knew that Gerald would soon be along to see to the horses. We found our friend pale and shivering, her ankle swollen and a gruesome cut on her shin. She claimed she'd sustained the cut at the same time as her sprained ankle, when she had stumbled and fallen after leaping down the main steps of the school. I looked around for an implement she could have used to hurt herself, but Marta saw me doing this and guessed my intention. She quickly grew wild with anger. Her voice rose to dangerous levels, and we had to leave before anyone heard her.

We went through the motions of the rest of the evening and, in my case, an almost sleepless night. I was so tired that I skipped morning duty, and finally snatched three hours' sleep between six and nine, when I was awoken by the insistent tolling of the cloister bell. I threw on my uniform and rushed down to Chapel. Walking in late, to the strains of the first hymn, I was shocked to see Max and Lloyd in the organ loft as usual. Max's face, though pale, was alive with some of its usual energy as he thumped away at the chords. I could barely stay awake for the duration of the service, at which lengthy prayers were said for Genevieve, but no real update given on her condition.

After Chapel I wandered toward the Main House, planning to return to Hillary, barricade myself in my room, and try to go back to sleep for a few hours. Then I would go to the clocktower to talk to Marta while everyone else was at Sunday lunch. As I climbed the steps into the Atrium, however, I heard someone yell my name. I turned to see Bella standing on the drive. She was dressed in her hockey kit with her Senior Patrol gown over the top, presumably as a concession to the Chapel dress code. "Where d'you think you're going?" she shouted.

"To Hillary," I called back.

"You're bloody well not," she said, stomping up the steps toward me. "We're playing Shrewsbury in fifteen minutes. Go and get changed."

I groaned inwardly. I'd completely forgotten about the match. Before the incident on the Eiger, Bella had been telling me for days that she was relying on me to score promptly, to give us an early lead. Now she spoke harshly, her flushed face close to mine. "I wouldn't have you in this match at all if I could help it," she said. "But the team needs you to win, so make sure you deliver the goods. Our little *lifesaver*."

She jogged away toward the Astroturf. I watched her go, unable to understand why she was annoyed that Sami and I had helped Genevieve. Until now Bella had been marginally less hostile toward me than the rest of the Senior Patrol, apparently on the basis of my prowess at hockey. In general, she seemed less invested than others in the bizarre system of loyalties, grudges, and avengements that operated at High Realms, instead being completely fixated on Games.

I joined the First XI on the Astroturf, having hastily pulled on my kit in the empty changing room, and saw Sylvia standing apart from the rest of the team, her face sallow. She looked exhausted. Bella glanced balefully at Sylvia several times while she delivered the pre-match briefing, and at me with certain anger.

The team from Shrewsbury now marched onto the Astroturf. Their coaches looked around for members of staff from our school, but there were none: extracurricular Games at High Realms were presided over by Bella and the team captains, and no Mags were involved. I watched the opposing team as they did their warm-up, noting that they were strong-looking and unfriendly. Glancing over at the Pavilion, I saw Sami settle himself on a bench under the canopy, wearing his waxed jacket and school scarf. He waved.

When the match began I knew at once that I hadn't overestimated Shrewsbury's power. They didn't break the rules, but they made us look gentle—which was saying something, because our team was infamously brutal. What was worse was that I realized how much I had come to rely on sheer aggression to win tackles and score goals. Their coach was the umpire, and she blew her whistle at us time and time again, awarding free pass after free pass and numerous penalties, calmly countering Bella's squawks of protest by quoting the rulebook.

I felt drained, and totally lacking in the exhilaration that hockey usually gave me. I lost tackles and missed easy shots, and felt Bella's hard glare on me with every blast of the whistle. I knew that I would be punished for this important failure, and a sickeningly familiar feeling of dread began to swell inside me.

Sylvia was playing badly, too, and she'd been rebuked more times than any of us by the umpire. I looked over at Sami, whose round face wore an expression of grim anxiety. With a terrible jolt, I saw that he'd been joined by Professor De Luca, who was also watching the game, his stick propped against the arm of the bench.

My anger then knew no bounds. The fact of Marta's father sitting there with impunity, having caused the harm he had, made me sick with rage. I chased a Shrewsbury midfielder and tackled her, hooking the ball toward me and making off with it toward the shooting circle. I ran with every bit of strength I had, fury coursing through my veins, and when a defender loomed in front of me I didn't slow down, but instead ran at her full pelt. She was stronger than I expected, and threw me to one side with the force of her tackle. I thrust back, and she retaliated by driving her stick under my foot. I stumbled and fell, my cheek striking the ground and the side of my face dragging along the Astroturf. The whistle blew.

I tried to sit up, but pain shot through my shoulder, forcing me back down. I felt warm blood on the side of my face, and a sharp stinging sensation. Lying on my side, I saw a pair of strong brown legs running toward me. Sylvia's face dipped into my line of vision, and I felt her warm hand on my uninjured arm. "Are you OK?" she murmured.

I nodded, dazed by pain. Sylvia called over her shoulder to Bella, who was jogging toward us from the other end of the pitch. "She's bleeding. She'll have to go off." She turned back to me, her body shielding me from the view of the other players. "You need to understand what happened on Bridge Night," she whispered. Then Bella jostled her out of the way, crouching down to look at my injury.

"Fuck's sake," she said. She glanced up at Sylvia just as I did the same, and we both saw that Sylvia's expression was full of concern so acute it was almost tender. Bella looked back down at me.

"This match is over," she said, and she stood up. As she did so she drove her knee hard into my stomach.

The pain was overwhelming. I retched, screwing myself into a ball on the ground. The umpire reached us and looked down at me, her face full of shock.

"What on earth—" she began, but Bella was already striding away across the pitch. As she pulled open the gate she barged into Sami, who was hurrying toward me.

"Come on," he muttered, helping me to my feet. I looked around at my teammates, at Sylvia, who was now impassive, and the bewildered umpire.

"Extraordinary behavior," she said, shaking her head. She was in her late thirties: a sporty, pleasant-faced woman wearing a Shrewsbury tracksuit. "I've never seen anything like it. I'm calling this match off. Come on, Shrewsbury."

Sami put his hand under my arm and helped me walk to the gate. As we passed through it, I looked up and saw Professor De Luca watching me from under the canopy. I met his eyes for a moment before limping away with Sami.

Sami took me to the infirmary. I didn't want to go, but the side of my face was bleeding badly, and we'd taken our only first aid kit to the clocktower. At one point I leaned against the rear wall of the Science Block, holding myself up while I retched.

I turned around to see Sami watching me. He handed me a tissue. "When Dr. Reza patches you up," he said, "see if you can swipe some extra antiseptic wipes and stuff."

"What for?"

"For that cut on Marta's leg," he replied. "I'm worried about it getting infected. It's so dirty up in the clocktower."

I looked at him properly as we moved away, and saw how troubled his expression was. *He knows what happened,* I thought, and was about to ask him when he said, "Marta's dad asked me how Marta had been doing at school, before the Genevieve thing. I said she was cleverer than all of us put together."

We'd reached the Hexagon. It was lunchtime, and dozens of students were strolling through the archway in their best Sunday outfits: sports jackets and paisley ties, skirts and shiny brogues. They chatted in the autumn sunshine, barely giving us a second glance, despite the blood dripping down my face. I couldn't hold back any longer. "Tell me what happened on Bridge Night," I said. "You know the full story, don't you?"

Sami's steady brown eyes met mine. "I wanted to tell you before, but Marta asked me not to."

"Tell me, Sami."

He took a deep breath. "I went over to the woods because I was worried about Marta, really. I found her pretty quickly. She was sitting on the ground on her own." He paused. "She said she'd been with Lloyd, and that he'd heard a noise and gone off to see what it was. And he hadn't come back. So I said to her, come on, let's get out of here. But she wouldn't come."

"Why not?"

"She wanted to wait for Lloyd," said Sami heavily. "He'd told her to stay where she was. So I sat down to wait with her, in this funny little clearing. Mar was shivering like mad— you know, she was only wearing a dress, that one of yours." I nodded, remembering her stumbling up the bank toward me. "Lloyd still didn't come back, so I persuaded her to come with me. Said I'd left you on your own, that you'd be worried. That seemed to rouse her, so we got going. And then I saw Lloyd and Max, behind a tree."

"They were kissing," I stated.

"Not just kissing." Sami's tone was bitter. "I heard Lloyd laughing at something, and I tried to take Marta another way, but it was too late—she saw them. I pulled her arm but she wouldn't move. Then I looked around," Sami went on, sounding strained, "and I saw Genevieve. She was standing a little way away, watching Lloyd and Max." He blinked, watching my reaction. "I thought she'd look angry, but she didn't. She looked . . . not even sad. She looked scared."

I swallowed. "What happened then?"

"Max realized we were there," said Sami. "He ran away,

and Genevieve followed him. I tried to get Marta to leave, too, but then Lloyd came out from behind the tree. He started saying all this stuff to Mar—how he'd meant to come back, and he really liked her, and it wasn't *personal*." Sami's voice was now sourer than ever. "Marta was crying. I wanted to— comfort her, but she . . . she pushed me away. Told me she was fine; that the only way I could help her was by not telling anyone—even you. She said the same thing to Lloyd. Then she ran off. I stayed with Lloyd. I told him what I thought of what he'd done."

I didn't say anything. *Why hadn't I asked sooner*, I demanded of myself, but Sami shook his head, seeming to read my mind. "I wouldn't have told you," he said. "I'm probably stupid, but I didn't want to break Marta's trust. I know how it feels to want to keep things to yourself. And I never thought Max and Lloyd would carry on seeing each other, not while Genevieve was on the scene. But sometimes I wake up in the middle of the night, and Lloyd's not there . . ." his voice trailed off.

I couldn't think what to say. I was deeply confused about one aspect of the story, the same thing that I'd been struggling to understand since I'd found out about Lloyd and Max in Major Gregory's office the previous day. "Why did Genevieve blame Marta? Why not Max? He's the one who betrayed her."

Sami sighed. "Lloyd's told me a bit about Genevieve and Max," he said. "Max fed Lloyd this story about how hard it was for him at High Realms at first . . . apparently they all thought his organ scholarship was pathetic. They tortured him," he added calmly. "Lloyd says things started to change after Genevieve's sister died. Genevieve had a sort of break-down. Didn't speak, didn't eat. Her parents wouldn't take her home. Sylvia stuck by her, but the others got impatient after a while . . . that's when Max saw his chance, and started to hang around her. He played the organ at Persie's funeral. Genevieve started to . . . trust him, I guess. He wrapped her up in all this kindness, and they fell in love. Or rather, *she* loves *him*."

"So why didn't she blame Lloyd?"

"She *does*, Rose. She hates him." He paused, looking inexpressibly sad. "I don't know for certain what happened in the lead-up to the Eiger," he said, "but I think Max must have tried to leave Genevieve. Genevieve must've been devastated—maybe she was looking for Lloyd, and came across Marta first. She must've said something to Marta about Lloyd, and Marta was defending him. She saw Marta as an easy target, but Marta wouldn't hear a word against Lloyd—despite what he did." His eyes were full of tears.

"Rose?" I turned to see Dr. Reza walking toward us. She stared at my bleeding face. "What's happened to you?"

"Only—only a hockey accident," I said, dazed by what I'd just found out, but Dr. Reza was looking at my hand, which was pressed against my aching stomach.

"Come with me," she said. "Sami, you go to lunch."

Reluctantly, I followed her across the Hexagon, trying not to show how much pain I was in. The clocktower rose above the other buildings, its red bricks glowing against the cornflower blue of the sky. I wanted to leave the infirmary as quickly as possible, so that I could go and see Marta before Sunday lunch was over. Sami telling me what had happened in the woods had only made me want to see her more urgently.

Dr. Reza pushed open the glass door of the infirmary. The

building was warm and quiet. The school nurses padded in and out of the small wards. Dr. Reza insisted on students staying in the infirmary when they were ill, believing—with some justification—that they would not be properly cared for in their Houses. She closed the door of her study behind us and gestured to me to sit on the examining table.

"Let me look at this," she said, turning my face to the light. I tried to stay still, but the nausea I'd clamped down since the incident on the Eiger was rising within me. It had been triggered by the revelation that not only had I been the only one of my four friends not to have known about Lloyd and Max, but also the fresh knowledge that Marta had wanted to stay with Lloyd in the woods, and that Sami had wanted above all to find Marta. A web of deep affection existed that I had known nothing about, and I felt stupid: naive and unsuspecting and immature. My stomach lurched. I clapped my hand to my mouth, but it was too late. I was sick on the carpet.

Dr. Reza placed her hand on my back, between my shoulders. When I'd stopped vomiting, she fetched a glass of water and some tissues. Then, "Come over here," she said, and led me to the sofa in the bay window. "I'm going to clean these grazes. It'll sting a bit, I'm afraid." She dabbed at the side of my face with an antiseptic wipe. "You've been in the wars," she said quietly.

I couldn't look at her. I felt deeply afraid; not only for Marta, but for myself. I was scared of what else Bella might do to me, and I was suddenly afraid of how little I knew about my friends. Not for the first time, I thought about what it would feel like to leave High Realms: to go back to London, to the warm flat in Hackney and my normal, perfectly adequate school, which finished every day at 3:30 p.m. and was closed at the weekends.

Whatever Dr. Reza read in my expression that afternoon, she didn't question me about it. Nor did she ask me more about how I'd got my injuries, or why I hadn't come to finish telling her what I'd started to reveal about Marta. She continued to minister to the cuts on my face, and as she did so she wiped away the few tears that I couldn't hold back, without remarking on them. In the silence that reigned between us, I felt I could have told her all kinds of things, asked for all kinds of help, but every time I tried to find the words my throat constricted with fear and emotion, and I could not speak. In the end I managed to ask, "How's Genevieve?"

Dr. Reza applied a plaster to the deepest part of the graze, on my cheek. "She's conscious."

"And is she—" I couldn't finish the sentence.

"It's too early to know whether there's been any lasting damage," Dr. Reza replied. She paused. "In slowing the bleeding from her head wound early on," she said, "it's very likely that you and Sami saved her life."

I stared at her. "Really?"

Dr. Reza nodded. She looked down at my arm, which I'd wrapped around my stomach to try to mute the pain. "This morning I attended the Senior Patrol briefing to give them an update on Genevieve's health. I told them what I've just told you. I did so in the hope that it might help with any difficulties you might be facing." She paused again. "I am very sorry," she said quietly, "if I misjudged things."

I could think of no reply. Dr. Reza got up and went to the sink in the corner to wash her hands. My stomach throbbed, and for a few seconds I wanted to jump up and scream at her for interfering. Then I remembered Sylvia's warm hand on my shoulder; her look of deepest concern.

There was a knock on the door. "Come in," Dr. Reza called, and a nurse put his head around the door.

"Sorry to interrupt," he said. "The police are here. They'd like to speak to Rose right away."

Nausea rose in me again, and I swallowed hard, darting a look at Dr. Reza. She looked back at me. I wonder now whether she saw the flicker of panic, of guilt, in my eyes, and guessed then—if indeed she had not since the beginning—that I knew where Marta was. If she did, she didn't show it. Nor did she try to shield me from the police. She simply nodded, dried her hands on a paper towel, and gestured to me to follow her out of the room.

Chapter 12

The police had set up camp in the Music School, on the opposite side of the Hexagon. I was worried about its proximity to the clocktower, but there was no time to dwell on this. A young police officer took me across the Hexagon and into the building, whose foyer contained a Steinway grand piano, and up the stairs to a small room on the first floor. Most of the school was still at lunch, but I could hear a clarinet being played softly down the corridor, and somebody practicing scales on the violin.

"Well, well," said a cheerful voice, the moment I stepped over the threshold of Practice Room 1. "Another wounded soldier!"

I smiled faintly. The remark had been made by a large, kindly looking man in his fifties, wearing the uniform of the Devon and Cornwall Police. He was accompanied by a younger police officer, whose face was pleasant but rather more shrewd.

"Take a seat," said the male police officer, pointing to a chair. The only furniture in the room was an upright piano, a couple of music stands, and two chairs that looked like they'd been brought in from the corridor. "I'm Sergeant Barnes," he said, bouncing a little on the balls of his feet. "This is my colleague, PC Werrill."

"Hello," I said, deciding that it would be best to be friendly. Beyond that, I had no kind of a plan. I sat down and tried to smile. "I'm Rose Lawson. Hillary," I said automatically.

"Yes, yes," said Sergeant Barnes jovially, sitting down on the piano stool. He nodded at my hockey kit and grazed face. "You've been keeping busy, I see!"

I nodded, trying to work out whether he was insinuating that I should not be carrying on as normal in these circumstances. Then I remembered that these police officers were probably not trying to catch me out, and that I should be capable of staying one step ahead of them in any case. "Yes," I said. "We had a hockey match this morning, but I fell over."

"Dear me," said Sergeant Barnes. "But I suppose it's taken your mind off what's happened. I can imagine it's been a bit upsetting for you, hasn't it?"

"Yes," I said truthfully.

"That's why we're here, Rose," said Sergeant Barnes, regarding me with a kindly expression. "We're going to look into what happened, to try to put everyone's minds at rest. And to do that we'd like to speak to your friend Marta, but it seems she's vanished. No sign of her anywhere on campus!"

"Er—no," I said.

"So," said Sergeant Barnes, "we thought we'd have a chat with you and your friends—Sami and Lloyd, is it?—about what happened on Friday, and see whether you've got any pointers about where Marta might have run off to. I take it you don't know where she is?"

"No," I said clearly. "No idea. We've been trying to think, but we just don't know." Voicing the lie felt different to hearing Lloyd say it. It felt less revocable. PC Werrill took out her notebook.

"Well, it's good you've been trying to puzzle it out," said Sergeant Barnes, folding his hands on his stomach. "And really, has nothing occurred to you or your friends, Rose, about where Marta might have gone?"

"No."

"Any places she talked about, for instance, that she might have tried to reach?" Sergeant Barnes's voice was almost coaxing.

"No," I said, more firmly than before. PC Werrill wrote something down.

Sergeant Barnes looked at me thoughtfully. "Did you see what happened on Friday, Rose?"

"I was there," I replied after a moment. "But I didn't see what happened."

"I see," said Sergeant Barnes. He scrutinized me for a moment, and I suddenly glimpsed a glimmer of perspicacity behind the jolliness. "But you were probably already aware of the conflict between Marta and Genevieve Lock, weren't you?"

He was working from the same premise as the High Realms authorities had, and that made me wary. I decided to downplay things as much as possible. "Not really," I said, trying to sound offhand.

"Really?" said Sergeant Barnes. His brow furrowed, and his expression of benign curiosity hardened slightly. "Are you sure about that, Rose? Your Housemaster tells us you're Marta's best friend."

"Well," I said, feeling slightly at a loss, "I am, I suppose. But I don't—it isn't . . ." I glanced at PC Werrill, who was now scribbling something else in her notebook, and realized, with an icy rush of fear, that they had caught me out. I had been complacent, and not nearly careful enough.

By the time Sergeant Barnes spoke, I'd guessed the gist of what he was going to say. "We had a word with your friend Lloyd earlier," he said. "He seemed to think that Marta might have headed to Oxford or Cambridge. He said she'd spoken to you all about a fascination with those places. Is that right?"

Maybe even distract them with some kind of false trail . . . "Yes," I said, trying to sound as though I was only just remembering, "yes, that's right. She did talk about that."

"Ah," said Sergeant Barnes. "Very good." He and PC Werrill now looked at me seriously, their arms folded. "So," he said, looking me in the eye, "you think I should contact my colleagues in those cities, do you, Rose? Ask them to keep an eye out for your friend, and send officers to the bus and train stations to see whether she turns up? It's a lot of resources, but I'm sure you'd like her found, wouldn't you? I'm sure you understand our need to talk to her."

My body was damp with sweat. I knew then that I'd under-estimated the police. My callow smugness; my assumption that I was the clever one had led me to open a chasm of contradiction between Lloyd's evidence and my own. We would be lucky not to be rumbled before the day was out.

"Yes," I said, trying to meet Sergeant Barnes's eye as I told the next lie. "Yes, I want you to find her."

They let me go shortly after that, with a knowing look in their eyes that told me they were on to us. I knew that I had to warn Sami about the police as soon as possible, as they would surely approach him next; and if there were further inconsistencies between his statement and mine, we would be in even greater danger. I dashed up to the Main House, my shoulder and stomach aching, and met a swarm of cheerful, well-fed students from all year groups emerging from the Dining Hall. I scrambled up the Eiger and looked down from the Lower Gallery, but there was no sign of Sami. I realized that he must have gone directly from lunch to the clocktower with food for Marta.

It was risky for me to go there, too, but if I was to intercept Sami I could see no alternative. I went the back way via the Classics department and the Ivy Door, the route we'd taken on Bridge Night, and somehow got myself over the wall by the bins. Then I ran along the rear wall of the Hexagon, down Lime Grove to the back entrance of the stables. I slipped beneath the clocktower arch and found the courtyard crowded with students dressed in cream jodhpurs and red hats, holding the halters of their horses and talking excitedly about the Sunday Hack. Nobody took the slightest notice of me. I slipped into Block C, through George's empty stall, and took the stairs two at a time to the clocktower.

My friends were gathered around the grubby mattress, on which Marta sat cross-legged. Lloyd was sitting on the edge of the mattress, his elbows propped on his knees, and Sami crouched next to him in front of the camping stove we'd found.

He was warming up the remains of a roast dinner in a small saucepan. Despite the strain of our situation, the sight of the three of them filled me with warmth and affection, chasing my nausea and resentment away.

"Hi, Rose," said Marta, who was holding a tin plate in her lap. She looked terrible. Her skin was gray, and her hair hung in lank, oily clumps. "What happened to your face?"

"Hockey. Bella."

She grimaced. "Sorry I was such a pain last night," she said quickly. "I didn't mean to—"

"Something's happened," I interrupted.

"I thought so," said Lloyd. There was an edge to his voice. "I tried to find you after the police spoke to me, but I couldn't. I got to Sami in time, though. We came up here to work out what to do."

"And to bring me lunch," said Marta, eyeing the contents of the saucepan.

"Yep," said Lloyd. He turned to me. "So what did you tell the police?"

Again I felt on the back foot, and annoyed with his tone of voice, which seemed to predict carelessness on my part. It seemed inappropriate in the context of his role in the chain of events that had brought us to this dank clocktower on a sunny Sunday afternoon. "They told me what you'd said about Marta heading for Oxford or Cambridge," I said. "I knew nothing about that, because you'd just made it up, so I'd already said we had absolutely no idea where Mar is and that we had no leads."

"And what did they say?"

"Not much, but they seemed pretty suspicious. Why did you have to go and tell them that before we'd talked about it?"

Lloyd watched Sami load Marta's plate with scraps of roast beef, potatoes, carrots, and peas and dribble gravy over it from the bottom of the saucepan. Momentarily distracted, I stared at this meal, wondering how he'd managed to transport the sauce. Marta began to shovel down the food. "Lloyd?" I demanded, when nobody spoke.

He looked up at me. "Because," he said reluctantly, "they put me under pressure. They said they were planning to bring in police dogs to search the Estate."

Marta's head whipped up. "*Dogs?*"

"Yes," replied Lloyd. "Don't worry," he said hastily. "I don't think they're actually going to use them. I think they're pretty much convinced you've run away from school, Mar. But I felt like I had to—you know—*encourage* that view."

"Thanks, Lloyd," said Marta, cramming a roast potato into her mouth. "I *would* like to go to Oxford, you know," she added, her cheeks bulging.

I didn't appreciate her lack of concern in the climate of heightened risk we now found ourselves in. "What made them think Marta's still at High Realms?" I asked.

Lloyd chewed his lip. I could tell that he knew the answer, and from the troubled look on Sami's face, he'd guessed it, too. Lloyd turned to face Marta. "Your dad's talked to them," he said. "He told them he's sure you wouldn't run away. Told them how much you wanted to come here." He sighed, and I saw real regret in his expression. "He's putting a lot of pressure on them to find you, Marta. He's upped the ante—he's told them you're vulnerable. I think . . . I think it's going to be hard to hide you here for much longer."

Marta's face drained of all color. She looked sadly at the

roast potato she'd just picked up, and put it back on her plate. I saw the pain in Sami's face, and the tension in Lloyd's, as we waited for her to speak. "Well," she said at last, smiling weakly, "it's good to know I hadn't underestimated him."

Sami glanced at Lloyd. "Mar," he said tentatively, "how long has this been going on for?"

"Which part do you mean?" Marta replied calmly.

Sami swallowed. "The stuff to do with High Realms," he said after a moment. I wondered whether he'd wanted to ask a different question and had lost his nerve. "Was he always weird about you coming here?"

She shrugged. "My father thinks boarding schools are dens of sin," she said. "Too much freedom. To be fair to him, he's never met Major Gregory." None of us smiled, and she sighed. "Drinking, drugs, sex . . . that's what he said goes on. Weren't your parents worried?" Sami and I shook our heads, and she paused, appearing to choose her words carefully. "My mother was different. She ordered the prospectus years ago, and we read it together. She thought it'd be good for me to spend some time away from home, with people my own age. She told my father it was more about that than the academic side of things. *He* said he was only trying to protect me from growing up too fast. But then she told him I wouldn't be able to manage at university if I'd only been homeschooled. He's always been determined that I'll go to university, because he's an academic himself."

"So she persuaded him?" asked Lloyd. We were all staring at Marta, who now sat in a shaft of pure sunlight that was refracted through the clock face, illuminating her dirt-streaked face.

"Yes," said Marta quietly. "Yes, she did. But after we lost her in February, he—well, he changed his mind. He became a bit dependent on me," she said tonelessly.

We sat in silence for a few moments. Somehow I could tell that Marta had given us an elliptical summary of a terrible course of events—that despite this glut of what was, for us, new information, there were many horrors still untold; much worse than the other secret Marta had kept from me, that I'd failed to ask Sami about. This smallest of gestures toward the true pain was enough, for now. It was enough to tell me what I had to do.

"Tell us how to help you," I said to Marta.

She looked up at me then, and smiled: a tired, sad smile that cut me to the core. She looked around the clocktower room, at its bareness and squalor, and then down at her hands, whose skin had regressed to the inflamed state they'd been in after Genevieve's attack. "There's only one way you can help me," she said quietly.

"Anything."

"Hide me here." She was not looking at the boys, but at me, her eyes bright and focused and clear. "You can hide me in this room for six months, until I'm eighteen, and then I'll be free of him. I'll never have to go back to his house. I'll never have to see him again."

We gaped at her. She gazed steadily back at us, her resolve plain. Dozens of thoughts whirled in my mind. I found Marta's idea both extraordinary and frightening. I tried desperately to think of alternatives; of ways to persuade her that to hide her in the clocktower room for so long was mad, dangerous, impossible; that it was asking too much of us. Before I could find the words, she spoke again. "Save my life," she said simply.

There was another long silence, and then Sami said, his voice quiet, "You'll be eighteen in six months?"

"I lied to High Realms about my age." Marta looked down at her hands. "I should be in the year above, but . . . I was desperate for a Millennium Scholarship." She gave us a small smile, and the four of us sat without speaking for a few moments.

Finally Sami spoke again. "OK."

Lloyd looked astounded. "What did you say?"

"We'll do it," Sami said. "At least—I will. I'll help you." He gave Marta a small smile. She returned it, and the mingled hope and relief in her expression tugged at my own uncertainty.

"I'll help, too," I told her.

Marta turned to Lloyd. "What do you think?" she asked, as if we were having a completely normal conversation.

Lloyd stared at us all with an expression that was half incredulity, half admiration. I could see his mind working; his agile brain laying out and evaluating the possibilities, the risks, the rewards. Finally he looked directly at Marta. She was watching him calmly, without any hint of desperation or pleading. Her head was tilted slightly to one side, and there was the glimmer of a challenge in her eyes.

"All right," he said at last. "I'm in. Let's give this a go."

Chapter 13

The police opened an official investigation into Marta's disappearance a full week later. In the meantime, Lloyd, Sami, and I were questioned on three occasions by Sergeant Barnes, but his tactics did not improve, and we continued to give nothing away. We deduced that Barnes was under significant pressure from the High Realms authorities and Genevieve's parents. A few days after we'd agreed to hide Marta, Sir Jacob Lock made a brief visit to High Realms with Genevieve's mother for a meeting with Dr. Wardlaw. Even if I hadn't recognized him from newspapers and the television I would have known immediately that he was Genevieve's father. They had the same haughty, angular features, and he twitched his blue tie straight in the same irritable way that Genevieve adjusted her gown. Although it was only the end of October, a poppy already adorned his lapel. Genevieve's mother meekly gripped his hand as they crossed the Atrium, their eyes flicking to the top of the Eiger as if to measure the distance their daughter had fallen. I found myself unable to pity them.

The fact that I could summon no sympathy for a couple who had already lost one child and whose other daughter's life was hanging in the balance should have been a warning sign. I was already losing my capacity to feel; or rather, all of my energy was being channeled in a single direction: to Marta. We had agreed to hide her with no thought or preparation for how hard it would be to do so—no understanding of how constantly, exhaustingly difficult it would be to conceal someone in plain sight. The fact that after a few days the police and the Senior Patrol gave up searching the High Realms Estate for Marta did not really help us. There was still a great deal of suspicion directed at us, Marta's closest friends; an assumption that we knew more than we were letting on, and we were watched closely by Major Gregory and other members of staff, as well as by Bella Ford, Jolyon Astor, and their cronies. The fact that Sami and I had saved Genevieve's life appeared to antagonize rather than mollify them.

We applied all our ingenuity to hiding Marta and keeping her as comfortable as possible. We rarely spoke among ourselves about what we were doing, instead relying on a kind of knowledge osmosis. Two factors counted in our favor: the extent to which we were hated by everyone at High Realms, and the busyness of the schedule. The former made it easier for us to conceal food for Marta from our plates at mealtimes, because we always sat by ourselves. It also meant that we weren't missed at evening gatherings or from lounging around in the Common Room, because we'd almost always been excluded from those spaces anyway. The latter enabled us to spend some time in the clocktower every day, because it was so difficult to keep track of people at High Realms. There were so many activities; so many procedures and formalities and duties, and this was helpful, because if you were asked where somebody was, or where you were going, you only had to make up something that sounded suitably High Realms, and you would generally be believed. As the days passed, I found myself lying with increasing alacrity. I found it comforting. It was creative, it had a purpose, it was successful. I believed my best lies myself.

Perhaps unsurprisingly, our most significant problem came in the form of Major Gregory. He was under pressure from Dr. Wardlaw and the governors, having effectively lost two offspring from the same family, and I think I might have felt sorry for him if he hadn't made our lives so difficult. He turned up at our rooms at unexpected times, he made sure other Mags reported any absences from lessons directly to him, and most annoyingly of all, he dealt us endless unwarranted WPs, which entailed spending hours in his office doing the most pointless tasks he could think of. We passed interminable evenings polishing shoes from the lost and found, reciting the names of Senior Patrols back to 1910, and memorizing every last detail of the obscure period of military history in which Major Gregory was currently interested. Worse than the tedium was the fact that it prevented us from getting to the clocktower to see Marta, who now depended on us to survive.

If we were going to be found out, I felt sure that it would be Major Gregory who foiled us—not because of any shrewdness on his part but through his sheer determination. His obsession with detail counted in our favor, because he was more interested in uniform checks and room inspections than he was in the welfare of people in Hillary House, but he had a relentlessly beady eye, and I think we would have been caught if it hadn't been for Lloyd. Perhaps as a result of his time in care, Lloyd was the most resourceful of the three of us by a long way. It was Lloyd who raided the school kitchens for tins of food when we couldn't get enough leftovers, Lloyd who tactically stole items we needed from different parts of the school so that they wouldn't be missed, and Lloyd who worked out the most discreet routes from Hillary to the clocktower so that we could get there undetected. When Sami and I made mistakes he was patient but firm, explaining where we'd gone wrong and how to avoid similar errors in the future. We soon realized that there was a part of Lloyd that relished the challenge we were facing. He saw what we were doing as a game of strategy; an adventure with a noble and necessary purpose, and the prospect of being outwitted by the likes of Major Gregory was not one he was prepared to contemplate.

As far as I know, Max and Lloyd didn't see very much of each other in the aftermath of the incident on the Eiger. The organ lessons stopped. Max kept a much lower profile than usual, and didn't hold court in the Atrium or at mealtimes as he had done previously. Apart from Sylvia, the Senior Patrol seemed to be shunning him. He and Sylvia visited Genevieve in the hospital twice a week, always driven by Dr. Reza in one of the school's Land Rovers. Reports filtered back that Genevieve was conscious, but very confused. With his girlfriend absent, Max had no reason to sneak into Hillary; no excuse to come and play the piano in the Common Room with Lloyd in the evenings, although we wouldn't have been there even if he had visited. When we weren't trapped in Major Gregory's office, we would either be trying to get to the clocktower—one of us going there and the other two providing cover—or going to bed early in preparation for getting up at half past five, the latest time it was possible to sneak down to the stables with no risk of meeting anyone.

Or so we thought. I made one of these predawn trips one morning in mid-November, about three weeks after the Eiger incident. My alarm clock woke me at ten past five, and I lay blinking in the pitch dark, trying not to fall back to sleep. *What does she need?* I asked myself, trying to remember what Marta had eaten last night. I got out of bed and pulled on my overalls and boots, shoving a package of leftover food from supper into my pocket. I looked despairingly at my desk, which was covered in unfinished work, including an essay that Miss Kepple had given me as a punishment for not completing the previous week's prep. If I didn't hand it in it would mean another WP, but I couldn't skip going to see Marta.

I crept out of Hillary and down the back stairs to Ivy Door, which opened into the courtyard with the bins. I heaved myself over the wall, trying not to squash the food parcel, and jogged through the grounds to the stables. The air was earthy and mild and fresh. There were no signs of life in any of the boardinghouses or the infirmary; no beady-eyed Mags or Senior Patrol or groundsmen at this time. Once the bane of my life, stable duty—and the fact that Major Gregory had refused to assign me a replacement partner—had become essential to Marta's survival. I felt some of the tension leave my body as I looped the stables and slipped through the clocktower arch, heading for Block C.

I was tugging the plywood board away from the concrete wall when I heard a noise behind me. I turned, concealed by Polly, to see a flash of red hair. Gerald was approaching the stalls, making crooning sounds to the horses. I crouched down, sweating. My instinct was to try to stay hidden, but if he came into the stall he would see me at once. I stepped out from behind Polly. "Morning," I said, as nonchalantly as I could, trying to push the plywood wall back with my foot.

He looked at me, a ripple of surprise disrupting his blank expression. "What are you doing here?"

"I've got morning duty." This was true, but it was still far too early to be at the stables: morning duty didn't begin until quarter to seven. I decided that annoying him would be the best diversion. "What are *you* doing here?"

"I'm Head of Horses. I can come here whenever I like." Gerald's tone was less hostile than I'd expected.

He stroked Polly's nose, his pale eyes flicking from me to her. "Are you coming out? I don't think she'll kick you, but better safe than sorry."

Moving would mean leaving the plywood wall exposed, but there seemed to be no alternative. I squeezed back into the main part of the stable. To my surprise, Gerald was wearing his school uniform and Senior Patrol gown, incongruous in the dirty environment of Block C. I'd never seen him out of his overalls and work boots, even the few times that I'd glimpsed him in the Dining Hall. He caught me looking him up and down and shrugged irritably. "Early study," he said.

"Oh." Early study meant a class before breakfast, usually as a remedial measure or a punishment or both. Genevieve and Sylvia called it preschool.

"I'm *supervising*," he shot at me. "I'm not stupid."

"I know." He was looking past me, frowning. Desperate to distract him, I pressed on with the conversation. "Which class?"

"I'm helping some Fifth Formers finish their art portfolios. I'm very good at drawing," he boasted, his chest swelling beneath his gown. "Have you been in the Columbus Common Room?" I shook my head. "There's two of my drawings on the wall. Briggs framed them. If I don't become a jockey, I'll be an artist."

"I thought jockeys had to be short. You're so tall—you're lucky." I knew I was overdoing it, but it seemed to work better than aggravating him. He bent down to pick up a bucket of feed, his cheeks flushed, trying not to look pleased. "Which other subjects are you taking?" I asked.

"Economics and Physics." He reached up and brushed some straw off Polly's head. "Same class as your friend," he said, looking sideways at me. "She was such a grind."

"She's clever."

"Maybe. But she's a coward. I wouldn't have run away," he said suddenly. "I'd have stayed to face the music. Then again," he added, "I wouldn't have left the job half-finished. I'd have fucking killed Genevieve Lock."

There was a long silence. *You're not serious,* I thought, but then I saw the hardness of his face as he poured feed into Polly's trough, and realized that he meant every word. At first I felt a kind of repugnance, but it left me more quickly than I expected. I remembered my old grief, my old anger. I wanted to say to Gerald, *Tell me what has happened to you. It will help.* But something stopped me.

"I've got to go," Gerald said. He looked at me uncertainly, as if he were about to say something else, but he seemed to read my silence as critical rather than hesitant. Before I could say anything, he turned on his heel and marched out into the courtyard.

I found Marta curled on her mattress, reading *Wuthering Heights* by the light of a torch. I noticed that its light had grown very dim, and added batteries to my mental list of things to bring next time we could get here.

"Morning," I said, extracting the package of food from my pocket.

"Hiya," she yawned, sitting up. "What's the latest?"

"Gerald was hanging around downstairs." I watched her tear off the sticky napkin and paw a handful of congealed pasta into her mouth. "We brought you cutlery," I reminded her, passing her a knife and fork from a box next to the mattress. Then I bent down to light the camping stove.

"I'm going to scrub down this mattress later," Marta said after a few moments, licking her fingers. "It doesn't smell great."

I glanced at her. The filthy, sagging mattress was a mystery that Sami, Lloyd, and I had pondered somewhat uneasily, as well as the presence of a small toilet and sink just below the clocktower room, which seemed to indicate that the clocktower hadn't always been boarded up. Lloyd said he thought that it might have been accommodation for stable hands many years ago. That evening Marta and I had planned to boil some water on the camping stove and make a project of washing her hair, which was in the worst state I'd ever seen it.

Marta seemed to read my mind. "I'm going to cut all my hair off," she said casually. "It'll be easier to keep clean. Can you bring some scissors when you next come?"

"That seems a bit drastic," I said, reaching for the tin of hot chocolate. I didn't want to bring her scissors if I could help it.

"It's not! I've always wanted to, but I've never been allowed," she insisted, shaking her head so that the greasy strands flew everywhere.

"You're just bored," I told her. "I'll bring some more books when I can."

"Thanks." Glumly, Marta inspected her hands, which were smeared with pasta sauce. "It's so weird being up here. I've never slept so much. Never *thought* so much. It's hard work, having nothing to do." Then she glimpsed my frustration, and looked guilty. "Why don't I do some of your prep for you?" she suggested. "Save you some time."

"You haven't got the books."

She waved her hand. "Don't need them. Tell me the topic, and I'll get started this morning."

I hesitated. Then, "I've got a commentary on one of Shakespeare's sonnets," I said. "It starts, 'My love is as a fever, longing still—'"

"Aha!" Marta rose onto her knees, swatting her sleeping bag out of the way. "I know it well." She beamed at me. "I can write that for you, Rose, no problem." Suddenly she looked downcast. "My father doesn't like that one."

I looked at her uncertainly. "That doesn't mean *you* can't like it."

"Is he still here? At High Realms?"

"I haven't seen him for a few days," I said truthfully, choosing not to mention how closely we had been watching Professor De Luca's movements, and how disturbing it was to have seen him from time to time in the Atrium, the Dining Hall, and once—most troublingly—emerging from Major Gregory's study.

Marta and I spent about twenty more minutes together. I made the hot chocolate, persuaded her to put on a clean school shirt—the only item of clothing I'd been able to bring—and reminded her to brush her teeth. She reluctantly complied, ranting about an argument she'd had with Lloyd about *Wuthering Heights*. "The problem with Lloyd is he applies his own logic to people in books," she grumbled, opening her notebook. "It just doesn't work. How're we supposed to know what we would do in certain circumstances—"

"He's just pragmatic," I replied. "He doesn't let his emotions get the better of him." I realized as I spoke that this wasn't always true.

"I suppose so." Suddenly Marta looked downcast. "I wish I was more like him, but I'm not. I've gone and fallen for him, Rose. It's—it's driving me mad." She said the words very simply and without shame, looking up at me with a trusting, hopeful expression that made me realize she'd wanted to tell me this for a long time. "Oh, I know," she said, in response to my surprise. "I would've told you before, but I couldn't find the words. I still can't, really. It's this huge thing, in here"—she pointed at her chest—"and I can't get it to make sense in *here*." She pointed at her head. "It's the one thing I can't understand," she murmured.

I bit my lip, trying to work out what to say. I'd known that Marta liked Lloyd, but I hadn't guessed the true extent of her feelings for him. Standing there in the clocktower room, I felt an oppressive pity for her that exceeded almost everything else I knew about her. Then I realized that I envied her, too;

envied her ability to be honest, both with herself and with me. She had expressed a difficult truth in an imperfect way, but I could tell from the way her shoulders had dropped from their hunched position that she felt better for telling me, even if I couldn't help her.

I heard voices outside in the courtyard. "I've got to go," I said automatically.

"OK," Marta said, looking up at me. "When will you come back?"

"As soon as I can. We can make hot chocolate again," I said, trying to sound reassuring.

"That'd be nice. I miss you, Rose. I miss hanging out with you—"

"I miss you, too."

"Even my mess?"

"Even your mess." I smiled. I wanted to tell Marta that I hadn't moved any of her things in Room 1A from the way she'd left them, apart from the bare minimum of tidying for an inspection, but then I heard Gerald shouting in the courtyard, and knew I had to get going. "See you later, Mar."

Lloyd, Sami, and I had different lessons for first study, so I had to wait until Elevenses to tell them about my encounter with Gerald. On my way down to the Atrium I scanned the crowds from the Upper and then the Lower Gallery, but there was no sign of them. I knew I would be a target if I hung around unaccompanied, so I threaded my way to the front door as quickly as possible, frustrated with the way my heart beat faster and my palms grew sweaty when people looked at me.

Out on the drive I found a dozen or so students milling

around in the weak sunshine. I saw Max sitting in the high, open doorway of the Chapel, leaning on his elbows with his long legs stretched out in front of him. There was a pile of music books by his feet. He raised his hand to me.

"Hiya." I went over to the steps. "How're you?"

"Oh, I'm fine," he said, but he didn't look it. His usually glossy hair was limp, and there were dark shadows under his eyes, and his breath smelled a little. He rummaged in the pocket of his gown and pulled out a packet of cigarettes. He tipped the packet toward me.

I shook my head. "I didn't know you smoked."

He laughed, but it was nothing like his usual self-assured giggle. "It makes me feel closer to Gin." He struck a match inexpertly.

"How is she?"

"Not great." He exhaled a cloud of smoke. "She's awake, but she doesn't seem to know what's going on. Doesn't know who I am." His hand shook as he raised the cigarette to his lips.

I didn't know what to say to him. If Sami was correct, and Max had wanted to leave Gin before the Eiger, his behavior now seemed strange; but he and Genevieve had been together for a long time, so there had to have been some feeling there. "I'm sure she'll get better," I said awkwardly.

"She might," he said. "But her parents are very angry. I would be, too, in their position—they've already lost one kid, and Gin's all they've got. Jacob wrote to me yesterday. He wants to press charges against Marta."

I swallowed hard as tension flooded my body. *How much worse can this get,* I thought, feeling sick. I waited for Max to show discomfort or regret, but he only smoked silently, looking out over the drive. Then, "Sylvia's so angry with me," he said suddenly, his voice shaking. "She said—" He stopped, and I followed his gaze to see Lloyd and Sami rounding the corner of the Main House. They were talking to Dr. Reza, who was walking between them.

Max drew on his cigarette, his expression unchanged, as the boys and Dr. Reza approached us. Dr. Reza watched him coolly for a moment and then turned to me. "Hello, Rose."

"Hello." I glanced nervously at Max, and then at Lloyd and Sami. I realized that they looked more tense than the cigarette alone warranted. "What's going on?"

The bell rang in the Main House as she took a step toward me. "The police are here again. They'd like a word with you all."

Max suddenly coughed: a guttural, panicked noise. "What about?"

"Beyond the obvious, I'm afraid I don't know," said Dr. Reza. She looked at the cigarette, which was glowing feebly between Max's slim fingers. "They don't need to see you, Max—it's just the others for now. You can go to class."

Clearly relieved, Max stubbed out the cigarette and got to his feet. He flicked the butt away and bent down to gather up his music books.

"Pick that up." Dr. Reza's voice was harder than I'd ever heard it. Max looked contemptuously at Dr. Reza, and I sensed the presence of an old grudge between them. Then, very slowly, he bent down to pick up the crushed cigarette, before leaving us to cross the empty drive toward the Main House.

Dr. Reza turned to us. "About the police," she began, drawing us into the antechapel, but before she could continue there was a loud shout—*Max!*—and we looked around to see

Jolyon and Rory stride out of Chapel Passage toward him. They didn't see us, hovering on the threshold, and the drive was otherwise deserted.

Rory was holding a rugby ball as usual, and, as we looked on, he drop-kicked it to Max, who shifted his music books beneath his arm and managed to catch it. A few books fell to the ground. "Hi, y'all," he called, an affable grin back on his face.

"Matey!" Rory ran at him, wrapping his arm around Max's neck and ruffling his hair. Max's head was pressed against Rory's chest, and then the hug became a headlock, and Max began to struggle, his feet scuffling against the gravel as Rory dragged him across the drive, still shouting playfully. Jolyon followed them. There was nothing out of the ordinary about this, but something in their voices that day made me run down the steps of the Chapel and follow them around the corner of the Main House. There they were on the lawn, half concealed by a clump of shrubs.

Rory and Jolyon had seized Max and laid him flat on his back, Rory holding his arms and Jolyon his legs. Pinned to the ground, Max chuckled feebly, as though this were just a joke after all—and until then, until that trusting laugh, perhaps it was. Lloyd and Dr. Reza had already started running across the drive toward them when Rory jumped on Max's right arm, crushing his wrist and hand beneath his smart black shoes. There was a sickening crack.

Max let out a terrible howl. For a split second Rory and Jolyon looked startled, as though they hadn't intended to cause real damage; and then they rushed away, ducking into the Main House via a side entrance, emitting a single whoop as they did so. Dr. Reza and Lloyd knelt either side of him and tried to prevent him from sitting up. Max's shoulders heaved as he cradled his right arm in his left, but he twisted his body away from Lloyd's touch, his face white and sweating as he slumped against Dr. Reza. As I looked on, the acute pain in his expression was overlaid with sheer terror.

Dr. Reza led Max away. Lloyd crouched on the grass, his head in his hands. Sami said his name, and he slowly straightened up. "Help me track her down," he said.

"Who?"

"Sylvia fucking Maudsley." His voice shook, and I realized he was even angrier than Dr. Reza. "She's poisoned the Senior Patrol against Max—*she* must have set Rory and Jolyon on him. I won't let her get away with this." He strode away, back around the corner and up the steps to the Atrium. Sami and I hurried after him.

"What about the police? They want to talk to us—"

"I don't give a shit about the police." At the foot of the Eiger, Lloyd paused. I glanced around the empty Atrium, desperately hoping that we would not be overheard. "I never thought they'd turn on Max," he said, his voice full of misery. "I thought he was safe." He turned and ran up the stairs, disappearing almost at once into the shadows of the Lower Gallery.

There seemed to be nothing to do but go to class. I knew it was unwise to try to evade the police, but I was in no hurry to meet them again, either. In our sessions with them over the past week we'd embellished the Oxford and Cambridge narrative, having agreed the details between us on one of our evening visits to see Marta. Marta had enjoyed this, and had contributed a number of ideas that she said would enhance the story's plausibility if it were relayed to her father. The tale seemed to have kept the police busy, but it felt like a ticking time bomb, because it would surely not be long before their investigations made it clear that Marta had in fact not traveled to Oxford or Cambridge. Furthermore, because we were always interviewed separately, it was very hard to stick to exactly the same story, and there had been several fractious moments when we reviewed what had been said and realized that somebody had revealed a piece of information too soon, or had got carried away and invented a new aspect of the story. There was a department of my muddled consciousness in which Marta *had* run away to one of those cities, and was now wandering happily among the dreaming spires, slipping into dusty libraries, biding her time until she was old enough to study there.

But this was a fantasy, as I well knew, and the opportunity to lose myself in it even temporarily was about to be snatched away. I was hauled out of class and marched down to the chilly Old Library, where I found Dr. Wardlaw, Sergeant Barnes, PC Werrill, and a somber man in a gray suit waiting for me. A minute or so later, Sami was brought in, and then Lloyd arrived with Major Gregory. The gray-suited man was introduced as Detective Inspector Vane, and we realized at once that he was a different kettle of fish to his more junior colleagues. He coldly informed us that an official inquiry had been opened into Marta's disappearance, alongside an investigation into the incident on the Eiger. We were to accompany him to the police station that very morning to answer some further questions.

It was the first time we'd left the Estate since arriving at

High Realms over two months ago, and if I hadn't been in the back of a police car I would have loved the drive through the rugged countryside, which glowed with color on that late autumn morning. In the quaint villages we drove through, we saw people walking their dogs, shopping, and pausing for a chat on the pavement, and those glimpses of people living their lives outside our sealed bubble gave me crippling pangs of doubt. Within the confines of High Realms, our decision to hide Marta seemed both rational and necessary, but out here in the real world it was as though a different kind of daylight was being thrown on the situation.

We were ushered inside the police station and taken to separate interview rooms. I was left alone for ten minutes, growing steadily more anxious, and then DI Vane entered, accompanied by a woman about ten years younger than himself, dressed in a dark suit.

"Hello there, Rose," she said, smiling at me as she and Vane sat down. "I'm Detective Sergeant Davies."

"Hi," I said nervously.

They settled themselves opposite me, DS Davies making rather a production of taking out her pen and notebook and switching on a tape recorder. The shuffling around reminded me of the start of a lesson, and gave me ample time to resolve that I would not make the same mistake with these two as I had with Sergeant Barnes.

DS Davies smiled at me again. "So, Rose," she said. Her voice had a lilting West Country burr to it. "You're a long way from home."

By now I was used to disconcerting opening gambits. I smiled back. "High Realms feels a lot like home now."

"Really?" she asked mildly, while Vane inexplicably drew a long horizontal line on a blank sheet of his notebook. "It must be rather different to London life. To Hackney," she added.

So the background check had been done. I wondered briefly what Major Gregory had told them, but then realized that I did not particularly care. "It is, yeah. But High Realms is great," I replied blandly.

She nodded, looking thoughtful. "It's certainly an interesting school," she said. "We've visited a few times over the years. On various matters."

I waited for a few moments before taking the bait. "Like—what?"

"Well, you'll have heard about the incident two years ago, for example."

"No." I would not make things easy for her.

"Persephone Lock. A very sad case." I shrugged, and my insouciance seemed to irritate her. "Suicide," she said abruptly.

I had to work hard not to gratify Davies with the reaction she wanted, which happened to be what I actually felt. I'd naively assumed that Genevieve's sister's death had been some kind of accident, and Davies's revelation shocked me, as she'd no doubt intended. As I grappled with my emotions, Vane looked at Davies disapprovingly. "Still, at least we already know our way around the place," she said, with a faint air of clutching at straws. "And so do the dogs."

"The dogs?" I kept my voice calm.

"Oh, yes," she said. "We have two. Sniffer dogs, you know," she added unnecessarily, but her voice had warmed up a little at the wariness in my reaction. "We want to make *absolutely* sure that your friend Marta isn't still on campus."

My entire body was sweating. *Stay calm,* I told myself. *She's probably just baiting you.* But as I groped for a response I realized that it didn't matter whether she was telling the truth. The intention was to scare me, because they'd guessed that I knew more than I was letting on, and they'd succeeded. But as I watched Vane write something down in his notebook, I realized that I wouldn't—*couldn't*—give up, in case different tactics were being used with Lloyd and Sami. The only strategy all three of us knew about was to pretend that we did not know Marta's whereabouts. I leaned forward.

"I really hope you can find her," I said. "We're so worried."

Davies nodded slowly. "You're close to her," she said. It wasn't a question.

"Yes."

"You've got a lot in common."

"In some ways. We're both Millennium Scholars. And both our mothers died," I added opportunistically.

Davies and Vane both raised their eyebrows. Vane wrote something else down, and I could tell from the motion of his pen that the final symbol was a question mark. "And—er—do you have any idea as to why Marta ran away?" asked Davies.

Her question surprised me a little. Up until now we had only been asked *where* Marta had gone. "I think she was very scared."

"Of what?"

"Of Genevieve Lock," I replied. "Genevieve bullied Marta from our first day at High Realms." The boys and I had decided that it was pointless trying to hide this from the police, even though it conferred a retaliatory motive on Marta. We knew that if we didn't tell them, another version of events would be spun by the staff and the Senior Patrol. We had also hoped that investigating the matter would distract the police. On this occasion it didn't work: DS Davies's next question was even more surprising.

"Was there anything else that Marta was frightened of?" she asked.

"No," I said, a shade too quickly.

There was a long pause. Davies wrote something down, apparently biding her time. The silence grew longer, and finally Vane cleared his throat. "You're probably aware that Marta De Luca's father is currently staying at your school," he said.

I nodded, although I had in fact thought that Professor De Luca had left High Realms. As I'd told Marta that morning, I'd last seen him two or three days ago. He'd been limping down the drive to the Gatehouse, where the school had put him up: a hospitable gesture in some ways, but made with High Realms's typical disregard for any kind of frailty or infirmity, because it entailed such long walks to and from the Main House. The longer Marta was missing, the less sense it seemed to make for him to be there, so I wasn't surprised when he appeared to have left. The police's information shocked me, but I tried not to show it. "Yes, I knew that," I said.

"Have you spoken to him at all?" asked Vane, scrutinizing me.

"Only once. The day after Marta ran away."

"What did you think of him?"

My mind whirred. "I thought—I thought he seemed . . . very worried about Marta," I said, telling the truth on the basis that if the boys were asked the same question, this apparent reality was the only fact we had in common.

Vane nodded pensively. "Does Marta get on with her father?" he asked.

This was much more difficult to answer. The risks seemed enormous, particularly if the police dogs succeeded in tracking Marta down. If I told the police that she had a poor relationship with her father, they might start to question Professor De Luca, in which case Marta would be in even more danger from him if he were not subsequently charged; and besides, we'd repeatedly promised her that we would not confide this information on her behalf. "I don't really know," I said. "Marta never spoke about her father much." The latter statement, at least, was more or less true.

Vane gazed at me, his blue eyes hard with skepticism. I sensed that he was intently focused on getting a result, and that he felt I was a pathway to it. "Are you quite sure that you are not aware of anything unusual in Marta's relationship with her father?" he pushed me.

This question was the most challenging so far. Watching DI Vane, I felt more and more certain that he was clever enough to have noticed something strange about Professor De Luca: something that the more junior officers had missed or glossed over. He'd deduced that something was amiss between Professor De Luca and Marta, and that it had a bearing on Marta's disappearance. The longer I was silent, the more he would think that he was on to something; but I needed time to work out what I should say.

I don't know how I would have replied if DS Davies hadn't diverted me with what she said next, or whether it would have made any difference to how things turned out. Even at the time, I realized how significant the moment was to Marta's fate; perhaps to her whole life. "Speaking of fathers," Davies said, "we had a word with yours this morning."

"What?" I said, totally thrown.

"Yes," she said, darting a disconcerted glance at Vane, who looked furious. She seemed to realize that she'd intervened at the wrong moment, with entirely the wrong idea, but she ploughed on. "We had to let him know that we were bringing you in, you see."

"Nice bloke," said Vane, who still looked annoyed, but was clearly resigned to following Davies's new tack. "He said you worked very hard to get into High Realms. He's extremely proud of you."

"And, obviously, he's rather worried about all this and its effect on your education," chimed in Davies.

She was beginning to irritate me. My conscience pricked as I stared at Davies and Vane. At that moment there was a knock on the door, and a young police officer poked his head in. "Phone call for you, sir."

Vane jumped up at once, unable to disguise his excitement. I guessed at once that the phone call was about Marta and was desperately afraid that it was the news that the dogs had sniffed her out in the clocktower.

I sat in silence for ten minutes while DS Davies watched me closely. Sweat poured from my body. I didn't dare take off my cardigan, because the room was not warm, and I was scared that my guilt would be obvious. And yet, I demanded internally, why did I feel guilty? In hiding Marta we had only good intentions. But the longer I waited for DI Vane to return, the more foolish I felt. If Marta were discovered in the clocktower, it would be immediately obvious that she couldn't have survived there alone, and although she would never willingly reveal who had helped her, it would be all too easy for the school and the police to guess. We would be expelled, and I would have to go home to face my father's disappointment.

Finally Vane returned. He passed a note to Davies, who read it and nodded briskly.

"Right," said Vane. He frowned at me. "We're almost finished here," he said, and fear swelled within me: surely this meant they'd found her. "We'll take you back to school shortly. I imagine you'll be back in time for afternoon lessons."

"OK."

"I'm sure you don't want to miss any more school. A hardworking girl like you. '

"No," I said, wondering where this was leading.

"It was interesting, talking to your teachers and your dad," said Vane, folding his arms and fixing me with a contemplative stare. "They all agreed on one thing, and that was that you're clever. *Extremely* clever. Mind works very quickly, they said." I couldn't think of a suitable reply to this, but Vane continued almost at once. "It's a funny old thing," he said. "My cleverest officers are sometimes the ones who jump to the wrong conclusions. They've got all these ideas firing around in their minds, and before you know it they've added two and two and made nine." I stared at him. "I don't blame them for it," Vane went on placidly. "Rushing things can be a side effect of being bright. The best ones among them are able to see when they've got it wrong, and the best ones among *them* can face up to it. They come to me and admit it. And then we work together to put things right."

I sat still, now not looking at him, but at the Formica surface of the table. My cheeks were burning.

"You see," said Vane gently, "mistakes happen. Rash decisions are made, particularly when you're under pressure. Nothing to be ashamed of, if your heart's in the right place. Sometimes emotions cloud our judgment—but things can be put right very quickly, before a lot of hard work is undone."

He knows, I thought dully. *He's giving me a chance to confess.* And how tempting it was to pour it all out to Vane; to confirm his suspicions and see whether he would save us. But there was something in his sanctimonious speech that stopped me. He was too much like the Mags; too secure in his authority over me. And louder than any other doubt, louder than all my guilt and strain, was Marta's voice ringing in the back of my mind. *It happened to me. I get to decide.*

DI Vane slid a small rectangular card over the table, halting beneath the damp pressure of my thumb and forefinger. I looked him in the eye and stepped further down the path of no return. "I've got no idea where Marta is," I said. "I hope you can find her."

Chapter 14

I was driven back to school by an unsmiling PC Werrill. I asked her where Lloyd and Sami were, but she either did not know or would not tell me. She took the coast road, and from the back seat I stared at the smooth expanse of gray sea. My entire body ached with tension.

As we pulled through the gates onto the long drive, another police car passed us, its driver raising a hand to Werrill. I craned my neck to see who else was in the car, but Werrill sped up. She parked next to the main steps, and I was surprised to see Sylvia standing at the top of them, surveying the empty drive. As I got out of the car, she started to walk back into the Atrium.

"Sylvia!" I must have sounded commanding, or perhaps desperate, because she turned around, her expression cold. "Who was in that car?"

She raised her eyebrows. "Why should you care?"

This was difficult to answer. Sylvia watched me struggle for a moment, and then shrugged. "It was Gerald."

"Why was he—"

"You know," Sylvia interrupted harshly, "no one would blame you and your little friends if you followed in Marta De Luca's footsteps."

"What?"

"Run away. Like her. Leave High Realms. Get out of here, before things get any worse. Why don't you just do that?" She paused, her eyes narrow and unreadable as they ranged over my face and body. "It would clearly be better for us, but what you don't seem to realize is that it would be infinitely better for *you* to—"

"You bitch."

"What did you say?"

"I said you're a bitch." Panic was rising in my chest, compounded by all the strain of the afternoon, the sight of Gerald in the police car, the lack of information—and here was a valid outlet at last. "As if *we're* the ones behaving badly—after what your friends did to Max. I hate you, Sylvia," I said, and the words surprised me, even though I meant them.

She looked at me quizzically, ignoring the indictment. "Max?"

"He won't be able to play the organ for weeks. I can't believe you told—"

"What on earth are you talking about?"

There was something in her voice—the slightest of tremors in those crisp, haughty vowels—that made me hesitate before telling her. "Rory stamped on Max's wrist while Jolyon held him down."

At these words, Sylvia's face paled, and I knew immediately that there was no way she had been behind the attack. She said nothing for a few moments. Then, "Is he badly hurt?"

"It didn't look good." I watched her expression as many things flickered across it: dismay, fear, regret. For the briefest of moments I glimpsed the hinterlands that stretched behind her hostility, and before I could stop myself I said, "I'm sorry. I thought you—"

"I know what you thought. There's a great deal you have no hope of understanding, but let me make two things very clear." Her dark eyes were hard again. "First of all, I would never harm Max Masters."

"But—"

"Secondly," she interrupted, "Rory and Jolyon may be Senior Patrol, but if you think I'd *ever* let those buffoons do my dirty work for me, you don't know me at all." She brushed past me, down the steps and toward the Hexagon, leaving me alone on the threshold of the Main House.

What followed was one of the worst, and longest, afternoons I spent at High Realms. I had no choice but to go to class, but it was impossible to concentrate, and I was told off time and time again for not paying attention. I was concerned about Lloyd and Sami and why they hadn't returned from the police station, but I was much more worried about why the police had taken Gerald away.

I was full of the old dread. I'd had a respite from it for a couple of weeks, because we'd been so busy sorting things out for Marta, but now it was back with a vengeance. I skipped prep and rushed up to Hillary to see whether Major Gregory was there. I wanted to ask him what was going on with Lloyd and Sami. There was no sign of him, so I went to my room. I found that it had been ransacked—presumably by the police—and that almost all of Marta's belongings had been taken away. I lay down on my bed and buried my face in my hands.

Somehow, despite the chaos of my thoughts, and the fact that it was only half past five, I fell asleep. The endless mornings of getting up before dawn were taking their toll, and I slept a hot, dream-filled sleep on top of my blankets. In my first dream, we had not hidden Marta. We'd found some other way to help her, but the dream would not tell me what that was. The second dream was more cruel. The clock face became transparent, and Marta could peer through it like Rapunzel looking out of her tower. She could see through every window of the school, and also into our souls. Seeing our torment, she walked sedately down the stairs from the clocktower room, through the stable, and into the courtyard. She stepped into the basin from which the stone horse reared and sank slowly into the ground, her body vanishing inch by inch. I watched her disappear, and in the dream my body heaved with unstoppable sobs, sobs that made my entire body ache, the likes of which I hadn't shed for four years.

"*Rose.*" I awoke to an urgent, whispered voice. "Wake up." I sat up, my body prickling with sweat. The room was very dark. I looked over at Marta's bed, wondering what she wanted.

"*Ro.*" A hand shook my ankle. I saw Lloyd and Sami at the foot of my bed, their waxed jackets zipped up over their uniforms. "Wake up, for God's sake."

"I'm awake." I wiped my damp face on my sleeve. "What's the time? Where've you been?"

"It's half past midnight." Lloyd pushed my legs to one side and sat down. Sami remained standing, his gloved hands gripping the bedstead. "We got back at about seven."

"Why didn't you wake me up? The police took Gerald away—"

"We know." Lloyd's tone was grim, and from what I could make out of his face, he looked exhausted. "We wanted to wake you up earlier, but Dr. Reza wouldn't let us. We went to the infirmary to see Max, and then she came up here with us to make sure Major G wasn't giving you a hard time."

"How's Max?" There seemed to be so much to cover that I could hardly get my bearings. I felt my old lockjaw panic, and swallowed hard, trying to stave it off. Sami answered.

"His wrist is badly broken," he said. "So're two of his fingers. He won't be able to use his right hand for months."

We sat in silence. As my eyes adjusted to the darkness, I saw that the strain in Lloyd's expression was even more acute than I'd realized. "Do you know why the police took Gerald away?" he asked me.

"No, I—"

"It's because of the dogs." Lloyd's voice was hoarse with tiredness. "I thought Vane was making it up, but Dr. Reza said they brought three Alsatians here this afternoon. Gave them a load of Marta's stuff to smell and let them get on with it."

"*Shit.*"

"Well, they didn't *find* her. Maybe all the smells in the stables are too confusing for them. But apparently the dogs *did* show an interest in Gerald. Started barking like mad when they got near him."

"Who told you all this?"

"Vane." Lloyd glanced at Sami again, and I realized that the tension between them was not the type I knew well by now—pressure mitigated by complicity; a shared burden—but mutual resentment. "At least," Lloyd went on bitterly, "he told *me*. He interviewed us separately."

"What did he ask you?"

"He knows we know where she is." Sami spoke flatly before Lloyd could reply. "It's obvious. *We're* obvious. We thought we were being so clever"—his eyes flicked bitterly toward Lloyd—"but it's only a matter of time before he works it out. Major Gregory's told him how close we were—*are*—to her. Genevieve's dad's putting pressure on him, too. Vane's got the measure of the three of us . . . he's made a mistake with Gerald, but that'll only make him more determined. The next time he comes here, he'll find her, I know it."

I stared at Sami, his words settling on me like a weighted blanket, dense and crushing in their implications. "You think we should tell Vane."

Sami nodded, unfastening his pocket and withdrawing the same card that Vane had given to me, which bore his name and phone number alongside the logo of the Devon and Cornwall Police. "It makes sense," he said quietly, putting the card down on my duvet. "We're going to lose Marta anyway, before too long. And," he went on, looking pained, "we'll be better off if we own up now."

"He's really got you wrapped around his little finger, hasn't he?"

"What?" Sami's eyes widened.

"Vane." Lloyd's voice was harsh. "You say he's got the measure of *us*. How would you know? He spoke to us all separately." There was a sneer in his voice as he asked, "Did he give you anything to eat?"

"What?"

"*Did* he?"

"A cup of tea and some biscuits—"

"I knew it." Lloyd's head snapped around to me. "Did you get anything?" I shook my head, and Lloyd laughed humorlessly. "Oh, mate. Did it all get a bit much? Did Vane ask you what your parents would think if—"

"Shut up." There was real anger in Sami's expression, and none of the humiliation I expected. "My parents have nothing to do with it. This is rich coming from you, Lloyd, after what you did to cause this nightmare—"

"No, you fucking don't. You don't get to bring that up, not now." Lloyd's fists were clenched, and I was suddenly afraid that he was going to hurt Sami. "Since the Eiger, I've been honest with you two. I didn't try to hide—I owned up to you about my part in this. And then we decided to do this *together*. We committed to Marta *together*. And who was the first to say yes to her?" He glared at Sami. "Rose and I came on board, despite the risks. Which are *still there*—except the consequences if we were found out now would be much worse."

"Vane said—"

"Oh, did he promise you it'd all be OK if we suddenly remembered where Marta is? Did he say the police would be *very grateful* for our help?" Sami started to say something, his voice trembling, but Lloyd overrode him. "Maybe that's true, mate. *Maybe* they wouldn't expel us, *maybe* we wouldn't be arrested. But unlike you, I'm not prepared to take the risk of finding out. I haven't got the luxury of being gullible."

"I'm being *sensible*," Sami said, his voice now shaking even more.

"That's another luxury I haven't got. Don't you get it? High Realms is my chance, my *only* chance to get on in life, do well, get into a decent university. That's *my* version of sensible, OK, Sami? I haven't got the backup you've got. You'd be fine without High Realms, your parents would make sure of it. They do the job you want to do, for God's sake—they'll be able to help you. They're richer than you'd like us to think, aren't they?"

"They're—that's not—what the fuck has that got to do with anything, Lloyd?"

"The fact you'd even *ask* that shows how easy your life's been." For a moment Lloyd sounded more sad than angry. "You two will always have a home to go back to, no matter what. You'll always be loved, forgiven, welcomed back—"

"You've got a home, too," Sami interrupted.

"Not an unconditional one." Lloyd's expression was harder than I'd ever seen it. "You're being very naive. I don't blame you. There's no reason you should know what I know . . . or feel what I feel. But I'm telling you now, if we get kicked out of here—if we get a criminal record—it'll affect me much more than either of you."

He got up and went to the window, staring out at the dark sky, while Sami and I looked at each other uncomfortably. I found myself remembering what Sylvia had said that afternoon. *Get out of here, before things get any worse.* I recalled the Marta in my dream, climbing into the fountain. I thought of Vane's phone call to my father, and of Lloyd's anxiety about Max, while Max seemed to care only about himself. "We're not being naive, Lloyd," I said suddenly. "We're trying to be careful. To look after Marta—but ourselves, too. We're not going to get anywhere by being unkind to each other."

"I'm sorry." Lloyd didn't turn around, but his tone was sincere. "It's Vane, he—he got to me, asking me about the children's home." He paused. "I can't help the way I feel. I—I'd rather they found Marta under their own steam. At least then we wouldn't have betrayed her, or ourselves. We'd have done everything we possibly could, and she would always know that. *We'd* always know that."

For a few moments we sat in implacable silence. Then Sami spoke, his voice softened by Lloyd's apology. "I'm not going to betray anyone," he said. "But there's one thing I want to say, Lloyd."

"Go on."

"There's a scenario where . . . we win, we keep Marta hidden till she's eighteen, but—morally, we lose."

"*Morally*—" Lloyd sneered, but it was Sami's turn to interrupt.

"I don't mean lying to Vane and the rest of them. I mean that—maybe keeping her hidden genuinely isn't the best thing for her. That it doesn't help her, even though she thinks it will. I mean that . . . *morally*, we fail Marta. Fail ourselves."

Lloyd was silent for a long time. Then he turned to look at Sami. His left hand was resting on the edge of my desk, his thumb running up and down the spine of my Math textbook. "I need to see her," he said at last. "I need to see Marta, talk to her. Today—Max, Vane, Gerald—it's been intense. I need to get my head straight."

"Then let's go to the clocktower." Sami's voice was calm. He picked up Lloyd's gloves from my bed and held them out to him. "Let's go and see her now."

Marta was awake, sitting up on her mattress with *Wuthering Heights* open in her lap. She was clutching her own torch, which was now emitting hardly any light. A couple of sheets of paper covered in her neat handwriting lay next to the mattress. We stopped in our tracks. Marta's shock of dark hair was almost entirely gone. "Hello," she said. "D'you like it?"

"It's—fucking hell—" I turned to Sami. He looked distressed, staring at Marta's cap of choppy stubble as though she'd insulted him.

"What's up?" she asked, her eyes narrowed against the beam of his torch.

He bit his lip. Then, "You look like a boy," he burst out.

"Don't be ridiculous," she snapped. "I look like me with short hair."

We were silent for a moment, and then Lloyd strode over to Marta. He knelt down in front of her, crushing the prep she'd done for me. "Marta," he said, sounding as though he was trying to force himself to stay calm, "what did you use to cut your hair?"

Suddenly she looked sheepish. "Scissors."

Lloyd glanced at Sami and me. "Have either of you ever brought scissors to this room?" We shook our heads, and he turned back to Marta, not even bothering to ask the question.

"I—I went downstairs," she said, her voice faltering. "To the stable. There's a pair for opening the feed bags . . . I used them and then I put them back. Nobody saw me, I promise."

Lloyd sat back on his heels, staring at Marta. Then he turned to me and Sami again. "Well, that's that mystery solved. Gerald's always in Block C. He must have used those scissors for something, and Marta's scent transferred onto him. Maybe even some of your hair . . . and then the dogs smelled *you* on him."

"Dogs?"

"Yes, Marta. The police have been here today, trying to hunt you down with a pack of dogs."

Marta's eyes widened. "I didn't hear anything."

"Well, you wouldn't, would you?" Now Lloyd's voice was rising in frustration. "You're up here, out of harm's way, while *we* take all these risks for you, and—" He stopped, breathing heavily, and I saw how angry he was, how humiliated. "You make me feel like a fool," he told her.

"Then I'm sorry," she said at once, looking up at him. "You're far from being a fool."

He ignored her. "We risk *everything* for you, every single day. And this is how you repay us—by being a fucking liability."

For a moment I thought Marta was going to grovel. Then she sat up straighter on her mattress, tossing her book aside. "I'm a liability, am I?"

"Yes." Lloyd's face was harder than ever. "You told us that you wouldn't—*couldn't*—leave this room."

"It's true!"

"So how come you're strolling downstairs like you've got nothing to fear, following your selfish little whims—"

"*Selfish,* Lloyd? Are you sure you want to have this conversation?"

Part of me wanted to cheer her on, but I knew that this was the entirely wrong moment to be challenging him. "I'm done with this," Lloyd said, getting up. He looked over at Sami. "You know what, mate, I'm sorry. You were right." He strode over to the door.

"Right about what?" There was real panic in Marta's voice. "Lloyd, where're you going?"

"I've had enough." Lloyd's hand was on the door handle.

"I've had enough of taking crazy, stupid risks for someone who hasn't even told me the reason I'm taking them."

There was a long, tense silence. Then, "What kind of reason would you like me to give you?" Marta's voice was tight and quiet.

There was an infinitesimal pause as Lloyd's eyes flicked to Sami. "I want you to tell us why you can't go home to your father."

This time the silence was thick and awkward. "Will a verbal testimony do, or shall I write it down for you?" I'd never heard Marta use sarcasm before. It didn't suit her.

"Just—tell us *something*. How bad can it be?"

Marta flinched violently. "I wouldn't ask that question," she said, and I was forcefully reminded of Genevieve on Bridge Night. "Or if you do, you'd better be prepared for the answer." Skepticism shimmered across Lloyd's face, and she pulled up her skirt, exposing her inside thighs. Nausea rose in my throat as the torchlight illuminated her burned skin: the vivid sores, the lustrous scabs, and the older scars, raised and mottled and violet. But as Lloyd, Sami, and I stared in shameful fascination, I saw there were far fewer fresh wounds than there had been when I'd first seen her press the match against her skin. Marta had been healing.

Marta tugged her skirt down over her grimy knees. "There you go," she told Lloyd dully. "And before you tell me again, I *know* I'm not normal. It's one of the only things I know for certain."

"Marta," said Lloyd. His face was creased with revulsion, and I knew he was regretting his ploy. "It's OK. You don't have to—"

"*No.*" Marta's head whipped up. "You said you wanted to know. And I get it, Lloyd. I understand that abnormal people make abnormal requests, and you've got to protect yourself from them." She looked him in the eye, and he stared back at her, his expression one of stunned curiosity.

"I used to be so brilliantly normal," Marta said, her voice now very quiet, "and I want to get my normality back. I really thought I could, if I stayed at High Realms long enough, with you three. I'd kill to be as normal as you are." She regarded us almost lovingly as we sat on the concrete floor around the mattress. "I still believe I could do it, if I don't have to see my father again. So I'll say the words for you, Lloyd, if it means you'll carry on hiding me from him. If I say them I'm afraid they're all you'll ever think about when you see me—I'm afraid we'll never be as we were before, but I'll take that risk for you, Lloyd. I've taken so many already." She swallowed, her hands balled in fists on her knees. "My first risk was to apply to High Realms, and then to do well enough to get a scholarship. My mother had gone, and I knew my father was against it. He'd told me over and over again that my education was *his* responsibility, his *honor.* When he taught me poetry, he said he was showing me the ways of the world, the secrets that most other people could only dream of tapping. He left these gaping gaps," she went on, her eyes flicking to each of us in turn, "in Math, Science, Geography. He wasn't interested in them . . . and it suited him that there were things I hadn't been taught."

"But you passed the scholarship exam." Lloyd's eyes were fixed on her.

"Yes." Incredibly, Marta smiled. She no longer sounded

defiant. "I taught myself enough Physics to get through those questions, and I *liked* it. I liked that there was nothing to discuss. No secrets—just science." She looked down at her hands. "Then the letter from High Realms came, and I knew straight away that it was a yes because the envelope was so heavy—you remember, they put all the uniform lists in there and stuff." We nodded, captivated in spite of ourselves. "I knew I couldn't hide it from him. I even thought he might be proud. So I told him. That was the third risk." She blinked, and I saw that in her mind she was there, poised on the cusp of these decisions all over again. "He didn't mention it for a few months, and I thought perhaps he was getting used to the idea. Then he started to insist that we study all day and all evening, too, as if we were running out of time. The table got so crowded with books that there was barely space to write. I didn't mind," she said, smiling again. "I thought it would be useful—and anyway, going along with it was the least I could do, because I was leaving him. Then my uniform arrived." Marta swallowed, pausing for a moment. I recalled the day my own uniform had been delivered, about a month before leaving for High Realms; how my father's eyes had moistened when I'd showed him. "My father suddenly came into the room while I was trying it on. He knew I was going—I didn't even have to say it. And he said, I won't stop you. You have my blessing.

"My final risk was accepting that blessing," she said. "A couple of days later, my father said we'd do our last morning of lessons. I was so excited—I thought he'd finally accepted that I was going to school; that he wanted me to be as well-prepared as possible. I went downstairs the next morning as usual. He was sitting at the head of the table. All the books had gone. He put his hands down on the surface," Marta said, her own fingers splayed over her knees, "and he said—I've taught you everything you need to know about literature. All you have to do is keep reading, and you'll be fine. But there's one lesson I can't entrust to anyone else. I can accept other people teaching you the things that don't matter. But this *I* have to teach you. I'm going to be the one to teach you about love."

At these words, I felt a new, shivering sickness, and tried to clamp it down. Marta hung her head for a moment, and then looked up, as if the sight of us would give her courage. "He did it. I couldn't stop him. There on that table, a month before I came here, he taught me his version of love."

I knew that the silence that followed was Marta's worst nightmare. She could only read it as disgust, because there had been so few silences between us. But I could not speak. I couldn't even move my tongue. I felt as though I would choke. I looked at Lloyd and Sami, desperate for them to say something, anything, but we were too late. Marta clutched her lower stomach, keening forward on the mattress, all her composure gone. "The pain," she said, her voice almost a moan. "Whatever I do, it won't go away. It's not even a memory. It's still there, so deep inside me. *He's* still there."

"Marta. *Stop. Stop.* Please, stop." It was Sami, and he actually had his hands over his ears. "Please," he said again, his face screwed up. "I can't hear it—I can't stand it. Don't say any more."

Marta's hands dropped away from her stomach. She looked at Sami with gentle disdain. His eyes were full of tears, but Marta's were dry as she moved her gaze to Lloyd. He was sitting with his forearms resting on his knees, watching Marta.

His expression was devoid of emotion: no disgust, no sadness, no pity.

"I don't expect you to understand," she told him quietly. "I'd rather you didn't even try. I'd rather you never thought about this again. I know you'll make the right decision, Lloyd. Even if it's not the one I want." At this, the first sign of confusion crossed Lloyd's face. "I trust you," she said. "If you won't hide me any longer, then I accept that's the right thing. And I know what I'll do." She looked around the clocktower room again: at the clock face through which moonlight filtered, the cobwebbed rafters that stretched beneath the ceiling. Her head tipped back, and I saw the startling gauntness of her face and neck. She looked, I realized, so little like us. "Please go," she said suddenly.

We found it easy to do as she asked. It was as she had feared: we didn't want to stay. We got to our feet, stiff with cold and shock and tension, and went to the door. I looked back at her. She was sitting in exactly the same position on the mattress, but she looked different. All the time we had known her, she had been so present, so alive, so determined. Now, she seemed irrevocably altered: as though, far from unburdening her, telling us what had happened to her had multiplied her trauma many times. She seemed now to occupy a different realm to us entirely, and whatever else we did for her, I feared that we would never truly reach her again.

Chapter 15

Did it change things, knowing the truth about what had happened to Marta? It must have. It must have made the task of hiding her feel more worthwhile, and less like a game that was getting out of hand. It must have raised the stakes in a new way, making us more determined to protect her, and more ruthless with those who—knowingly or unknowingly—tried to stand in our way. I say *must have* because the shock of what we heard that night has affected my memory of the days and weeks that followed. I recall what happened, but it is much harder to pin down all that I felt.

Years later, somebody asked me whether I would have continued to hide Marta if she hadn't told us what her father had done to her. I resented the question. Even at the time, it was clear to me that Lloyd believed there was an imminent risk of Sami and me turning Marta in, or he wouldn't have forced the confession he hadn't needed to hear. I can't say whether Lloyd was right or not, but the more important question is whether we reacted to what Marta told us in the right way. After that night, all three of us believed that everything we said and did in Marta's presence had to be much more carefully considered. The abstract drained from many of our conversations. It was hard to talk about our families, about relationships, sex, even about literature with or in front of her, without fearing that we might be causing her untold pain. We refrained from complaining about anything; from telling Marta about our everyday struggles and woes, because they were so trivial compared to what had happened to her.

None of this was what Marta wanted. Since being in the clocktower, she'd always loved deep conversations, hearing gossip from school, drinking in our petty stresses and strains and offering advice. She loved arguing—a passion heightened by the glut of excess energy she accumulated sitting around with very little to do. She wanted to be one of us, on an equal emotional footing. She'd told us about her father under duress, and now that it was said, she made it clear that the subject was off-limits. That was her prerogative, but it meant that for a long time we did not name it—either with her, or among Lloyd, Sami, and me. If we had to refer to it, we were primly euphemistic.

I never felt lonely anymore. I cherished solitude as I tried to come to terms with what had happened to Marta. On easier days, I simply grappled with the unfairness of it, the brutality, the perversion. At other times I couldn't stop myself imagining the rape itself. Picturing it seemed wholly inappropriate; an invasion of Marta's privacy, but the visions came to me time and time again, swarming into my mind and solidifying into visceral, technicolor detail whenever I closed my eyes to sleep, or tried to read or hold a conversation. Most of the time I was a witness to what Marta's father was doing, a helpless shadow hovering next to the discarded books. That was bad enough, but on the worst nights, when my imagination was at its most punitive and outrageous, I became Marta herself. I was pinned down, a hand on each of my shoulders, and I was being forced to have sex. I'd imagined sex so many times, sometimes even longed for it, and although the actual physical sensation was elusive, in those invented scenarios I'd been ready, willing, passionate. I had never contemplated the version that now stubbornly occupied my mind, crowding my imagination with its violence and indelible shame. I felt that I would never want to be close to anyone in my life.

But my friends still needed me, and I could not avoid them. Sometimes, very late at night, Sami would come to my room and get into bed next to me, sighing quietly and falling asleep almost immediately. I would lie awake, hearing his slow, deep breathing and noting his perfect stillness, which was so different to the breathy snuffling and restless fidgeting that had characterized Marta's sleep. I would turn onto my side, being careful not to touch him, and stare at the contours of his face; at the dark shadows beneath his eyes. These days Sami often left entire meals untouched, and as he lay next to me I saw how the weight was falling away from his body, leaving his jawline sharp and his cheeks hollow. He spent the night in my room more and more often, but he never talked to me about how he felt, and I didn't ask him.

Even when we weren't with Marta or planning the next trip to the clocktower, it was hard to escape thinking about her. The Missing Person Enquiry grew more high-profile by the day, fueled by frequent television and radio appearances by Professor De Luca in which he begged piteously for her safe return. The photograph of Marta that he gave to the media had been taken when she was ten years old: a tiny, androgynous child gurning at the camera, her green eyes glittering beneath an unkempt fringe. To my surprise, the press came down firmly on Marta's side, running headlines such as SCHOLARSHIP KID HOUNDED OUT and THEY LET HER DOWN. There was a gleefulness about the way the left-wing papers castigated High Realms, and a fresh bout of gloating ensued when they discovered that Marta's disappearance had been precipitated by a dispute with the daughter of the Leader of the Opposition. It wasn't long before they found out that Genevieve was still in a very bad way in the hospital, and they had to change tack. I expected the newspapers to home in on Sir Jacob and Eliza Lock's double trauma, but Genevieve's sister was never mentioned in the reports.

Meanwhile Lloyd, Sami, and I were questioned by DI Vane and his colleagues several more times. On each occasion, Vane hinted more heavily that Marta had serious music to face if and when she was ever found. To our great relief, nothing came of the police questioning Gerald. He denied any knowledge of Marta's whereabouts, and the police reluctantly concluded that the dogs had slipped up. No statement was made about this to the school, which transpired to be a grave mistake. Everybody knew Gerald had been hauled in for questioning, and for weeks afterward he was subjected to relentless, vicious taunting about kidnapping Marta and keeping her a prisoner. I had a feeling Max started the rumor, because it was exactly the kind of thing he found funny, but it was difficult to tell because almost everybody propagated it. Gerald looked more miserable every time we saw him.

By the end of November, Vane was growing frustrated with the lack of results, and was clearly beleaguered by the pressure from the school, Genevieve's parents, and Professor De Luca. He took it out on us, but we didn't give in. Now that we knew exactly what Marta was hiding from, we became even more determined not to let anything slip, but we also agreed between ourselves that it was best not to invent any more red herrings. Consequently, we spent the majority of the interviews in almost complete silence, while Vane grew hoarse with pestering us. His persistence meant that we missed hours and hours of lessons, but somehow we managed to stay at the top of the Rankings, with Lloyd and Sylvia generally vying for *summa cum laude* position in Marta's absence.

Marta was very troubled by Genevieve's prolonged stay in the hospital. It was always the first thing she asked us about when we entered the clocktower room, and as it gradually became clear that Genevieve was unlikely to ever fully recover, she grew even more distressed. "How has it come to this?" she asked, over and over again. She also became very frightened about what awaited her when she finally left the clocktower room. Being eighteen would absolve her from contact with her father, but it wouldn't protect her from the police. If anything, her fate at their hands would be even worse when she became an adult.

Lloyd joined Sami and me in trying to console Marta, but it was obvious that he, too, was worried about Genevieve—although for a different reason. The longer she was in the hospital, the more harshly the likes of Jolyon and Rory persecuted Max. They came after us, too—one night they dragged us out of bed and forced us to drink a three-week-old pint of milk, which made us sick for days—but it was Max they really wanted to punish. He was the person who had ascended their hierarchy, gained their trust, and betrayed one of their own. We expected Sylvia to share this anger, and perhaps privately she did; but whatever she felt, we soon realized that she was trying to protect Max. On one occasion we saw her wade into a terrible scene on the Upper Gallery. Rory and Jolyon were trying to force Max over the rail, bellowing recriminations as they did so. Just as Rory grabbed Max's legs to expedite things, Sylvia approached from behind and put her hand on his shoulder. She leaned forward and spoke quietly in Rory's ear. Rory's face immediately turned white, and he dropped Max's legs, walking away from the scene without a word.

"I think she wants Genevieve to be able to make up her own mind about him when she's better," Sami surmised, when I asked him why he thought Sylvia was bothering to protect Max. "She doesn't want him finished off by mob justice before that." He was probably right, but I still found Sylvia's behavior puzzling. For someone so keen on wielding power, she seemed indifferent to the fact that her defense of Max was diminishing hers. She was far less visible around school, and in the lessons I shared with her she was taciturn; almost indifferent. Once or twice I allowed my eyes to rest on her while she worked, but she did not raise her gaze to mine, or give any indication that anything out of the ordinary had ever passed between us. So I went back to my work, which had become my refuge from the almost unbearable tension I endured day after day: a safe haven of beautifully abstract problems, solvable conundrums, and answers that could be found in books, if only I looked hard enough.

Throughout November the temperature in the valley plummeted. We took the risk of running an extension lead up from the stable to the clocktower to power a small electric heater, but we could only use it late in the evening, when we could be more or less certain that nobody would come into Block C. As a result the clocktower was bitterly cold on an almost permanent basis. We tried everything to keep Marta warm—all the clothes we could find, rugs, hot water bottles, an extra camping stove—but nothing truly thawed the room, and toward the end of November she developed a hacking cough. Even before that, the eczema on her hands had grown far worse as a result of the cold and her anxiety. She never complained, but we knew it was painful.

We started to think about Christmas. The holidays would begin in mid-December and last for a month, and we had no plan for Marta during that time. Leaving her in the clocktower seemed both impractical and cruel. The most obvious issue was food, but there was also the question of company—she couldn't be entirely on her own for four weeks. We even began to wonder whether we could temporarily move her to somewhere near one of our homes, but we soon abandoned that idea. The police were still searching for her, and if she went to a bus or train station there was a risk she would be recognized. Marta never mentioned it, but we could tell that she was worried, too; and, as November slid into December, the temperature continued to slump, her cough persisted, and it felt to us all as though she would be in the clocktower forever.

Inside High Realms, the atmosphere was different. Serious work began to tail off from the beginning of December. The Senior Patrol were planning the Sixth Form Christmas Ball: a tradition of dizzying importance that took place in the large rooms off the Lower Gallery. There would be dancing, food, drink—a sanctioned single glass of champagne or wine, or one beer; and then all the illicit booze smuggled in via the groundsmen or imported from home. Lloyd was asked to play the piano and take photographs. Despite everything, I found myself looking forward to the party.

Then, on the second Saturday in December, I suddenly realized that it had been over a week since Vane had last questioned us. I dared to believe that this meant the enquiry was tailing off. I played hockey under a clear-blue sky, the match made even more enjoyable by the fact that Sylvia wasn't there, because she'd gone to visit Genevieve in the hospital—and felt stronger and happier than I had in a long time. Afterward, I returned to Hillary to complete my final pre-Christmas assignments. Since the Eiger I had taken to working in the relatively safe haven of 1A, rather than in the Straker Library or one of the Prep Halls, which were supervised by the Senior Patrol.

I was immersed in an essay when there was a quiet knock on the door. Frowning, hoping it wasn't a Senior Patrol Inspection, I went to open it. To my surprise, Sylvia was standing in the corridor. I took an involuntary step backward. "Hi."

"Hello." She was wearing the High Realms winter overcoat, a blue Raleigh scarf, and a black felt hat that wasn't part of the uniform.

"What is it?" I asked, trying to sound nonchalant.

She raised an eyebrow. "I was hoping to come in."

Against my better judgment, I stood back and allowed her to step past me. It was about four o'clock, and the winter dusk was gathering outside. I switched on both bedside lamps while Sylvia waited calmly. She was eyeing Marta's bed, from which the sheets and blankets had been stripped, and the bare shelves above it.

"You can sit down, if you like," I said, indicating an empty chair, but she perched on the edge of my bed. Her cheeks were slightly pink.

"I went to see Genevieve this afternoon," she said after a few moments.

I nodded. I had expected this. My entire body was tense, waiting for my punishment to be meted out. Then, "She seems to be getting better."

"Oh." I was unable to keep the surprise out of my voice. "That's—that's great."

"Yes." Sylvia nodded, and I could tell that she was trying not to show her sheer delight. "She recognized me straightaway today. They think she'll be home by Christmas."

"Amazing."

She nodded again and rested her hands on her knees, which were encased in woollen tights. Wearing tights rather than socks was a privilege granted only to the Senior Patrol. "We had a bit of a chat," she said. "Genevieve more or less remembers what happened on the Eiger now, and she wanted me to pass on a message to you."

"Right." I could not keep the surprise out of my voice. "What is it?"

At this Sylvia got up, and crossed the room to the left-hand window, looking through it at the darkening grounds. I watched her impatiently as her eyes took in the view that contained Marta. Then she turned to me. "Shana says your friend comes here at night."

"Does she?"

"Yes." She considered me for a moment. "I'd be careful with that, if I were you."

I couldn't let her hypocrisy slide. "Bella spends almost every night in your room."

"Not anymore, actually." Sylvia glanced at me, and then continued as if she hadn't changed the subject. "Genevieve isn't going to press charges against Marta for what happened on the Eiger. She's going to tell the police exactly that as soon as possible. She also intends to speak to Dr. Wardlaw, to—er—set the record straight."

I stared at her, unable to take in what she'd said. "What do you mean, set the record straight?"

"She's going to tell Dr. Wardlaw that what happened was a private matter between herself and Marta and she doesn't want Marta to be punished for it."

I was silent. Then I realized something. "Does Genevieve know that Marta's gone missing?"

"Yes."

"So why is she giving me this message?"

"I suppose," said Sylvia evenly, "it's so that you can tell Marta if she happens to get in contact with you."

I was silent again. There was a lot that I didn't understand, and I was finding it hard to trust the messenger. I watched Sylvia cross her legs on the window seat. She looked back at me with an unusually patient expression. "Why is Genevieve doing this?" I asked.

Sylvia looked thoughtful. "She feels that there are reparations to be made."

"Reparations?"

"Yes. There were one or two occasions on which Genevieve

247

and Marta clashed." I looked at Sylvia incredulously, but she went on in the same indifferent tone. "Gin acknowledges that Marta behaved decently in not snitching on her about one of the incidents in particular. She'd like to honor that decency with her own . . . discretion."

"Right." I was deeply skeptical, and it didn't help that Sylvia had erased herself from the references to bullying Marta. "Am I really expected to believe this?"

Sylvia looked surprised. "Why would you not believe it?"

"Because Genevieve *tortured* Marta. She made her life a complete misery. You *know* she did," I exclaimed in response to her stony expression. "And you were just as bad—you baited her, you got Gerald to ask her out—"

"Oh, that." Sylvia's tone was dismissive. "That was nothing to do with Marta, really. That was just my little joke to cheer Genevieve up. She was having a very bad day."

I stared at her. "You played a cruel trick like that to cheer Genevieve up? That is *fucked up,* Sylvia. This place," I said, suddenly exasperated, "this whole place is totally fucked up."

For a moment Sylvia looked shocked, even confused, and I realized that it probably never occurred to her to question the values of the High Realms regime, or the behavior that counted as normal within it. She was brainwashed by her own prestige within that regime and by her intransigent loyalty to Genevieve. Suddenly I felt a bizarre kind of sympathy for Sylvia. Her warped morality highlighted how little she knew about the real world; how she had been damaged by being forced to live in a place where only the fittest could flourish. We would never be able to understand each other.

"Look, Rose." It was the first time I'd heard Sylvia use my

name. "It makes no difference to me whether or not you believe me. I promised Gin I'd pass on the message about Marta, and I have." She got up from the window seat, smoothing down her skirt, an elegant figure even in the dowdy High Realms uniform. She paused, and I looked up at her from my seat on Marta's bed. "Tell your friend to stop coming here at night," she said. "You're being watched."

You're being watched. We already knew that we had to be very careful about where we went and when, but Sylvia's warning had unsettled me. I wondered whether I should delay going to see Marta until I'd spoken to the boys, but Genevieve's reprieve felt too significant to keep from her, even though I knew that Marta would be as cynical about it as I was. I waited in Room 1A until I heard Major Gregory shouting at people as he left Lower House for Higher Mags' Tea. Then I left Hillary via the back way, wearing my overalls so it would look like I was doing evening duty.

As I made my way downstairs, I found myself daring to hope that Sylvia had been telling the truth. If Genevieve really didn't press charges, the police could not hound Marta for her part in what had happened on the Eiger, and when she escaped the clocktower she would have much less to fear from them. Dr. Wardlaw was a different matter, but as I ran across the rugby pitches in the gathering dusk, I dared to hope that she would not expel Marta. Just the thought of her one day returning to school, to our room, to lessons together, filled me with a joy I hadn't felt since October.

I dashed through the Labyrinth and into the Hexagon. The courtyard was busy with students hurrying back from sports matches, red-cheeked and mud-spattered and talking excitedly about the Advent Carol Service, which would begin in half an hour. Lloyd was due to make his debut on the organ, covering for Max. I mingled briefly among the students, and for once I didn't feel excluded from their happiness. *It's going to be all right*, I thought. *We'll save her, and it won't have been for nothing. Her life will be fine.* The clocktower rose strong and still above the cluster of buildings. Marta was up there, waiting for her supper. I didn't have any food for her, but I had something much better: the prospect of freedom.

I was walking so fast, and was so wrapped up in the anticipation of telling Marta the good news, that at first I didn't notice Professor De Luca waiting under the northern arch of the Hexagon. "Rose," he called from the shadows.

"What are you doing here?" I couldn't disguise my shock. It was the first time I'd seen him since Marta had told us what he had done. According to the news, he'd been combing the country for her for weeks.

Professor De Luca limped toward me, leaning heavily on his stick. I wanted to run away, but forced myself to stay put. As he drew closer I saw that his eyes were red and watering and he was more gaunt than ever. "We need to talk," he said.

His overfamiliar tone sickened me further. "You shouldn't be here," I said, taking a step backward.

"I need to speak to you," he repeated. "Will you walk with me?"

"*Walk* with you?"

I saw at once that he'd misunderstood me. "I know I can't hop, skip, and jump like you," he said, his voice hoarse and aggrieved, "but I can still hobble pretty much any distance.

I suppose you have no idea how unusual that is after a major stroke."

I shrugged. "I'll walk with you," I said reluctantly. I felt I had no choice; that it would look suspicious to refuse. "But I haven't got long."

He nodded and gestured through the trees. By now it was very nearly dark. Students hurried past us in overalls and jodhpurs. In the distance I heard the cloister bell begin to chime. We entered the courtyard, which was lit by dim orange lamps on the walls of the stables, and began to walk slowly around its perimeter. I caught the smell of manure that I usually hated. Today it was almost comforting.

"Did you know," said Professor De Luca abruptly as we passed the Senior Patrol block, "that Marta could read and write from the age of three?"

"No."

He nodded. "She learned very quickly," he said. "Her mother and I barely had to teach her. She saw us working, you see, and wanted to copy us. We bought picture books for her, but she refused them. I found her poring over my copy of the *London Review of Books* when she was six years old."

None of this surprised me. "Why are you telling me this?"

"As soon as she could craft full sentences, she wrote fiction," he said, ignoring me. "Little adventure stories, animal tales— fairy-tale stuff, you know. She wrote hundreds of them. We never stopped her. They were lovely stories. A bit far-fetched, but that's children's imaginations for you. She sat on my lap and read them to me . . . that was always the highlight of my day."

I didn't say anything. We were approaching the clocktower, and I hoped to get Professor De Luca through the archway before Marta heard the sound of his voice. I decided that we would walk down the path to Donny Stream and then loop back around the barns to the Hexagon, where I would try to shake him off. I wondered whether anyone else knew he was here. "She's always written a lot," said Professor De Luca, limping a little faster to keep up with me. "Stories. Diaries. Letters."

I tried to turn left to pass through the clocktower archway and bumped into him, as he did not move with me. He shook his head. "I would rather stay in the light."

I paused. "OK."

We continued past Block C, the cloister bell chiming steadily in the distance. The upper half of the stable door was open, and I glanced in to see Gerald feeding apples to Polly, Margot, and George. At the sound of our footsteps he looked up, and scowled at me.

"And, of course, she wrote to me from High Realms," Professor De Luca went on, as though there had been no break in the conversation. He was breathless. I looked to one side and saw that his lips were blue. It was a cold evening, I thought, but not that cold.

"What did she write to you about?" I asked, partly to humor him. We were almost at the end of the second side of the quadrangle. I decided that after one circumnavigation I would force him to return to the Hexagon with me. We were currently far too close to Marta for comfort.

"It's funny you should ask," replied Professor De Luca. "There was one letter in particular I wanted to share with you." He pulled a crumpled sheet of paper from the pocket of his ragged coat. With a jolt, I saw Marta's neat handwriting, and her trademark red ink. I remembered her crouched over her desk in 1A, painstakingly making the case to stay at High Realms.

"*'I've made good friends here,'*" Professor De Luca read. "*'My best friend is Rose. We share a room. You said there would be dormitories—but it's just the two of us. I've told her things. I trust her.'*"

He stopped reading, and watched me beadily. I shrugged. There was no way I was going to provide him with any commentary. When no reaction came, Professor De Luca shook the letter open again and repeated: "*'I've told her things. I trust her.'*"

We'd reached the final side of the quadrangle, but I was no longer focused on getting Professor De Luca back to the Hexagon. I felt that it was better to allow him to get whatever he wanted to say off his chest, and to try to deal with it here and now. "What do you want?" I asked bluntly.

He stopped walking and turned to face me. To my horror, his eyes filled with tears as he leaned heavily on his stick, his body listing to one side. His jacket hung open, revealing his fragile frame beneath a threadbare sweater. His collarbone protruded sharply beneath the mottled skin of his neck. "I want my daughter back," he said.

"The police are looking for her—"

"They're giving up. There hasn't been a single sighting of her . . . they have no leads. Soon they will stop searching." I stared at him. I didn't know what to say. "It will be left to me to find her," he said. "And I know that you can help me."

I shook my head, backing away from him: he had extended his free hand and was reaching for my wrist. "I can't. I don't know where she is."

He gazed at me, and I saw that beneath the tears his gray eyes were fixed on me with deep skepticism and dislike. "'*I trust you,*'" he repeated. "My daughter trusted you. You know things you shouldn't, Rose."

He was goading me, I knew, and I would not take the bait, would not hurl back at him that yes, I knew things I should not; things I loathed knowing—things I should not know because they should never have happened. I tried to move away again, but he followed me with surprising speed, his stick scraping on the gravel. "She's told you some of her stories," he cried, his voice carrying across the now deserted courtyard. "You've swallowed them down, and now you're keeping her from me." He lowered his voice, knowing that I was listening. "You are very foolish, Rose."

I wheeled around. My resolve to stay calm, to not be drawn, was scattered to the four winds by Professor De Luca's indictment, and I was filled with an anger the likes of which I'd never felt before in my life. "Don't you dare call me that," I said.

His eyes narrowed as he realized he had found his mark. "You are immoral," he told me. "You've taken her from me. You've been gullible—you've believed things you shouldn't."

"Don't be so fucking patronizing!"

"You patronize *me*," he said coldly. His voice shook as he hobbled toward me. "You're trying to deceive me, but it won't work. Do you know what it feels like to lose someone you love? Marta is all I have—my only strength—my only joy—"

"You've got a funny way of showing it!" My voice was close to a snarl. I was seconds from running away from him. I felt uncontrollably angry and was frightened of what I might do if I stayed near him.

"You don't understand. She is all I've got. Without her, I am nothing. Since her mother left—"

"*Left*? You're mad! She's dead!" I cried.

For a moment he looked totally thrown. "What do you mean?"

"Marta's mother is *dead*!"

He shook his head. "No."

I stared at him, breathing heavily. A small smile twisted his lopsided mouth further. "Oh," he said, and his amusement grew more tangible by the second. "Oh, I see."

I suddenly felt sick. I glanced involuntarily up at the clock-tower, desperate for Marta to interject, to explain this vilest of misunderstandings. I was speechless.

Professor De Luca shook his head slowly, the smile still playing on his lips. "Marta's mother is not dead," he said, and began to limp toward me again. "She abandoned us. My wife left our house one night in February of this year, and my daughter and I haven't seen or heard from her since." He stopped a few feet away, watching me closely, a gleam of triumph in his cold, watery eyes. "I did warn you," he said quietly. "You need to watch your back. She is a master story-teller. She can draw people in . . . but also drive them away."

We stood facing each other in the empty courtyard. The sky was now a deep, inky black, peppered with the brightest of stars. In the distance I heard the organ. *O come, o come, Emmanuel.*

I met Professor De Luca's eyes, feeling strangely calm. He gazed back, and I saw the misery and shame that was both the fuel and the product of his evildoing. I took a step toward him.

"You were right about one thing," I told him.

"Which was?"

"That wasn't the only story Marta told me," I said, and I raised my arms and pushed Professor De Luca with all the strength I could muster. My hands met his bony shoulders and he was thrown backward, stumbling momentarily and then sprawling hard on the dusty gravel. I walked away, feeling nothing but anger. His soft groans were quickly drowned out by the sound of the organ.

Chapter 16

Baked beans," Sami read, ticking an item off a list. "Apples. Tinned peaches." He put down his pen, rummaging in the backpack. "What about crumpets? They don't spoil quickly."

It was the day of the Christmas Ball, and the penultimate day of term. Sami, Lloyd, and I were in the boys' room, packing up Marta's provisions for vacation. We would be leaving High Realms in the morning.

"She needs sixty-three meals," said Sami, consulting his notebook. "Three a day for twenty-one days. Thank God we're coming back early." Major Gregory had told us that we were expected back at school a full week before everyone else, to start preparing our university applications. At first we'd thought this seemed premature, but we soon realized that the events of the term meant that Major Gregory was prepared to leave nothing to chance in his campaign to get us into top universities.

Sami was running his finger down the list of food, looking troubled. "I'm worried she's going to run out."

"Relax," said Lloyd, who was sitting in front of the door, putting together the components of an expensive new camera. It was school property, but he'd purloined it for the evening to photograph the Ball. "We can always nab some stuff tonight."

"*How*? Dinner jackets don't have big pockets—and anyway, it's canapes, not tins of soup." Sami looked upset. "And what are we going to do about drinks? She shouldn't drink too much of the water from that tap, it might not be very—"

Lloyd paused, turning a lens cap over in his hands. "Max has a load of mixers in his room," he said.

"So that's where you've been disappearing to every other night," Sami said irritably. "I should've known."

For a moment Lloyd looked uncomfortable. Then he said, "I want to make sure he's doing OK. He's been through the mill. His hand is still agony, he can't move his fingers—"

"I'd rather not know, Lloyd." Sami's tone was flat. He crammed another packet of biscuits into the backpack and zipped it up. "My parents are coming at nine tomorrow," he told Lloyd, "so make sure you're ready."

"Oh, yeah." Lloyd looked more sheepish than ever. "I meant to tell you . . . Patrick and Sheila phoned me the other day. They said—well, they're expecting me back at their place for Christmas."

"What? But you said—"

"I know."

Sami raised his eyebrows. "OK," he sighed. Then he turned to me. "Can you help Lloyd take the drinks to the clocktower tomorrow morning?"

"I'll help you get them there," I told Lloyd, "but I'm not going in."

Sami and Lloyd exchanged a look that was half-exasperated, half-anxious. I'd told them about my conversation with Professor De Luca the day after it had taken place. They had been disappointed to hear that Marta had lied about her mother being dead. Lloyd, like me, was angry with her, although in a condescending sort of way that suggested he'd expected nothing less. Sami maintained that Marta must have had a good reason for lying to us, and together with Lloyd he'd continued to take food to her. For me it was different. Since speaking to her father I'd continued to help the boys behind the scenes, but I hadn't gone to see her in the clocktower, or communicated with her in any way.

"She really misses you, you know," said Sami in a low voice. "She's so miserable."

I fiddled with the label on a packet of shortbread. "What do you want me to do about it?"

"Come on, Rose. Go and see her. Talk to her."

"I can't. I'll say something I'll regret and make her even more unhappy." This was a real fear of mine. There was a simmering anger inside me that shoving Professor De Luca hadn't quenched, and I didn't want it to flare up with Marta just before we were due to leave her on her own for three weeks.

Sami sighed again. "She wants to explain—"

"*Explain*," I repeated. "Not deny?"

"No." Sami looked frustrated. "She told us it's true. I'm sure there's more to it than that, Rose—but she won't talk to us. She wants to tell you personally." He paused, scrutinizing me with a pained expression.

I looked at his anxious face, and wished that the sphere of hardness in my throat would dissolve. Not for the first time, I wondered about giving in, and going down to the stables with Sami to make up with Marta before vacation. But then

Lloyd asked the question that was preoccupying me more than anything else. "Doesn't this make you doubt the other stuff she's told us?" he asked Sami.

Sami shook his head with a conviction I deeply envied. "Not in the slightest," he said quietly. He got up and swung the backpack over his shoulder. "See you at the party, I guess."

By six o'clock, Room 1A was virtually bare. Major Gregory had decreed that all our possessions were to be taken home for vacation, despite the fact that we would be returning to the same rooms in the New Year. I emptied the bookshelves and wardrobe, cleared my desk, and piled everything into the two huge trunks that had lived under my bed for three and a half months. While I worked, I found myself thinking about Marta again. Marta had always got in the way more than she'd helped with this sort of task, but she'd never failed to make things more entertaining.

I flopped onto the window seat and gazed out at the dark grounds. The clocktower was just visible against the horizon. I thought of Marta inside it, alone with her books and camping stove while the rest of us got ready for the party. She was facing three weeks without human contact, and then a further three months in one room with only us for company, for one hour a day. It was a risk and a sacrifice of a magnitude that I still found hard to comprehend. In my heart of hearts I knew that the reason she'd barricaded herself in the clocktower should be more significant to me than the lie she'd told. But the discovery of that lie had pricked me in a new and painful way, compounded by the secret Marta had already kept from me. For three years I'd worked hard to make my grief manageable. I had rationalised it, compartmentalized it, even made it my friend. I knew my grief better than I knew myself.

If only she'd lied about something else. I got up from the window seat and went to the sink to wash my hair. It was easier to do it there than risk the showers just before an evening event. I bent over and immersed my head in the warm water, closing my eyes.

"Oi. Ro-Ro." My ears, just above the surface of the water, heard the door slam and footsteps move into my room. "Things aren't that bad, surely?"

I pulled my head out of the water and swept back my wet hair, trying to look dignified. Max and Lloyd had entered, wearing dinner jackets and carrying a four-pack of beer. Max's right arm was still in a sling, pinned up against his left shoulder. The school camera hung on a strap around Lloyd's neck, and he raised it to take a photo of me. "*Don't,* Lloyd. And can't you knock?" I demanded.

"Not when I'm trying to avoid two kinds of trouble at once," he said, as Max flung himself down on my bed. It was like the incident on the Eiger had never happened. "Major G's on the prowl, and so's bloody Bella. Think she's spoiling for a fight."

"Why?"

"Don't ask me. Want one of these?"

"Go on, then," I said grumpily. Max snapped the elastic tie and tossed us each a can. "Where's Sami?"

"Now that is a *very* good question," said Lloyd, cracking open his beer as Max started to laugh, rolling around on my duvet. "Sami is a man of mystery," he said. "He's going to the party with a *date.*"

I stared at Lloyd, as Max continued to laugh uncontrollably. "Who?"

Lloyd snorted with laughter, too. "Ingrid Crichton. The lass he got off with on Bridge Night."

"*What?*"

"She asked him yesterday! Mental." Lloyd sat down on my bed, pushing Max's legs out of the way. "Sorry—I should've used her full title. The *Honorable* Ingrid Crichton." He took a swig of beer, grinning.

"But I thought—" I hesitated, remembering that I couldn't mention Marta in the present tense in front of Max. Lloyd's eyes flashed as he sensed her name in the offing. "I didn't think they'd be very well-matched," I amended lamely.

"Well, no. Ingrid lives in a stately home. Her father owns half of Northumberland and avoids the tax that pays Sami's parents' wages," said Lloyd succinctly. He slurped his beer. "Apparently she really likes Sami, and I think he's into her—but he doesn't seem to want people to know about it."

"Why not?"

"Well, in your case, he probably thinks it'd make you feel lonely," Lloyd said baldly. Ignoring my consternation, he went on, "You'd better hurry up, Ro. It starts in twenty minutes."

I carried on getting ready, feeling annoyed and condescended to. For all I knew Lloyd was right, and Sami felt sorry for me, which was not something I wanted at all. Sulkily, I put on the dress I'd worn for last year's prom at my school in Hackney. It was made of red, flowing silk, with a scooped neckline and low back. Max whistled as Lloyd did it up for me. "You look gorgeous," he said. "Have you got a date?"

For a moment I thought he was suggesting we go together, and then I came to my senses. "No," I said awkwardly.

"Oh, well," Max said, smiling mischievously, "you won't be the only one. Everyone seems to be single or breaking up at the moment. Everyone apart from Sami, that is."

"Who's breaking up?" Lloyd asked, opening my wardrobe to check his reflection in the mirror on the inside of the door.

"Shana's given Jolyon the boot. Apparently he invited himself skiing with the sheikhs over Christmas and she realized he doesn't care about *her*, only her money. She's a bit slow on the uptake, if you ask me." Max laughed at his own joke, his fingers twitching in his sling. "And Sylv and Bella, of course, RIP—"

"I didn't know they'd broken up," Lloyd said, helping himself to my hairspray.

"Well, no, they've kept it pretty quiet. But that's why Bella's in a bad mood."

"I knew," I said without thinking, and Max glanced at me.

"They were together for ages, but they were never particularly compatible," he said smoothly. "Bella's so . . . *coarse*, somehow. And fucking *obsessed* with Games. I think that's how she could put up with Sylv spending so much time with Gin, you know—Bella always had her own thing going on. But Sylvia's an incurable romantic—"

"*What?*" I said, before I could stop myself. I sat down on Marta's bed, staring at Max.

Max nodded. "Oh, yeah." He regarded me for a moment, appearing to enjoy my reaction. "Sylvia is the most romantic person I know," he said authoritatively.

There was a short pause, and then Lloyd spoke for me, his tone deeply cynical. "Max, mate," he said, "just to check— we're talking about *Sylvia Maudsley* here? Sylvia Maudsley, Vice-Captain General?"

Max nodded, taking a delicate sip of beer. "You've got to remember that I've known Sylvia for over five years," he said pompously.

"So explain."

"Well, when we first started at High Realms, Sylvia wasn't like she is now. She was clever, sure, but she was awkward. We all were, to a certain extent—we were *eleven*, for God's sake—but Sylv was shy, she was a bit . . . *gawky,* you know?" He caught my incredulity, and leaned forward. "Oh, I know she's gorgeous now. Even more so for the fact that she doesn't know it." Max looked pointedly at Lloyd. "In those days Sylvia's temper was even worse than it is now. She used to fly off the handle at stuff . . . have meltdowns, that kind of thing. I remember Dr. Reza taking her aside, trying to work out what was going on . . . but it was obvious to me what set her off each time."

"Which *was*?"

"Disloyalty," Max said simply. "It's the red flag for her—she can't bear it. She takes it incredibly personally."

Lloyd was scrutinizing Max. "Why?"

Max paused. "When you start boarding school it's . . . well, it can be tricky." He gave an uneasy laugh. "If you don't keep busy enough, you get lonely. Until Third Form you sleep in these huge dormitories . . . have you seen them? On the second floor?" We shook our heads. "They're a bit bleak. People cried at night. I remember Dr. Reza would walk around with a little torch, checking on us, but there's only *one* of her, you know?" He paused again, and hummed a fleeting, incongruous tune to himself. "It's hard for you guys to understand," he said casually, "because you came here at sixteen—we're grown-up now. Back then, we were children. We felt like we'd been abandoned."

I glanced at Lloyd, whose background Max appeared to have completely forgotten. As I expected, he looked sullen, leaning against the wardrobe with his arms folded. "You're saying that loyalty became Sylvia's coping mechanism," he summarized coldly.

"Her *survival* mechanism," Max corrected him. "She hated the way people would shift between cliques—friends one minute, enemies the next. She had an older sister here, you know—Hermione Maudsley, she was Captain General—but Hermione wasn't interested in Sylvia, even though it was obvious that Sylv wasn't very happy. I remember trying to talk to Sylv about it," he went on, and I imagined the twelve-year-old Max, as alone as Sylvia herself, trying to bond with her over their shared isolation. "But she wouldn't talk about how she felt; she never does. She devoted herself to Gin, to forming this close friendship that nothing and nobody could touch. Until Bella and I came along, that is." He smiled an odd, self-satisfied smile, which faltered when he saw that Lloyd and I were unimpressed. "Loyalty is the way Sylvia *does* friendship," Max stated loudly. "Sticking by her friends no matter what, protecting them, fighting their battles for them—that's how she shows she cares. And it's the way she showed her love for Bella—unwavering loyalty, even when things weren't going well. *That's* what I meant by romantic, OK?"

"She must've been devastated when Bella broke up with her," Lloyd muttered.

"Oh, it was the other way around. *Sylvia* left *Bella*." Max smiled, and I didn't like the trace of glee I could detect in his expression. "Having to do that has crushed Sylvia, I can tell. On top of Gin not being here—well, she's not having the best time."

I was silent. I was fascinated by this glut of new information about Sylvia, but I was also struggling to credit all of it. Some of the biographical details were implausible enough, and smacked of exaggeration, but above all Max's comments about her character seemed both presumptuous and uncharitable. Sylvia had, after all, spent much of the past few weeks trying to protect him. Without her intervention, he would have suffered even more, but Max's ego appeared to have recovered to the point that he'd forgotten this.

Max seemed to realize that he'd overstepped the mark, because he changed the subject. "You know how everyone's been joking about Gerald kidnapping Marta?" he asked. Lloyd and I nodded uneasily. "Well, yesterday Jolyon and Rory decided to follow him. Just to see where he goes, you know? They lost track of him for a bit, and then they found him knocking one out in the barn. He'd hidden this *crazy* stash of porn there—not the tame kind that Rory's got; some really hard, twisted stuff. And he was *crying*. Actually sobbing, as he was doing it."

"*What*?" Lloyd looked appalled. "What happened?"

"Rory and Jolyon had a field day." Max glanced down at his injured hand, a strange expression on his face. "They took away all the porn, and they've told *everyone*."

"Seems kind of infantile," Lloyd murmured. He'd taken a seat on my bed next to Max, and was fiddling with the ring pull on his can of beer. "Can't you say something to them?"

"What would I say?" Max asked, in a bright, over-reasonable tone. ""Hey guys, sorry to interrupt, but would you mind being a bit less infantile?"" There was something rigid in his smile as he put his head on one side to consider Lloyd. "I'm not sure that'd do anyone any good."

"Maybe not in the first instance, but—"

"But I should play the long game of moral superiority!" Max sang, sitting up straighter on my bed. His arm jerked in the sling. "Yes, that's right! I should wage war on infantilism! I should be more like you, Lloydy: mature and pure of heart." He was still singing the words, making them into a kind of ceremonial chant, his forefinger beating time on my bedstead. Despite his smile, I heard a tremor in his voice as he cried, "Down with infantilism!"

"OK, OK." Lloyd held up his hands in a resigned way. "Calm down." But Lloyd was right, I thought. For all that High Realms prized autonomy and self-reliance, there was a peculiar breed of infantilism at play there, with the grudges and the lashing out and the relentless tit-for-tat that meant nobody had the chance to grasp the point of being good and kind.

"I am calm." I watched Max stretch out his good arm and rest his long fingers around Lloyd's kneecap. "Calm, and wise, and a fucking realist." He grinned at us both. "Are you ready to go?"

I'd grown so used to High Realms, and had been so immersed in all that was going on, that I'd forgotten how grand our school was. On the night of the Christmas Ball, I was reminded of how imposing High Realms was determined to be, and how it was a world—and a law—unto itself.

The Atrium, the Lower Gallery, the Old Library, and the Salon were transformed that evening. Ivy had been wrapped around the banisters, intertwined with tiny, delicate lights. Everywhere else was candlelit. The high-ceilinged rooms with their polished floorboards had been emptied of furniture, apart from a few long tables around the edges, which bore vast quantities of food and drink. The walls of the Old Library had been draped with gold and silver hangings. A string quartet played buoyantly in the Atrium. In each room there was an enormous Christmas tree, dug up from the woods on the Estate. The tree in the Atrium was the largest I had ever seen in my life. Its tip—adorned with a single gold star—reached the banister of the Lower Gallery.

I'd never been in the Salon before. Its ceiling was even higher than the Old Library's, and its walls were not hung with portraits, but frescoed with beautiful, faded images of hunting. A fire was lit in the enormous hearth, and a grand piano had been pushed into the middle of the room. Lloyd left me to my own devices as soon as we got downstairs, saying he had to warm up, and Max went with him.

I wandered in and out of the vast rooms by myself. There had been a special, early evening Bridge Night, to which I had not been invited ("If I see you there," Bella had hissed to me at lunch, "it'll be the last party you ever go to'), and now the attendees were drifting up to the first floor, smelling of cigarettes and cider, their cheeks flushed and their shoes muddy. They seized glasses of champagne from the silver trays circulating with the Dining Hall staff and knocked back their contents. The noise in the Old Library was just reaching a crescendo when I spotted Sami walk in with Ingrid Crichton.

I hurried over to him, determined to prove that I didn't care who he was dating. "Sami!"

"Hiya," he said, smiling tightly. "How's it going?"

"Fine," I said, noticing that the hem of his trousers was muddy. "Hi, Ingrid."

"Hello there," she replied coolly. I knew her a little from hockey, and from the only class we shared, Math, at which she struggled. She had a long, aquiline nose with slightly flared nostrils, and red hair that tonight cascaded to her waist.

"Lloyd's going to be playing soon," I told them both. "Want to come and watch?"

"Maybe in a bit," Sami said, sounding nervous: Ingrid had laid her long-fingered hand on his forearm. "See you later, Rose." They drifted off to the drinks table, leaving me standing by the door on my own. I stared after them for a moment, feeling more alone than ever, and then turned to move into the Salon. As I did so, I found myself face-to-face with Sylvia.

I hadn't seen her for a few days, and my first impression was that she looked different. She was as elegant as ever, but her face was pale, and she'd grown thinner. She wore a simple black dress, and her hair was swept into a careless gathering at the nape of her neck. I glanced at her feet, which were encased in expensive-looking shoes with narrow gold straps. There was no mud on them. "Hello," she said.

"Hi." I swallowed, not wanting to get into an argument. "I was just—"

"If you're going to get a drink, I'll have one," she said. There were dark circles beneath her eyes, and her hand shook slightly as she raised it to smooth a strand of hair back from her face.

"All right." I went to the drinks table and picked up two glasses of wine. *What is going on,* I thought. I returned to Sylvia and handed her a glass.

"Thanks," she said, and took a sip. Her eyes darted around the room. "For fuck's sake," she snapped.

I followed her gaze to a corner. Gerald was skulking there by himself, a bottle of beer in his hand. Rory and Jolyon were standing a few feet away, and I was surprised to see that Max was with them. As we looked on, Max used his good hand to imitate what Gerald had been doing in the workshop that afternoon. Rory and Jolyon sniggered, and Max looked gratified. "At least they're not beating him up," I said to Sylvia.

"I wasn't aware that it had anything to do with you," she shot back. I raised my eyebrows; I couldn't help myself. I saw a flicker of something pass across her face, and then her anger solidified. I shrugged, and walked away from her.

The party was growing more raucous. We were only supposed to have two drinks each, and there were staff on duty to police this, but they weren't very committed to the task. Even Major Gregory was flushed and unsteady on his feet, his bow tie askew as he talked to Mr. Briggs. I hung around in the corner of the Salon for a while, watching Lloyd play Chopin while people chatted around the piano. Max wandered over and perched on the stool next to Lloyd, leaning over him to turn the pages.

"Hello, Rose." I turned to see Dr. Reza standing next to me, dressed in her usual jeans, cardigan, and sneakers. "I haven't seen you for a while. How are you?"

"I'm OK." I felt that to elaborate would be to open an emotional fissure that I was unable, this evening, to confront.

"Are you missing Marta?" she asked shrewdly.

I shrugged. Then, "Dr. Reza," I said suddenly, "why did you sign Marta off Games? When we first arrived, I mean."

Dr. Reza looked at me. It was several moments before she said, "The reason I gave to Marta was that she was very underweight."

"But what else?"

She was silent again. At last she said, "You know better than most that Games at High Realms are anything but that—a game. When I first met her, I thought Marta wouldn't be able to cope with sports, on top of everything else. I felt—I *feared*—that she'd been through enough."

I stared at Dr. Reza. She looked steadily back at me, and I felt again what I'd felt at the end of my interview with Vane. I felt seen, but with Dr. Reza there was no hint of accusation or disappointment. To hide how upset I was, I said harshly, "You told Marta she had to start doing Games. On the morning she disappeared."

"I thought it would be better coming from me." Dr. Reza's tone was heavy.

"What do you mean?"

She looked at me in surprise. "Major Gregory decreed it," she said. "I held him back for as long as I could, but he'd noticed that Marta was settling down; that she seemed much happier in herself. I thought so, too, but I still didn't want her to have to face Games. Major Gregory said he wouldn't allow her to be excused any longer unless I could give him a medical reason. I couldn't, but I wanted to be the one to give Marta the news. I told her she could come to me if anything—"

"This fucking school." I knew I shouldn't swear in front of her, but the words came before I could stop them. Tears stung my eyes. I walked away from Dr. Reza, weaving through the crowds toward the grand piano.

As I reached him, Lloyd's piece came to a climax. He played three final, ebullient chords, and then jumped to his feet and bowed to the applause, his arm around Max's shoulders. Then he picked up a glass of wine from the top of the piano and drained it in one. "Shall we dance?" he asked me, grinning.

I shook my head, still stung by Dr. Reza's revelation, but he grabbed my arm and pulled me on to the dancefloor. Fast jazz was now playing through speakers. I gripped Lloyd's strong hand and tried to move with him. "I can't see Sami and Ingrid anywhere," I said over the music, and Lloyd laughed.

"If what Max says about her is true, Ingrid will be expecting more than just a snog under the mistletoe." Lloyd pulled me closer, his hand against my lower back, dipping his head so he could speak into my ear. "It'd be good for him to start seeing someone. He needs a distraction, to stop him getting so worked up about Marta. Same goes for you, Ro."

"You don't know what I need."

He shrugged, steering us deeper into the throng. The song changed and he swung me around. "You both need to have faith," he said. "I reckon we're going to manage it."

"Manage what?"

"To save Marta. We've come this far! The police have lost

interest . . . I think it's gonna work out, Ro, I really do. We've done six weeks already." Lloyd leaned back, grinning sloppily. He put his warm hands on either side of my face. "Imagine it, Rose. Imagine the day she can be free." I closed my eyes for a moment, trying to obey him, but the image that swam in my mind's eye wasn't of Marta. It was of myself: an unburdened Rose walking by Donny Stream, whose conscience was as peacefully clear as the water that rushed alongside her. The Rose I saw would never have to tell another lie in her life.

Lloyd seemed to sense that he hadn't convinced me. "Oh, Rose," he said. He tilted his head back for a moment. "You're beautiful, you know. Everyone says so." He dropped a kiss on my forehead and let go of my hands. "I'm going to find Max," he told me, and then he was gone, striding away through the crowd.

The music was now very loud, and I didn't want to hang around with nobody to dance with. I slipped out onto the Lower Gallery, which was dimly lit, cool, and quiet after the frenetic atmosphere of the Salon. The string quartet was still playing downstairs. I turned down a side passageway, heading for the toilets. In the gloom I walked straight into two people pressed together against the wall.

"Look where you're fucking going," said an aggrieved, aristocratic voice. Ingrid Crichton adjusted her dress, looking furious.

"Sorry," I said, but I was looking at Sami. He was leaning against the wall, his collar undone and his eyes unfocused. "Are you OK?" I asked him.

"Rosie," he said, reaching out. "Is it you?"

"It's me." Sami was the only person who called me Rosie.

He got hold of the end of my hair and pulled gently. "I missed you," he slurred.

"*Missed* her?" Ingrid was eyeing him in disgust.

Sami fixed her with a baleful stare, lolling sideways against the wall. "Go away," he told her. Her eyes widened, and she turned on her heel and marched off down the corridor.

"That wasn't a very good idea," I told Sami.

He nodded languidly. "I agree."

"Shall I take you up to Hillary?" I asked, but he suddenly leaned toward me and put his lips on mine. They were wet and soft and tasted of vodka. "Hey," I said in surprise, moving my head away. "What're you doing?"

He shrugged, putting his hand against the wall. "Wanted to kiss you," he said. "You look so pretty in that dress."

I was half-amused, half-annoyed. "You need to go to bed," I told him.

His head drooped slightly. Then: "I miss Marta," he said, his voice suddenly clear. "I love her."

"I know," I said, glancing around to check that the corridor was still empty. "But shh, Sami. We can't talk about her here—remember?" His eyes became unfocused again, and I reached for his arm. "Let me take you back to Hillary—"

"I care about her more than *he* does," said Sami distinctly, trying to twist out of my grasp.

"OK, but—"

"He's manipulating us, Rosie. He wants us to think he's all alone in the world, but those foster parents of his write to him every bloody week."

"Come on, Sami. Let's go to bed."

"I don't think so," said a cold voice, and we turned to see

Ingrid and Bella striding down the corridor. Ingrid pointed, and Bella seized me and dragged me into the toilets.

The door banged closed behind us. "Get out," Bella said to the couple who were kissing by the sinks. They didn't need to be told twice. My heart was pounding in my chest.

"You've really pissed me off," Bella told me. She rammed the plug into one of the sinks and twisted on the hot tap. Ingrid stood with her back to the door, her arms folded.

"What have I done? Apart from existing."

"Existing would be enough," Bella snapped, rolling up the sleeves of her velvet suit.

"But?" The bathroom was filling with steam.

"But what?"

"You said existing *would* be enough. That suggests there's something else." I wanted to keep her talking for as long as possible, hoping that Sami still had enough presence of mind to find Lloyd and get help.

"Don't be smart with me," she snarled. The sink was now full, and she wrenched the hot tap off. "I know you like washing your hair in your room, freeloader, but tonight we're doing things differently."

I tried to back away, but she grabbed my arm, motioning to Ingrid to do the same. Together they forced me over to the sink. Clouds of steam were rising from the water. The plumbing in the Main House was very old, and the hot taps were notoriously lethal. Ingrid and Bella clamped themselves on either side of me and put their hands on the back of my head, forcing it down. I struggled, trying to kick them, but they were too strong. I stared at the water, growing ever closer as the muscles in my back weakened.

My forehead was the first to touch it. A thousand knives pressed into my skin, followed by a searing, acid agony. I struggled harder, trying to stop any more of my face coming into contact with the water, but it was no use. My neck felt like it was about to break. I squeezed my eyes tightly closed, bracing myself for immersion.

Then all of a sudden the pressure was released, and I stumbled to one side. I fell to my knees, dimly aware of Bella and Ingrid staggering backward.

"*Leave* her, I said!"

I struggled to my feet. A third figure was visible through the steam.

"Get out," she was saying, but she wasn't speaking to me. "Get out right now." Ingrid scuttled away at once, but Bella remained. Sylvia dropped her voice. "Bella. That's enough. Leave her alone."

"Oh, I see how it is." Bella spoke with her usual brusqueness, but I saw pain in her expression. "Two and a half years, Sylv. *Two and a half years,* and you just drop me—"

"Bella," Sylvia interrupted, "we've talked about this. You're going to be fine."

"You've decided, have you?" Bella's voice cracked. "I wish I could believe you, Sylv. But I'm not like you. I let myself *feel* stuff. I let myself cry—" and I saw that her eyes were filling with tears; that the ferocious, physically indomitable Bella was crying, in front of me and Sylvia.

Sylvia was watching her coldly. "This isn't the time or the place," she told Bella, who emitted a kind of strangled howl, turned on her heel, and ran out of the bathroom.

A few moments passed, and then Sylvia strode to the cold

tap and turned it on. "Put your head under this," she ordered. My skin was so painful that I obeyed her without question, dipping my head and allowing the icy water to run across my forehead. I felt vulnerable in that position, and stood upright as soon as I could. Sylvia was leaning against the wall, watching me silently.

"You stopped them," I said.

She shrugged. "Bella's always been a bad loser, but that's no reason to take it out on you."

"But you—"

Her eyes flashed. "I what?"

Be careful, I told myself. My forehead throbbed. "You— don't like me," I said limply.

She shrugged again. "I've been very angry with you. That's not the same thing."

"You hate me." The words left my mouth before I could stop them.

Her head jerked up and she looked at me as if she didn't understand. "*Hate* you?"

"Yes."

"You're not used to how it works here," she said impatiently. "We are loyal to our friends. There are . . . things that can't be tolerated. I have been loyal to Gin."

"Well, congratulations." At her mention of loyalty I suddenly felt angry. "Your *loyalty* has made me fucking miserable. I hope it's brought you some pleasure, at least." I made to move past her to the door, but she reached out quickly and put a hand on my wrist. Her skin was cold.

"Nothing brings me pleasure anymore," she said.

I stared at her. There were tears in her dark eyes, and

exhaustion was etched in her handsome features. I remembered how much I'd admired her devotion to her friends in the early days. I remembered her keening over Genevieve's motionless body. I remembered her defense of Max, and how she had immediately come to find me to pass on Genevieve's message. Most of all, I remembered Max's description of her, which I hadn't been able to bring myself to believe: the slight, dark-haired child who'd become the powerful person in front of me.

"Things do bring you pleasure," I told her, almost coaxingly. "What about hockey?"

A couple of tears rolled down her cheeks. She nodded mutely, wiping them away with the back of her hand. Again I turned to go, knowing that she wouldn't want me to see her crying, but then she spoke. "Hockey makes you happy, too. I've seen it."

I looked at her, unable to hide my surprise. "Yes."

"Can we—" Sylvia stopped, and took a deep breath. "I want to get out of here. Will you come with me?"

We left the school by the front door, the way Marta had run on the day of the Eiger. The air outside was so cold I almost gasped. We ran across the drive and down the dark avenue of plane trees toward the Pavilion.

Sylvia ran up the steps, her black dress flying behind her. She pulled open the door and reached inside. There was a series of loud, metallic clicks, and the floodlights came on over the Astroturf: dozens of them, searing through the darkness.

"We'll be seen," I said, my teeth chattering.

Sylvia looked down at me from the doorway of the Pavilion. Her pale skin gleamed in the white light. "I don't care," she said. "I don't care about anything anymore." She darted into the darkness of the interior and returned with two hockey sticks. "Here," she said, tossing one to me.

We slipped through the gate and onto the Astroturf. Sylvia kicked off her shoes, and I did the same. Then we were running across the pitch barefoot, passing to one another as we did six mornings a week, trying to trick each other, grinning at our own deftness and skill. Our breath rose in great clouds. The cold air was all around us, and the Main House with its many lights loomed large against the blackness of the night. I thought of the warmth of the party inside, but I did not want to go back.

Then Sylvia passed to me more quickly than I expected, and I had to leap forward to reach the ball. My foot caught the hem of my dress and I stumbled, landing on my hands and knees in the middle of the pitch. The ball scudded away, but Sylvia didn't chase it. She knelt down in front of me, her eyes meeting mine.

"Something else for pleasure," she said softly, and raised her hand to my cheek. She cupped my face briefly with her hands, and then she kissed me. Her lips were soft, softer even than Sami's had been. It was a softness that made me feel weak, and at first I was full of shock. I didn't understand. But perhaps, I thought, there was no need to understand. It was enough, for now, to feel: to feel Sylvia's lips on mine and her arms around me, and to lean in and kiss her back, with all the feeling that I had. And I kissed Sylvia under the deep black sky, with the harsh floodlight all around us, and while I kissed her I knew no fear.

PART III

Chapter 17

Dear Rose,

I'm writing this to give to Sami, in the hope he'll bring it to you. Perhaps I'm wrong to do this. Perhaps I should wait for you to come to me. But, you see, I'm afraid that you won't come. And then this will grow and grow between us and I will lose you—my best friend—forever.

I'm not saying that to be manipulative. I'm not saying <u>that is why I lied</u>, or <u>I lied because I so desperately wanted to be your friend</u>. It wasn't that, at all.

I lied to you because it was better than the truth. I can't speak the words of the truth. I might be able to write them— some of them—here, if I pretend that it's a story. I will try.

My mother, Maria De Luca, is an academic and a writer. She's a very intelligent, creative person. As I grew up, she wrote articles, essays, books. She wrote poetry and a play. She became more and more well-known. People wanted to hear her speak, to read her work. I remember scooping up her letters from the mat and bringing them to the study she shared with my father. Sometimes I would read them to her while she—and he—worked. People, particularly women, loved her. She was an icon.

At first my father was tolerant, even supportive. He'd claimed to be a feminist—even taking my mother's name when they got married—but he gradually became very resentful of her success. It was more than jealousy—it was possessiveness, because he had to share her with who he sneeringly referred to as her "acolytes." His feelings gradually morphed into cruelty. He was unfathomably cruel to her. I wasn't supposed to know about it, but I did; of course I did. She tried to protect me from knowing, but it was happening in the same house. He was always kind and gentle with me. That was one of the worst things.

When I was fourteen my father had a stroke. He was weaker as a result, but it made him harsher in other ways. He began to suspect that my mother would try to leave him. He was frightened of this. She was his carer, but it wasn't really about that. He wanted to control her. And he was very afraid that she would take me with her. One day when she was out, he told me that he thought my mother might be going away. He said that if I went with her he would find us and he would kill her. He would not kill me, he said. He loved me.

I believed him. He'd almost killed her on several occasions. And so last year, when my mother told me, in secret, that she was planning to run away, and asked me to come with her, I said no. I didn't tell her why. I just said that I wanted to stay with my father. She must have seen this as a betrayal. After all, he'd always been so kind to me, while doing terrible things to her. But I couldn't tell her the truth about why I would not go with her. I thought if I did, it might stop her leaving, and I desperately wanted her to go. She was losing her will to live, in a very literal sense. She wasn't eating. Not sleeping. Not working. Not writing. She barely spoke—even to me.

She left in February, during the night. That afternoon, while my father was in the bathroom, she'd told me that she would come back for me in a few weeks' time, in case I changed my mind about wanting to stay. I knew that if my father caught her coming back he would kill her. So I told her not to come back; that I didn't want to go with her. There was no time to explain. My father returned to the room, and that was the last time I was alone with my mother.

She left. I don't know where she went. She just disappeared. For the first three months or so, I thought that she'd settled down somewhere else, that she was writing another book, another play, more poems—that she'd recovered. I thought I would walk past a bookshop one day and see her new book in the window.

But Rose, she hasn't come back. I'd told her not to, but there was not a single part of me that really thought she <u>never</u> would. I suppose I assumed she would make a life for herself and that she would somehow fetch me and that we would escape him together. But she didn't come back—and then I gave up waiting, and came to High Realms. She could never have predicted what would happen between February and September. She'd only known my father's kindness to me, and his cruelty to her.

So I prefer to tell myself that my mother is dead. It's plausible, but it's also easier than acknowledging that she chose not to come back, that she left me with my father. She never once checked that he hadn't turned on me. He did. You know that already.

I know that I've hurt you. But this is the lie I've told myself in order to keep living. It's the lie I cling to, and even as I write this and acknowledge again that she may not be, I know I will continue to fantasize that she is dead. I can't hide that from you. But I am desperately sorry. For the lie I told you, which was wrong, and for the pain I've caused you, which I despise; and for all of this, which I know is spoiling your time at High Realms.

Love,

M.

I finished reading and looked up. Sami was sitting on the end of my bed, watching me. Our eyes met.

"Well?" he said quietly. "Does that explain things?"

I swallowed. "Yes."

It was Saturday afternoon in late January. Lloyd was practicing the organ with Max, and Sami had gone to the clocktower with lunch for Marta before coming to find me. The boys and I had been back at school for a fortnight. Lessons, Games, and duties were underway, and it was almost as if we'd never been away, except that we now had to attend university preparation classes three times a week with the Head of Drake House, Dr. Lewis. She'd spent the first few sessions trying to make us decide which subject and universities we were going to apply for. Sami had chosen Medicine at Oxford, for which he would be coached by Dr. Reza. Lloyd and I were still ambivalent about our next steps.

I was glad to be back. Until I went home I hadn't realized how institutionalized I'd become. I'd grown unused to helping prepare meals and washing up afterward, to warm baths rather than harried showers, to domestic peace and quiet rather than the constant commotion of Hillary House. I spent entire afternoons lying on my bed in the silent flat, staring at the ceiling, trying to process the events of the term. Over Christmas itself my father took several days off from driving his cab, and we walked all over London together: Greenwich, Fulham, Kilburn, Ealing. I found myself missing the colors and the textures and the clear air of the countryside.

I could tell that my father noticed a change in me, but he didn't comment on it or ask me questions. He'd followed Marta's case closely in the newspapers. A couple of times he mentioned how concerned I must be about her, and when Professor De Luca made a final appearance on TV just before Christmas to appeal for her safe return, I heard my father say quietly to himself, "Poor chap." He turned to me and asked what Marta *had been* like as a person. "She's not dead," I snapped before I could stop myself, and he gave me a strange, searching look that I felt took in everything I did not want him to know. From then on, my father took a step back. He cooked my favorite food, suggested films he thought I'd enjoy, helped me with my vacation assignments. I was enveloped in the sort of care I'd lived without for fourteen weeks, and I found it stifling.

Sami wrote to me several times from Leeds. We'd agreed that we wouldn't say anything explicit about Marta in our letters in case they were intercepted, but I could tell he was worried. It was such a long time for her to be entirely on her own, and we were concerned about her physical welfare as well as her mental state. *I seem to be very hungry all the time,* Sami wrote in late December. I knew it was a reference to Marta, and to the fact that we had only been able to get hold of the bare minimum quantity of food that she would need. *Is it very cold where you are?* he added pointedly, and I felt a stab of anxiety about the temperature in the clocktower.

Lloyd wrote, too. He'd gone back to his foster parents for two weeks before going to stay with Max in Chiswick, which I knew hurt Sami's feelings. Lloyd's access to information was useful, though. He wrote to tell us that Genevieve had been discharged from the hospital on Christmas Eve, but had refused all contact with Max. Sylvia had been to see her at home in Berkshire, and had passed on that it looked like she might be able to return to High Realms before Easter. Then Lloyd wrote to me and Sami to say that Sylvia was hosting a Millennium party at her parents' house in north London. Max was going, but the three of us hadn't been invited. I wasn't exactly surprised, having heard nothing from Sylvia since the night of the Christmas Ball, but I found that I was thinking about her much more than I wanted to. I wondered how she would act toward me when we returned to school.

Over Christmas my concern for Marta lapped against my resentment about her lie, eroding it in places, but accentuating it in others. It didn't help that I was at home, in the flat I'd lived in with my mother, which still held so many memories of her. I thought of the final Christmas we'd spent together. I'd leaned against her soft, depleted body while we watched TV; she'd kissed the top of my ear with cracked lips. I found myself freshly astonished at the thought that I would never know that affection again. I felt that I could have borne any length of separation if only I could be sure that I would meet her again at the end of it. But I knew that this was impossible, and as the vacation continued I withdrew further and further into myself. My sadness grew, and it began to occupy almost all of the space in which other emotions—compassion, empathy, hope—normally lived. I felt frozen and hard. I wanted very badly to get back to school, where distractions were plentiful and there was limited time to think.

Now we were back at High Realms for second phase, but I still hadn't visited Marta. Lloyd and Sami had raced to the stables as soon as we'd arrived, their pockets stuffed with treats from home. An hour later they'd returned to Hillary Common Room very subdued. Marta had greeted them, but had otherwise barely spoken. She'd eaten less than half of the food we'd left her. Her cough was bad, and her skin was more inflamed than ever. "She just wants you, Rosie," Sami said, looking at me beseechingly, but I had not gone to her.

I raised my eyes to Sami's, and saw the pain in his expression. I couldn't share the contents of the letter with him, and I knew that he would not have dreamed of reading it before handing it to me. I also knew that his heart was still breaking for Marta; that his mind was racing through the horror of what she had suffered. I couldn't bear to cause him any more distress, or to go on resenting Marta for a moment longer.

"Shall we head to the clocktower after Dr. Lewis's class?" I asked.

He looked quickly at me. "What?"

"Let's go and see Marta," I said.

He beamed, relief and joy cutting through the anxiety on his face. "Oh, Rosie," he said, and hugged me. I rested my forehead briefly on the tweed of his blazer before we separated,

Sami bounding to his feet. "Come on," he said happily. "Let's go to class."

Three hours later, Lloyd, Sami, and I strode over the fields toward the stables. It was a cold day with a stiff breeze, and, at half past four, the daylight had already almost faded. Dr. Lewis had kept us in her study for longer than usual, haranguing us to decide on universities and subjects and scaremongering about the mock exams, which would take place in the third week of February. Ultimately I'd chosen English at Oxford, and Lloyd had opted for Philosophy at Cambridge, just to get her off our backs. Then Sylvia, Jolyon, and Rory had arrived for their session, and Dr. Lewis had released us. In a continuation of her behavior toward me since Christmas, Sylvia had thrown herself into an armchair next to the window, barely giving me a second glance. I was so focused on going to see Marta that this had caused me less pain than usual.

We entered the yard that lay between the barn and the clocktower. A small bonfire was burning in the corner, and the otherwise gloomy area smelled enticingly of woodsmoke. As we crossed the yard, trying to keep a low profile, we heard sobbing.

"Rose," said Sami warningly, but I was already walking quietly toward the door, which was ajar. I stood to one side and looked through the gap. It was very dark inside the workshop, but I could just about make out a large figure sitting on a stool in the corner, his back to the door. Gerald's head was in his hands and his shoulders were heaving. He was trying to stifle his sobs, but every few seconds I heard a guttural moan of sheer misery.

I knew better than to try to comfort him. I tiptoed back to the boys, and we left the yard as quickly and as quietly as we could, all of us feeling disconcerted. We slipped into Block C. In my distracted state, retracing these familiar footsteps, I'd almost forgotten that I had not seen Marta for such a long time. It was only as we hurried up the concrete stairs of the clocktower that I remembered what had passed between us, and I felt both hopeful and apprehensive about our reconciliation.

Sami reached the top of the stairs first. He knocked briskly and pushed open the door.

"All right, Mar?" I heard him say. "Look who's here!"

I stepped into the clocktower room. It had changed significantly since my last visit. It was untidy again, almost squalid, and smelled sour. A small tent had been erected in the middle of the room, beneath the rafters. The boys had told me about this, explaining that it was an idea of theirs to try to keep Marta warmer at night, but I was unprepared for how pitiful the sight of it would be, like a camping trip gone badly wrong. The interior was piled with several sleeping bags and numerous blankets, and the electric heater was positioned in front of it, facing inward.

Marta was crouched in the mouth of the tent. It was dark in the clocktower room, the only light coming from a small paraffin lamp we'd suspended from one of the rafters at the end of October. I stared at my friend through the gloom. She was thinner than she had been when she'd first arrived at High Realms. Her face was sallow and grubby, and her eyes were large and round in their sockets, which seemed to have retreated into her skull. Her short hair stuck up around her head in unkempt, dirty spikes. She was dressed in an old Columbus House tracksuit that I'd found for her in the lost and found in October.

She got to her feet, stepping unsteadily out of her tent and onto the concrete floor. Her hands when she placed them on the ground to help herself up were gleaming red and scaly with eczema, and as she stood up to face me I saw that her neck was similarly inflamed, the skin almost purple in places.

"Rose?" she whispered, looking at me. Her voice was very hoarse.

"Hi," I said. I was deeply shocked by her appearance, but a bubble of joy was swelling inside me, dissolving the grains of hardness that had settled there. It was Marta, my best friend, and how could I have left her? I suddenly felt ashamed.

"Did you get my letter?" Marta's eyes flickered to Sami, who was standing to one side, with Lloyd.

"Yes, I did."

"And do you—forgive me?"

"I—" I began, and she rushed at me. There was a moment in which Lloyd started forward, as if he thought Marta was about to attack me, but she flung her bony arms around my neck and hugged me fiercely, her cold cheek pressed against my warm one. I felt her tears run beneath my shirt collar, and wrapped my own arms around her as if I would never let her go.

When we finally broke apart, Marta was trembling. She picked up a filthy towel from the floor next to the tent and wiped her tearstained face with it. "I've missed you so much," she said.

"I missed you, too," I said, and it was only as I spoke the words that I realized how lonely, how confused I had been.

But foremost in my mind was the harm I had done. Looking at Marta, I knew at once that her physical state was only the surface of the damage that my refusal to see her had wrought. But she smiled tremulously at Lloyd, Sami, and me, and the boys came forward to where Marta and I stood, grinning and patting both of us on the back.

We stayed with Marta in the clocktower for several hours, that cold evening in January, and they were some of the happiest we ever spent as a foursome. For once we threw caution to the winds and ran the extension cord up for the heater, but the real warmth came from our togetherness, our conviviality. We made hot chocolate on the stove, and talked and laughed and bickered as we always had. We felt the old, inexplicable safety in numbers. The color started to come back into Marta's hollow cheeks, and every so often she darted me a look of pure happiness. For the first time since coming back to school I forgot about the fact that Sylvia was ignoring me. I dared to believe that the four of us would recover from the estrangement of Marta and me, that it would become just another thing that had happened; another bad thing that we had been able, through our collective resilience, to overcome. Healing, I thought, was something all four of us were becoming good at.

Chapter 18

The next day was Sunday. Buoyed by the happy evening we'd had together, I spent the morning filled with a lightness and warmth that seemed to seep to my every extremity, thawing all the parts of me that had been frozen. Suddenly, the fact of it being a new year—a new millennium—took on a new significance. 2000 was the year that Marta would be set free. She would turn eighteen in two months' time. There was an end in sight, and what was more, we now had a template to work from. We knew how to keep her safe, keep her alive. There were fewer secrets between us. We would survive.

After Chapel I went to Sunday lunch with the boys and Max, wearing a new skirt and a black cashmere sweater that had been my father's Christmas presents to me. For the first time I felt indistinguishable from the other students in their chic outfits. Lloyd, Max, and I chatted away, eating large platefuls of roast pork, raising our voices to hear each other over the din. But Sami was subdued, pushing his mashed potatoes around with his fork. Every so often he slipped some food into a napkin. He wasn't even particularly discreet about it, knowing that Max was too wrapped up in himself to notice.

"You OK?" I asked Sami as we left the Dining Hall. We crossed the Atrium and stepped out onto the chilly drive.

"Later," he said quietly, but Lloyd and Max were already drifting away, barely glancing back. In the early days they'd often wandered off by themselves, and they seemed to have fallen back into their old ways. "It's Ingrid," Sami now said to me, grimly.

"Oh," I said, surprised. We started to walk aimlessly through the plane trees where a few First Formers were playing with a cricket ball. "Well—what's the matter?"

"She seems to *like* me," muttered Sami. "She sent me letters over the vacation. Invited me to stay at her dad's bloody castle. And now she keeps turning up at mine and Lloyd's room, wanting to—you know—hang out."

So they were sleeping together. "Do you . . . like her?"

"Sort of. I dunno." Sami kicked at the path, plunging his hands deep into his pockets. "It's weird. I *want* to like her, you know? Sometimes I find myself thinking, she's OK, she's not a bad person . . . but I don't trust her, Rosie, not even for a second."

I nodded. I thought Ingrid was despicable, but now did not seem like the right time to say this. We walked a little farther, and then Sami said in a great rush, as if every syllable were dangerous, "I feel like Ingrid *needs* me. But I can't be needed by her, Rosie. Every bit of care I give her is a second I'm not caring for"—he lowered his voice—"for Marta. I see Marta getting weaker every day—"

"D'you think she is?" I interrupted, alarmed.

"Yes." Sami looked at me, his face creased with worry. "That cough, and the eczema, and not eating . . . all of that's bad enough, but—she's not well, Rose. She doesn't talk like she used to. She doesn't wash. She doesn't even argue with us." He swallowed, looking at me with eyes that seemed ready to fill with tears, and I realized the extent of his pain. "I asked my parents for advice," he told me. "Don't worry," he said quickly, seeing my expression, "I didn't tell them it was about Marta. I just said . . . a friend. I could never tell them what we're doing—they'd be so disappointed."

I swallowed. "What did they say?" I asked, not knowing whether I wanted to hear the answer.

"My father said she should be getting professional treatment, to help her cope with what's happened to her. I know he's right, Rose. She's locked up in that clocktower twenty-four hours a day, seven days a week. It's—it's trauma after trauma. It's mad."

His eyes were now full of tears. He turned away from me, wiping his face angrily on his sleeve. We stood silently under the trees for a few moments. Amid my irritation that Sami had confided in his parents, I realized that if he were a different person he would blame me for Marta's decline. It was partly attributable to me; to my decision to be absent from her.

"Sami," I said, and he slowly turned back to face me. "It'll be OK. We can help her."

"How? It's beyond our—"

"No, it's not." I sincerely believed this. "I'll go and see her today. I can help her, I know I can."

He looked bleakly at me, and a single tear ran over his cheek. "Do you really think so?"

"Yes," I said, firmly. "I'll go as soon as the Sunday Hack is over, Sami. I promise."

A few hours later, I was in Block C, hastily mucking out. I scattered fresh straw over the floor, filled the feed containers, replenished the water barrels. Then I leaned over the door of the stalls and fed an apple each to Polly, Margot, and George. I'd taken to doing this lately, with a strange notion that I was compensating them for their patient complicity in our decision to hide Marta.

After our conversation that afternoon, Sami and I had wandered into the Straker Library. I'd made my way to the first floor, to the Drama and Poetry sections. I'd run my fingers lightly along the plastic-coated spines. Larkin. Lessing. Lowell. *De Luca*. My scalp had tingled as I'd tugged the book out of its place. It was called *A Truthful Heart*.

I'd knelt down on the carpeted floor and started to flick through the play. It was dedicated to *My adored and adoring husband, Nathaniel De Luca*. Its premise—a chance meeting between Virginia Woolf, Emily Dickinson, and Ibsen's Nora—was strange, but it told an unexpectedly beautiful story of personal fulfillment and redemption, ending in an almost hallucinogenic underwater world with very different rules to our own.

I hadn't needed to find the play to know that Marta had been telling the truth in her letter. To me, the letter had been a bit like reading a commentary on a difficult text. Added to what she'd told us in October, it elucidated Marta in a way I found almost depressingly sensical. I'd found myself feeling grateful that I hadn't known any of it in the first few months of my friendship with her. It meant I had taken Marta on her own terms: as she, of course, had wanted and planned.

"You know," a clear voice now rang out behind me from the threshold of Block C, "for somebody who doesn't ride, you spend rather a lot of time in the stables."

I wheeled around to see Sylvia leaning over the half door, a hard hat dangling from her hands. Her hair was disheveled and her cheeks flushed, and she was wearing an old Raleigh sweater. I'd seen her many times over the past fortnight, and we'd spent hours together in lessons and on the hockey pitch, but they were the first words she'd spoken to me since we'd kissed.

"It's my duty," I said, trying to keep the guilt out of my voice.

Sylvia nodded disinterestedly. "Want a hand?"

"I've almost finished," I attempted, but she'd already swung open the lower door and marched into the stable in her long boots and filthy jodhpurs. She picked up a brush from the shelf and went over to George's stall. I was worried about her proximity to the way into the clocktower, and also about the small pile of things for Marta that I'd left by the feed bucket: a clean towel, *The Importance of Being Earnest*, and some cereal bars.

"I was wondering," Sylvia said abruptly, without looking up from brushing George's mane, "whether you might like to come riding with me on Tuesday afternoon."

"I don't know how."

"It isn't hard." She ran her hand along George's back. "That's a great play, isn't it?" she added, gesturing to *The Importance of Being Earnest*.

I ignored this. "How do you know how hard riding is? You've probably been doing it all your life."

She nodded thoughtfully. "Since I was three. But really, it's fun. We can go out into the countryside—away from school."

"Right." I suddenly felt irritated. The fact of not knowing how was only one of my objections to going riding with Sylvia. "That's convenient."

"What do you mean?" She looked puzzled.

"You'd rather not be seen with me."

Her eyes flashed. "You misjudge me. Don't come riding if you don't want to, but don't sling insults around just because you're in a muddle about how the fuck you feel."

At first I felt enraged that Sylvia was claiming the moral high ground. I wanted to hurl an insult back at her, and then withdraw into my hard-won carapace of independence, but I forced myself to look at her properly. In her tatty riding clothes she seemed different to how she looked in her Senior Patrol gown. I *was* confused, and that wasn't entirely Sylvia's fault. Nor was it her fault that she'd been trained to meet any rejection, any pain, with aggression.

"It's not that I don't want to come with you," I said, forcing myself to stay calm. "But you need to give me some time to think. You owe me that much." She looked angrier still, but the memory of how I'd been treated over the past few months made me go on, looking her in the eye. "I'm not asking you for an apology, Sylvia. But you hurt me. I need time to—"

"*Hurt* you?" she demanded. "How have I—"

"Stop." I spoke more harshly than I'd intended, and Sylvia's eyes widened. "I get that we're different, Sylvia. I get that this—" I gestured around at the stable, and toward the Main

House "—is your world, not mine. I get that you're Vice-Captain General, whatever. But *you* kissed *me*. You kissed me for half an hour on the fucking Astroturf, over a month ago, and you haven't spoken a word to me since. In *any* world, Sylvia, by *anyone's* standards, that's hurtful." I stopped, swallowing hard at Sylvia's impassive expression. "You're so clever," I said to her feebly. "Why can't you understand that you've hurt me? You're making me feel like I've gone mad."

There was a long silence. Sylvia looked back at me. I expected her to turn on her heel and march away, but her eyes were now bright with a mix of comprehension and chagrin. For the first time, I felt that the balance of power between us had shifted. Even so, I feared that what I'd said would drive her back to the Main House to start a new war against me.

Of all things, I didn't expect what she said next. "I think I do understand, actually. About being hurt, I mean. It does take time. It *is* taking time." She looked down at her hands, which were chapped and muddy, and then back at me. "Let me know," she said curtly, and she walked away, across the courtyard toward the Hexagon.

Washing had always been difficult in the clocktower. There was no hot water, and until that Sunday, no receptacle larger than a bucket. Something had to be done. I crept into one of the workshops and found a large plastic tub full of dirty horse blankets. I tipped these out onto the floor and slipped back to Block C with the tub.

Marta had been tidying. She'd moved her tent into the corner, where it looked a little less forlorn, and had rolled up the sleeping bags and blankets. Another area housed the camping stove and the plates, bowls, and cutlery that we'd managed to steal from the Dining Hall. She'd lined up her books—a surprising number of them—against the wall under the clock. As I returned with the tub, she was adding *The Importance of Being Earnest* to her collection. She smiled at me, but she looked exhausted, as though the effort of clearing up the room had drained her. Her cheeks were hollow and her skin had turned a faint yellow color. Her eyes narrowed when she saw me putting a large saucepan of water on the stove. "I thought a warm bath might help your skin," I said.

"That'll take ages." She eyed the plastic tub.

"We've got time. The boys aren't coming down for another hour."

We sat together on the mattress and did a crossword from a book that Sami had given her for Christmas while we waited for three pans of water to boil. Marta perked up a bit as we worked on it, but after a while she sighed restlessly and put down her pen. "Tell me what's going on in school," she said. "I feel like I'm missing so much."

"You're not," I said automatically, before realizing that this wasn't strictly true. "Well—something weird did happen at the end of last term."

"What?"

I told her about kissing Sylvia on the Astroturf. Marta's green eyes widened, and a grin started to spread across her face. "Bloody hell," she commented. "Is she a good kisser?"

"Yeah," I said bleakly, fiddling with my pen.

Marta chuckled, and then coughed. "What a fucking story for the books," she said. "I used to think she was a terrible person."

"So did I."

"The way I see it," Marta said, with a trace of her old confidence, "even if she was a bad person *before*, she'll already be getting some of your goodness, Rose. It'll seep into her."

"I'm not a good person." I glanced awkwardly at Marta, unable to bring myself to talk about our estrangement. Then, "I feel guilty all the time," I told her, suddenly realizing that she was the only person who could help me unpick the paradox. "I feel guilty for doing something I believe is right."

"Hiding me, you mean?"

"Yes."

Marta looked thoughtful. "Why do you think that is?"

I gazed around the clocktower room, which was still so inhospitable despite our attempts to improve it. After a moment's hesitation, I gestured to the eczema on Marta's hands, her grubby tracksuit, her pallid face. *Trauma after trauma.* "Because . . . you're not very well. Because we can't help you get better."

"Oh, Rose." Marta's eyes were bright with empathy. "You shouldn't feel guilty about that. The way I am . . . that's not your fault. There's not much to be done with me, you know." She smiled sadly. "Anyway, you *do* help. Every time we talk, it helps me. It's all in the gray matter, Rose."

"The gray matter?"

Marta leaned forward. "The bits in between all the scary stuff, the big decisions. The times we're just together, hanging out. You look at me and we laugh and every time, every *single* time, it reminds me that you don't think I'm disgusting."

"Of course I don't think you're disgusting."

She shrugged. "I get it, though," she said suddenly.

"I understand why you feel guilty. *I* feel guilty, you know, because of everything you and the boys are doing for me. It was all I could think about, the whole time you were away. I had a lot of time to think," she said, laughing hollowly, "and I kept wondering how you cope with all this. But then I realized . . . at least in your case, Rose, it's probably the same reason *I* can cope with it."

"What's that?" I realized how much I'd missed Marta's insights; her often disarming way of cutting to the chase.

"You and I can cope with this because it's not the worst thing we've been through," Marta said simply. "We've both already faced the worst thing. Your mum—my dad. Nothing will ever be as bad as those things, will it?"

I didn't know what to say. I didn't know whether to prioritize the unforeseen wave of grief that Marta's observation had elicited, or respond to the fact that she'd mentioned her father for the first time since telling us what he'd done. I sensed that she wanted to talk about it with me, and even though I knew I would struggle to find the words to reply, I was determined to try, for Marta's sake, and as part of my conscience-assuaging compensation for refusing to see her. All too quickly, however, Marta seemed to misread my silence as sadness. She reached out, putting her cold hand on mine as we sat cross-legged on the mattress.

"What I meant," she said hesitantly, "is that I think the worst part might be over, for both of us. I can see the light. I couldn't before Christmas, but I can now. There's less than three months to go, Rose. Three months—and then I can leave here, and start again. Somewhere nobody knows me. I'll still see you and the boys, of course." She paused, her hand still on mine. I felt its chill thawing as it absorbed the warmth of my skin. "That doesn't mean you don't need some help to get through the rest of this. That's partly why I think you should go out with Sylvia, if you want to. I think she'd help you." She paused again, and suddenly smiled. "Maybe you'll get to be in the Senior Patrol."

I realized that the third pan of water was boiling. I got up and poured it into the tub, and put another pan on the stove. I turned to see Marta watching me. "Sylvia was cruel to you," I forced myself to say.

Marta shrugged. "I suppose she was, a couple of times," she said blandly, "but it was in the service of loyalty to Genevieve, wasn't it? She's loyal to her friends—she's not so different to us, really. And all of this"—Marta gestured around us—"this is *my* fault. I was the one who slapped Genevieve."

Silence again. "Do you regret it?" I asked at last.

Marta's face was drawn. She gazed at the steam rising from the tub, and down at her mottled hands. "Oh, I don't think so," she said quietly.

"But—"

Her head snapped up. "How could I regret standing up for one of my best friends?" She returned my stare with an obstinacy familiar to me from the early days. "I'd do it again, Rose. In a heartbeat."

I looked down at the bath. I felt depressed, and more than a little angry. Until this point I'd believed that Marta and I were on the same page, but it was now horribly clear that we weren't. Her declaration seemed to throw back in my face everything we'd done for her; to suggest that it wasn't significant because it could, if necessary, be repeated. For the first time, I found myself thinking that Marta was selfish. "Why are you so into him?" I asked abruptly. "He betrayed you." *He's still seeing Max,* I wanted to say, but I couldn't bring myself to.

There was a truculent gleam in Marta's green eyes. "Anyone can make a mistake. We've just talked about the fact that Sylvia—"

"It's not the same thing, Marta."

"Maybe not." I glimpsed a scintilla of spite in Marta's expression. "You asked me what I see in Lloyd. Well, I see that he and I are both alone. We both have no one at home who really cares for us. But also, Rose, I *want* him. I want to *be* with him. Do you understand?"

I stared at her: at the avid set of her jaw, the defiant tautness of her neck. I did understand, and yet in some ways I did not. I sensed that Marta had guessed that I'd never slept with anyone; had seized on it and was treating it as a weakness, as the High Realmsians had done. A spark of hostility flickered between us, and swiftly died when we realized that we did not want to—that we could not—argue, and least of all about this. "I never want to be far from you, Rose," Marta said suddenly.

I paused, and then nodded. "Ready?" I asked her, pointing to the tub, and Marta nodded reluctantly.

"Don't let Lloyd and Sami in," she said, pulling her tracksuit top over her head. She stepped into the plastic tub, shivering. I turned away to give her some privacy, but it was impossible not to glimpse the maimed condition of her body. There were twice as many scars as there had been on our second day at High Realms, now creeping down her thighs almost as far as her knees. Her arms, chest, and back were covered with eczema.

Marta's teeth were chattering. I'd added too much cold water to the makeshift bath, and the air temperature in the room was too low for her to have any chance of being comfortable.

"Do you want to get out, Mar?"

"Might as well do my hair while I'm in here," she said, her voice trembling with cold. "Can you help me?"

I knelt down and poured lukewarm water slowly over Marta's head, watching her cropped hair flatten over her scalp in a sleek, gleaming cap. Then I rubbed shampoo into her hair. She leaned back, her eyes closed, and despite the goosebumps all over her body, she looked more relaxed. I pressed my fingertips into the top of her head, massaging it.

"That's nice," she murmured. I poured the rest of the water gently over her head, watching the dirty suds stream into the bath.

She got out soon after that, and got dressed in clean clothes that I'd brought for her. Then she sat cross-legged in the mouth of the tent and toweled her hair dry until it stuck out around her head in a clean, fluffy halo. I passed her a tube of emollient cream, and she dabbed it on her hands and neck.

"Let's have something to eat," I said, pulling out the food that Sami had filched from lunch. We'd decided that from now on we would share meals with Marta as often as possible, because she generally ate more when she had company. I poured a tin of rice pudding into another saucepan and put it on the stove. I felt a sudden, soaring contentment.

We sat in the tent and ate the leftover pork and vegetables and mashed potatoes, which Sami had transferred into a plastic container and wrapped in a napkin. I asked Marta a question about an essay I had to do for Miss Kepple that evening, and she grew animated as she gave me her opinion, waving her fork around and talking with her mouth full. The rice pudding began to bubble on the stove.

Then we heard footsteps on the stairs, and Marta grinned, color showing in her cheeks. "I *know* Lloyd will agree with me," she said, and she leaned out of the opening of the tent, watching the door eagerly. It swung open. Gerald stood in the doorway.

For a few moments the three of us simply stared at each other in total shock. Gerald's expression was one of sheer incredulity. I noticed how large he was; how his frame filled the doorway. He was wearing his overalls and steel-toed boots, and a rope was looped over his shoulder and across his body. He looked around the clocktower room, taking in the home we'd made: the tent, the stove, the tins of food stacked against the wall, the tub full of grimy water. Then he turned his gaze to Marta.

"Well, well," he said slowly.

"Gerald," I said, my mouth dry. "Gerald, please—"

"Shut up." He dragged his hand across the back of his mouth. He was shocked, I could tell; almost as deeply as we were. He shifted the rope slightly. I tried to catch his eye, and as he stared back I saw that his eyes were bloodshot and swollen.

"Sit down," I said wildly. "We can talk about this, Gerald—"

He shook his head. "Save your breath." He glanced at Marta. "You're as mad as they all said you were," he said softly.

She looked at him pleadingly and said nothing. Her face was white.

"I'm going now," Gerald told us. "Enjoy your meal." And with that he was gone, closing the door quietly behind him.

I looked over at Marta. She was deathly pale, clutching her fork in one hand. Then she leaned to one side and was violently sick on the concrete floor. Helplessly, I put my hand on her back, feeling the bones under my palm as her body heaved, and all the food she had consumed was expelled from her body by the intensity of her fear.

Chapter 19

No." Sami's voice was almost a moan. "No, no, no, no, no—"

"Shut up," Lloyd snapped. We were in the boys' room in Hillary, where I'd found them peacefully finishing their prep, their books spread out around them. I had barely been able to form the sentence to tell them what had happened. In the moment I first saw them, I had wondered about simply *not* telling them; pretending it hadn't happened. Our deepest fear was realized. It was our worst nightmare: the thing we'd dreaded most, since the very beginning.

Lloyd got up from the desk and went to the window. He stared out of it, biting his lip. Sami's head was buried in his hands. Then he looked up. "We have to get her out of here."

"What?" Lloyd turned around.

"We need to move Marta." Sami reached for his jacket. "We need to get her away from this fucking school—away from him." He tugged on his shoes. "Rosie, come with me."

"Wait a minute." Lloyd went to stand between Sami and the door. "That's not a good idea."

"Have you got a better one?"

"Yes, actually." Lloyd put his hand against Sami's shoulder, preventing him from getting past. "I'm going to talk to him, Sami. I'm sure he can be reasoned with. Just calm down, and—"

"*Calm down*?" Sami stared at him, his face red with disbelief. "I can see how much you care about her, Lloyd, if you can be calm right now—"

"There's more than one way of caring." Lloyd's voice was harsh. "Back off," he said dismissively, as Sami opened his mouth to argue. "I'm going to find Gerald. I'm sure we can sort this out."

"For all you know he's already—"

"I don't think so." Lloyd shook his head, his expression serious and calculating. "He's got too much to lose by doing that. Or rather—too much to gain." For a moment he looked troubled, and then he glanced at me. "Will you come with me, Rose?"

"This is ridiculous." Sami got to his feet. "I'm going to get her out of there. I should have done it ages ago," he said. His voice was close to a sob.

"Sami," I said, trying to keep my voice level, "I don't think we should move her. If Gerald thinks we're trying to give him the slip, he'll be furious. I think—I think Lloyd's right. We need to talk to him."

There was a short silence in which we all looked at each other. Then Sami said, his tone resigned, "Fine. Let's go." He got to his feet, doing up his jacket, but Lloyd shook his head.

"No," he said. "I'm sorry, Sami, but I don't think you should come. You're too worked up. *No*," he said more loudly, in response to Sami's shout of protestation, "I mean it. You're too close to her. You care too much."

Sami looked at him mutinously. "So I'm supposed to just stay here?"

"Do what you like, but you're not going to the clocktower."

He turned to me, his expression desperate. "How was she, Rose? When you left her?"

I thought back to how I'd left Marta: glassy-eyed and silent on the mattress, alternating between frozen immobility and uncontrollable shaking. She hadn't even reacted when I'd said I had to go. Lloyd shot me a look of warning. "She was OK," I said at last, hating the lie. "I told her we'd take care of it."

"Rose, come with me." Lloyd opened the door. "We won't be long," he told Sami, gesturing for me to follow him.

Lloyd and I soon realized the flaw in our plan: we had no idea where Gerald was. There was no sign of him in the stables, barns, or workshops. As a last resort, Lloyd ran up to the clocktower room to check whether he'd gone back there, while I kept a lookout downstairs.

When Lloyd came down his arms were full of items from the clocktower: the tin opener, a broken plate, even pens. His hands trembled as he thrust them into my arms and turned to seal the entrance. I swallowed, feebly hoping that he'd confiscated the objects as a contingency, but he shook his head. "She's hurt her arm," was all he said.

"We should stay with her—"

"*No*, Rose. It's too risky—this is exactly the time of day we'd be missed. I've taken away what she was using, and everything else dangerous," Lloyd said. I knew from his sick-ened expression that he'd seen something bad. "We need to sort this out," he said, a new urgency in his tone. "Let's try Columbus—maybe he's taking early roll call."

We ran to the Hexagon, where the Sixth Form of Columbus House was based. As we approached the double glass doors, Max burst out of them, stumbling down the steps toward us.

"Whoa! He*llo* there!" His hair was disheveled and his color high, and he reeked of alcohol. "What're *you* two doing here?"

"We're looking for Briggs," Lloyd said, glancing repressively at me. "You all right?" he asked, as Max lurched to one side.

"I'm fucking fine. Lloyd," he said, slinging an arm heavily around Lloyd's shoulders, "Lloydy, you know the bit of St. John Passion I played this morning—d'you remember?" He sang a couple of lines, his voice clear and tuneful in the empty Hexagon.

"Yeah, I remember—"

"I've played that piece *dozens* of times. I know it like the *back of my hand*," Max said, holding his right hand up to the darkening sky, "but today I made a mistake. Bars six to nine . . . I fucked them up. My fingers still aren't right." His face crumpled. "Did you notice?"

Lloyd hesitated. "No, mate. It was beautiful." He reached out, his hand brushing the curve of Max's jaw, but within seconds Max had pulled away, and was lurching across the Hexagon toward the Main House. Lloyd stared after him for a moment.

"Come on." I pushed open the door to Columbus House, and he followed me inside, to the small lobby where the signing-in sheets were. We heard music and laughter coming from the Common Room to the left. Lloyd peered around the door.

"He's not in there."

"Let's check upstairs." We glanced at the room list at the foot of the stairs. As a Senior Patrol member, Gerald's name was among those at the top of the list, in a single room.

We slipped up the stairs, glad that there was nobody around. Visiting other Houses without good reason was contrary to the segregationist policy of High Realms, and generally warranted a WP. When we got to the top floor, Lloyd marched up to Gerald's door, his fist raised ready to knock, but I grabbed his arm. "We need to take it easy. Not . . . scare him."

"He won't be scared," Lloyd replied scornfully, and before I could say anything else he'd thumped on the door. There was a pause of a few seconds, and then Gerald opened it. His face hardened.

"We've come to talk to you." Lloyd lowered his voice, glancing around the empty corridor. "Can we come in?"

Gerald hesitated. He looked even wearier than he had done on the threshold of the clocktower room a couple of hours ago. His eyelids were swollen, and now that we were close up I saw that his face was creased with premature lines. To my great surprise, he shrugged.

I'd never been in a Senior Patrol bedroom before, and my first thought was that it would be worth propping up the tyranny of High Realms just to get one. Gerald's room had a high ceiling and wood paneling like the Main House, but the more modern feel of the Hexagon was evident in the vast window that took up most of the back wall. Lloyd and I stared at the view. It encompassed the paddocks, the Chapel, and miles and miles of green fields in which sheep were scattered in the tranquil January dusk. The neatly made bed was a single like ours, but the other furniture was more grand: a larger desk, an armchair, and a handsome wardrobe whose doors Gerald had covered with postcards and drawings. Moving closer, I saw that the postcards were mostly reproductions of famous paintings of horses. I recognized *Whistlejacket* and some anatomical drawings that I thought might be by da Vinci. Gerald had painstakingly copied each of them in pencil or pen, creating a gallery that must have taken him hundreds of hours.

"What do you want to talk about?" Gerald's voice jolted me back to reality. I turned to see him standing with his back to the window, his arms folded. The sleeves of his overalls were tied around his waist, and he was wearing his usual grubby T-shirt.

Lloyd sat down on Gerald's desk chair. "Have you told anyone what you saw this afternoon?"

"Nope." I felt a premature rush of relief, which was tainted by spotting an empty bottle of communion wine on the desk behind Lloyd. Max's stained lips swam in my mind's eye.

"Well, that's good." Lloyd crossed his legs, leaning back slightly. "Wanna sit down?" he asked Gerald, indicating the armchair.

"Fuck off."

"Suit yourself. I'll get to the point." Lloyd's eyes were fixed on Gerald. "The thing is, mate," he said, "we can't allow you to tell anyone about Marta."

"*Allow* me?"

Lloyd shrugged. "You're not to fucking tell anyone, OK?"

"Or what?"

"Or I will make your life a misery."

"Nice try. My life is already a heap of shit." Gerald's tone was bitter, almost despairing. I looked at Lloyd. He was going about this entirely the wrong way, but I couldn't work out how to intervene.

There was a short silence. "OK," said Lloyd. "We'll make it worth your while."

Gerald glanced at him. "How?"

"Well—how much do you want?"

There was another long silence in which Gerald and I stared at Lloyd. After a few moments, Gerald said politely, "My parents have a forty-thousand-acre farm and three houses. I'm an only child. I'm all right for money, thanks."

"Right." Lloyd chewed his lip. "Fine." There was another uncomfortable silence. I was about to speak when Gerald crossed the room to his bed, bending down to pull something out from underneath.

"I've got something to show you," he said. He was holding an art portfolio. "This is my A-Level coursework," he said. "Worked on it all last term and finished it over Christmas. It's due in tomorrow."

"OK." Lloyd nodded. He glanced at me, clearly perplexed. There was a long pause in which Gerald appeared to be waiting for something. He looked from me to Lloyd with an air of expectation that was almost pleading.

Finally, and very reluctantly, I asked, "Can we have a look?"

Gerald passed the bulky portfolio to me, and I took it to the desk. I untied the black ribbon that bound the folder. The first page comprised one large photograph of a naked woman lying on a satin-covered bed, her legs wide apart and her finger placed coyly on her lips.

I looked up at Gerald. "What the hell—"

"Look at the rest of it."

Slowly, Lloyd and I turned the heavy parchment pages. Gerald's portfolio had been ravaged of its original work and plastered with pornography. In some cases the images had been carelessly pasted over drawings that Gerald had made directly on the paper, the edges of his meticulous work still visible. In other places, pieces that he had stuck in had been ripped out and replaced with glossy sheets from magazines. As I turned the pages, the pictures became more sordid and offensive. The women's poses became demeaning rather than sultry; they were forced into grotesque positions; their eyes were trapped and unhappy as they performed acts that made my skin prickle with embarrassment. The final three images were of the same, very young woman. In the first photo she cowered against a wall, her eyes wide. In the second, she had been flung onto her back, handcuffed. The third showed her being penetrated by a man whose back was to the camera. I turned the page, feeling sick to my stomach, and saw a scrawled message on the final sheet. *Some new material for you. The closest you'll ever get.*

Lloyd and I looked up at Gerald. He was watching us closely, his eyes glistening. Lloyd glanced down again, at the handwriting on the final page.

"So," said Gerald, "there you go." He rummaged under the bed again and withdrew a plastic bag from a supermarket, tied at the top. He undid the knot and showed us the mass of shredded paper inside. "They were my drawings," he said. His voice shook slightly. "I don't see why I should help you," he told Lloyd baldly, "when you're in league with the person who did this."

Lloyd swallowed. I longed for him to try to deny Max's involvement, but he did not. "What do you want me to do?" he asked quietly.

"Get him to leave me alone."

"How can I do that?"

"If you want your little friend to stay safe, you'll think of a way."

"I'm not in league with him," said Lloyd suddenly. "I'd never do anything like—"

"Don't give me that shit!" Suddenly Gerald was shouting, his pale face flooded with color. "You're *fucking* him, aren't you?" Lloyd stared at him. "I've known Max Masters longer than you have, *mate*—I know what he's like. He and I were actually *friends*, once."

"What the fuck?"

"First Form—we were in the same dorm. Max used to be in Columbus. Bet he didn't tell you that." Lloyd shook his head, and Gerald sneered at him. "Oh, yes. We were good mates—until he decided he wanted to get in with the cool kids. He started putting it about that I was after Genevieve Lock's sister."

"And were you?"

"No, I fucking wasn't! Persie and I were *friends*, OK? She loved horses; she hung around the stables all the time. That's how I know about the room in the clocktower—she found it, she used to go up there to get away from it all. One day I saw her run into Block C, crying. I followed her, to check she was OK. I saw her going up the stairs, so I went up, too, to comfort her. Max saw us coming out of the stable later on." Gerald's expression was full of pain. "He didn't want to be friends with me anymore, but he wouldn't let me have another friend, either. *He* has to be the one people want to be around; *he* has to be Mr. Popular. At any fucking cost."

Lloyd swallowed. "What happened after Persie died?"

"Max ramped it up. Told Jolyon and the others I'd been harassing her. Which I never, ever did." He stared at us, his eyes full of tears, and I found that I believed him. "Dr. Reza found out and got him moved to Raleigh, away from me, but it was too late. I've been treated like shit ever since."

I glanced at Lloyd, who looked crestfallen. He hadn't known any of this, I could tell. I felt a jolt of pity for him, but I knew we had to focus on Marta. Lloyd swallowed. "I'll talk to him. I don't know how much good it'll do, but if it means you won't tell anyone about Marta, I'll try."

"You've got two days." Gerald's voice was harsh. "Two days to get him to come to me and apologize for all the shit he's put me through. *On his knees.* Or I'll go straight to the police about her. I'd enjoy that, after what they put me through before. *Don't* tell me you haven't got the influence," he said loudly, as Lloyd started to argue, "because it won't wash. I've got the measure of both of you, OK? He never wanted Genevieve Lock for a second, the manipulative bastard. He wants *you*."

There was a short silence, and then Gerald marched over to the door and opened it. "Get out," he told us, his eyes full of tears. He was still clutching the carrier bag of his ripped-up artwork. "Get the fuck out of my room."

Lloyd and I stumbled through the pitch dark to the Main House and then up the stairs to Hillary, not speaking. The temperature had dropped, but my relief at reaching the warmth of the Common Room was short-lived: we were late for roll call, and Major Gregory gave us both a WP. "Where is Mr. Lynch?" he demanded.

We guessed at once that Sami had gone to the clocktower. "Perhaps he's got a late rugby practice, sir," said Lloyd feebly, but there were no Games on Sunday evening, and Major Gregory knew it.

"You will spend the evening in my office until Mr. Lynch returns," he said.

So Lloyd and I were back on the hard chairs. It was maddening not to be able to take any action, given how little time we had. After about half an hour, Major Gregory began to make phone calls to different parts of the school in pursuit of Sami. We listened as he phoned Reception, the Straker Library, even the Gatehouse. Finally, and very reluctantly, he phoned the infirmary. "I see," he said curtly, after a short conversation with Dr. Reza. "Send him back as soon as you've finished with him." Lloyd and I glanced at each other in surprise. "He's being treated for an allergic reaction," Major Gregory told us dismissively. "Go to dinner. Your WPs will be on Tuesday afternoon."

Lloyd went straight to the Dining Hall in search of Max, but I had no appetite. I went to 1A, which was freezing cold, and tried to do my prep for the following day, but I was too full of worry about Marta, disgust at what Max and his cronies had done to Gerald, and tension about what might follow to be able to concentrate. I hated my inability to do anything constructive, and knowing that Sami was not in fact with Marta made it a lot worse. I wanted to talk to Lloyd about how he intended to approach Max, but I heard Major Gregory's heavy footsteps in the boys' corridor above, and didn't dare go upstairs to find him.

In the end I went to bed very early, planning to sleep for a few hours and go to the clocktower in the middle of the night. I got out all of my warm clothes—some for me to wear, and extra for Marta given the drop in temperature—and set my alarm for two o'clock. I fell asleep almost immediately.

I was awoken by the pressure of a body on the bed beside me. I jumped, shifting away. "Rose, it's me." It was Sami, his voice soft. He sat down next to me on top of the blankets. I could just make out that he was wearing his overcoat and woollen hat. "Can I put the light on?"

I nodded, and he switched on my bedside lamp. His face was pale; almost white, and his clothes were damp. "It's snowing," he said quietly.

"How come Dr. Reza let you come back in the middle of the night?"

"Dr. Reza?"

"You were in the infirmary . . ."

"No, I wasn't." Sami frowned. "I've been with Marta." He pressed his lips together, and I saw a new, dire strain in his face. "Rosie—we have to tell someone about her. Tomorrow. It's gone too far."

"What's happened?" I sat up, pulling my pajamas straight.

The mystery of the infirmary could wait. "Lloyd and I spoke to Gerald, and I think—"

"She's cut her arm," Sami said.

"But Lloyd took away—"

"She pulled a spring out of her mattress," he interrupted me flatly, "and she used the sharp end to gouge several times into the skin of her bicep and remove a chunk of flesh about this big." He held his thumb and forefinger almost an inch apart without looking at me.

For a moment I could not speak. Then, "Did you—help her?"

He dragged his eyes from the opposite wall to find mine. "What do you think?" he asked quietly. He looked old; resentful. "What else have I ever done, Rose? I'm going to be a doctor." His voice cracked. "I know a bit of first aid, so I could just about stop the bleeding, and I could clean the wound, and I could make a bandage out of a spare shirt, and I could sit with her until it bled through the cotton . . . and I could compress it again, and clean it again, and wrap a new bandage around it—" He let out a small sob. "But I couldn't make her say a word, Rose, or look at me for a single second, or persuade her to leave that awful room with me—"

"Sami. Sami." Helplessly, I reached for him. He was freezing cold. A tear ran over the back of my hand. "Sami, please. It's going to be OK."

"No, it's not." He turned to face me, and my hand dropped. "I'm so frightened for her, Rosie," he said. "I'm frightened she won't survive. I've never been so frightened in my life. I think . . . I think it's over, Rose. We need help. It's time to give in."

We sat in silence for a moment. As I took in what Sami had said, I realized that he'd voiced the very thing I had been frightened of since October, when Marta had told us what her father had done.

"OK," I said. "OK." I reached for him, properly this time, and helped him undo the buttons on his coat. I pulled it from his shoulders, and he took off his hat and got under the covers beside me. He put his head down on the pillow, and I laid mine down next to him, and we looked at each other in the lamplight. I felt a complicated relief.

"I'll go back to the clocktower soon," he said, his voice low with exhaustion. "She can't be on her own."

"I'll come with you." I put my hand on his cheek again. "You're still cold."

"You're warm," he said. Very gently, he moved his hand so that it rested on my side, just above my hip. I felt the chill of his skin through the fabric of my pajamas, but I didn't resent it. "I love your warmth, Rose," he said.

"I'm worried I'm cold. It's painful, but I can't change." The truth came: familiar, yet unspoken for so long.

"No." Very gently, he slid his hand under my pajama top. "There's nothing cold about you. You're warm, and you're brave, and you care." His hand moved down slightly. "I couldn't have done any of this without you."

The weight of his hand against my skin was comforting: more than comforting. I looked at Sami, at the shape of his face, his mouth, nose, eyes; the features I knew so well. He was so good, so unselfish. He had never harmed; only helped, and loved, and carried on loving. "I want you," I said.

He didn't look away. There was no trace of greed, or

satisfaction in his expression as he moved his hand lower, and said quietly, "Are you sure?"

"Yes. But slowly." It was so easy to tell him. I had thought it would be the worst thing in the world to have to ask: that I would be paralyzed with shame. But the opposite was happening to my body as Sami moved closer and kissed me, long and tender, and his hand roamed deeper, his every motion gentle, his eyes open to see as well as feel my reaction; to know, and to respond. His movements were not expert, not clumsy, but entirely his own. And instead of tension, loneliness, and fear, I felt warm and alive.

Even a little later, when I felt a short, sharp pain—the sensation I had thought I would never be able to face—I felt strong. A new power came to me as I held Sami in my arms, his body now as warm as mine, and we rocked against each other, fierce and free. I felt Sami's tears fall on my skin as he smoothed my hair back from my forehead. "It'll be OK," I told him, and in that moment I believed what I was saying. "We will be OK."

Chapter 20

As is so often the case, things seemed very different in the morning. Sami and I stayed in the clocktower until six o'clock, keeping watch over Marta, who lay silent and sleepless on her mattress, unresponsive even as we outlined what Gerald had demanded from Lloyd. Her arm would not stop bleeding. We ministered to it as best we could, unwrapping the soaked material and swabbing it with salt water, but the wound was even deeper than Sami had thought. We ran out of clean shirts to make bandages from. In the end, Sami cut a towel into strips, which we wrapped tightly around her arm.

It was still snowing as we rushed back to Hillary for early roll call. I felt exhausted, almost delirious, but I had to get dressed in my uniform, wash my face, brush my teeth, and present myself in the Common Room. Things were already worse than they'd ever been, but I tried to tell myself that the nightmare was coming to an end. We were going to bow out, for Marta's own good.

Lloyd watched Sami and me coldly as Major Gregory took roll call. Afterward, as the herd started to move toward breakfast, he beckoned to us. I looked at Sami, and he shrugged. *Fine,* the shrug seemed to say. *Let's get it over with.* We followed Lloyd to a quiet corridor two stories below Hillary. He paused next to a window, leaning on the radiator beneath it. I looked out at the grounds, now cloaked in whiteness beneath a heavy gray sky, and realized I'd completely forgotten to go to hockey that morning.

Lloyd fixed Sami with an unfriendly stare. "You've made a quick recovery."

"I wasn't in the infirmary."

"How mysterious." Lloyd looked angry. "I *told* you not to go to the clocktower. We have to follow a plan, Sami."

"Yeah, right. Go along with your shit plans while she gets closer and closer to hacking off her own arm. Have you spoken to Max?"

"I tried. He was too drunk. I took away everything Marta could've used to—"

"Lloyd, we're going to tell someone where she is," Sami interrupted. "Rose and I have decided. We're going to tell someone today."

Lloyd folded his arms, staring at us. "Fuck me," he said after a few moments. "That is the worst timing I've ever heard. Absolutely appalling."

"Lloyd," I said, "she's hurting herself. We can't deal with it anymore. She's in danger—"

"And you think turning her in will stop her doing that? Reckon she'll be looked after better by other people, do you? Reckon they'll care more about her than we do?"

"She needs *medical help*," Sami said, his voice trembling. "She needs *treatment*—"

"She'd be sectioned," Lloyd said loudly. "They'd take one look at her and section her."

"And that would be fine! If it got her the help she needs, it'd be for the best. Not every state-funded institution is evil, Lloyd, despite what you want us to think—"

"Oh, give me a break." Lloyd spoke over Sami, his tone harsh. "You think you're so *reasonable*, don't you? So *strategic*. If I thought it'd help," he went on, pointing disdainfully at Sami, "I'd remind you that it wouldn't do your chances of getting into medical school any good if you were arrested. Have you ever tallied up how many lies we've told to the police? Have you stopped to think about what it would look like for us to turn her in *right now,* just after Gerald found her—like our hands were forced?" Sami and I stared at him, horrified. "No, I didn't think so. But none of that matters compared to what really gets to me, which is how *fucking* cowardly you two are. This isn't really about getting Marta help, is it? It's just that you two've got scared, just when she needs us most."

"I'm not scared for myself," Sami retorted. "I want to look after her myself, but she needs proper help."

"Yeah, and handing her over to the authorities without her permission is taking away the thing she wants most—her freedom. Freedom to decide stuff for herself," Lloyd snapped. "Oh, and do enlighten me. Who were you actually thinking of telling? Your precious mentor, I suppose?"

"She'd help us. I'm sure she would. She's got a duty of care—"

"I agree, she *might* help us. But you know what that duty of care means, Sami? It means her *telling other people*. And *other people* means Dr. Wardlaw and the fucking police. *And* your parents. And you know what—if Dr. Reza's as caring as you seem to think, if she's as good and kind and reasonable as you say—what would she think of the state Marta's in? She's hardly going to think you've done a brilliant job looking after her, is she, if she saw her arm and the rest of the—*get away from me*," he spat, as Sami took a step toward him, his jaw clenched. "Don't touch me, you idiot. You don't want anything else on your conscience, do you?"

At that moment the bell rang, shrill and unforgiving. Sami stepped away from Lloyd, looking devastated. Lloyd glanced at his reflection in the window, straightening his tie. "We are not losing this battle," he told us. "Not on my watch. I'm going to talk to Max today. Fill Sami in about that, will you?" he added to me, and strode away down the corridor.

The sky cleared as the day continued, and winter sun glinted on the snow, sharp and brilliant. I sat next to the window in Math, feeling the chill of the air through the glass, trying to stay awake.

I couldn't concentrate on my work, instead dwelling on the past twenty-four hours. Events were spiraling out of our control, in a new and more frightening way than before. I tried to think about what was genuinely best for Marta. It had always been hard to separate this from the morass of other considerations that swirled around our decisions: what Marta wanted; what was actually possible; what would hurt or inconvenience the fewest people. In this case, Marta's silence made it harder to know what was right. Part of me agreed with Sami that she was beyond our help—that she was a greater danger to herself than she'd ever been—but we had thought both of those things before, and had somehow pushed on.

Much as I hated to admit it to myself, I believed Lloyd had a point about Marta's right to choose.

My mind was so full, and my anxiety so acute that I barely thought about the fact that I had had sex with Sami until lunchtime, when I ate for the first time since one o'clock the previous day, and my brain unfogged a little. As my plate emptied and my mind cleared, I became more aware of my body. It felt more or less the same as yesterday. I thought of Marta, of the gaping disparity between our experiences, and felt a sadness for her that had a different complexion to the kind I'd known before. I looked over at Sami, who was eating lunch a few tables away with Ingrid—the sight of whom gave me brief pause for thought—and felt a rush of affection for him, for what we had done, for the pleasure he had given me. I felt no guilt or shame. I watched Sami for a while longer, wondering whether doubts would march into my mind, but nothing happened. It felt simple, and it felt done with.

I left the Dining Hall in search of Lloyd. I was deeply annoyed with him, but I wanted to find out whether he'd managed to talk to Max. I tracked him down in the Salon, where he was practicing Brahms on the grand piano. When he admitted that he hadn't spoken to Max we argued again: fiercely, implacably, careless with Marta's name and each other's feelings. As I left the Salon, my eyes stinging with tears, I saw Sylvia halfway up the Eiger, pausing in exactly the spot from which Lloyd said Genevieve had fallen.

She looked up at me, her dark eyes soft and serious in the alabaster paleness of her face. Slowly, she climbed a few more stairs, until she was standing just below me. "Hello," she said.

My vision was still blurred by incipient tears. "Hi."

"Is everything all right?"

I began to see Sylvia more clearly. I recognized her expression as similar to when I'd fallen over during the hockey match: it was full of concern. "I'm fine," I said. Then, suddenly, "I'll come riding with you tomorrow," I told her. I wanted to mollify her, in case she'd heard Marta's name, but it was much more than that. Seeing Sylvia in front of me in the deserted Lower Gallery, the strain and anxiety I felt was dissolving, supplanted by a warm feeling in the pit of my stomach. "I've got a WP from Major Gregory, but after that."

Sylvia smiled, and for a moment she was a different person. "I'll speak to him," she said. "I'll tell him you're seconded to me. Then we'll have more daylight."

I nodded. She took a step toward me, but at that moment the bell rang for fourth study, and she turned away, striding along the Lower Gallery with her usual imperiousness.

That night Lloyd finally tracked Max down, and Sami and I stayed with Marta in the clocktower again, doing a four-hour shift each. I took the second half of the night, relieving Sami at two o'clock. He pointed silently to a new pile of bandages and left the room, his shoulders slumped in exhaustion. I sat down on the concrete floor next to the mattress, huddled inside my High Realms winter coat.

Marta hadn't eaten or even spoken since being discovered by Gerald. Now she was fast asleep, her face gray against the crumpled sleeping bag. Every so often she coughed in her sleep, the sound hoarse and unsettling. Her eyelids rippled as she dreamed. I watched her for a few minutes, unable to envy her troubled repose, despite my own extreme tiredness. *This could be the last night,* I thought to myself, hating my ambivalence about that prospect. I got out my prep.

A few hours later, just as I was nodding off against the whitewashed wall, I heard the mattress creak. I opened my eyes to see Marta trying to look through the clock face, her hand cupped against the glass. It was pitch dark outside.

"Morning, Mar." I spoke softly, so as not to startle her.

She turned around. The upper arm of her sweater was stained a deep red where the bandage had soaked through. "What's the time?" she asked quietly.

"It's quarter past five." We looked at each other, acknowledging how few hours were left before Gerald's deadline. I shifted, my body stiff after so many hours on the floor. "Can I look at your arm? Just to—"

She looked down at her bloodstained sleeve as though it was nothing to do with her. Wordlessly, she walked over and sat down in front of me. She pulled her sweater over her head and sat there in a short-sleeved Raleigh lacrosse shirt. She did not shiver.

As I peeled off the makeshift dressing, I had to stop myself gagging. She'd aggravated the wound in some way, and now it was even deeper and more jagged than before. Not knowing whether I was doing the right thing, I swabbed the edges with a clean piece of shirt, while Marta sat there mutely, looking to one side. Then she turned to me. "What's going to happen today?"

I couldn't think what to tell her. *Whatever happens, you will be safe,* I wanted to say. *We will always look after you.* But I could guarantee neither statement. "What do you want to happen?"

"I want Lloyd to choose me," she said, "and I want to stay sane." Her eyes gleamed in the light of my torch. "But most of all, I want to live. I really, really want to live, Rose."

We sat together, the cold air pressing against us. I looked at Marta, trying to see her clearly, properly, objectively. There were many things I wanted to say, but none of them were fair; none of them were appropriate for her to hear in her current state. *You want to live, but you're destroying yourself. You want to live, but at what cost? You want to live, but you don't care what happens to us.*

Then I realized that there was only one thing that mattered, and only one thing I could control. I reached for her hand. "I want you to live, too," I said.

The morning light came, and with it normal life, in which I somehow had to participate. I mucked out the horses and went to hockey. It was getting harder and harder to feel any connection with my surroundings. The sense that we were running out of time, that by the end of the day we could all have been arrested, or expelled, or both—that all our efforts for Marta could have been for nothing—was pressing down on me like a giant pair of hands. My knees felt weak. I wanted to lie down in the snow and sleep for a hundred years.

Bella wouldn't allow me to practice with the team, instead ordering me to run fifty laps around the pitch as a punishment for missing the previous session. I stumbled around the perimeter, slipping on patches of compacted snow. The cold air stung my face. *Wake up,* it seemed to say. *You need your wits about you.*

Then it was time for lessons, and I went to them. I listened to the Mags, I wrote down answers, I handed in the bad prep I'd done—but everything felt as though it was happening to somebody else. At Elevenses, with six hours to go, I threw up in a bathroom on the third floor, and then slumped on the linoleum, resting my aching head against the cool tiles of the wall.

After that, and again at lunchtime I went to look for Lloyd. He was nowhere to be found. I wanted an update; to find out whether he had made any progress with Max, but there was no sign of either of them. The first lesson after lunch was English, but both Max and Lloyd were absent. Sylvia was late, and when she arrived Miss Kepple immediately sent her to report Lloyd's absence to Major Gregory. Sami and I stared at each other across the horseshoe of desks, unable to concentrate on our essays. I could tell that Sami was just as terrified as I was.

After class, Sami and I trudged along the corridor toward the Eiger. We were exhausted, and our practice essays had been deemed substandard by Miss Kepple. I felt a quick tap on my shoulder, and turned to find Sylvia behind me, her cheeks slightly flushed. "See you at the stables in fifteen minutes?"

"What?"

"We're going riding, remember?"

"You're *what*?" Sami looked scandalized—*how could you, right now?*—but Sylvia paid him no attention.

"You said you'd come," she told me strictly. "I've worked it out with the Major. Now go and get changed."

Twenty minutes later I met her outside the Senior Patrol stable. Sylvia was holding the halters of two horses: her own, and a much smaller one. It was a pale gray, and looked almost sleepy as it stood patiently next to Cleopatra. The latter stamped restlessly, jerking her head against the halter. Sylvia patted her neck.

"Relax," she told her, as she led the horses over to the mounting block. "On you get," she said, guiding the gray horse into position. "Beau's very chilled out," she added.

I stood next to the mounting block, unsure what to do. Sylvia motioned encouragingly, but when I didn't move, her eyes narrowed. "You have sat on a horse before?"

"No."

She frowned. "But everyone at High Realms has riding lessons. As soon as they arrive. *Everybody* here knows the basics," she said, as though I were trying to trick her.

"Well, I don't," I replied, irritated. "Gerald never offered us lessons."

At the mention of Gerald's name, a flicker of something passed across her face: an emotion more acute than annoyance. "Well, there's no time like the present," she said after a moment. "Stand on the mounting block, put your left foot in that stirrup, and hoist yourself up."

I stared at Beau, who blinked. *Nothing to do with me,* he seemed to say. "But—"

"Oh, come on, Rose," Sylvia snapped, as though I were about to spoil her plan. But she put her hand out for me to hold as I stepped hesitantly onto the mounting block, and didn't smirk as I swung myself clumsily onto Beau's back. I felt dizzy; far higher up than I had expected. My instinct was to lean forward and put my arms around Beau's neck, or simply get off, but Sylvia had other ideas.

"Put your foot in the other stirrup," she ordered, before

hopping nimbly onto her own horse. Briefly, she showed me how to hold the reins, and how to squeeze Beau's flanks with my heels. We proceeded sedately out of the courtyard, under the clocktower arch, and onto the path that ran alongside Donny Stream. Beau followed Cleopatra, so that I did not even need to steer. After a minute or so Sylvia glanced behind her.

"There's no need to look so worried," she said, her tone teasing. I smiled weakly, concentrating on staying upright on Beau's swaying back. I looked down at Donny Stream, unable to hear its usual pleasant, gurgling sound, and saw that it had frozen over.

We continued along the path for a mile or so, to the edge of the Estate. Here Sylvia slid off Cleopatra and opened a gate for me to pass through. She jumped back onto her horse and grinned at me.

"Ready to trot?" she asked, and clicked her tongue without waiting for an answer. Cleopatra set off at a smart pace, and my reins jerked as Beau followed. Suddenly we were going much faster, and the bouncing had become more like jolting. We were crossing a huge, snowy field, and I was dazzled by the sun on the pure white of the ground. Then Sylvia was cantering, her hair flying out from under her hat as she rode toward a thicket of trees on the edge of a hill. My thighs were agony as I finally caught up with her, cold sweat stinging the back of my neck.

"That wasn't funny."

She shrugged. "Sorry," she said unapologetically.

She led me through the trees and onto a bridle path that snaked gently up the hill. There was nobody around. Everything was covered in snow: the branches of the tall trees, the fences, the high verges. The air was cold and clear. I gulped it down, my sweaty hands gripping the reins, feeling the morning's nausea finally recede. But nothing was sorted. We were facing our direst challenge yet; were probably mere hours from being expelled, or arrested, or worse. Marta was alone and terrified, and here I was, out riding with Sylvia as if nothing had happened. I felt ashamed.

"Sylvia," I called. We were nearly at the top of the hill. She turned in her saddle. "I want to go back."

"Just a bit farther. The view's amazing at the top. That's Donny Stream, you know," she added, gesturing to a bright, sinuous river in the distance.

"I have to get back to school."

She frowned. "Why?"

"I've got—something to sort out. With Gerald."

His name slipped out unbidden, as though my mind wanted to unburden itself of just one secret; to mitigate my torment by sharing it. Perhaps, too, I wanted to punish Sylvia: for my chafed thighs, and my aching legs and lower back, caused by her refusal to slow down. I'd guessed something was amiss between them, and when I said his name again I was sure of it, watching her face go as white as the snow that surrounded us. Slowly, she dismounted.

"Get down," she said, coming over to Beau. She held out her hand, and I obeyed her, sliding unsteadily down to the hard ground. Sylvia tied the horses to a tree, and then returned to me, gesturing to a bank below a drystone wall. Sprigs of heather were poking stiffly from beneath the snow. "We can sit on my coat."

We looked out over the glittering white valley. I saw High

Realms in the middle distance, the clocktower spire glinting in the winter sun. My stomach was churning again. Sylvia glanced at me. "I don't know what your business is with Gerald," she said quietly, "but I need to warn you about him."

"Warn me?"

"Yes." She stared over the valley: the jagged patchwork of snowy fields, and the glistening ribbon of the river that Donny Stream grew into. "He's dangerous, Rose. He's completely—"

"Max and your lot are tormenting him," I interrupted. "Do you know what Max did to his art portfolio?"

"I heard about it." Sylvia bit her lip. "Max is becoming a bit of an issue."

"An *issue*? Sylvia, you've been protecting him since October. And you're Vice-Captain General. If you wanted to stop him from bullying Gerald, you could. And if Gerald's dangerous, it's partly your fault."

She looked as though I'd hit her. "Don't say that," she said, her voice shaking slightly. "Please don't say that." I was shocked to see her eyes fill with tears. "You're right," she said, "I *have* been trying to protect Max. I don't care about him, but I care about Gin. I care about keeping Max safe so that she can make a proper decision about him when she comes out of the hospital. I know I'm failing, but—"

"He doesn't want her, Sylvia." I thought of what Max himself had told us about Sylvia's fixation on loyalty. "He needs to let her go."

"Rose—please." She looked at me, her expression sad and serious. "You may be right. I don't know for certain—nobody really knows that except Max, do they? But I do know that *she* loved—*loves*—him. He was her lifeline, Rose."

"You're talking about Genevieve's sister." Sylvia nodded mutely. "Did you know her?"

"Yes," she said. She stared out over the fields. "Yes, of course I did."

"Did you like her?"

"I liked her very much." Sylvia paused, her fists clenched on her knees. "Genevieve adored her. When Persie died, I didn't think Gin would be able to carry on. I thought she'd have to leave High Realms. I tried to help her, but really it was Max who got her through it."

"Gerald told me Max spread rumors about him and Genevieve's sister," I said.

Sylvia hesitated. "That's true. He did."

"And did you—"

"I didn't join in, if that's what you're thinking. I don't gossip. Anyway, I knew Persie and Gerald were just friends. Awkward misfits together—although she was worth ten of him." Sylvia blinked, and looked sideways at me. "I knew he wasn't into her because he was always after me," she said haltingly. "*Constantly*. I didn't know how to handle it."

"What do you mean?"

"Before I was with Bella," she replied, "he used to ask me out all the time. He wouldn't take no for an answer. I suppose I wasn't very kind to him about it, but I didn't know how else to be. I was trying to work out who *I* was—what I wanted—and being pestered by him constantly didn't help. I started to get a bit scared of him. I still am."

I watched Sylvia for a few moments, realizing how significant it was for her to admit any kind of weakness, let alone fear. "What's he done to you?" I asked at last.

She was silent for a moment, her hands curled around her knees. Then she dipped her head, not looking at me. "He assaulted me. A few days before the Christmas Ball."

"*What?*"

She ignored me. "He asked me to go with him, as his date. I said no, of course." She shrugged bitterly. "I think it was one rejection too many."

"What happened?"

Sylvia glanced at me. "Do you really want to know?"

I didn't want to hear it, but I needed to know the truth. "If you can tell me," I said, "then yes, I want to know."

"I was working on my own in one of the Reading Rooms," she said quietly. "He tracked me down. He asked me to go to the party with him, and I said no. Told him I thought he was acting desperate. Told him we'd been through it all before. I said too much—I've only got myself to blame." She stopped, and looked at me. "I don't know if I can say it."

"Tell me."

"I'm frightened—"

"I'm here."

"He held me down on the chair," she said abruptly, "and he forced my legs apart. He—he pushed his fist inside me. Said— *this is what you like, right?* Fuck," Sylvia said, tears streaming down her cheeks. "Fuck, Rose, it was so painful. I can't describe it. It was like—no other pain I've ever known. I didn't stop bleeding for days. I thought I was going to have to go to the hospital." Suddenly she retched, her whole body buckling, and she turned away from me, her hand over her mouth.

I gave her a few moments, and then I reached out and pulled her back around to face me. I looked into her eyes, allowing her to see that I had understood, that I was sorry, that I still wanted her. She leaned forward and rested her forehead on my shoulder. Her body heaved with one sob, and then she was still.

After a minute she sat up, gripping my cold fingers in hers. "So you see, Rose," she said thickly, "you need to be careful. I don't want you to get hurt. I've got my revenge, but if he hurt you—"

"What do you mean?" Her face had hardened as she spoke.

"I couldn't let it slide, Rose. It took me a while to think of the right punishment, but today I finally sorted it."

"What have you done?"

"I got him demoted," she said. She wiped her eyes on her sleeve. "He's not in the Senior Patrol anymore. He's not Head of Horses."

"*How?*"

"It doesn't matter." She turned around, checking on the two horses. "They'll have taken away his gown by now," she said flatly. "Hey—what're you doing?"

I'd scrambled to my feet. The knowledge of what Gerald had done to Sylvia, combined with his punishment, had filled me with a new kind of fear. I had to get back to school, to intervene in whatever was going on between Lloyd, Max, and Gerald. "I've got to go," I said, looking down at her. "Right now. I can't explain," I told her as she started to protest, "but please—it's important. *Please*, Sylvia. Help me get back."

She stared at me. "OK," she said, after a few moments. "Let's go."

We both rode back to High Realms on Cleopatra, leaving Beau tied up on the hillside. "I'll go back for him," Sylvia said, "and walk them both home." *Home.* I had never thought of High Realms as home.

As we cantered into the small courtyard enclosed by the barns and workshop, I saw Lloyd up ahead, running toward Block C. I struggled to dismount from behind Sylvia. "Lloyd!"

He turned around, looking puzzled. Then he saw me and came toward us, beaming. "Ro," he said, his eyes flicking between me and Sylvia, "Ro, what're you doing?"

"I need to talk to you." I tumbled off Cleopatra's back, landing heavily on the gravel. Lloyd put out his hand to steady me.

"Ro," he said again, "it's OK. I've done it—I've persuaded him—everything's all right." I stared at him. "Everything's going to be all right," he repeated. "Sami knows, too."

"All right?"

"Yes." I leaned against him for a moment, unable to believe he had managed it. "Max is looking for him now," Lloyd said, and I needed no further explanation. Max was apologizing to Gerald. Marta was safe, for now.

"Have you told her?"

"I was just going there." Lloyd gripped my hand. "Come with me?"

Sylvia frowned, her boots crunching on the gravel as she jumped down from Cleopatra. "What's going on?" she asked, but Lloyd and I were grinning at each other, and did not reply. "OK," she said after a moment. "I'm going to get a spare bridle, and then—"

"Thank you," I said, turning around. "Thank you so much for bringing me back." I took a step toward her and kissed her, long and hard, my hand gripping the back of her riding jacket. "See you later?"

"Yes," she said, looking stunned, but Lloyd and I were already running away across the courtyard toward the stables and Block C.

It is a mark of my naivety—stupidity, even—that Lloyd's news drove from my mind both what Gerald had done to Sylvia, and Sylvia's punishment of him. As we rushed into the stable, as we tugged at the plywood, even as we rushed up the concrete stairs, all I could think about was the relief, the joy that we were bringing Marta; the way her face would break into a smile when we told her; the gratitude she would feel . . . we had done it. We had saved her again.

Even when we opened the door of the clocktower room and saw Gerald in there, a part of my brain refused to believe that everything had not turned out all right. *Max has already spoken to him,* I thought. *He's already apologized, and Gerald has come to tell us he'll keep the secret.* It was absurd, but it was better than the reality, which my eyes and then my mind struggled to absorb: the clothes strewn on the floor, the tins that had been kicked aside and rolled into the corners, the empty and gleaming patch of floor where the mattress had moved or been moved over it.

Whenever anything very bad has happened to me after that day, I remember the immediate, sickening nostalgia of that moment. I remember longing to be the person I had been thirty seconds before, running up the stairs with no knowledge of what Gerald had done. I didn't want to turn the clock back, but rather move to a different time zone entirely; a parallel region in which Gerald had made a different decision—it *was* a decision—and had not raped Marta. I remember that Lloyd took even longer to accept it—kept asking what was going on, saying he didn't understand, even when we saw the stain on the sleeping bag; even when Gerald stood up from the upturned bucket he'd been sitting on, head in hands, and we saw that his belt was loose, that his chest and arms were smeared with blood from Marta's arm. "She fucking stinks," he told us.

And then there was Marta. She was still sitting—lying, really—on the mattress, slumped against the wall, wearing the thin lacrosse T-shirt. The bandage had fallen off her arm, and the wound was leaking blood down to her wrist, and over the towel she'd pulled over the lower half of her body. She looked up, but didn't seem to recognize me at first.

Gerald ran away. Lloyd and I sat with Marta, not saying anything. I remember that Lloyd went to fill the basin with water, and wordlessly put it next to Marta as though it was what she needed first. I remember thinking that she wouldn't want anyone near her, and keeping my distance, only asking once whether there was anything I could do for her. "Sit with me," she said quietly, and so I moved onto the mattress, sitting against the wall about a foot away from her. She curled up and rested her head in my lap. After a few minutes, when I was sure it wouldn't startle her, I put my hand on her head and stroked her cropped hair, trying to transmit tenderness through her scalp. We'd washed her hair just two days ago.

A few hours later, Marta asked Lloyd and me to leave. We were reluctant, but it seemed cruel to argue with her. As we walked numbly through the Hexagon, we heard someone calling our names, and I saw Sami burst out of the infirmary and run toward us. "Guys," he said, breathless and sweaty, "guys, something's happened—"

We looked at him, silent and heartbroken, and said nothing. Sami didn't seem to register our distress. "It's Professor De Luca," he said. "He's had another stroke—a bad one. He's in the hospital, he's unconscious. Dr. Reza said—she thinks it's likely, it's *very* likely . . . that he'll die." He stared at us, oblivious to our grief-stricken stupefaction, and spoke with reproachful urgency. "Don't you *see?* If he dies, Marta will be free! Genevieve's already forgiven her—she's not going to be prosecuted. It'll be over," Sami said, his eyes shining, "this whole thing, this whole nightmare—it'll be over forever." He reached for me and Lloyd, an arm around each of our shoulders, and pulled us toward him. "I love her," he said into Lloyd's coat. His voice was muffled, but I heard his relief, his ecstasy, even as something inside me broke. "I've always loved her. The minute she's free, I'll tell her. I'm going to tell her how much I love her."

PART IV

Chapter 21

If there is such a thing as a picturesque brawl, it took place at High Realms on a bitterly cold evening in January 2000.

The fight started on the snowy grass of the Hexagon. Seconds after Lloyd and I told Sami what Gerald had done, we glimpsed him trying to sneak back into Columbus House. Sami and Lloyd ran to him, dragging him back down the steps and into the middle of the courtyard. Blood splattered across the snow as Lloyd broke Gerald's nose with his first punch. The second strike was Gerald on Sami: a blow that flung Sami face-first into the snow.

Then Gerald ran, blood flying from his nose. We chased him through the Labyrinth, down Chapel Passage, and on to the drive. It was dusk: the sky a deep blue, the moon rising over the Main House. Patches of ice were forming on the ground. I remember skidding to a halt as Lloyd and Sami caught up with Gerald. I looked past the three of them to the Gatehouse. Beyond it was the road, and beyond the road were the high and peaceful hills of North Devon, their contours so familiar now. *Leave this place,* I thought. *Run away.* "Help us, Rose," Sami snarled, and I did.

We got Gerald under the arms and pulled him bodily up the steps of the Chapel. Nobody stopped us because nobody was there. Everybody was at prep or showering after Games or at a briefing in their Common Room or perhaps—this was High Realms, after all—keeping a low profile somewhere, avoiding other violence. I remember reaching behind me to push open the door, my fingers clammy on the gnarled wood, and the three of us hauling Gerald into the freezing and deserted antechapel. There, Lloyd pinned Gerald to the floor, a knee on each shoulder, and allowed Sami to hurt him. After a while, I couldn't watch.

I remember thinking, *Gerald is stronger than this*. I felt sure that he could have thrown Lloyd off, and easily wrestled Sami to the ground. Perhaps he was weakened by his broken nose, but I don't think so. He barely struggled as Sami kicked every inch of his body. As Gerald's resistance waned, so too did Sami's aggression. His desire to punish Gerald seemed to drain from him with the tears that were pouring down his bleeding cheeks, and he stumbled backward, crouching down with his head in his hands. "If you go near her again, I'll kill you," he moaned, and as I looked down at Gerald trapped beneath Lloyd, I knew that we had broken him.

Then Gerald did throw Lloyd off, but he didn't try to run away again. Instead he made for the tight spiral stairs that led to the organ loft. Despite his injuries, he got up them quickly. Lloyd chased him, yelling for Sami and me as he realized or guessed what Gerald was planning, and Sami and I scrambled up the stairs, too, and joined Lloyd in that tiny organ loft and together the three of us pulled Gerald back from the railing over which he was trying to climb with a view to throwing himself, head first, into the nave of the Chapel.

We sat together on the cold floor of the antechapel for half an hour after Gerald had stumbled away, until our next steps became urgent and unavoidable. Lloyd would take Sami to the infirmary—his lip was so badly split that it would need stitches—and I would go to Marta. "Don't tell her about her father," Sami implored me, and I nodded.

I would go to Marta. *I will go,* I told myself over and over again, as I stalled by going up to Hillary to change my blood-stained clothes. *I will go to see her,* I pledged as I dropped into the Dining Hall—it was my turn to get Marta's supper, after all—even as I sat there eating food I wasn't hungry for; even as I felt Sylvia's hand brush my shoulder as she passed me. After supper I walked straight out of the front door of the Main House and across the drive, not bothering to use the back route even though it was late. I wanted somebody to stop me, but nobody did. Evening duty had finished, and the stables were quiet.

Even as I entered the clocktower room, I wanted to leave. I hoped that Marta would tell me to go. She was lying on her side on a pile of cushions that she'd draped in towels, reading *The Importance of Being Earnest.* Bruises had formed around her mouth and on her cheeks. The little camping stove burned cozily next to her.

I sat down at the end of her makeshift bed and watched her read the play. She was completely absorbed in it, her eyes occasionally flickering with amusement. Then, just as I was about to offer her the food I'd brought—grapes, crackers, cereal bars—she suddenly groaned, sitting up and looking down at her lap.

"Fuck," I said, before I could stop myself. "Marta—"

"It's OK." She put the book down, shifting on the cushions. "It's OK," she repeated, her voice hoarse, but firm. "Pass me some of those bandages, would you, please? *Rose,*" she added, when I didn't move. She pointed to the strips of towel we'd made for her arm. I reached for a couple, noticing how depleted the pile was. She wiped up the blood as well as she could, and then held out her hand for more bandages.

"I could get—" I began, but she shook her head almost impatiently.

"Thanks, but these are better." She put the stained bandages to one side. "Would you pull the basin over here?" Her tone was polite, detached.

I did as she asked. Marta washed her hands in the freezing water, and I gave her the only intact towel to dry them on. "I need some more trousers," she told me. I nodded, getting up at once, but she shook her head. "It can wait till morning. Stay and talk to me."

I sat back down, watching Marta rearrange herself carefully on the pile of cushions. She was on her side again, wincing every time she moved. She pulled the book toward her. "I love this play," she murmured.

"Marta," I began. "Marta, it's going to be OK."

She looked at me almost pityingly. "Let's talk about something else," she said, her tone horribly polite again, and that gentle dismissal—the clear sign that I was no use to her beyond the practical—was crushing. Then I saw her eyes drift to the book next to the mattress, and somehow I knew what to do. I began to ask her about the play—about the characters, the themes, her favorite lines and scenes—and she answered my every question thoughtfully and with precision, flicking through the play to find quotes.

After an hour or so, she started to become very drowsy, but as I was getting ready to leave she suddenly sat up again. I reached for the bandages, but she shook her head. "Rose," she said, "tell me. Did it really happen to me? Was Gerald here?"

I stared at her. Her eyes were bright with hope, but oddly glazed. "You see," she said, her voice now trembling a little, "I feel as though—as though maybe it *didn't* happen. The pain's gone. You're here. Nothing's really changed. I wonder whether maybe . . . maybe it didn't happen." She swallowed, looking at me beseechingly. "Did it?"

There was a long silence. Somehow I knew that she would believe whatever I told her. Marta had placed herself in my hands. If I told her Gerald hadn't come here, hadn't raped her, she would accept the untruth as fact, as her living memory, as the real past rather than fiction. It would bring her comfort. She would eat, she would sleep. The lie could be my gift to her; my atonement for failing to protect her.

I'd told so many lies, but I couldn't do it. "I'm sorry," I said. "I'm so sorry, Marta. He was here." *He forced you to have sex with him. That's why you're bleeding.* "We're going to help you. You're not alone—"

"Shut up." Her voice reeked of disappointment. She looked down at her bruised and swollen wrists, at the stains in her lap. The glaze had dissipated from her eyes, and we shared the same reality again. "I hoped you might be able to understand," she told me, her tone vindictive, "but you can't. You're so innocent, aren't you, Rose? Your life is charmed. Your life will be beautiful. I wish it were mine."

I wanted Sylvia, but I couldn't go to her. I didn't even know where her room was, or whether she shared with anyone. But I couldn't be alone. I went to the infirmary, knowing Sami would be there; knowing that if Dr. Reza had discharged him he would have come straight to the clocktower.

It was late, and the place was deserted, but a whiteboard showed who was in which room. Sami had a single. I went there and found him lying on his back, fast asleep, his arms flung out either side of his body. The bedside lamp was on, and he was fully dressed apart from his blazer and tie. I moved one of his arms and lay down next to him.

His eyes flickered open. "Rose?" His speech was thick from his split lip, which had been cleaned and stitched.

I couldn't talk to him. His whispered questions—*How is she? Did you tell her about her father? Has she gone to sleep?*—all went unanswered. I lay next to Sami with my head on his shoulder, and didn't speak a word. Finally he sighed. He shifted onto his side and wrapped his arms around me, and we lay like that for a minute or so. "Can I stay here with you?" I asked, my face pressed against the soft wool of his school sweater.

I felt him nod. I felt something else, too, and didn't resent it; but Sami rolled away from me, his pale cheeks suffused with red. "You should go," he murmured, passing his hand over his face.

I shook my head, moving closer to him again. "It's OK." I kissed his hot cheek, putting my arms around him, pulling him closer. I had no idea what I wanted, but I was certain of what I did *not* want: to be alone, anywhere, ever again. I would have done anything not to be alone. As I pressed my lips to Sami's neck, I knew I would do anything he asked me, if it stopped me being alone that night.

He asked me for nothing. It was only later, after things had got even worse, that I thought back to that night in the infirmary and allowed myself to remember how, after half an hour in his arms, it was me who asked Sami—first with dignity, then with urgency, and finally cravenly—for sex. The greater his reluctance, the more desperate for him I became. I felt as though nothing would comfort me that night apart from Sami giving me what I wanted. When he finally consented, I wanted it no less. I was seeking the same power I'd felt three nights previously; all the power Marta knew she'd lost, and resented me for possessing. But that night, that second time, although there was no pain, I felt no pleasure; no power. I felt nothing at all: only a hollowness; an unconquerable dismay and regret that the real power I could have wielded that night—the power to make Marta believe that Gerald hadn't touched her—had been beyond me. I could have saved her, but I had summoned her back to this world. Already on that night, I knew that my cruelty would haunt me forever.

Chapter 22

Wake up, Rose." The words were whispered and urgent. "Wake up."

I sat up, squinting against the light spilling into the room from the corridor. Next to me, Sami rolled over, sighing in his sleep. Dr. Reza was standing next to the bed, wearing a dressing gown. "Major Gregory is here," she said. She reached down and put her hand against Sami's cheek. "Wake up, Sami. Major Gregory wants to speak to you both."

Her expression was impassive as we pulled on our clothes. "You were missing at late roll call," she told me. "It's one o'clock in the morning. He says he's been looking for you." I buttoned my cardigan, trying to stop my hands shaking. "You were here."

"I—"

"You came to the infirmary," she broke in, "having been sick after dinner. You had a temperature, and I kept you here for observation." She frowned, looking at Sami, whose split lip was swollen and purple. "You slipped on the ice, Sami." He was fumbling with his tie, looking up at her as trustfully as a child. "Come with me," she said, and we thrust our feet into our shoes and followed her into the corridor.

She had not shown him into her study. Major Gregory

was standing in the dark waiting room of the infirmary. The shoulders of his greatcoat were dusted with fresh snow, and his face was drawn with familiar anger, which intensified at the sight of Sami and me. "Sit down," he said to us, and we obeyed him. Dr. Reza stood behind us. She placed her hand on the back of my plastic chair.

"I am inclined to send you home tonight." I'd expected to hear the words long before now, and when he spoke them they came as a kind of relief. "Your lack of respect for this school is staggering."

"Sir," Sami began, his speech still impeded by his split lip. "We—"

"Silence." Major Gregory cut him off. "I have something to tell you." He paused, chewing his lip. For a few bizarre moments, I felt completely disinterested in him. "You are aware that Professor De Luca, Marta De Luca's father, had a stroke yesterday afternoon." He waited. "You are aware of that fact," he repeated.

"Yes, sir."

"Professor De Luca was still conscious when he went into hospital," Major Gregory said. "He told the doctors something very troubling. He said it many times before he lost consciousness. Knowing who Professor De Luca is, and what he has been through with his daughter, your friend, the hospital passed the information to us." We waited, listening intently now, and I could feel tension in the small part of Dr. Reza's hand that was touching my shoulder. "He said—" Major Gregory broke off as the door of the infirmary opened and Lloyd stepped over the threshold. "I told you to wait in my study, Mr. Williams," he snapped.

"I know." Lloyd's tone bordered on indifference. He looked exhausted—wearier and more defeated than I'd ever seen him—as he took in Sami and me on adjacent chairs, and Dr. Reza standing behind us. I was suddenly very aware of my rumpled clothes, my loose collar and disheveled hair. Lloyd's eyes narrowed a fraction.

"Why have you disobeyed me?"

"Because Rose and Sami are my friends."

Major Gregory gaped at him. "This is unacceptable beha—"

"Nicholas," Dr. Reza broke in, as Lloyd took the seat next to mine, "it's the middle of the night. Please tell Rose and Sami what you have to say."

For a moment I thought Major Gregory was going to shout at Dr. Reza, or even attack her. There had always been something psychopathic about him—an unnerving dearth of empathy or care—but I'd always assumed that this was partly performative, or at least that it was a reasonable consequence of his exasperation at the rings that were run around him. I'd wanted to believe that beneath Major Gregory's fastidious-ness and snobbery he was, after all, a human being with a conscience. Watching him in the infirmary that night, I knew I had been wrong. Our Housemaster was committedly cruel and self-interested; devoted only, and with inexplicable fervor, to getting the results he wanted for Hillary House. We, the Millennium Scholars, had never been anything more or less to him than a punt that might or might not pay off: a pathway either to accolades and glory, or ridicule and humiliation.

"Some new information has come to light," Major Gregory said at last, his voice icy and quiet. He looked straight at me as he said, "Before he became unconscious, Professor De Luca said the same thing several times. He said, *Rose Lawson knows where Marta is. Ask her.*"

For a long minute there was complete silence in the waiting room. Sami and Lloyd were motionless either side of me. I became aware again of the slight pressure of Dr. Reza's hand against my blazered shoulder. I realized that I was completely unafraid, and I looked my Housemaster in the eye as he spoke again. "I am not going to ask you that question," he said softly. "I will not ask you because Marta De Luca's whereabouts are not my concern. We removed her from the school roll before Christmas—she is no longer my responsibility. I have no interest in her, and I don't care whether you know where she is, or have ever known. I don't care whether she is alive or dead. My concern is for the honor and reputation of Hillary House and High Realms. Do I make myself clear?"

Lloyd, Sami, and I nodded slowly, and Major Gregory took a step closer to us. "You will therefore understand my decision," he stated, "to put the three of you under house arrest. You will not be permitted to leave your rooms for ten days." Sami groaned quietly, and Lloyd started to say something, but Major Gregory raised his voice. "It has been a very long time since I last issued this sanction. It is justified now because the three of you are distracted to the point that you are failing to meet your scholarship commitments. You were permitted to attend this school, completely free of charge while others pay tens of thousands of pounds a year, to fulfill a duty and to meet certain criteria. You are currently doing neither."

"We're still top of the Rankings," Lloyd hissed, but Major Gregory shook his head dismissively.

"The Rankings are only a small part of what you were

admitted to this school to accomplish. In case it is unclear to you, let me tell you that your role here, first and foremost, is to get into the best universities in the country, if not the world, and for that achievement to have been enabled by High Realms. Dr. Lewis tells me," he went on manically, "that neither of you, Mr. Williams and Miss Lawson, have shown the slightest interest in working on your university applications or preparing for the mock entrance examinations, and that you were only induced to choose a subject when she threatened you with a WP. She further tells me that as things stand, Mr. Lynch, your chances of being accepted to study Medicine are very slim indeed."

"That's not true," Dr. Reza said. "Nicholas—"

"No." Major Gregory shook his head. "There will be no discussion. The three of you will accompany me to Hillary House tonight, and you will spend the next ten days in your rooms. A Mag or a Senior Patroller will be stationed outside at all times. Meals will be brought to you. Your Mags will send work, and any spare time you have over and above completing it will be spent revising for the mock examinations. Any dissent now or during this period will result in the duration of your house arrest being doubled."

"*Nicholas,*" Dr. Reza began again, but he cut her off.

"I don't want to have to humiliate you, Dr. Reza, but be assured I would not hesitate to do so if you try to obstruct this sanction. Get up," he said to Lloyd, Sami, and me, and we did so with terrible resignation, knowing that the slightest provocation would make him do what he had threatened.

We walked out into the thick, dark night, which was the

coldest I'd ever known at High Realms. The air seemed to contain icy pins, which pressed painfully against my face and hands. I shivered uncontrollably as we walked toward the Main House. Neither Lloyd nor Sami looked at me. Dr. Reza was talking quietly but firmly to Major Gregory, making various stipulations about our house arrest. We entered through the Ivy Door, and the familiar institutional warmth of the school was crushing to me. It was the warmth that Marta had not felt for months, and must surely doubt she would ever feel again.

The first two days of house arrest came as a surreal, guilty relief. I was so tired that the extra sleep was welcome. With visiting Marta and morning duty off the cards, I could sleep until the rising bell rang at quarter past six, and then lie in until half past eight, when Major Gregory came to 1A with the day's work. On the first morning I opened the door to him in my dressing gown, a mistake I would not repeat. He immediately tacked two days on to the original ten, for Lloyd and Sami as well as for me.

After my physical energy had replenished a little, and I was able to see my situation more clearly, I began to struggle. The events of the past few days replayed themselves over and over in my mind, their horror sharpening every time. Most often, I ran through the last conversation I'd had with Marta, and the way I had failed her. To be forced to abandon her without an explanation was bad enough, but for this to happen off the back of such a severance of trust gave me a feeling of guilt so overpowering that I was sick, several times a day, in the wastepaper bin in 1A. Afterward I opened the window and lay on my bed, limp and empty, allowing tears of self-pity to leak from my eyes. 1A grew cold, and I wanted it to. I wanted to suffer.

After three days or so, it occurred to me that Marta might run away. Apart from her injuries, there was nothing to stop her doing so. The clocktower room wasn't locked, and she knew that there were many hours of the day and night in which she could slip away unnoticed. It was almost too painful to imagine how she must feel, what she must be thinking. One moment we had been there for her; the next, Gerald had raped her, and we—her friends, her lifeline—had disappeared. We hadn't had a chance to tell her how we'd punished Gerald, so she must be terrified of him returning. I curled up on the window seat and stared at the clocktower, wishing I could teleport there. I tried to remember how much food and water Marta had. In my heart of hearts I knew that worrying about provisions was a waste of time. Marta would not be eating.

There was no possibility of escape from 1A. A Mag or a Senior Patroller was stationed outside twenty-four hours a day, even escorting me to the bathroom down the corridor. The only other time I was permitted to leave the room was for a brief walk every day: one circuit of the Main House, accompanied by Major Gregory himself, either first thing in the morning or last thing at night. In Major Gregory's view, the walk was clearly the thing that prevented house arrest from being an actual infringement of our human rights, but for me it was by far the worst part of the day. I didn't see many people, but by day three the relative liberty of those I did see—their ability to walk at their own pace, to go to breakfast when they liked within a certain window, to talk to their friends—was more than I could stand. By day three, I was counting all my waking hours, but the nine days that remained of house arrest seemed so impossibly infinite that I gave up. I wondered how Marta coped with her hours of solitude and inactivity; which techniques she used to mark and hasten the passage of time. We had never discussed it, because she'd never complained.

Gradually, the absence of most of my coping mechanisms began to take its toll. I hadn't realized the extent to which I'd been sustained by the unabating schedule of High Realms. In precluding proper thinking time, the daily grind had, in fact, been my strength and stay. Without lessons, hockey, and the company of Lloyd and Sami—who were at least spending house arrest together—I began to sink into depression. I could do the work the Mags gave me, but I did it all mindlessly and without enjoyment. On the evening of day three, Bella was stationed outside my room. At the end of her shift she came in and told me that she was firing me from the First XI. This extended period of absence from training was the final straw, she said. My position on the team had always been controversial; it had been a trade-off between the way my presence divided the team and damaged morale, and my skill at the game, which, Bella said—as a final dagger—was undeniable.

By day four—the first day of February—I was beginning to wonder why Sylvia never appeared as one of the Senior Patrollers who rotated as my guard outside 1A. At first I dared to hope she'd been assigned to Lloyd and Sami's room rather than mine, but as the days went on and there was no sign of her, I came to the conclusion that she was avoiding me. She must have decided that I wasn't worth the hassle of being associated with. With this realization came a surprising amount of pain. I felt frustrated with myself: I barely knew Sylvia, and yet I'd allowed myself to get attached to her. Reviewing the facts of who Sylvia was and the things she'd done, the ways she'd hurt me in the past, I couldn't believe how naive I had been. I told myself sternly that the fact I was missing her was a function of my acute loneliness rather than anything else. When I realized that I was still yearning for her, I forced myself to remember that her demotion of Gerald had tipped him over the edge, with shattering consequences. *Her pride meant that Marta suffered,* I tried to tell myself, but it was like trying to force corners into a circle. My heart had gone its own way, and my mind would not be separated from it.

Finally, on the afternoon of my fifth day of house arrest, there was a knock on the door, and Sylvia entered without waiting for an answer. She looked around Room 1A and then at me, slumped on the window seat. "Goodness me," she said crisply. "Standards have slipped."

She was right. I hadn't bothered to make my bed or put away any clothes for days, and my desk was strewn with bad essays and incomplete work. I'd swapped my uniform for a tracksuit as soon as Major Gregory left that morning, and had not washed my hair since the start of House Arrest. Sylvia, meanwhile, was immaculately dressed in her uniform and Vice-Captain General gown. She was fresh from lessons, from action and purpose, and I could not bear it. "I can't stay long," she said briskly, advancing to the middle of the room. "I've got something to tell you."

I had no appetite for news, which would surely be bad. I went to my bed and curled up facing the wall. Ignoring this, Sylvia said, "Genevieve is coming back to school in two weeks' time. Dr. Reza told us this morning. I've just spoken to Gin on the phone—she sounds very well. Her speech is completely back to normal."

I didn't bother to open my eyes. "Why are you telling me this?"

"I thought you'd be interested."

I did not reply. There was no chance that Genevieve's return to High Realms could impact me in any way but negatively. I could not imagine seeing her, the person with whom the nightmare my life had become had started. As if from far away, I heard Sylvia say, "Gin coming back is good news on several fronts."

"I'm happy for you," I said mechanically, still staring at the wall. "You'll have your best friend back."

"Well, yes." There was unmistakable joy in Sylvia's voice. I heard a creak as she sat down on the window seat. "I've missed Gin very much. That's why I'm organizing a party to celebrate the announcement of her return."

"Right."

"It's going to be on Saturday night. It's the first Saturday of the month, so all the Mags will be at the pub. We're going to host it in Raleigh Common Room—it's the biggest one."

"I'll be thinking of you."

"Perhaps I should be clearer," Sylvia said loudly. "I am throwing a party on Saturday night that the entire Sixth Form will attend. All the Mags, including Major Gregory, will be at the pub in Lynmouth until past midnight."

I let her words sink in, and then I rolled over and stared at her. She'd shrugged off her gown and was sitting on the window seat with her legs crossed, surrounded by its black folds. Behind her the sky was a clear, cloudless blue. She looked at me steadily. "Is there anyone else you would like me to tell about this?"

I swallowed. My mouth was very dry. "Lloyd and Sami," I said. Sylvia nodded.

Slowly, I sat up. Realizing the significance of what she'd told me was like sinking into a warm bath, cooled only by nagging incredulity and confusion. "Why are you doing this?" I whispered, and within seconds she was beside me, kissing me hungrily, tenderly, for a very long time. The feel of her, the smell of her after so many hours of isolation was dizzying, overpowering. She was fresh air after days of suffocation; she was softness after the hard stone of solitude. As she kissed me, her power seemed to flow into me, restoring some of the hope I thought I'd lost forever.

Some time later, we sat next to each other on my bed with our backs against the wall. I let my head rest on her shoulder. "Why didn't you come sooner?" I asked, hating how plaintive I sounded.

"I had to be very careful," she replied. "Bella and the others . . . they know there's something going on between us. It took me a few days to have the right conversations. I needed to make sure we'd be safe, today and going forward. One visit isn't enough for me, Rose."

I closed my eyes, feeling tears rising. "Nor me."

"This is very hard for you," she said softly. Her lips brushed my hairline, and then she lifted my chin so that we could look at each other. Her eyes were the rich, dark brown I remembered, but for the first time I noticed that they contained tiny flecks of green. "Trust me," she said. "Trust me to get you through this, Rose, because I swear to you that I can."

After that, she came every day. Her influence within the Senior Patrol was such that they protected our time together by distracting Major Gregory and the other Mags. They did so with practiced deftness and total dedication. When I expressed my surprise at her colleagues' willingness to do this, Sylvia shrugged. "We've always helped each other," she said, but I knew that what they were doing was above and beyond the norm.

She didn't ask me why the boys and I had been placed under house arrest. She held Major Gregory in almost total contempt, but I was also realizing that she wasn't an inquisitive person. If confidences weren't forthcoming, it wasn't her style to coax or niggle. She told me she'd been at boarding school since she was seven, and I came to understand that her way of caring was primarily determined by that fact. People were paid to care for Sylvia—to feed her, to wash her clothes, to provide her with an education the world envied—but they were not paid to care *about* her; to be more than perfunctorily interested in her emotional well-being. As such, Sylvia's own way of caring was based on practical help, favors, and protection from obvious danger or disadvantage. Nor did she seem to be familiar with the sort of meandering conversations in which unburdening takes place without you realizing it. She told me she wanted to be a lawyer, and her style of communication was so forthright, so unequivocal, that I wasn't surprised.

But none of this meant that Sylvia didn't help me, or that she wasn't suffering herself, in a way, and for a reason that I was too wrapped up in myself and my separation from my friends to grasp. I should have realized more quickly that something was wrong, because in all ways but one Sylvia was amazingly tender. At first I struggled to understand how someone so publicly irascible could privately be how she now was with me: endlessly gentle, respectful, appreciative. She made it clear that she adored me, and I felt the same way about her. Slowly, our wary mutual fascination gave way to affectionate familiarity. Sometimes Sylvia would sit on the floor while I had a bath, gazing at me with a total lack of inhibition. In those moments, I wanted to speak through the clouds of steam rising from the water and tell her *Please, go to the clocktower. Get help.* Something—some residual disbelief that this was real, that she was good—stopped me.

Very tentatively, we began to talk about what had happened between Genevieve, Max, and Lloyd. Sylvia filled in parts of the story that I hadn't known or understood: that Max had come to Sylvia's room the night before the Eiger, asking for her advice about his plan to leave Genevieve, and she'd urged him to reconsider, or at least not to tell her about his feelings for Lloyd. Max and Genevieve had spent the night in the organ loft. During first study—which they'd both skipped—he'd told her he was leaving her. "I shouldn't have gone to English that day," Sylvia said, her voice shaking. "I knew he was going to do it; I knew how devastated Gin would be. I should've been there for her." Her humility made me ache for her in a way her asperity never had.

Most cautiously of all, but with a certain determination on both sides, Sylvia and I talked about her betrayal of Lloyd in

Major Gregory's study after the Eiger. More cracks appeared in Sylvia's pride as she told me how much she regretted what she'd done. "I was so terrified . . . I thought Gin was dying. I thought I'd lost her forever. I'd never been spineless before that, and I hope I never will be again." She paused, her eyes full of tears. "As soon as I said it, I realized you didn't know that Genevieve had seen Max and Lloyd together. And I knew you *had* to find out . . . that nothing would make sense until you did. Do you remember calling out my hypocrisy, the morning after the Eiger?" I nodded. "Nobody had ever confronted me like that before. It jolted me—it made me think. I'd always been . . . curious about you, but right there and then, I realized I wanted you." She paused again, and spoke with difficulty. "You know, I tried to persuade Max to stay with Gin because I genuinely thought it was best. I thought it was right to stick with people no matter what. Now I know . . . that might be true for friendship, but it's not true for romantic love. If that fails, you can't stay with the person. I was all muddled up, Rose, and that's why I didn't leave Bella sooner, and come to you."

I realized I wanted you. The words made me shiver with joy, but soon afterward Sylvia had to go. It was the day before the party, and she told me she had things to sort out. The following morning she told me that everything was arranged, that Lloyd and Sami had been briefed, that they would come to my room at ten o'clock when the party would be in full swing. "You'll have an hour and a half together," she said. "You must have missed them so much."

My reconciliation with Lloyd and Sami might have been joyful and more long-lasting, had it not been for the fact that we were desperate to see Marta. The boys came to 1A at the appointed time, wearing their thick coats and boots, and after they'd both hugged me—brusquely in Lloyd's case; more warmly in Sami's—we set off through the dark, deserted school, hearing the thud of music coming from Raleigh House.

The familiarity of slipping out of the Ivy Door was bracing, despite my fear about what we would find in the clocktower. As we crossed the rugby pitches I started to run, and Lloyd and Sami followed me, the wind driving against our faces. As we approached the clocktower arch, Lloyd reached for my arm. "If she's not in there, don't panic," he told me.

The horses stamped restlessly as we entered Block C. We wiped the rain from our faces, and Lloyd led the way upstairs. The closer we got to the clocktower room, the more certain I was that the room would be empty; that Marta had run away. Then Lloyd pushed the door open, and we saw our friend. She was crouched in the far corner of the room, surrounded by screwed-up pieces of paper, writing something in her notebook. She barely glanced up as we entered.

"Marta." Sami went to her immediately, crouching down in front of her. "Mar, we're sorry. We can explain." He broke off, staring at the piece of paper she was writing on. "What're you doing?

She didn't answer, instead bending over and writing more feverishly. She muttered something to herself, running her free hand through her hair. Lloyd shone his torch on her, and she looked up in alarm: a tiny animal in headlights. Her face was very dirty. "What are you doing, Marta?" he asked, his voice very loud and clear.

To my surprise, she smiled at him. "I'm writing a letter," she said. "Will you post it for me, when it's done?"

Lloyd glanced at me. Marta was behaving as though we had last seen her ten minutes rather than ten days ago. Before we could say anything, she looked directly at Lloyd. "Will you?" she repeated.

He blinked, and then seemed to pull himself together. "Well, maybe. You're a Missing Person, remember." He paused. "Who's the letter to?"

"My father," Marta replied. She was looking up at him, still smiling. "I'm not going to be a Missing Person for much longer, Lloyd. I'm getting out of here." She bent over the letter again.

Lloyd, Sami, and I looked at each other uneasily, and with a distinct sense of anticlimax. Sami was patroling the clocktower room, biting his nails, looking at Marta's possessions as if they were dangerous. Lloyd cleared his throat. "So, Mar—what are you saying to your dad? I thought you didn't want to have any contact with him." I admired him for staying calm, because I felt the opposite, watching Marta scrawl her letter. She still hadn't looked at Sami or me.

"I'm doing him a deal," she said. "It's what I should have done all along. I'm telling him that I won't tell the police about what he did to me, if he promises to leave me alone."

"Right." Lloyd bit his lip. "And how—how d'you think he'll take that?"

"Well, I don't know," Marta said. She paused in her writing, looking thoughtful. "But I'm making myself very clear to him, Lloyd. I'm explaining exactly how he made me feel—and why what he did was wrong. I've had plenty of time to think about it, after all." She laughed. "I wrote a letter to my friend Rose, too, when we fell out. It helped then, so I thought I'd try it again."

There was a short silence. Sami stopped pacing, and glanced between me and Marta, clearly confused. "Marta," he said, pointing at me, "Rose is here! Didn't you see her come in?" Marta bent lower over her letter, still writing frantically. "*Marta*," Sami said, more urgently this time. She shot me a look out of the corner of her eye, and shook her head.

"That's not Rose," she said.

Lloyd stood over Marta, his arms folded, as Sami knelt down next to her. He beckoned me over, and I bent down next to Lloyd and Sami. "Marta," Sami said again, "Rose is here."

"It's me, Mar," I repeated, trying to look her in the eye.

She looked at me properly then, her eyes blank. "It's nice you've come to visit me," she said politely, "but don't tell anyone I'm here, will you?"

For a moment Sami looked relieved, but Lloyd frowned. He crouched down. "Who's that, Marta?" he asked, pointing at Sami. "Can you tell me his name?"

"What the f—" Sami began, as Marta shook her head, smiling peaceably at Lloyd.

"I don't know him," she said.

Lloyd swallowed. "And . . . do you know who I am?" he asked, his voice slightly hoarse.

"Of course. You're Lloyd," Marta replied at once, still smiling at him. "You're Lloyd, and I love you." She put the lid on her pen, placed it on the floor, and shifted over the concrete to where Lloyd was kneeling. She moved onto his lap and put her arms around his neck, burying her face in his shoulder.

There was another long, terrible silence in which Sami and

I looked at each other, stunned, and Lloyd's eyes flicked from one to the other of us over Marta's head. She was completely motionless, curled on his lap like a child. Lloyd's body dwarfed hers. His arms hung limply by his sides as he stared at Sami and me, his expression devoid of his usual smooth confidence. Then I saw that Sami was mouthing something at him, his face contorted with misery. *Hug her.*

Slowly, obediently, Lloyd raised his arms and put them around Marta, his hands joining on her back. She wriggled a little in his embrace, nestling closer against his chest. She sighed deeply, and the four of us sat in silence for a while longer. I heard the rushing of the wind outside, rain pattering on the clock face, and the horses rustling downstairs. Sami was sitting cross-legged with his head in his hands, not looking at any of us. Lloyd's arms were around Marta, his head resting on hers, his eyes large and solemn in the torchlight. I couldn't see Marta's face. As I looked on, she turned her head slightly so that her face was touching Lloyd's neck. Her right arm drifted down his body.

"No. No. Marta, *no.*" Lloyd tipped her off his knees, holding up his hands as though to prove his innocence. Marta was jolted onto the floor, looking even more startled than Lloyd. She looked at him curiously. Then her hand groped for him across the concrete.

"Lloyd," she said. "Lloyd, you said you wanted me—in the woods—don't you remember? I'm sorry I couldn't be with you then, but I'm ready now."

"*No!*" Lloyd's shout seemed to awaken her. He scrambled to his feet, backing away from her. "That was months ago, Marta—it's done with—it's over. It's not for now, Marta. Stay away from me," he said, taking more steps backward until he was almost at the door. She was crawling toward him.

"Marta," I said quietly. She whipped around. "Marta, leave him. Come here." I reached out for her, knowing she would not come.

"I don't know who you are," she told me, her voice shaking. "You're frightening me."

"I don't want to frighten you." I struggled to my feet. "I won't hurt you, Mar. It's me—Rose."

She looked up at me, and for a moment I thought she knew me. Then she started babbling. "He *did* want me. I promise you he did. He said we'd be good together—he kissed me in the woods! You don't believe me, do you? Rose would believe me, I know she would—"

"I do believe you. I do." I sank to my knees in front of her, putting my hands on her shoulders, but she shook me off, looking petrified. "I believe everything you've ever told me, Marta. I promise you, I'm Rose. I can prove it. You remember," I said, swallowing hard, "you remember telling me about what your father did—"

"*No!*" Marta screamed, drawing her knees up to her chest, flinging her head back as she had on that night. "How *dare* you mention that in front of him?" She brandished her arm at Lloyd. "It's *you*, isn't it, you cunt, you've turned him off me—you've told him I'm dirty, I'm damaged goods, that's why he doesn't want me anymore—" She screamed again, even more loudly, and the boys and I looked at each other in terror. "Oh my God," she said, her voice suddenly quiet.

"What?"

"I've realized what it is," she said, looking me dead in the eye. "You want to kill me, don't you?"

"Of course I don't—"

"You do. You want me dead. *He* does, too. My father. Why else would he have—" She stopped, swallowing. "I want to kill him." She let her forehead drop onto her knees, her fists clenched. "I will kill him."

Then Sami slid across the floor toward her. I remember expecting his face to be blotchy with tears, but it wasn't. His eyes were completely dry as he said her name. She looked at him sightlessly, indifferently, but he spoke again, his voice quiet. "He's dying," he said. "Your father's dying, Marta."

"What?" she whispered.

"He had another stroke," Sami said, "a couple of weeks ago, he's in the hospital, we don't know whether he's still—" His voice trailed off as Marta stared at Sami. We watched her, three points of a triangle around our friend.

Finally she spoke. "I don't understand," she said slowly. Her eyes gleamed with sudden lucidity. "You said this was two weeks ago."

Sami swallowed. "Yes, nearly—"

"But you—you haven't been here. For days and days . . ." Marta wiped her mouth on the sleeve of her tracksuit, her eyes darting around the room. "How long is it since you've been here?"

"Ten days," said Sami quietly. "Major Gregory put us under house arrest. We weren't allowed to leave Hillary—they guarded our rooms—"

"All of you?"

"Yes."

"I don't believe you," Marta said at once. "You're lying—you didn't want to come—you've turned against me—"

"How can you say that," Sami said tremulously, "after all we've done to look after you?"

He couldn't have said anything more destructive. Marta screamed a third time, launching herself at Sami from the floor. She pinned him down, biting and scratching at his face, shrieking at him, as he lay there and did nothing, not even raising his hands to defend himself. I tried to pull her off him, but she was unfathomably strong, her body twisting against mine as I grabbed at her. Finally Lloyd came and seized her, lifting her off Sami as easily as if she had been made of cotton wool and putting her into a kind of headlock under his arm.

"Get out," he told Sami, whose nose was bleeding. "Get out of here and go and get something to block that door with. *Go*," he said, gripping Marta more tightly, and as she opened her mouth to scream again he put his hand over her mouth, almost inside it, deadening the sound. "Rose, get me one of those bandages." He jerked his head at a pile of clean bandages we'd made weeks ago for her arm. Sami ran out of the room.

Lloyd was hurting Marta. Her struggling was attenuated as he gagged her with the bandage, her legs kicking against him more weakly. She choked against the material. Lloyd dragged her over to the mattress and forced her down onto it, crouching down in front of her as he held her in position.

"Rose," he said over his shoulder, "Rose, come here. Witness this."

I went to them, kneeling next to Marta's limp form on the mattress. "I know I haven't always done the right thing," Lloyd told her quietly. Her eyes widened as she groaned against the cloth, and he raised his voice a little. "But I won't allow you to say I don't want you because of your father, Marta. It's not true, and it's not fair on either of us." He stroked her hair once, and got to his feet. "Go back to Hillary," he told me. "Take Sami with you."

"But—"

He shook his head. "Please, Rose," he said, and the unfamiliar entreaty in his voice made me obey him. I got to my feet, and, without looking at Marta again, I stumbled down to the stable. There I met Sami, who was carrying two large blocks of wood, the front of his sweater covered in blood. When he saw me he let the planks fall to the ground.

"We've failed her," was all he would say, his voice shaking. "We've failed Marta." He was crying bitterly. I pulled him out of Block C into what was now a violent storm. The cold wind scoured our faces as we battled down Lime Grove. My arm was through Sami's, trying to keep him moving, but as we passed Drake Cottage my emotions caught up with his, and I couldn't support him any longer. I let go of his arm and started to run, ducking my head against the driving wind and rain. At first I felt Sami at my heels, but even after the stasis of house arrest my legs were powerful and fast. It wasn't long before I'd left him behind.

Chapter 23

The storm raged around High Realms for the rest of the night, buffeting the thin glass of 1A's window. When I finally managed to fall asleep, shortly after dawn, the whistling of the wind penetrated my dreams to become the white noise of the radio I'd put on at night after my mother died. In those dreams I was a parody of thirteen-year-old Rose Lawson, whose life was exaggeratedly pure, despite her grief.

Shortly after nine o'clock I was woken by Sylvia, who arrived at 1A dressed in her riding clothes, carrying two cups of coffee from the Dining Hall. Her hair was disheveled, but she otherwise looked as smart as usual. I could just about hear the cloister bell chiming over the wind. "Why aren't you in Chapel?" I asked groggily.

"Good morning to you, too." She sat down on the edge of my bed as I slumped back onto the pillows, the horrors of the night seeping back into my consciousness. "I got a reprieve," she said, "because so many trees have come down on the Estate. The Major tasked us"—she meant the Senior Patrol—"with riding out with him first thing, to record the damage . . . obstructed paths and so on. They're still at it." She yawned. "Move over, would you?"

I shifted toward the wall, and she lay down next to me on top of the covers. "How was the party?" I asked, trying to sound normal.

"A roaring success." Sylvia stretched out and closed her eyes. "Although Max rather let the side down. He's nervous about Gin coming back . . . he knows it's not going to be easy. He was so drunk by half past ten that I sent him to bed. He was still being weird at breakfast." I nodded. I felt extremely tired, almost unable to process what she was saying. "How were Lloyd and Sami, then?"

"They were fine."

"Only two days left of this," Sylvia said, rolling over. "Let's go back to sleep for a bit," she said unexpectedly, closing her eyes, and soon she was breathing slowly and evenly, her expression serene and unguarded. I watched her for a minute or two, aware that it was the first time I'd seen her asleep. I put my head down next to hers on the pillow.

After what felt like only a few minutes, I felt myself being shaken. "Rose. *Rose*." Sylvia was kneeling on the bed, looking down at me. "Wake up. Wake up, Rose."

I tried to answer her, but I couldn't speak. My mouth was filling with saliva, but my throat muscles were frozen: I couldn't swallow. I was gagged, gagged like Marta. The image made me scream internally. I hit out with my hand, hard, trying to feel something—anything—and it met the wall. Sylvia grabbed my arm.

"Rose," she said again, "don't hit the wall. Hit me, if you have to." She put one hand either side of my face, holding it still so I had to look at her. "Hit me," she repeated, but when I looked at her I couldn't see my Sylvia. I could only see her standing next to Genevieve as the latter blasted Marta with the hose. I hit out again, involuntarily this time, and my hand connected with Sylvia's nose.

"Blimey," she said, her hand over her face. She leaned forward, blood seeping between her fingers onto the pillow. The sight of the vivid red soaking into the white jolted my senses, and my jaw loosened.

"I'm sorry," I said. "I'm really sorry, Sylvia."

"What's the matter? You were moaning." A line of blood snaked down Sylvia's wrist. Her expression was unusually tentative.

I couldn't tell her the truth, so I told her something else I feared. "Sometimes I dream you've turned on me. I dream it's September, and . . ." I swallowed. *And I had Marta, but I didn't have you.* "I still hardly know you. We hardly know each other."

"What would you like to know?" Sylvia reached for a tissue, staunching the blood that was trickling from her nose. "What would you like to know about me?" she repeated, putting her other hand against my cheek.

I curled up on my side. I was being dishonest about the cause of my nightmare, but Sylvia now looked confused, even suspicious, so I had no choice but to continue. "Where do you live?" I asked stupidly.

"London. You know that."

"Yes, but where?"

Sylvia sighed, wiping her nose. Then she spread two tissues on top of each other on the pillow and put her head down next to mine. "My parents' home is in Hampstead," she said.

"Do you go to the Heath?"

"Sometimes. In the holidays. And when we were smaller."

"We?"

"My sister and I. You *know* about my sister, Rose."

"Only her name. Tell me about her." I moved my head a little closer to hers on the pillow.

"Her name's Hermione. She's twenty-one."

"What's she like?"

"Arrogant," Sylvia said unironically, "but not as clever as she thinks she is. She's always pissing people off." She paused. "She's at Oxford."

"She went to High Realms, right?"

"Yep." Sylvia tilted her head to blot another drip of blood. "She's going out with Rory's older brother. Everyone says she's very beautiful."

"*You're* beautiful." I moved a strand of her hair out of the way of the blood. "What about your dad?"

"Oh, he's harmless. He's a historian. He puts up with a lot."

"From you?"

"No!" Sylvia scowled at me. "I'm hardly there. No, from my mother."

"You said she was the breadwinner."

"She's also an alcoholic." Sylvia looked scornful. "My mother makes Hermione look meek and mild. I know I can be a bit snappy, but when you spend your evenings with an alcoholic laywer you have to be able to stick up for yourself. Honestly, this place is so *relaxing* compared to home."

I was silent for a moment. "You'll be a better lawyer than her," I said.

Sylvia shrugged. "That's the idea."

"Do you think Max is an alcoholic?" I asked suddenly. Sylvia shook her head.

"No," she said, "no, I don't think so. I mean—I'm sure there's more than one way of being an alcoholic, but he's nothing like my mother. But he's very muddled up at the moment. I don't know what's going on inside his head, but he needs to sort himself out. I'm . . . worried." She paused. "I'm worried about you, too, Rose."

"About me?"

"Yes." She put her hand on my cheek. "There's something wrong."

We lay there in silence. I knew that I hadn't managed to distract or delude Sylvia, but I was afraid that if I said anything at all I would break down and tell her everything. I couldn't tell her about Marta, nor was I ready to tell her about the devastation inside me. There were parts of me that I knew had broken forever by seeing Marta the way she had been last night, by the knowledge of what had happened to her, and by the fact that we had failed so completely to help her. Tears did come then, silent and swift. I turned my face so that it was pressing into the pillow. Still, for a long time, Sylvia said nothing.

"Rose," she said after a while, "I'm going to suggest something. I imagine you'll be a bit surprised." I lifted my head to look at her, and she leaned over, kissing the tears on my cheeks. "I think you should talk to Dr. Reza."

"Dr. *Reza*?"

"I think she might be able to help you. She helped me."

"But Sylvia, you don't trust anyone."

"Not true. I trust you, Rose." Sylvia blinked, as though the words surprised her. "You're right—I don't *entirely* trust Dr. Reza, but I've known her for a long time. And she was my only option."

Just in time, I realized that she was trying to tell me something. "When?"

"After Gerald attacked me," she said quietly, "I went to see her. I . . . I *had* to go and see her. My body wasn't healing, and the pain was getting worse every day. I tried to get day leave—I thought I'd find a doctor in Barnstaple or Exeter—but Keps wouldn't sign it off. So I had no choice."

"You didn't *tell* her?"

"Not then. I couldn't. I was . . . I've never felt so ashamed." Sylvia pressed her lips together, looking down at the blood-stained tissue. "But Rose, she didn't ask me what had happened. She asked me what my symptoms were. I told her, and she prescribed me antibiotics. Gave me her phone number and told me to ring her over the holidays if I wasn't getting better. Just as I was leaving, she asked me to come and see her as soon as I got back to school for second phase."

"And you did?"

"I had an appointment, so I had to." Sylvia looked at me as if I'd asked something very dense. "I was better by then, but I went along, mostly to make sure she was going to keep it to herself. I'd checked it all out. After we turn sixteen, she's not allowed to share medical information about us without our consent."

"Right."

"Anyway, I told her I was better. She looked at me for a bit, and then she just said, "In every way?" And I just . . . I didn't know what to say. I had this whole speech prepared about how she needed to keep her mouth shut and leave me alone. But then she asked that question, and I suddenly realized that I'd reached the limit of what I could live with. I hadn't told anyone at all, Rose, but I found myself telling her what Gerald had done to me."

I stared at her. I couldn't believe it: that Sylvia, of all people, had confided in Dr. Reza; and that nothing and nobody had forced her to do so. I saw that her eyes were dry, that she was calm.

"What did Dr. Reza say?"

Sylvia swallowed. "She didn't say anything for ages. She just listened. And afterward—well, for a while I didn't notice that she wasn't saying anything, because I was . . ." She took a deep breath. "I was upset. Then I did manage to look at her, and I thought she was angry with me again. We've had our ups and downs over the years. She knows I've never been very nice to Gerald—she used to get at me about it." Sylvia stopped, and I saw true regret in her expression. "I remember exactly what she said. She said, "I want you to know that you haven't lost any power here. The power is still all yours, and I'll give you any help you need. You only have to ask.""

The rain had stopped. 1A was very warm and quiet. "She helped you demote Gerald," I said at last.

Sylvia nodded slowly. "Yes. I thought punishing him would save me, but it was telling Dr. Reza, and then telling you, that really helped. I won't assume it'd be the same for you. But if you need to, go and see her." Sylvia paused. "That's not the only reason I told you this, Rose."

"Why else?"

"I—" She stopped. "I wanted to tell you because . . . well, you must be wondering why I can't—why I haven't done more than kiss you. I want to explain," she said, tears suddenly coming to her eyes, "that it's not because I don't want to, or that I don't love you, Rose. It's because I *can't*. My body doesn't—it won't work that way anymore. I can't have sex, and I don't think I ever will be able to again. He's taken that away."

"Sylvia, no." I finally reached for her, feeling her face bury into my neck, her body trembling in my arms. I felt an uncontrollable anger. "Sylvia, I don't think it's forever. But if it is, we'll work it out. I won't leave you."

"You won't?"

"No." I'd never been more certain of anything. Suddenly, despite everything, I smiled. "I thought you assumed I don't know how," I told her. "I thought that was the reason."

She paused, and then she smiled back at me through her tears. "Well, do you?"

"I've never tried."

"With *anyone*?"

"Well—with someone. With Sami. Twice."

"I see." Sylvia rolled onto her back, pulling her sleeves over her hands to wipe her eyes. "Well, that's a bit different."

I watched her carefully. "Are you angry?"

"No!" Sylvia suddenly snorted. "No, I'm not. We've all been there."

"*Have* you?"

"Oh yes." She looked at me thoughtfully. "It was a long time before Bella," she said. "I think I was in Third Form."

I stared at her. "You were *thirteen*?"

"Don't be judgmental." She tapped me on the nose. "I went through a phase of being completely besotted with Max, for some reason. I went to every single Chapel service he played at—"

"Hold on." I was struggling to take in this new information, which she was throwing out as though it were ancient history. "You slept with *Max*?"

She shrugged. "Like I said," she replied, "I really wanted to." She smiled, looking oddly sheepish. "I was interested in finding out whether it would bring about a real connection."

"And did it?"

"Well—not exactly." Sylvia grimaced. "It was just bloody uncomfortable, to be honest. But I think . . . I think being vulnerable with each other, working out how to do it . . . it *did* sort of bring us closer. I didn't feel great while it was happening, but afterward, I remember feeling like I had some new power. Max and I stayed up all night talking. Telling each other secrets. That was the best bit."

"Did you do it again?"

"Once or twice. Then Max got together with Gin, and that was that. We've never told anyone." She looked at me slyly. "Max can be very charismatic."

"Oh, shut up."

Sylvia nodded unrepentantly. "And then you transferred your affections to someone rather different. *Sami Lynch*. My, my. How was it?"

I paused. The memories were private, but Sylvia had been honest with me that afternoon, and I felt closer to her as a result. "It was special," I said at last, choosing to focus on the first time, and immediately regretted my choice of word when Sylvia mimed vomiting over the edge of the bed. "No, seriously. Sami's so—*thoughtful*. It was . . . it felt like it was more about me than about him."

"Well, he'd had Ingrid to practice on, hadn't he," Sylvia said dispassionately. "You've got her to thank for your lovely night of—"

"Stop it, Sylvia. I wish I'd never told you."

"I'm very glad you did." Suddenly she was serious. "Truly, Rose, I am. Even if it does make me even more sad that I can't be with you in that way . . . at least for now." She pressed her lips together, looking down at her hands. "I'm very glad you told me," she repeated. "You're right. It's good for us to know things about each other."

Silence swelled between us. Then, "Sylvia," I said before I could stop myself, "why have you never asked me about Marta?"

She looked at me carefully. "What do you mean?"

"We've talked about so much else. The Eiger . . . Genevieve, Max, Lloyd . . . but you've never asked me about Marta."

Sylvia looked down at the bloodied tissue again. She pulled at its edges until it fractured in the middle. "What would you like me to ask you?" she said quietly.

Silence again. I saw a new sadness in Sylvia's expression, and lingering shame. She'd been honest with me about a terrible thing that had happened to her, and had expected nothing in return, but now I'd nudged at an unknown between us. How unknown, I could not tell. We'd been close for a very short time, but Sylvia had already deduced that something was wrong, over and above the strain of house arrest. She might not have asked me directly, but she'd dropped hints. She knew the lengths I would go to for my friends because she would do the same for hers. Before I could say anything, Sylvia spoke again, her voice still soft. "In my experience," she said, "people tell you things when they're ready."

I looked at her, and she looked at me, and the significance of the moment burned in my throat and behind my eyes and in the tips of my fingers. "There's a room in the clocktower," I said. "Marta's hiding in there. She couldn't go home to her father, so she asked us to hide her there until she turns eighteen."

In the calmness of her nod, the steadiness of her gaze, I sensed a kind of relief. "How long?" she asked.

"Since the day Genevieve—"

"No, I meant how long before she turns eighteen?"

"Four weeks."

Sylvia nodded. "Doable, then."

We were lying on our fronts, very close to each other. We raised our eyes to the window, which was speckled with bulbous, glistening raindrops. The sun was coming out. I gazed at the crest of a faraway hill, and for a few soaring moments my life opened out before me: a pasture rather than a tunnel. *Doable.*

Then Sylvia spoke again, more abruptly. "When did you last see her?"

"Last night." Images of Marta flashed across my mind, vivid and painful. "Last night, during the party—" It was suddenly extraordinary that she had not known this.

"Did you all go? You, Lloyd, and Sami?"

"Yes."

Sylvia sat up, reaching for her blazer and gown. "I've got to go."

"But Sylvia—"

"Fucking hell," she muttered, thrusting her arms into the sleeves. "Fuck—*fuck*."

"What's the matter?"

"There's something I need to deal with."

"Are you angry?"

"I'm furious," she said, looking down at me, and panic rose in me like bile. She was angry, she was leaving, she was going to punish me. "It's dishonorable," she said, "*he's* dishonorable—"

"*Who?*"

"Max." Sylvia swung her gown around her, tugging her hair out of her collar. "He saw you last night," she said, "I'm sure of it. I'm sorry, Rose. This is all my fault. I only hope I'm not too late to fix it—"

I scrambled off the bed, sweat springing to the surface of my skin. "Why—what makes you think he saw us?"

"There's no time to explain," she said, pulling on her shoes.

"I'm coming with you." I wasn't allowed out; I wasn't even dressed, but I knew I couldn't bear the strain of waiting, all over again, for news. I grabbed some items of uniform. To my surprise Sylvia didn't argue, but went to my wardrobe and dug out the garments I was missing.

"Come on," she said, the second I was ready. "There's not much time."

We ran through Upper House, down the spiral staircase and across the Common Room. A few students were already returning from Chapel. They stared at me with hostile curiosity, and a couple started to say something, but Sylvia drew herself up and glared at them, and they sidled away at once. I followed in her wake as we began the long descent to the ground floor, hugging the edge of the Main House to avoid thoroughfares. I remember seeing the storm-blown Estate out of every window we passed. Clouds were sailing across the sky, obscuring and then liberating the sun every few seconds. The phases of brightness threw into sharper relief the many fallen trees and flooded lacrosse pitches and, farther afield, sheep huddled together on the hills. Twice, I glimpsed the clocktower, and the burnished hands of the clock made it our beacon, a star to navigate by.

As we strode along, Sylvia muttered an explanation. "I think Max must've gone to Hillary to see Lloyd after I sent him away from the party. Lloyd wasn't in his room, or yours, so Max went to look for you all . . . he must've seen you."

"I don't see how he managed to—"

"When Max is drunk he gets these ideas in his head. He can be so—*determined*. Did you all come back from the clocktower together?"

My heart sank. "No. Sami and I came back first."

"He must've seen Lloyd, then."

"But even if he *did*, he wouldn't turn Lloyd in—"

"Rose, you don't know Max like I do." Sylvia's tone was urgent. "When he's feeling insecure there's no knowing what he'll do. He becomes vindictive. He's worried about Genevieve coming back. They haven't had a proper conversation since before the Eiger. He thinks she's going to make him pay. He's going to try to claw back some influence and glory, I know it, and he thinks he can do that by breaking the story of where Marta is—"

"He wouldn't betray Lloyd."

"Rose, please. Stop being naive." Sylvia rattled the handle

of a door on the ground floor, which would not yield. "If I can get to him before he does anything stupid, then it's only four more weeks." She put her shoulder against the door. "Help me," she said. I added my strength to hers, and together we burst out into brilliant sunshine and a cold breeze.

We started to run along the perimeter of the Main House. "There's a side door into the Chapel," Sylvia murmured. "He'll probably still be in there after the service." We hurtled around the corner of the East Wing and there, right in front of us, examining the Ivy Door, was Detective Inspector Vane. He smiled coldly at Sylvia and me, his gray scarf rippling in the wind. "Good morning."

"Hello, Detective Inspector." Sylvia's tone was calm. Her hand closed briefly around mine, concealed by the folds of her gown. I couldn't understand how she knew who Vane was.

"Hello there, Sylvia." Vane's eyes glimmered contemplatively as he surveyed her. "Long time, no see."

"Three years." Sylvia gathered her gown around her. "What are you doing here on a Sunday?" she asked.

Vane's eyes narrowed. Sylvia must have come across to him as haughty, even rude, even though her tone was far less commanding than usual. She was also objectively and disarmingly beautiful, and I could see that this fact had neither escaped Vane's notice nor put him at ease. "The police investigate serious allegations immediately, whatever the day of the week," he said smoothly.

Sylvia's hand brushed my wrist again. "I see," she said. "Is there any way I can assist you, Detective Inspector?"

"As a matter of fact, there is." Vane's eyes darted between Sylvia and me. "I'm looking for Maximilian Masters," he said, and my panic intensified. Sylvia had been right. "The Gatehouse told me I would find him in the Chapel, but he's not there. I'd also like to speak to Major Gregory."

"I see," Sylvia said again. I could tell she was thinking hard. "Major G is out riding," she said. "Assessing the storm damage, you know—"

"And Maximilian?"

"I'm sure we can track him down between us," Sylvia said suddenly. "There are only a few places he could be at this time of day. Rose, why don't you check the stables?" I stared at her. "There's a chance he might be saddling up to join the others," she said, "but I *think* he's more likely to be in the Music School. I'll take you there, Detective Inspector." Vane nodded curtly. "See you later," Sylvia told me firmly, and she marched Vane away toward the Hexagon.

I hovered for a moment, feeling totally thrown. There was no reason I couldn't have accompanied Vane and Sylvia, as the Music School was en route to the stables, but Sylvia clearly wanted me to go a different way. Furthermore, I was sure that Max was very unlikely to be in either the stables, because he didn't ride, or in the Music School: with Chapel just over, he would have no reason to be practicing. I wrestled with my next move before concluding that my only option was to follow Sylvia's obscure plan. I ran across the sports pitches and down Lime Grove to the barns. As I jogged, I wondered desperately why Lloyd had not found a way to warn me about Max and the police. *Perhaps he's given up,* I speculated miserably, remembering his look of disgust as Marta tried to embrace him. *Perhaps he wants out.* With a sickening jolt, I realized that more could have happened between them after he'd told Sami and me to leave.

A few windswept Second Formers were mucking out Blocks B and C, but the stables were otherwise deserted. From the Second Formers' baleful glances I gathered they'd been told to cover my morning duty while I was under house arrest. I couldn't get into the clocktower while they were there, so I awkwardly began to help them to get the job done more quickly. After about forty minutes, which seemed the longest of my life to date, Sylvia entered Block B. "You're reprieved. Go back to the Main House," she snapped at the Second Formers.

"This is a fucking mess," Sylvia told me, the second they'd scurried away. "I didn't think we'd actually *find* Max here or in the Music School, and we didn't—but then Vane insisted we check the Chapel again, and he was there. Clearly he'd hidden in the organ loft and crept out, thinking the coast was clear."

I stared at her. "Why would he hide from Vane if he got in touch with him?"

"God knows, but my guess is he's lost his nerve. He looked fucking terrified. Now look, Rose," Sylvia said, her face pinched with tension, "Max can't have told Vane exactly where Marta is, or Vane would've come straight here."

"Vane will get it out of him now." I sat down on an upturned bucket, letting my head fall between my hands. Sylvia came and crouched down in front of me.

"We've got a bit of time," she said softly. "I saw Max's expression when I turned up with Vane. He regrets phoning the police, I know it. I didn't say anything—I couldn't—but I stood behind Vane and *looked* at Max—tried to make him

understand what a mistake it would be to—" She was interrupted by a sudden, bloodcurdling scream from the clocktower
above.

For the first time, I ran up the stairs to the clocktower with
Sylvia at my heels. As we rounded the corner Marta screamed
again, even more loudly this time, and I saw a makeshift
barricade: planks of wood nailed across the door, with barely
a gap between them. Lloyd had wedged the largest block under
the handle. "Rose," Sylvia said, her voice full of shock, "you
didn't tell me she was locked in."

"She *wasn't*." I stared at the barricade. Not only had Lloyd
failed to warn me about the police; he'd also stopped me getting
to Marta. I heard Sylvia's feet clatter on the stairs, and within
moments she was back, carrying a saw. Together we hacked
at the middle planks of wood. "I'm here!" I called to Marta,
hearing the thin wail of my voice echo in the stairwell.

After five minutes or perhaps fifty, during which Marta
screamed three more times, we managed to open the door.
Sylvia and I burst into the clocktower room. My eyes went
immediately to the mattress, but Marta wasn't on it. She was
curled in a ball under the clock face, surrounded by blood
and vomit.

"Jesus Christ." All the color left Sylvia's face. "Rose, she's
split her head open—" Before I could stop her, Sylvia had gone
to Marta and knelt down in front of her. She reached out and
touched Marta's arm.

I wish that Marta had screamed again at that point. It would
have been less terrible in so many ways, even though—and
perhaps *because* of this fact—it later turned out that Vane was
on his way to Drake Cottage with Max, and might have heard

her. But instead of screaming, my best friend raised her head from her hands and stared up at Sylvia with glassy eyes that seemed stupefied. She said nothing. Then her gaze traveled to me, and I knew that she remembered nothing of what I'd told her was going on between me and Sylvia, nothing whatsoever of that final conversation before Gerald had found us, and that in Marta's unwell mind, this was another betrayal—and perhaps the final one. She believed that I had brought Sylvia here to punish her. For the briefest, most tantalizing moment I thought I saw a flicker of lucidity in Marta's green eyes, and I grasped her wrists, ready to explain. Then she let out a great, shuddering gasp, and with abrupt, inexplicable strength, she pushed me and Sylvia aside and ran at the wall, colliding with it with a sickening crack of bone on concrete.

Chapter 24

Three hours later, Sylvia escorted me back to Room 1A, entering Hillary ahead of me to check that the coast was clear. She didn't stay very long. We sat on the window seat for a few short minutes, and in the end it was Sylvia's troubled, unresentful silence that galvanized my decision. I turned to her. "I know we can't keep Marta there for four more weeks. Can you give me three days?"

Sylvia stared at the floor. Her expression reminded me of how she'd looked at Genevieve's injuries on the day of the Eiger. It was far greater than shock: it was profound fear; not for herself but for somebody she loved. I reached out and put my hand on her wrist, trying to transmit a confidence I didn't feel. After a few moments, Sylvia nodded. "OK. I'll try and sort Max out—and keep Vane at bay." She exhaled shakily, then got up and brushed down her gown. "I'll make sure you can get out at night," she said, her voice strained. "There'll be someone outside your door, but they won't stop you leaving. And they'll take notes to Lloyd and Sami for you, if you want. Good luck." Her hand brushed my cheek, and then she was gone. The sharp click of the door as it closed felt like an ending.

Over the course of that Sunday afternoon, the wind dropped

until a perfect stillness settled over the Estate. The trees were still barren of leaves, but when I opened the window the air had a sweetness to it, as though spring was seizing its chance in the wake of the storm. I could hear the soft bleating of sheep again, and the hourly chiming of the cloister bell. Dusk descended quickly, that cold evening in February, but I didn't close the window.

I made no attempt to contact Lloyd and Sami, or to make any kind of plan. I thought only, and obsessively, of Marta, whom Sylvia and I had left sleeping. We'd sat with her for almost three hours, trying to stop her screaming and running at the wall. The first impact had aggravated the cut on her forehead, but somehow it hadn't knocked her out. It took the combined strength of Sylvia and me to hold her back each of the six times she tried again. At last Marta slumped, gray-faced and exhausted, on the concrete floor. She moaned softly to herself, curled tightly in the fetal position. When her guttural breathing evened out and we were sure she was asleep, Sylvia and I lifted her onto the mattress and tied her to it with ropes that she brought up from the barn. She found a first aid kit, too, and I looked on numbly as she swabbed the blood from Marta's forehead and cheeks. Before Sylvia and I left her, I'd leaned over her to kiss her on the cheek, murmuring that I would be back later. Her eyelids had drifted open and she'd half smiled at me.

For the very first time, I was grateful to be without Lloyd and Sami. There was nothing they could do to help. Lloyd had given up in favor of Max, or struck some self-preserving deal with him; and Sami, I knew, was too emotionally raw to act rationally. The compassionate pragmatism of my one other ally, Sylvia, had endured for the afternoon, but she'd now returned to the fold. I didn't blame her. I was alone again, and I was glad.

I slept for a couple of hours and went to the clocktower just after one o'clock, my boots crunching on the frosty grass. As I let myself into the stairwell, I felt dread drape itself over me like a cloak of cement. *Please let her be all right,* I thought, my throat tightening and my palms growing damp. I pushed open the door of the clocktower room, which we hadn't barricaded.

Inside, all was calm. Marta was fast asleep on the mattress, her breathing slow and regular. I shone my torch around the room, checking that everything was as we'd left it. The room was cold, but spotlessly clean. It reeked of the bleach that Sylvia had used to scrub away the vomit and blood.

One of the buckets still had vomit in it. I took it downstairs and sluiced it out with the hose. As I crept back into the clocktower room, Marta stirred. "It's Rose," I said, touching her cheek. I began to untie the ropes that bound her to the mattress. "You're safe," I told her. "It's only me here."

Marta's eyelids fluttered, but her eyes didn't open. Then she groaned something, sounding very groggy. I helped her sit up, and she slumped against me, her face pale and sweaty. Before I could pull the bucket toward her she'd started to be sick, retching limply in my arms, vomit dribbling down her front. I couldn't reach anything else, so I wiped her mouth on the sleeve of my shirt. "Sorry," she murmured.

"Don't say sorry." *It's not your fault,* I wanted to say. I helped her lie down again, and reached for some water. "Have some of this."

"You were here earlier," she said thickly, her thin fingers gripping mine. "With Sylvia."

"Yes." I couldn't tell how lucid she was. "Yes, I was."

Marta nodded languidly. "You're going out with her."

I hesitated. "Maybe."

She nodded again, leaning against me. I shifted slightly so that she could lie down with her head on my thigh. "Tell me about school," she said quietly, her eyelids drifting downward.

Again I hesitated, but I could see that she was already nearly asleep, and probably wouldn't hear me. So I glossed over house arrest, and recounted a compilation of real and fabricated stories: an English lesson on *The Wild Swans at Coole,* the frost sparkling on the Astroturf, our forthcoming mock exams, and an increase in the Straker Library borrowing allowance, which had been brought about by Sylvia. Suddenly Marta spoke, her eyes still closed. "Do you love her?"

"Yes." I put my hand on Marta's forehead, just below the jagged scar.

"And you love me," she said drowsily, "don't you?"

"Very much."

"Does Lloyd?"

I hesitated. "Yes," I said.

Her grip on my fingers loosened then, and I was sure she really was asleep. I eased her head off my leg and lay down next to her, pulling the sleeping bag over us both. *Sleep,* I thought. *Sleep until Sami comes* . . .

I woke up to find Marta fidgeting. I rolled over and flicked on my torch, looking at my watch. It was ten past six. "Rose?" Marta whispered. She was crouched on the edge of the mattress, her knees drawn up to her chest. Her eyes were wide and frightened. "I can't breathe," she said. "I'm suffocating." She gasped, pressing her fist against her throat. "I don't want to die."

"You're not dying. I promise you're not." Now Marta was panting as though she'd run a race, her thin shoulders rising and falling in jagged movements.

"The air in here—it's stopping me breathing. It's holding me down." She gasped for air again, and emitted a kind of wail. "Rose—"

"Shh. It's OK." I knelt down in front of her. As I held her wrist, I could feel her pulse racing. Her body was damp with sweat; her hair stuck to her forehead and cheeks. "I'm going to get Sami," I said automatically. "I won't be long—"

"Please stay. I don't want to be alone." She gasped again: this time half gag, half retch. "I can't breathe. There's no air in here. I need to go outside, Rose. I need air."

I glanced at the clock face. The first signs of light were seeping cautiously through it. Then I looked down at Marta, who was still trembling uncontrollably. "Don't leave me," she managed to repeat.

"I won't." I made my decision quickly. I wanted to make Marta happy; to atone for what I was having to do to her. It was still early enough to be safe, just for a few minutes. "I'll take you outside."

She looked at me disbelievingly as I got to my feet. "Really?"

"Yes." I went to one of the piles of clothes and found a warm jacket and woollen socks. "Wear these. It's cold out there."

She looked down at herself, still breathing heavily. Her T-shirt was stained with fresh vomit and old blood. Below that she wore a pair of my pajama trousers, folded over several times at the waist. "Can I get dressed?"

I helped her into some clean clothes, washed her face and combed her lank hair. Then we crept down the stairs, Marta clutching my hand, and I helped her through the gap between plywood and cement. I went ahead to check that the coast was clear.

Then we were both outside Block C. It was dawn in the middle of February, and the air was so cold it felt almost solid. The sky was a deep, deep blue; the moon and the stars just faded. We were surrounded by the muted noises of the untroubled horses; their shuffling and occasional snorts, and by the tentative chirruping of birds. The fountain dominated the courtyard. I took in the horse's hooves as they scrabbled at the air and understood for the first time that the sculpture depicted joy, not desperation.

Marta exhaled deeply, her breath rising around us in a translucent cloud. She dropped my hand. "Rose," she said. "Rose." She seemed so overwhelmed that I thought she might collapse, but she stayed standing, her eyes wide and alert. "Thank you."

"Let's go to Donny Stream." I knew I was getting carried away, but I couldn't bring myself to take her back upstairs. Out here, she seemed more like the old Marta, the Marta I could help.

Marta looked at me in surprise. I saw how pale she was; how the natural light—despite its faintness—made her look otherworldly. "Can we, really?" she asked.

"Yes." I led her through the clocktower arch, past the barns and workshops. She was moving timidly, and I forced myself to slow down, to remember how fit and strong I was compared to her. She took hold of my arm.

"Is this the way you come to see me?"

"Sometimes. We take different routes," I said, suddenly proud. "We usually go in and out of the Main House the same way—the Ivy Door, by the bins. But then we mix it up."

Marta nodded. She was breathing quickly again, her chest heaving, but this time it seemed to be with the effort of walking. We were nearly at Donny Stream, and Marta looked down the frosty bank to where water rushed over its rocky bed. "You've done so much for me, Rose," she said quietly. Her speech was totally coherent. "How will I ever repay you?"

I looked at her. At times I had been unable to believe that there would ever be a point at which Marta would be well enough to know what we had done for her. This morning she seemed different. I watched her gulp the air, her eyes shining. "You don't have to pay us back, Mar. We're doing this because you deserve it." I felt my throat thicken as I realized that I wasn't afraid of her that morning. "And because we love you."

"I'll love you forever." Marta saw my damp eyes and squeezed my hand. She gave me a shy smile. "That's why I want to repay you, Ro. By the time we're thirty, I'll have done that."

"Why thirty?"

Marta looked thoughtful. "Thirty seems doable," she said at last. "Thirteen years is plenty of time to get better, go to university, get a job. I wonder what job I'll have." She frowned.

"Do you . . . do you think you're getting better?"

"Yes," she said, "yes, I really do, Rose. I feel . . . Well, I feel sick all the time. I *don't* feel like my old self. But sometimes, now, I can see her. I can hear her. She's calling me back. She calls me by name."

"But she's Marta, too?"

"Yes." She started to walk down the bank, her movements

jerky. I followed her. "I recognize her. She's me when I was ten. She doesn't do much except read, and write stories, and do lessons with her parents, but she's happy. If I didn't have her, I wouldn't believe I can get better, but I see her so clearly sometimes, Rose. On the best days I go inside her head. It's great in there."

"What's great about it?" We only had a few minutes, but I wanted her to keep talking.

"She believes people are good and kind." Marta stopped at the edge of the stream, her eyes on the water. A few birds were already washing themselves prettily in the shallows. "I won't ever think that again. Only you and the boys are good. '*Everything has gone from me but the certainty of your goodness.*' D'you know who wrote that?" I shook my head.

"Virginia Woolf." In that moment she was the Marta of September and early October. "I know you're doing all you can for me. Beyond the call of duty." Stiffly, she bent down and trailed the fingers of her good hand in the stream. "It's so cold!"

I knelt down next to her, putting my hand on her shoulder in case she lost her balance. "The call of duty is different for best friends," I said. "You would've done the same for me."

"I would. But you'd never have ended up like me."

"Anyone could, Marta."

We started to walk along Donny Stream. "You know," Marta said, half laughing, "I always hated Chapel. But I keep thinking of that hymn . . . we sang it a few times." She paused. "'*He makes me lie down in green pastures. He leads me beside still waters. He restores my soul.*' It's a nice idea, don't you think? To believe that your soul can be restored?" Her eyes flickered to the fervent stream, the fields ahead of us, and up at the sky, which was now hesitantly suffused with pink. She shivered, tugging her coat sleeves over her hands. "I guess it happens for some people."

"I believe it will happen for you." I remembered what Dr. Reza had told Sylvia. "You still have power."

"I know." She stopped again, turning to me. "I need to ask you something, Rose. Before I lose control again—it could happen at any time, I know it." She shivered again. "I want you to find help," she said.

"What do you mean?"

"Help for me." Her jaw was set, and her expression of determination belonged to the old Marta. "Which means help for you, I suppose. When I'm awake . . . when my head's clear, I know this isn't working, Rose. You're all doing everything you can to make me better, and I *will* get better . . . I believe I will, but I'm scared, Ro. It's like a game I don't want to play," she said, blinking rapidly. "Behind one door there's Marta, telling me I'm going to survive. But behind another door there's a giant pair of hands. They grab me and tell me it's over. They tell me that people like me . . . they just *don't* survive. The worst thing," she said, swallowing, "is they tell me I'm hurting other people by being alive."

"Don't listen to them," I began, but Marta shook her head violently.

"I believe them entirely." She stared at me. "It's logical, Rose. So much badness has been put into me . . . I'm full of it, I'm bursting at the seams with badness. Now it's seeping out of me—into you, Sami, Lloyd. Even I can see that." Her voice shook.

"No." I couldn't let her think it for a second longer, even though I knew she was speaking the truth; that her decision was the same one I'd come to. "Marta, we're fine. We want to care for you—"

"Rose." Marta touched my wrist. Her fingers were very cold. She looked me in the eye, and I saw how weary she was. "Please . . . don't argue. I can't waste this time, when my head's clear and I can explain stuff. You're doing everything you can to make me OK, but I've realized I can be *more* than OK. I can be happy again, Rose, I know I can. There must be a way. I need you to find help, Rose."

There was a long silence. Marta and I stood together in the long grass, surrounded by the dissonant dawn chorus and the placid gurgling of Donny Stream. The pink sky was now overlaid with strips of bright orange. "When?" I asked eventually.

Marta reached for my hand. "Today."

I felt tears rising. "It's too soon—"

"No, Rose. I know myself today. Tomorrow might be different. Save my life." She looked into my eyes. "Save yourself. Save *yourselves*. Your exams are coming up. Tell someone today, Rose."

I didn't know what to do. I felt a deep, cold fear. "I don't want to lose you," I said.

"You won't." Marta's voice was soft. "Even if they take me away, I'll come back to you. I'll come back to you as the *whole* me. I could be with Lloyd, and not harm him. I could find my mother, and do her no harm."

I looked at her differently then, and realized again how ill she was. Our realities were so distinct, and yet Marta was claiming to know herself; to know what she wanted. "OK," I said. "Today."

Marta smiled. Then her gaze drifted behind me. "I've just seen a deer in the trees," she said.

I turned. She was pointing into the woods on the other side of Donny Stream. The nascent daylight hadn't penetrated them yet. "Are you sure?"

"I'm completely sure." She looked around. The sun was just easing above the horizon, casting its light over the dew-sodden grass. We'd walked farther than I'd realized, and we were almost at the spot where we'd had the picnic in October. "This place," she said. "It's so fucking beautiful. I'd forgotten just how beautiful it is. Or am I just crazy, Rose? Have I been inside too long?"

"You have been inside for a long time," I said. "But you're not crazy." I paused, reluctant to disrupt her contentment. "We've got to get back, Mar. It's quarter to seven."

"OK." She put her left arm in mine as we started to walk back along the stream. "D'you remember Lloyd telling us about that deer he saw, ages ago?" she asked.

"I remember. We were in 1A."

Marta grinned at me. "That was the happiest time of my life. I felt so . . . optimistic. *Everything* was possible. I always think about that time, you know, when my brain will let me." We were walking slightly uphill, and Marta stopped, breathing heavily again. "I'm so unfit."

We paused, Marta leaning on my arm. The weight of her was nothing to me. The birdsong all around us was becoming raucous and insistent, as though they were urging us back to the clocktower. But Marta's face was ashen, her head drooping as she clung to my arm. I looked up the slope, wondering whether I should try to give her a piggyback. I saw Lloyd and Max striding along the top of the bank, hand in hand.

Marta must have felt my body stiffen, because she looked up, too. She saw Lloyd and Max at once, and she watched them for a few moments as they walked. Max tossed his head back and laughed, the sound echoing all around. In that moment he was the Max I'd fallen for in September: handsome, confident, full of joy.

They saw us, too, of course. They were absorbed in each other, but I don't think there was ever a time at High Realms when Lloyd, Sami, and I weren't looking over our shoulders. Lloyd was the wariest of the three of us, and so that morning he glanced around and behind him, and inevitably down toward the stream, where Marta and I were standing. He didn't pause, but Max must have sensed his dismay as Marta had sensed mine. They stopped, and the four of us gazed at each other.

Not a word was spoken. I saw immediately that Max hadn't known about Marta before that moment. I didn't understand how it could be so, but his expression was one of such profound shock—his wide eyes and slightly open mouth rendered him almost childlike—that I knew that the entire premise on which Sylvia and I were working was false. Most clearly, I remember that Max didn't overreact. In fact, he barely reacted at all. He must have understood that it would be wrong to confront us, or to alarm Marta in any way. He said something quietly to Lloyd, and the two of them walked on.

I took Marta back to the clocktower. By then the sun had just crept over the horizon. I remember that Marta didn't appear to be as troubled by seeing Max and Lloyd as I'd feared.

She pointed out a couple of things that I was too preoccupied to notice—a colony of rabbits playing in the grass, a kingfisher diving from a mossy branch—and talked about coming back to school in September. "I can't wait to see this place in the snow," she said. I thought of what Major Gregory had said about her removal from the school roll, my throat aching with anger and sadness.

Sami was waiting for us in Block C, his hair disheveled and his face pinched. "What the *fuck*—" he began, but when he saw Marta he stopped. "Oh, God. Are you OK?"

"I'm fine. I'm just tired." She smiled at him. "I'm going upstairs now. Rose will explain."

Sami looked from me to her. "What's happening?"

"Only good things." Marta stepped toward Sami and gave him a one-armed hug. "Don't worry," she said. "Thanks to you, I'm OK. I'll see you in a bit, Sami."

Then she turned to me. "Thank you for taking me outside," she said simply.

"That's OK." I wanted to hug her, cling to her, but she looked exhausted, and I knew it wouldn't be fair. "See you very soon, Mar."

She nodded. "I'll be waiting." She turned around and slipped into George's stall, past his bulky body, and behind the plywood wall. We heard her slow footsteps on the stairs.

Sami and I stood there, looking at each other. He started to say something, but I shook my head, going over to stand in front of him, resting my forehead on his overalled shoulder. "She's ready to go," I said, as his hand fell on the back of my neck, cool and gentle. "Let's find Dr. Reza."

Chapter 25

There were things about Dr. Reza's room that I hadn't noticed the first time I'd been in there, just after Marta had hidden herself in the clocktower. It was part sitting room, part doctor's office, and it looked out onto a little garden full of roses. As the nurse showed us in, I saw Max sitting on the sofa in the bay window. Dr. Reza occupied an armchair opposite him. She looked up, taking in Sami in his overalls and me in my pajama trousers, which were damp to the knees from the frost. I knew immediately that Max had told her, even before Dr. Reza asked us, "Is she all right?"

I looked at Max. I didn't want to discuss Marta in front of him, even though I knew there had been time for Lloyd to tell him things. "Where's Lloyd?" Sami asked Max.

"He's gone to say goodbye," Max said, as though it were obvious, and I understood that we had already lost some of the control we'd fought so hard to retain. I glanced at Sami.

"I'm going back there," he told me. I knew it would be useless to try to persuade him otherwise, so I nodded, and Sami left the room, followed by Max a few moments later.

Slowly, I took Max's seat. I put my hands on my knees

and looked up at Dr. Reza, feeling lightheaded with fear. She looked back at me in a very simple way, and there was long silence between us in which I wrestled with the mistakes I had made, the delusions I'd been comforted by, the uncertainty I still felt. It was so difficult to face her alone, without Sami and Lloyd by my side. "Would it help," Dr. Reza said quietly, "if I asked you questions?"

I shook my head. I could feel the narrative slipping away from me like water between cupped hands, and I knew that questions, however well-meaning, could misdirect me as I tried to tell her the truth. "I don't know where to start," I said.

"Start at the beginning," she said, and so I did. I told her about the early days, about the burning and the bullying, about Bridge Night, about Marta's determination to stay at High Realms. As the story tumbled out of my mouth, our blindness and complacency became so clear to me that I was filled with self-loathing. Released from within me, our reasons for what we'd done sounded as shallow, as nonsensical as I had feared. "We had to protect her," I said, but an image of Marta in her current state suddenly swam before me, and I couldn't go on, couldn't face telling Dr. Reza any more, even though I hadn't got to the crux of the matter; the true reason we'd continued to hide Marta.

She went to the door and locked it, and then came to sit next to me. "Where is Marta now, Rose?"

"She's in the clocktower. She's been there since October."

"Are you telling me," Dr. Reza said slowly, "that you, Sami, and Lloyd have been hiding Marta in the stables since Genevieve fell down the stairs?"

"Yes," I said. Panic rose in me as I saw Dr. Reza's

astonishment. It was too late to go back. I had told her, it was done, and all I could do now was attempt to put the information in its proper context. "But she—"

"Just a moment." She held up her hand, her brown eyes fixed on mine with the utmost seriousness. "I—I think the explanations can wait. I'm sure you did what you thought was right." Dr. Reza paused, and the words *you thought* blared in my mind. She glanced at her watch. "Max said . . . he seemed to think that Marta didn't look very well. He said she had a head injury. He thought it looked like she needed medical attention—perhaps quite urgently."

I felt a quick shiver of irritation. I only had myself to blame, but this kind of interference was exactly what I'd hoped to avoid. Dr. Reza looked at her watch again. "Rose?"

"I'm going," I said suddenly. I got to my feet. The loss of control was giving me such a feeling of panic that it overrode any fear about what Dr. Reza might do, and whom she might tell. Marta was more important. She needed me.

"Rose, wait a moment." Dr. Reza had moved quickly to stand in front of the door. "Please don't be frightened. Max was only trying to help."

"I'm not frightened." I tried to step past her, but she moved again, blocking the handle. "Get out of my way."

"I think you're terrified," she said quietly, trying to look me in the eye. "I think that's why you're here now, Rose, and that's why you're being aggressive—"

"Fuck you." I didn't know what I'd expected from telling her, but I felt no shred of relief—only an enervating frustration; a weariness of always trying to act rationally, comfort, protect. I wanted to attack Dr. Reza, to finally expunge some hurt.

"Rose," she said, "calm down. One question, and then you can go back to Marta."

I took a step backward, breathing heavily. "Fuck you," I said again, mindlessly.

"Can I ask you one question?"

"Fucking *ask* it, then," I snarled, wheeling around, leaning over to plant my hands on the arm of the sofa. I felt very dizzy. A strange noise roared in my ears, and I could barely hear Dr. Reza as she spoke.

"Why did you come here this morning, Rose?"

I looked up, trying to take in her expression, but my vision was grainy. I was seeing double through a dense fog, and my body was drenched in sweat beneath my pajamas, and even though most of my weight was being supported by the sofa, I could barely stand. "Because Marta asked me to," I said, and then I crashed onto my knees, my head colliding with the soft leather.

I came to on the carpet, with Dr. Reza kneeling next to me. She put her hand on my forehead, its coolness soothing to me despite my anger. "When did you last have something to eat?"

I struggled to sit up, but the oppressive dizziness returned. Dr. Reza got up and went to a cupboard, returning with a carton of juice. She put the straw into it and handed it to me, helping me sit up. I drank, feeling helpless and foolish, and again Dr. Reza waited. As my vision cleared, I realized that she was looking at my sleeve, which was stiff with Marta's dried vomit. "Have you been sick?"

"No, I . . ." I tipped my head back, closing my eyes. "Marta was. She's—she's being sick a lot."

"Why has she been sick, Rose?"

"I don't know, I . . ." I could see Dr. Reza properly now. Her face was creased with concern. "Marta lost herself," I said limply.

There was a short silence. Behind the closed door of Dr. Reza's office I could hear the infirmary coming to life: the murmur of nurses' voices, the rattle of equipment, somebody coughing. I could smell toast, but, despite my lightheadedness, I didn't feel all hungry. I felt tired, and stupid, and disappointed.

Dr. Reza was watching me. Suddenly she reached for my hand. "Rose," she said, "if I thought it would help Marta—and you—I'd take over now. I'd make all the decisions for you both. But that wouldn't be right. I know some things, and I've guessed others, but I don't know half of what you've been through, I can see that."

"It's Marta. So many bad things have happened to her."

"I hoped it wasn't the case," Dr. Reza said. "I hoped I was wrong about Marta, but . . ." She looked up, through the window to the brilliant morning outside. "I could tell as soon as I met her that something was badly wrong. I tried to gain her trust, but I asked her too many questions, much too soon. I wanted to help, and I believed time was of the essence . . . I wish I'd handled it differently, and not driven her away." She paused. "When it came to you, Lloyd, and Sami, I saw how guarded you were about Marta. There was something you wanted to tell me, but you couldn't. I decided to wait, to stop asking questions—to avoid making the same mistake I had with Marta. I kept an eye on you; I tried to make your lives here easier when I could. I hoped you'd tell your parents at Christmas—"

"We couldn't. Marta needed us," I said, and as soon as

I said the words I was flooded with their truth, and with the relentless pressure of being needed so much, in so many unfulfillable ways, by someone I really loved. I pulled my hand away. "We've done all the wrong things—we've broken the rules—"

"The rules weren't made for someone like Marta," Dr. Reza said. She watched me closely. "That's why we need to be careful. We need to make sure your efforts don't go to waste. You've managed to protect Marta for a long time—"

"You don't understand," I said, tears coming to my eyes at the horror of what she still did not know. "We *didn't* manage it, we've failed—she's so ill, she'll never get better—"

"People do get better. I promise you, there are ways of making people better." Dr. Reza looked at her watch for a third time. "Now, Rose, we need to make a plan. We need to—" She was cut off by an urgent rapping on the door. Both of us jumped.

"Sit there," Dr. Reza said quietly, helping me on to the sofa. "Don't say anything unless you have to." There was another rap at the door. "Trust me," she said, squeezing my hand, and then she crossed the room to answer the door.

"He saw Sami." Sylvia's presence filled the room, vivid and powerful. She was dressed in her hockey kit, her hair in the immaculate braid she used for sports, holding her stick like a billy club. In seconds, she was sitting beside me on the sofa. "Max saw *Sami* two nights ago, not Lloyd. Sami told Max that something's happened with Gerald. Nothing about Marta at all. I've just got it out of Max." She looked at me, hard. "What's been going on, Rose?"

I swallowed. "Max . . . Max didn't see Lloyd?"

Sylvia shook her head. "Max said Sami told him that something happened with Gerald," she repeated. "He phoned the police about *Gerald*, not Marta. Vane knows nothing about Marta at all, and nor did Max until half an hour ago. Vane's taken Gerald in for questioning."

There was a long silence in which I was flooded with guilt for believing that Lloyd had betrayed Marta. Sylvia looked from me to Dr. Reza. "I'm frightened, Dr. Reza," she said abruptly. "I'm frightened that Rose is going to lose Marta like Gin lost Persie."

I swallowed. "What happened to Persie?"

"She killed herself."

"I know that, but—"

"High Realms was the wrong school for her," Sylvia said baldly.

"What do you mean?"

"Persie was . . . different." Sylvia paused. "When she first came here I thought she was going to be like Gin. She was good at lacrosse and riding. She was always top of the Rankings. The Mags liked her, she was brilliant at music . . . she could've found her niche if she'd wanted to. But she didn't. She used to say the strangest things . . . she used to *do* strange things." She swallowed. "At first we tried to help her. Encouraged her to settle down, lean into the things she was good at, like we'd had to. She just . . . she just *wouldn't*. She wasn't interested in being the same as everyone else." Sylvia paused. "Gin loved Persie, but she struggled with how different she was. With her being friends with people like Gerald. She wanted Persie to be like her—she tried to make her conform. Told her she'd be miserable if she didn't. After a while we . . . we just gave up. We didn't shield her anymore. And of course, she started to be bullied. Gin was firm—and I agreed—that we wouldn't intervene. She'd made her bed, and she'd have to lie in it." Sylvia looked down at her hands. "It got very bad. We didn't know *how* bad until later, but"—she swallowed again, her voice shaking—"Persie suffered."

I stared at her. "*Why* didn't you help? When you realized what was going on?"

"We *did*, Rose. After a couple of months I told Gin we couldn't stand back any longer. We'd heard about something that had been done to Persie. Something particularly—humiliating." Sylvia looked sickened. "She had to go to the infirmary. We came here to find her; went to the room they said she was in. She was dead. The nurse had left her to sleep, and she'd taken an overdose of acetaminophen."

I stared at her, and then at Dr. Reza, unable to fathom her negligence. She shook her head sadly. "It was just before my time," she said. "The previous doctor was sacked. I got the job here just after Persie's funeral."

"I didn't do enough," Sylvia said, her voice thick with grief. She turned to me. "Marta reminded Gin of Persie. Her vulnerability . . . how volatile she was . . . Persie was like that. I could see that from the very start—it's why Gin couldn't stand Marta. She even *looks* a bit like her. Every time Gin saw Marta, she was reminded of what she'd lost."

I said nothing. My instinct to suppress the truth was still there, paralysing my ability to speak. Then I realized that there was no longer any reason not to tell them. Marta had asked for help, and it was only my own fear, my own revulsion, that was stopping me telling Sylvia and Dr. Reza the truth. "Maybe Marta *is* like Persie," I said. "But it's more than that."

"What?"

"Her father—did something to her." Even after all this time, I couldn't say the words. "Marta was afraid it would happen again if she went home. So we hid her in the clocktower, but two weeks ago Gerald found her. He raped Marta." The second statement was easier.

There was a long silence, and then Sylvia spoke, her voice very quiet. "When?"

I couldn't look at her. "On the day he was demoted."

She slid away from me to the end of the sofa, her whole body shaking. Far away, in the Main House, I heard the breakfast bell. "I should have come to you months ago," I said to Dr. Reza, and that confession, more than any other, delivered an agonizing cocktail of sadness and relief. "I left it too long."

Dr. Reza got up from the armchair and came to sit on the sofa, between Sylvia and me. She took Sylvia's hand. "I understand why you didn't come," she told me. "Marta's been through terrible things, but it's not too late to get her proper—*medical*—help." She paused. "You all did what you thought was right," she said carefully, "and you don't deserve to suffer any more. Seventeen is very young, but I'm afraid it's old enough in the eyes of the law."

"What do you mean?"

She ignored my question. "How is Marta today, Rose?"

"She's frightened—"

"What is she most frightened of?"

"Of being alone. Of being left behind." It was so easy to tell her, now that she'd heard the worst.

"She won't be alone." Dr. Reza's voice was firm. "But she needs to be properly assessed, by people who have experience in Marta's kind of trauma."

"Where? How?"

"There's a place about an hour from here. It's a clinic, not a hospital. A former colleague of mine works there—I trust her completely. I think we should take Marta to her. You and I can go, too," she said swiftly, seeing my dismay. "She won't be on her own for a second, I promise."

"She'll be terrified—"

"Rose, please. Listen to me." Dr. Reza spoke urgently. "These psychiatrists, the people we're taking Marta to—I know it's hard to believe, but they will have seen cases like this before. Perhaps not Marta's exact profile, but that doesn't matter. They're trained, there's a procedure, they'll know how to keep her safe, how to start treating her. She *can* be treated, Rose. It won't be easy. But based on what you've told me, I think she's going to need the best care, as soon as possible."

"She won't trust them—"

"They'll be used to that, too." Dr. Reza got to her feet, looking down at Sylvia and me. "I'm going to go and see Marta now. I'll be very careful," she said. "I promise you, I'll look after her."

"I'm coming with you."

"No, Rose." She crouched down in front of me. "Coming with me might seem the best thing to do right now, but it's not the right decision for the rest of your life. We need to get Marta out of here without her being seen, without her being linked to you. Or there's going to be a lot of explaining to do, to people who might not want to understand." Dr. Reza looked at Sylvia. "What do you think, Sylvia?"

Sylvia looked up. She wiped her eyes. "I think you're right," she said quietly. The three of us looked at each other, and suddenly there was no hierarchy between us: we were just three women making a plan. "Rose, I want Marta to be OK, but if they find out you've hidden her for so long . . ."

Dr. Reza got to her feet again. She looked out of the window to the rose garden. "All being well," she said, "we'll take Marta to the clinic tonight. I'll ask them to send a car—not an ambulance—during the night, so that we can get her out of High Realms quietly. I'll make sure she knows we're going with her, Rose. I'll stay with her all day." She went over to a cupboard near the examining table and started to pull out bandages, material for a sling, medical gloves—all things I knew she wouldn't need, because they were already in the clocktower.

"What should I do now?" I asked Dr. Reza. "If you're staying with Marta, what should I do today?"

Dr. Reza turned to me, her arms full of supplies. "Go and get dressed," she said. "Go to breakfast. Go to school. Sit in the sunshine. Play hockey, do your homework." She looked from Sylvia to me. "Love each other. Don't fall out over this." She gave me a brief smile as she went to the door of her office. "Have courage, for one more day. It's nearly over."

It was the first day of a false spring: eight hours of dazzling sunshine and implausible warmth, and my memories of that day are suffused with a golden glow.

I followed Dr. Reza's instructions, and found that I was able to eat a large breakfast before going to lessons. It was our first day back after house arrest, and I found the noise of the school—the one thousand busy, untroubled High Realmsians—oppressively loud. As I left Latin, Bella came up to me and sheepishly told me she was a player down. Would I consider helping the First XI thrash Stowe? *Of course,* I said, and walked away, ignoring her expression of surprise.

Lloyd and Sami were in class, too. Their faces were carefully blank, but we were so accustomed to reading each other that I could find trepidatious relief in Lloyd's expression, and something more complex in Sami's. I wanted to talk to them both, particularly Sami; but there was no time. At Elevenses, Lloyd murmured to me that Marta had accepted Dr. Reza's appearance in the clocktower more calmly than he'd expected. In English, Miss Kepple had opened the windows of her classroom to the cloudless sky and the sweet smell of the outdoors.

Did we still feel like a team, the boys and I? The answer is no, but I would have trusted either of them with my life. *Really?* Sylvia asked me later on. *Always,* I said.

All day, as the winter sun soared over the Main House and the playing fields swarmed with lacrosse matches and the groundsmen carried desks up to the Old Library for the mock exams, I thought of Marta. For so long, visits to the clocktower had been woven into the fabric of my days, my thoughts, my emotional landscape, and without an appointment to go to the clocktower I felt superfluous, supplanted. I'd been assured that Marta was safe, and she was going to be even safer. *People do get better,* Dr. Reza had said. But

Marta was not *people*. She was Marta, my Marta; and no one understood her like I did.

At three o'clock, Sami shouted my name as I was dashing down the steps of the Pavilion to the Astroturf. I rushed to him, knowing something had gone wrong. "Come with me, Rosie," he said. Ignoring Bella's yells and Sylvia's dismay, I ran with Sami through the plane trees and across the drive, down Chapel Passage to the infirmary, to Dr. Reza's room. There, lying on the sofa, wrapped in blankets, her head in Dr. Reza's lap, was Marta. She was fast asleep, her chest slowly rising and falling, her tufty hair sticking up around her head. Her head was bandaged. Her arm hung from the sofa to the floor, her fingers gently curling inward.

"How—" I began, looking at Dr. Reza, but she shook her head, putting a finger to her lips. She looked at me, and I read a new sadness in her expression. *One o'clock,* she mouthed to me. *Meet here at one o'clock tonight.*

I wanted to stay with Marta, but I was needed to play in the match. I skidded on to the Astroturf just as the whistle blew, and as I played, as I ran and passed and tackled and scored three times, I realized that I was free. Whether I had wanted to be liberated or not, I *was* now free: I could choose my path according to what was right rather than what had to happen. I could help people who were not Marta, people who needed me, people who'd been patient and selfless while I was consumed by caring for her. The whistle blew: we'd won. The floodlights were coming on. I sank to my knees on the Astroturf, pressing my forehead against the prickly surface, and tears of selfish relief streamed down my cheeks.

"Help me with her," I heard a voice say, and a pair of strong arms pulled me to my feet. It was Bella. She clamped her arm around my shoulders, and Sylvia put hers around my waist, and they walked me off the pitch and toward the Main House as my tears continued to fall: unstoppable, painful.

The showers in Raleigh were empty. I sat on the tiled floor and cried while Sylvia found soap and towels and ran the water until it was warm. I took off my hockey kit and stood under the shower, but my tears would not cease. I sat down, feeling the water hammer on my head and shoulders.

"Come here." I thought Sylvia was going to pull me out of the shower, but she knelt down and rubbed shampoo into my hair, and soap over my neck and back. Water ran down her arms, soaking her shirt and skirt, but she took no notice. She rinsed my hair and passed me a towel. "Go to my room," she said. "I'll tell Major Gregory you're not well."

For the first time, I lay in Sylvia's bed. The sheets were cool against my skin. I closed my eyes, but I wasn't ready to sleep. I couldn't dial out of the feeling of needing to be somewhere else, with somebody else. I thought of Marta's peaceful face as she slept; of Dr. Reza's competent, compassionate gaze as she watched over her. I thought of the treatment Marta was going to have, and how little I knew about the doctors who would look after her.

Then Sylvia was in bed next to me, her damp clothes discarded on the floor. I laid my head on her shoulder, and she stroked my hair, saying nothing at all. Doors began to open and close around us as people in Raleigh House got ready for dinner. It all seemed so far away. Sylvia didn't move. She held me close to her, and I knew there was no deadline, no point by which I had to have pulled myself together.

Relief came, slowly and not without pain, and with it more tears, and something I hadn't expected. I felt something inside me giving way. As Sylvia held me, the dregs of my fear of her leaked out of me. We looked into each other's eyes and suddenly it was as if nobody and nothing else existed: only the two of us, and the love that had taken us both by surprise. I put my hands on either side of her face. Some people would have asked, *Why didn't you tell me sooner?* I knew Sylvia would never ask me that. I closed my eyes, feeling her mouth on my neck.

Then she was holding me differently, and the final secrets between us fell away, swiftly and simply and with greater tenderness than I could have ever imagined. The things we did that evening amazed me so much that I felt helpless—but I felt entirely safe in my vulnerability. I wanted Sylvia to have all of me, in that moment and forever. And although I knew that Sylvia hadn't fully healed—how could she, how could anyone?—it didn't matter, because she knew she was safe, too. I was inside her, and she was inside me, and there were long moments of perfect, blissful release.

I slept a deep, dreamless sleep, waking at twenty to one. Sylvia had set the alarm, but she didn't stir as I pulled on some clothes and crept out of Raleigh House. I headed for the back staircase.

Pausing at the Ivy Door, I looked down at my carelessly assembled outfit: my hockey shorts and socks, and Sylvia's school shirt and cardigan. *We need to be very careful,* Dr. Reza had said. I knew that if Major Gregory saw me like this when I arrived back at High Realms he would haul me into his office for questioning. There was just enough time to go to

Hillary and change. I ran up endless flights of stairs, through the thick silence of the Main House. I remember glimpsing a diffident crescent moon through the windows, and feeling grateful that the grounds would be very dark that night.

The sash window was still open in Room 1A, and the room was very cold. I slipped between the two beds to the wardrobe and found a clean shirt—stiff with the starch they used in the laundry—a skirt, Hillary tie, cardigan, and long socks. My blazer was still in the changing rooms. I rummaged at the bottom of the wardrobe, eventually extracting Marta's old blazer, which she'd discarded when Dr. Reza had found her a smaller size. I put it on.

Can we sense tragedy, before it happens? Is there an obscure murmur, a flicker of the light, a tremor in even the oldest and sturdiest of buildings? On that cloudless night I remember the gentlest of cool breezes entering Room 1A through the open window. It was my reminder to hurry, to get to Marta, and so I strode to the door. As I opened it, I heard a scream. From behind, outside, below: a scream.

What do I remember? I've told this story as clearly as I could—as rationally as I've been able, in the circumstances, to achieve—but to write the fact of Marta's death is to finalize it, to suffer again that banishing of all hope, all meaning, all joy. After that night, my notion of justice moved on to a different scale. I no longer work to a system of what is deserved, or earned, or commensurate. Too often, there's no rhyme or reason to what we suffer.

Marta, my Marta. It was such a dark night that I could barely see her from the window of 1A. As I looked down, my vision clouding with fear and then denial and then those first inklings of indelible grief, the lawn began to be illuminated. Lights were being switched on in all the floors below me, one head then another emerging from the open windows, and the silence of the night was rent by the shouts and screams and moans of tens, dozens, hundreds of teenagers.

Marta, our Marta. Lloyd, Sami, and I got to her—they tried to stop us; even Dr. Reza didn't want us to go near her broken body, but we had to be with our friend. We knelt around her as we had so many times before, stroking her, running our fingers through her hair, holding her hand. The dampness of the grass; the freezing temperature of the air; the warmth of Marta's blood as it left her body. The instinct, the need to lie across her, to cradle her in my arms overridden by the knowledge that this was the last time the four of us would be together, and that she was not only mine to hold.

Marta, Marta. All too soon, they took her away: not quietly to a new beginning, but with blue lights and noise to a cold, cold room. They took my best friend; the purest love I've ever known. Marta: who loved books and poems and Physics and school and loving and being loved. Possessor of a brilliant mind, a brilliant memory, a brilliant and unexpected smile. Persecuted, but full of empathy. Victimized, but never a victim. In all ways but one, a survivor. Marta, I would do it all again, and this time you would survive.

Chapter 26

April 2012

We meet at Paddington. Sami's early, and anxious. Sylvia is late, overexcited by a new case. Lloyd arrives just in time, dismissing his small entourage at the ticket gates, posing for photos with several members of the public. They ask him where he's going. "To Devon, on a private matter," he says, and won't elaborate. It's the first year we've seen him be accosted like that.

We sit around a table in standard class, eating sandwiches. "Why couldn't we have gone in first class?" Sylvia grumbles, but Lloyd shakes his head. He can't be seen to travel in style. "This isn't work," she argues.

"We *look* like we're working," Lloyd replies, indicating Sylvia's papers spread over the table, the pink ribbons gathering crumbs. "You could be my special advisor, Sylv."

"Maybe when your lot are actually in government," she says drily. She looks down at her papers, which are stamped with our chambers' logo. I read the claim upside down. Sylvia's prosecuting, as usual.

Sami's opposite me, leaning against the window, his eyes

occasionally drifting closed for a few seconds. He's probably come straight from a night shift at King's, doing the best he can in an overworked, underresourced department. I see him more than the others do, and I know he's doing well—that he's admired by colleagues and patients alike. But he claims it's hard to evaluate success in psychiatry. A patient's outcomes can seem good, but they'll suddenly relapse. I know he won't talk much today. These trips back to High Realms are hardest for him.

We've made the journey every year since 2008. That was the first year all four of us finally finished studying, training, applying, and actually had jobs: jobs we're lucky enough to be passionate about, that pay us well enough to enable us to endow the scholarship. It was also the first year we were satisfied that the regime at High Realms had truly changed for the better. We believe it's a safer place now.

More importantly, 2008 was the first year they would have us back. A new Director of Studies had been appointed, and she'd done much more than her due diligence on what took place in February 2000. I suppose she wanted to be prepared for when people—prospective parents, and the odd journalist at a loose end—asked her about it. She'd talked to Detective Inspector Vane, who'd mellowed a bit since our last encounters with him. Then she'd invited Lloyd, Sami, and me back to school to speak to her.

At first we'd refused to go. After Marta died, we'd been unceremoniously removed from High Realms. We weren't even allowed back upstairs to pack our things: our trunks had been waiting in the Atrium when we were brought back from the police station. The school had wanted to put as much distance between itself and us as possible. "A failed experiment," we were called in a leaked letter. They didn't say a word about Marta. Dr. Reza was fired. On the same morning we were sent home from High Realms, Gerald was released without charge, and went back to school to complete his education. Five days later, on the same day that Sylvia wrote to me to say that Genevieve had returned to High Realms, we'd heard that Professor De Luca had died in his sleep.

Perhaps unsurprisingly, it took a long time for Lloyd, Sami, and particularly me to be exonerated from any direct involvement in Marta's death. Dr. Reza reported that she'd left Marta asleep in her study while she went to meet the psychiatrists on the front drive and show them the way to the infirmary. She didn't lock the door, thinking that I would arrive while she was gone. It's difficult to know exactly what happened between Dr. Reza leaving the room and her finding Marta on the lawn fifteen minutes later. Lloyd, Sami, and I pieced together a version of events, but to the police, who didn't know Marta, it made suspiciously little sense.

We think Marta woke up, panicked at finding herself alone, and made her way to the Main House, entering through the fire door. If she'd done so a few minutes later she would have bumped into me, but she must have crept up the back stairs to Hillary—perhaps then going directly to Room 1A, where she thought I would be. Sami is certain that Marta came to his and Lloyd's room first. Lloyd was in Max's room, and Sami was in bed with Ingrid. They were both asleep, but Ingrid thinks she remembers half waking at the sound of the door closing. She wouldn't tell the police in case she was implicated—and she only provided Sami with an alibi very reluctantly, because she was breaking the rules by being in his room. They broke up because of that, but whenever we talk about that night, Sami mentions what Ingrid thinks she heard.

I have no alibi between leaving Sylvia's room and kneeling next to Marta's body, and only Sylvia's word for it that I'd been in her room at all. I suppose it was this gap, the coroner's discovery of Marta's old injuries, and the months of lying to the police—to which we freely confessed—that made Vane suspect I'd accidentally killed Marta. Perhaps he was simply aggrieved that we'd duped him. Either way, he decided something had got out of hand, that I'd panicked, that there'd been some kind of skirmish between Marta and me in Room 1A that had resulted in Marta tumbling to her death. In his view, Lloyd and Sami were covering for me. There was no proof, but the absurdity of the claim meant I had no appetite to fight him or anyone else—no burning desire to set the record straight, because Marta was gone, and High Realms had turned its back on us, and there was no point. We didn't even tell Vane what Gerald had done to Marta, because there was no proof of that, either. The trial was set for January 2001. Then, in November 2000, after I'd spent nine months at home in Hackney, inert with grief, my father received a letter from a barristers' chambers in central London.

I don't think Detective Inspector Vane or Barnstaple Crown Court had ever seen the likes of Araminta Maudsley, Esq. She was—and still is—the most fearsome barrister I've ever met: waspish at best, and at worst withering, contemptuous, devastatingly rude. From the word go, Araminta behaved as though the case against me should never have been brought.

"Your asinine theories are ruining lives," she railed at Vane. "These young people have been through enough. They should be at *school*, playing hockey and having midnight feasts and *snogging*." She summoned me to her wood-paneled room in Gray's Inn and demanded to hear the whole story. She barked questions throughout, staring over my shoulder, her eyes narrowed in concentration. When I couldn't go on because I was crying too much, she poured me a shot of whiskey. "Drink this," she said curtly, "and keep going. You can't afford me, even without these fucking intermissions."

I couldn't drink the whiskey, but I managed to tell Araminta what Marta's father had done to her, and what Gerald had done to her. "Context!" she shouted, her tone unchanged, and weary of obfuscation I supplied it, including—after some hesitation—what Gerald had done to Sylvia. I was almost certain Sylvia hadn't confided in her mother, and, as I watched the color drain from Araminta's flushed face, I knew I'd been right. She reached across the table for my glass, her hand shaking. "Have you told the police this?" she asked. I explained the allegation Max had made, and Gerald's swift exoneration when Max had been unable to say whom he had assaulted. Araminta's face contorted into an expression of derisive confusion. "Why would Max bother to report a crime without a plaintiff?" she snapped. I explained that Max hadn't phoned the police out of a sense of justice, or any kind of altruism, but because he'd believed that if he could get rid of Gerald from High Realms, he would be more secure in Genevieve's esteem when she returned to school.

Araminta listened to this, and nodded slowly. "A blessing in disguise," she muttered. Seeing my surprise, she snapped,

"Even if Max had given them a name, I doubt that Gerald would have been prosecuted. The law is utterly feeble in such cases." She drained her glass, her face screwed up in pain. "He's more use to us this way, the bastard." The following week, she interviewed Gerald in preparation for calling him as a witness.

The trial started badly. The prosecution berated Lloyd, Sami, and me about why we'd hidden Marta in the clocktower, easily presenting it as a reckless, arrogant decision with fatal consequences. The worst thing was that we more or less agreed with them. Marta had been dead for nearly a year, and we were missing her more than ever. We doubted our actions more with every question we were asked.

Sami was in a bad way when he took the stand on the third day of the trial, and Araminta's opposite number—an Old High Realmsian himself—was irritable after an unproductive morning. "Even if we accept that you deceived the police for the apparently noble reason of protecting Marta De Luca from her father, whom you claim was abusive to her," he snapped, "my colleagues and I are unable to understand why, as highly intelligent, promising young people, you were unable to see the wisdom, the *necessity,* of seeking help from one of the many trustworthy adults who surrounded you at one of the finest schools in the world?" The barrister drew breath, and there was a resounding silence in the courtroom.

Finally Sami spoke, his tone flat. "Marta couldn't go home to her father," he said slowly, "but that wasn't the only reason she wanted us to hide her in the clocktower." He gazed across the courtroom. "She wanted to stay with us. With one of us in particular." The barrister looked incredulous, and Sami shrugged again. "Her mother had run away. You can believe what you like about him, but I'm telling you her father was evil. She'd always been homeschooled, so she didn't have any friends. She knew we loved her. We were all she had." He looked down at his hands, resting on the rail in front of him, and then up at the barrister. "What would you have done?" he asked, and his question was a plea rather than a challenge.

I'll never know what Araminta said to Gerald before the trial, but the evidence he gave under cross-examination was crucial. After Araminta had set the scene, emphasizing the extreme conditions under which we'd agreed to help Marta, Gerald testified that he'd seen her in the clocktower in January 2000. He said she wasn't locked in, and seemed reasonably well; that his regular presence at the stables meant he'd seen us coming and going, caring for Marta until the day she died. He'd seen Dr. Reza moving her to the infirmary; had overheard her telling Marta what was going to happen that night. He'd been aware of Marta's mental health declining, and of our concern for her welfare, evinced by the increased frequency of our visits to her and the things he'd seen us taking into the clocktower. "They were obsessed with keeping her safe," he said, shooting a nervous glance at Araminta.

Araminta shuffled her papers. "Were you aware," she asked calmly, "that Marta De Luca was pregnant when she died?" The horror on Gerald's face was unmistakable. I looked around at Lloyd, whose expression was all shock, and at Sami, who looked heartbroken. That very evening, Araminta ordered Sylvia to report Gerald's assault on her. Three days later

Gerald, Lloyd, and Sami were summoned to take DNA tests. They showed the only thing they could show, and prompted by Araminta, we told the police what Gerald had done to Marta.

By this point we were daring to hope that we might win. The atmosphere in the courtroom was different; the jurors' expressions less censorious. But there was still the question of what Professor De Luca had done to Marta, and the fact that nobody really believed us. Having discussed it at length among ourselves, Lloyd, Sami, and I decided to submit three new pieces of evidence: evidence we'd hoped we would never have to reveal, because to do so meant betraying Marta's trust in us. But Marta was dead. Professor Nathaniel De Luca was dead, too, and could not be brought to justice for what he'd done to his daughter and, before that, to his wife. We had no idea whether Dr. Maria De Luca was alive, but it seemed crucial to set the record straight. I would be lying if I claimed there was not also a part of us that wanted Dr. Wardlaw and Major Gregory to be punished for how remiss they'd been in their treatment of Marta. So we handed over the note Marta had scrawled to me on the day of the Eiger, the letter she'd written to me after Christmas, and the letter she'd written to her father in the clocktower shortly before she died. The last one was the hardest to read.

The evidence more than satisfied both judge and jury, and Lloyd, Sami, and I were cleared of nearly all charges, receiving a caution each for wasting police time. All we wanted to do was go home, but Araminta insisted on taking us out for a drink. She'd had nearly a bottle of wine when she fixed the three of us with a stare that was unnervingly like Sylvia's. "I couldn't tell you before," she said. "About Gerald, I mean. I had to give us the element of surprise. I wanted the judge to see the difference between your reaction and his. I was sowing the seed to bring him down."

"Do you think that will happen?" Sami asked quietly.

Araminta pursed her lips. "His parents will be able to afford a lawyer who's almost as good as me. But at the very least, I'll drag his name through the mud. Nobody will *ever* want anything to do with him."

Very occasionally, Lloyd, Sami, and I talk about what we did. We never intend to. The conversation comes into being without warning, started by whoever feels the need to rake over the past. It's happened in all sorts of contexts. A walk through the woods in autumn, outside a crowded bar in high summer, in text messages late at night. When the urge to talk comes to one of us, the rest of us don't resist it. We owe each other that much.

We know we made many wrong decisions. We know that if we'd acted differently, Marta might have lived. We are certain that we'll carry our guilt and our grief with us forever. But sometimes—and I think this is the naivety, or perhaps the arrogance, that enabled us to do what we did—we force ourselves to recall the conviction and the love that drove us. *We were doing what Marta wanted,* Sami still insists. I find this difficult. I think the boundary between selflessness and selfishness is murky, and I know that Marta wanted, above all, to live.

We never chastise each other for our mistakes, our missteps. We acknowledge that the point at which our teamwork fractured was the point that tragedy struck, and so we've buried all the hatchets, and any vestiges of resentment, as I think Marta would have wanted. Besides, we cannot be at all certain that different actions would have yielded a different outcome.

We can never again be the teenagers who sprinted across the rugby pitches toward the clocktower, our pockets stuffed with food and our hearts pounding with jeopardy, but we are the same people. We are still clever, loyal, ambitious, stubborn, neurotic, lonely people: people consumed by complicated, joyless pride. It's the same pride that took us to High Realms in the first place. It's the same pride that got us to university, despite the fact that we'd been expelled from one of the best schools in the country with no qualifications. It's the same pride that still drives us to do our best, in our jobs now rather than for the Rankings. And it's the same pride that made us blinkered to the presence, the obvious and undeniable goodness, of the one person at High Realms who could have helped Marta. That, I know, is what Miss Kepple would have called *hubris*.

Isobel Reza picks us up from the station and drives us to High Realms. She's a doctor in a village about five miles from the school. We always take her out for a meal after the scholarship meeting. Life was very difficult for Isobel after Marta died, but we never lost touch. She wrote to me regularly for three years.

She says she hears that High Realms is continuing to go from strength to strength in terms of personal care. Until recently, she had a dozen students in her consulting room every term, terrified of being caught out of school, asking for help with all manner of things. Now, apparently, there's a new doctor at High Realms, several nurses—one of them specializing in sexual health—and a counselor. Day pupils are now admitted, which Isobel thinks is a good thing. "Less of a pressure cooker," she says.

Sylvia wants to know whether Isobel will come to London for my thirtieth birthday party in September. Isobel looks sideways at Sylvia in surprise. "Are you organizing this?"

"Yes, seeing as it's being held at my house." Isobel can't help but raise her eyebrows, which Lloyd spots.

"We're as confused as you are," he tells her brightly. He nudges me, but I don't say anything. Isobel nods warily.

"How's Genevieve?" she asks Sylvia.

"Oh, she's very well. The twins are . . . a delight." Sylvia yawns ostentatiously. "The christening's next month."

Isobel doesn't drive up to the Main House, but parks by the Gatehouse. She gets out and hugs us all, even though we'll see her later. She holds me for longer than the others, as the old grief rises in my chest. "You did what you thought was right," she says to me quietly: the same sentence she's repeated to me for years, since the day Marta died. "So did you," I say, and she kisses me on the cheek, her eyes full of tears.

I breathe in the smell of the Atrium as we wait for Professor Ling, the new Director of Studies. It's cool in there, and all around us are the familiar sounds of lunch being cleared, classroom doors slamming, a thousand pupils settling down for two hours of lessons before Games, prep, duties. A member of the Senior Patrol walks us up the Eiger to the Old Library. He's calm and pleasant, with no hint of a swagger.

Coming back is painful, but now we feel it's worthwhile. The scholarship is one way of honoring Marta's memory; of enabling a part of her to exist here, in the place she wanted to stay. When Professor Ling first suggested it we thought she was mad, but when she followed up with a sincere, fulsome apology for High Realms's failings, and a pledge to improve things, we decided to think about it. Still the richest of us by a long shot, Sylvia said she'd pay the lion's share.

We sit around a table in the Old Library with Professor Ling and Miss Kepple. Profiles of the shortlisted applicants are scattered in front of us, as well as their essays. Every year, we choose a poem for the candidates to respond to. We always try to find one that meant something to Marta—she loved so many that we don't think we'll ever run out. A couple of months ago, Sylvia remembered a lesson in which she and Marta had argued strenuously about Louis MacNeice's "Snow." "She adored that poem," she reminded us. "I tried to say it was about chaos and confusion. Marta thought it was about infinite possibility."

The candidates' responses to "Snow' are predictably varied. After an hour's debate, we award a full scholarship to the Sixth Form of High Realms to a young woman from a state school in Norfolk. In her references her teachers describe her as "effervescent, determined, endlessly curious."

We walk down to Donny Stream. It's a bright day in late spring, the time of year we never spent at High Realms as pupils. The breeze ruffles the new leaves on the trees. We drink everything in. The stables are deserted: they don't keep horses at High Realms anymore.

Cautiously, we begin to talk about Marta. For so many years, we didn't. We were all in different parts of the country, recovering in different ways and at different paces. When I finally joined her at Oxford, Sylvia was surprised by the ongoing intensity of my grief. "Were you in love with her?" she once asked me at the end of a long dinner, and straight away I thought of Sami: of how much, how steadfastly, how unselfishly he'd loved Marta. "No," I said truthfully, and she looked relieved.

I told Sylvia about a time in Room 1A, just before the Eiger, when Marta had asked me about love. She'd been speculating on what it felt like to experience real, reciprocal, romantic love. "Do you think it'll be amazing, Rose?" she'd asked. "D'you think it'll be the best thing in the world?" I'd struggled to answer, and Marta had nodded seriously. "If I found someone who loved me, and I loved them back," she'd told me, "I'd never, ever let them go."

Lloyd, Sami, and I walk down the grassy bank to the water's edge while Sylvia hangs back by the barns. The boys and I crouch down and dangle our fingers in the water. "She was extraordinary," Lloyd says suddenly. "The most incredible person I've ever met."

Sami nods. "I'll love her forever," he says.

"Me too," Lloyd and I say together, and we laugh. There's a pause. "Does Sophie know how you feel?" Lloyd asks Sami.

"I told her before we got engaged. I think she gets it." Sami grins at us, and glances back up the bank to where Sylvia is waiting. "On which note, Rosie," he says, "I've been meaning to tell you . . . it's so stupid, you not being with Sylvia. She made a mistake, but she's really sorry. She loves you. She wants to *marry* you." Lloyd frowns at him, but he shrugs. "Life's too short for secrets. Even nice ones."

I think about it. Marta's words echo in my mind. *I'd never let them go.* I look up the bank to where Sylvia is standing with her back to us, arms folded, staring up at the clocktower. The memory of her betrayal—a fling with an older, extravagantly successful barrister from our chambers—still stings. Then I remember how she helped me in the days before Marta died, and her support in the long months and years afterward. I think of the days I thought I couldn't go on, and all the reasons Sylvia gave me to do so.

Lloyd, Sami, and I climb back up the bank to the stables. "Sylvia," Lloyd calls. She turns around. For a moment I think she's going to walk away, back to the Main House and home to London without me. But then she strides toward us, and as she gets closer I see the love that possesses Sylvia; that still drives everything she does. I see her compassion, which even seven years at High Realms could not erase. She falls into step beside me and I take her hand. Lloyd, Sami, Sylvia, and I walk back to school together in companionable silence, the four of us bound by love, loss, and enduring hope. We dream of the future.

Acknowledgments

I wrote *The Four* in several phases, beginning in September 2020 and completing the final draft in March 2023. The duration of the process, and the world and life events that took place during it, mean that there are a lot of people to thank. I will do so in roughly the order that they contributed to the arduous, joyful, maddening, exhilarating, excruciating process of writing a novel.

Thank you first and foremost to Hannah Medlicott, the best listener I know, who absorbed my ad-libbed synopsis in Haworth in August 2020 and galvanized me to get started. And then to keep going. And to start again. And to finish. Hannie, you're my hero.

Thank you to my wonderful friend Felicity Bano for your support and kindness at Chichester Road and beyond. You never failed to make me feel like I could do it.

Thank you to Jessica Lazar for reading those early chapters in the Summer House in October 2020, and for not letting on that they were terrible. If you had, I might have given up. Thank you for feeding back on later drafts with your infallible instincts. As an artist and as a friend, you have my enormous admiration and gratitude.

From the bottom of my heart, thank you to Tim Bano for the memorable Carne Cottage/Stepper View trip of December 2020, during which I wrote those tricky middle chapters while storms raged and the world fell apart around us. Thank you for staying calm, and for your loving friendship, always. It means the world to me.

Thank you to Gail McManus for being the best mentor I could wish for. You have counseled, encouraged, and empowered me beyond measure. Thank you for telling me to *just get it done*. Thank you for being so utterly dependable and unerringly wise, and for proving that there are very few problems a good spreadsheet can't solve.

Thank you to the endlessly erudite Dr. Sophie Duncan for your astute feedback on an early draft, and for your assistance later on in the process when I was pitching to agents.

Thank you to Arifa Akbar for reading the second draft in summer 2021 and for your warm and constructive comments at a difficult stage in the process.

Thank you to Kate Mosse for the many hours of invaluable advice you've kindly given me, and for being inspirational in so many ways. I'm truly grateful. Thank you to Greg and Felix Mosse for your warm encouragement.

Thank you to my great friends Thomas Bailey and Emma D'Arcy for all your support over the years, with this book and so much else. Thank you for your creativity and openness. Thank you, Tom, for a phone call you probably won't remember, that helped me work out how to start again. Thank you, Emma, for always helping me see the wood for the trees. Thank you both for the plays, the adventures, and the love.

Here's a big one: thank you, thank you, Katy Guest, for

being the legendary editor that you are. Thank you for your incisive commentary, your astute diagnostics, and your ability to hone in on detail while never losing sight of the whole. Thank you for never solutionizing: it meant I wrote a better book. Thank you for becoming an unexpected, truly brilliant friend.

Thank you to Diane Pengelly for reading the first few chapters and gently suggesting that they had a few too many words in them.

Thank you to my incredible friends Isabel Marr and Lara McIvor for lots and lots of good jokes and for helping me believe in myself (and for not allowing me to take myself too seriously).

Thank you to my great pal Monica Dolan for your help and support when I set out to find a literary agent, and for your sound advice on so many occasions.

Thank you to Professor Tom Kuhn for reading a late draft and for your perceptive comments.

Thank you to Rosie Kellett for doing the same, and for all the cooking and the love over the years.

Thank you to Jackie Ashley for the invaluable introduction to Gillian Stern, without whose expertise I seriously doubt *The Four* would have had this magical journey. Gillian, thank you for your insight and good counsel, and for guiding me so deftly through those heady weeks of agent meetings. I will never forget the help you gave me.

I shall now join the ranks of those thanking Cathryn Summerhayes for her inimitably stylish and effective agenting. Cath, thank you for being a jumpsuited legend of genius ideas, indefatigable hard work, and steadfast support for this neurotic author. I do not know how you also manage to be fun (and funny), nor how you manage to make camping look glamorous, but you do. You changed my life, and I appreciate you very much.

Thank you to Lisa Babalis for an absolutely indispensable set of notes. You were right about everything.

Thank you to my wider team at Curtis Brown: Jess Molloy, Annabel White, Katie McGowan, and Georgie Mellor. Thank you to my incredible team at UTA: Jason Richman, Addison Duffy, and Meredith Miller.

A huge thank you to the exceptional Daisy Goodwin, for your boundless generosity, intelligence, and compassion. Your support has made all the difference.

Thank you to my wonderful team at HQ, and above all my talented and tireless editor, Cicely Aspinall. Cicely, thank you for believing so staunchly in *The Four*. Thank you for your incomparable skill in edits both macro and micro; for your patience and understanding; for your ability to dive deep into emotional matters while simultaneously dealing with technical aspects of plot. I'm so grateful to you, Lisa Milton and Kate Mills, for making my experience as a debut author such a thoroughly positive one. Thank you to Seema Mitra for your attention to detail, Kate Oakley for the gorgeous cover, map, and endpapers, and to Sian Baldwin, Emily Burns, and Becci Mansell for everything that is (at the time of writing) still to come!

Thank you to my wonderful editor at William Morrow, Danielle Dieterich, who has welcomed me so warmly and with such skill. I feel so lucky to be working with you.

Thank you to Georgina "Guru" Moore for the warm and

generous introduction to the world of book publicity, and for all your advice and support.

Thank you to Joe Keel for your robust pragmatism and unwavering support. I could not wish for a better sibling.

Thank you, Maow, for being my rock. (And for the place-holder title.)

And finally: thank you, thank you, thank you to Gillian Keel, for reading me all those books. Those stories were where this journey began.

About the Author

Ellie Keel is an award-winning producer and activist. She is the founding director of the Women's Prize for Playwriting, a literary prize and campaign for gender equality among writers for the stage in the UK and Ireland. In January 2024 she was the youngest producer ever to win Producer of the Year in the Stage Awards. She is based in London. *The Four* is her debut novel.

About the Author